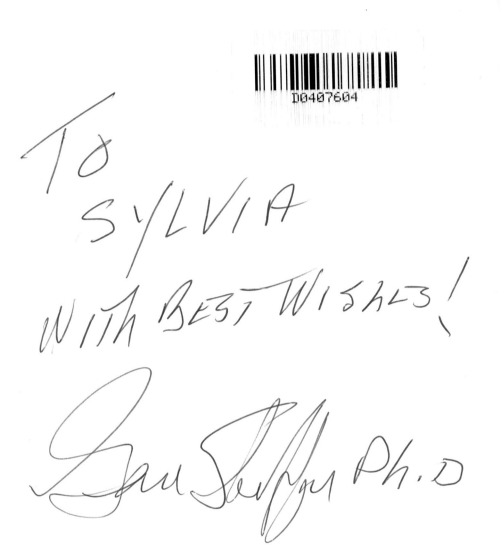

To SYLVIA
WITH BEST WISHES!

Dan Stauffer Ph.D

THE CROSS

THE CROSS

Where the power of love
overcomes the love of power

GENE SHAFFER

THUNDER RIDGE PUBLISHING

The Cross
Copyright © 2006 Gene Shaffer
Thunder Ridge Publishing

For further information contact:
Thunder Ridge Publishing
PO Box 3869
Prescott, AZ 86302

Printed in Canada

Gene Shaffer
The Cross

1. Author   2. Title
Library of Congress Control Number: 2005909245
ISBN: 0-9774141-0-8

Registered WGAW 4-10-2003
Registration No. 862829

ACKNOWLEDGMENT

$\mathcal{E}$ven as a writer, I find it difficult to thank the many individuals who helped me through the years in preparation and research on this project.

My profound love and gratitude to Nancy, my bride of over 50 years, who kept her hand on the tiller while I navigated the mysterious effects of the Cross of Calvary on the characters in this book.

Thanks to Imam Machmoud, Father James, Rabbi Isaac and Reverend Ed(who recently passed away), for patiently explaining the critical aspects of their creed while opening my eyes to the esoteric facts and beliefs of their respective religions.

This manuscript could not have been completed without the assistance of my long time friend; Janet McKewen-Smith, whose skills at typing and editing helped produce a story of great magnitude.

Special thanks to Bill Bonanno, a fellow writer, for his enthusiasm and wise counsel. His never-ending efforts to have this manuscript see the light of day is greatly appreciated.

Nothing can repay Gary Abromovitz for his magnificent efforts and many hours of toil in the vineyard of research and editing. His imprint is found in the pages of the manuscript.

My sincere gratitude to John Forsythe, a consummate actor and friend, that many years ago lit the torch which led the way through the labyrinth of creative writing.

To my sons and daughters, and Grandchildren, forgive me for the incalculable hours spent in research and writing at the expense of quality time with them.

Gene Shaffer

SYNOPSIS: THE CROSS BY GENE SHAFFER

In the last year of the first decade of the new century, we follow the heroic efforts of an American Cardinal of the Catholic Church.

Join Justin Kennedy, biblical scholar extraordinaire as he leads the Vatican in its unrelenting quest for the mightiest symbol of Christianity.

From its secret repository in ancient Palestine, the Quadrate Christogram of the man from Galilee is brought forth and revealed to the world.

Wonder at the effect the artifact has on Judeo-Christian philosophy as it merges with the esoteric enigmas of, the Shroud, the Robe, the Chalice, and the Ark of the Covenant.

The mount of Moses known in biblical times as Gebel Musa is situated almost at the midpoint of the southern peninsulas between the strategic gulfs of Aquaba and Suez.

No one can comprehend the Sinai, even the bible terms it 'a great and terrible wilderness', a place where Christians, Muslims and Jews revere.

A place where Moses talked to God and God answered him. It is the land of the prophets Elijah and of Abraham, the patriarch, who feared God more than the dangers of the wilderness as he walked its rocky paths.

The sandal prints of Mary and Joseph with the child Jesus were made here as they fled the evil of King Herod.

No one can explain why this magnetic almost supernatural vortex of land has commanded our attention over thousands of years.

Is the lost cross of Jesus secreted here awaiting its discovery?

The stage is set, scenery in place and the curtain parts…the omniscient hand of God directing the players in the drama surrounding the heraldic insignia of Jesus Christ.

Join the odyssey, which has its roots in the writings of the Codex Vaticanus that discloses the missing pages of the Book of Mark, final verses of the fifteenth chapter, which had been hidden for over two thousand years. Learn of leather scrolls discovered in an obscure monastery, as an American Cardinal of the Catholic Church finds the key to unlock the mystery that has eluded mankind for two centuries.

Witness a tumultuous Papal election as the Cardinal is catapulted onto the throne of Peter and becomes the first American Pope.

Follow his reign as Constantine II, punctuated by the unrequited love of a nun, deep divisions of loyalty among the fractionalized Curia, murder, blackmail, ransom, suicide, scandal, pedophilia, clandestine sexual encounters, and a covert unauthorized attempt by Mid East commandos to retrieve the stolen artifact discovered on Israeli soil.

Witness secret meetings of American religious zealots and a Muslim terrorist group; all overshadowed by a secret so awesome it could destroy the Catholic Church.

The secret; locked in tapes recorded by Vatican psychiatrists which indicate that the American Pope has possibly gone mad.

Revisit the trial of Jesus, the Last Supper, the raising of Lazarus and the betrayal by Judas Iscariot. Experience the crucifixion as the American Pope drifts between sanity and insanity while he envisions himself as Judas and a witness to these events.

All overshadowed by the intrigue of Vatican Politics.

THE CROSS

The search for, the discovery of, and the effect upon humanity of the cross on which Jesus Christ was crucified.

The story-line entwines with characters woven in the fabric of various plots, characters and events rich in the tradition of the Roman Catholic Church, including an American Cardinal, a beautiful archeologist nun, a Papal death, a tumultuous election to the Chair of Peter of the first American Pope, signaling dramatic and earth shaking changes in the Catholic religious community.

Intrigue manifests itself with political jealousies between members of the Curia, foreshadowing blackmail, suicide, sexual trysts and murder.

Involvement of foreign powers of Israelis and Arabs in the affairs of state of the Vatican. All overshadowed by the unrequited love of the nun toward the American Cardinal.

How the curative Cross as an emblem will bring people of all religions to a new understanding of the faith of Abraham, the father of all mankind. An understanding destined to bring peace throughout the world, all in the name of God.

The possibility exists for mankind to live in freedom and harmony – all we must do is find the key. The key to be found in the American Pope.

To My Father, Who Believed In *The Cross* Only
At The Very End, Not Unlike The Participants Who
Witnessed The Event On Calvary

PART ONE

CHAPTER ONE

$\mathcal{A}$merican Roman Catholic Cardinal Justin Kennedy sat comfortably in window seat 2A of the supersonic Boeing AliItalia X-7 en route to Rome, Italy, looking out his window and viewing the curvature of the earth from 66,000 feet. The digital speed read-out on the bulkhead in front of him read Mach 2.3, almost two and a half times the speed of sound. Although he had made this three and a half hour flight from Boston's Logan International Airport over twenty times in the past, this trip was different. He was being summoned to return to the Vatican by the Pope.

He sipped the Italian vintage wine from the signature papal goblet and relaxed in the oversized Corinthian leather seat reserved for first class. Closing his eyes for a moment, his mind began drifting to an earlier time, when a young priest tutored him in the Greek classics and taught him to read and understand Latin fluently by the time of his first communion. When he graduated Loyola Marymount University at age nineteen, he could converse in eight languages, effortlessly switching among them, as his professors challenged his unique ability. The Catholic Church recruited his talents and Justin entered the priesthood when he was twenty years old. Attached to the Vatican as a linguistic expert in the department of religious antiquities, he was assigned to translate ancient dialects of Hebrew, Aramaic, and Sumerian origin. He was chosen by Pope Alphonse to accompany him and write the holy masses and addresses to be spoken in various languages by his holiness. Academically, he flourished in the environment that honored him with the opportunity to serve. But, there was a dark side. Justin became a percipient witness to the backstabbing and jealousies that flourished in Vatican political circles. He learned early that he had no particular use for the pompous young Cardinal from Germany whom he would later confront after being elevated to Cardinal Justin Kennedy of the United States of America.

"More wine, your Eminence?" the steward asked as Justin opened his eyes at the intrusion. He looked into the half-full goblet resting on his leg.

"No, not now, but most assuredly later," he smiled.

He glanced at the briefcase in the chair next to him and decided he could wait no longer. He reached for the briefcase, opened it, and took out the classified folder. The Papal seal, embossed in wax, clearly indicated it had not been opened. The folder was marked "Cardinal Justin Kennedy **CLASSIFIED**", and was dated March 15, 2009.

The Cardinal anticipated that the contents of the folder related to a continuing disagreement between Justin and the Cardinal from Germany, his Eminence Kurt Wilhelm. Justin was seeking Vatican funding for archeological excavations he believed would unlock the two thousand year old mystery pinpointing where the Cross of the crucifixion was buried. Cardinal Wilhelm opposed the funding claiming it constituted frivolous expenditures of Vatican funds that could be better used to feed the poor, his favorite charity. Justin, interested in a more balanced approach that included feeding the soul, saw discovery of the priceless relic as a means to rekindle faith.

Wilhelm was a giant of a man at over six feet three inches tall. He was respected by many, feared by most. Extremely muscular at age sixty, he was an imposing figure as he towered over the other Cardinals. The ugly rumor that his father had been a member of the Hitlerian S.S. leadership had never been proven, yet he knew the stigma remained and added to his mystique. His head was meticulously clean-shaven. The bald appearance and thick German accent gave him the commanding presence of a general prepared to lead his troops into battle. If you closed your eyes you could picture him as a military man during World War II marching his men over the rolling hills near the Skoda automobile factory, where the German enigma-coding machine was built outside of Prague. There was no mistaking his Arian heritage.

Kurt Von Wilhelm, as a youth was studious, intense and athletic. His leadership on the soccer field spilled over into his academic endeavors. However, as a spurned lover, he sought solace in the priesthood upon graduation from the University of Hidelburg.

From the beginning, his superiors in the Catholic Church took notice of his dedication and zeal.

A meteoric rise from Priest to Bishop, then to Archbishop was accomplished in 15 years. A stunning promotion to a financial post at the Vatican began paving the road for his sought after goal of becoming a Roman Catholic Cardinal.

Once accomplished, he set his sights on the great prize of the papacy, an unrelenting mosaic of alliances, back room deals, patronage and border-line blackmail.

He was both respected and feared. Welheim could be cruel yet at times benevolent.

His dark side was his sexual drive and involvement with Marcella De La Sant, the former wife of Hosni Khatabi an Arab arms merchant.

His encounters with the countess at her villa near Rome took on the vestiges of a Roman orgy. He was matched perfectly with the Maltese Countess whose own sexual drive exceeded the clerics.

He would insist Marcella verbally relate her experience with the gang rape she experienced as a teenager. She obliged, often embellishing her ordeal with descriptive words that always brought him to a rapid climax.

Wilhelm destined to change the face of history in the Roman Catholic Church.

His nemesis, Cardinal Justin Kennedy was Cardinal Wilhelm's enemy in the very real sense of the word and he would do anything to derail the American Cardinals growing popularity.

Justin Kennedy had the innate ability to master languages with ease. He was fluent in Latin at age seven, thanks to the efforts of a local parish priest in his hometown of Boston.

He became fluent in Arabic, French, Hebrew, Italian, Spanish, Russian and obscure ancient languages. His teachers were astounded at the ease which he continued to add dialects to his knowledge. Justin often joked that his head injury as a young man 'scrambled' his brain waves, which in turn converted his mind into a language computer.

Justin's skill was honed as he visited various mosques and synagogues and engaged in conversation with the religious leaders in their language.

It was during this time, at age twenty-one he decided his vocation as a Roman Catholic priest. His assignment to the Vatican as a linguistic expert with the department of religious antiquities started his rapid rise in the Roman Catholic Church.

Having the attention of the late Pope Francis II, he would travel with his holiness, writing the masses and addresses to be spoken in the various languages by the Pope.

The foreign Catholic community was always amazed by the Popes ability to speak their language. Few were aware Francis knew only his native language and it was Kennedy who coached his Pontiff with pronunciation and inflection, often using phonetics.

Many were jealous of the American Bishops close relationship with Pope Francis II and were further inflamed when Justin was named Cardinal just prior to the Popes death.

Justin Kennedy was not a politician, rather he portrayed himself as a biblical scholar, but destiny was about to change his life forever.

Justin, on the other hand, did not possess the temperament to intimidate his colleagues like his German nemesis. At age forty-eight, he was one of the youngest prelates ever selected to the Sacred College of Cardinals. He was a Cardinal who never had a parish or a pulpit. The title was conferred in recognition for his expertise in linguistics, biblical translation and interpretation. Soon to be triggered by the information in the classified folder, those skills would be put to good use.

Wilhelm had aspirations of ascending to the Throne of Peter. It was well known that Pope Alphonse, at age eighty-seven, had serious health problems. Justin, if successful in finding the Cross, would be a serious competitor for the throne, although the thought of such a happening was not even considered by Justin. Wilhelm was shrewd, knowledgeable in Vatican politics, and would not hesitate to eliminate those who might conceivably be a challenge to his selection. He believed he had the upper hand in being the next Pope since his traditionalist views of Church doctrine were supported by a majority of the factions within the Curia.

Wilhelm had thrown every financial hurdle in Justin's path trying to restrict monies allocated to archeological exploration. Nevertheless, he recognized that the Catholics of the world needed a restoration of faith. Acts of sexual abuse by priests as well as accusations of homosexuality and collections of child pornography could no longer be swept under the rug simply by transferring offenders from parish to parish. The loss of parishioners would deplete Vatican coffers continually needed to settle huge damage claims being faced by the Church. Wilhelm needed time. Time to find an acceptable solution. He also needed the position of authority, now held by Pope Alphonse. If the Cross was to be found, he knew faith would be restored. Wilhelm had a choice, either prevent the Cross from being found in the first instance, or be the prime player in its discovery. Millions of Catholics would flock to see the holy Cross, as well as members of other faiths who might be very generous with their money given the opportunity to cleanse their sins and become empowered with renewed religious convictions. Mass conversions to the Catholic faith were certainly possible. Wilhelm didn't care. His first goal was ascension to the Throne of Peter. He would take credit for the positive effects of the relic after his primary goal was accomplished.

One hour remained before the supersonic aircraft would touch down in Rome. Even after having flown in the aircraft several times before, Justin was always surprised at the heat generated in the cabin during descent caused by friction and speed of the aircraft. The X-7 was a relatively small plane, contrary to what most people believed. There were two seats to a row on either side of the aisle.

Justin opened the classified folder and read the confidential memorandum requesting translation of three parchments found during an archeological expedition in Russia. It mentioned that the parchments bore unusual markings and inscriptions and could be the missing three pages from the Book of Mark.

Some years before, Justin found the earliest version of the Codex, the index of all Catholic writings, stored in the stacks of the Vatican library privy only to the highest order of the clergy. That early version detailed the number of pages in the Book of Mark, identifying three more pages than that recorded in later versions of the Codex.

Justin continued reading. The memorandum described three page numbers circled in blood red ink. The mark of the Cross was affixed to each page in ink different from all the other handwritten pages of the Codex. The ink change and why the page numbers were never recorded in any subsequent version of the Codex remained a mystery Justin felt was his mission to uncover. Was it possible the mark of the Cross-on only these three pages was a clue from an ancient scribe who may have been sworn to secrecy under penalty of excommunication? Possibly a clue to the location of the Cross of the crucifixion? These thoughts and more went through Justin's mind until he was interrupted by the sound of the lowering of the landing gears of the supersonic jet.

He returned the memorandum to its folder, put the folder in his briefcase, and placed the briefcase under the seat in front of him in preparation for landing. Details not mentioned in the memorandum were to be saved for the in-person meeting Justin was summoned to attend, for security reasons.

The X-7 banked to the left on its approach to Leonardo da Vinci Airport. Justin focused his eyes on the familiar scene below and viewed the Coliseum, the Imperial Forum, and the monstrous cake-like Victor Emanuel monument. He watched the green Borghese Gardens disappearing under the wing of the jet. The Tiber River to the southeast of Rome leading the way to the upcoming Piazza di San Pietro and the Dome of the Basilica were now coming into view. The one hundred and eight acres of the Vatican were clearly visible. What would Michelangelo have created, Justin wondered, if he had experienced the view of his city from five thousand feet?

The aircraft touched down and taxied to the private terminal reserved for the plane. A special customs unit was located just inside the terminal, an added benefit for those who could afford to fly on the supersonic jet. Justin deplaned, completed customs quickly and without incident, and was met by Vatican security guards who led him to the black limousine emblazoned with the Papal Seal.

The limousine made its way toward the Vatican drawing the attention of onlookers recognizing the Papal Scal and trying to get a glimpse of who was behind the dark tinted windows. Justin paid little attention to the street scenes of Rome. Rather, his mind fastened on the subject that if proven, would shake the religious world to its molten core. It was times like these when he felt like a half pair of scissors, unable to cut out the pattern of his life. His destiny was controlled by a higher being. His arrival into the Vatican proper went smoothly. The grounds were little different than from the time Pope Symmachus had it built on the slope of Mons Vaticanus in the year 500.

Justin was ushered briskly through the underground labyrinth of the papal palazzo, past unblinking statues of marble that stared into forever. Then he was left alone after he entered the antechamber of the Sistine Chapel, called the Sala Regia, which originally served as a reception area for princes and royal ambassadors. He stood quietly scanning the powerful frescoes depicting momentous turning points in the life of the Church.

"Ah, my dear Justin. Welcome home!" Monsignor Enrique Capelli's voice startled him from his reverie as he was enfolded in an embrace. Their golden pectoral crucifixes clanged together, a seeming violation of the silence of the room. Just behind Capelli stood a woman.

"Eminence, may I present Sister Mary Frances," Capelli said holding her elbow as she genuflected and kissed the hand Justin proffered. The Sister was wearing a habit made of black serge fabric that fell softly from the neck to the top of her shoes. A white coif made of starched linen covered her neck and framed her face. She wore a simple silver ring symbolizing that the final vows had been taken. A large cross on a silver chain hung from her neck. Her dress was symbolic of holiness, cleanliness, simplicity, and purity. Her tanned face confirmed the dedication to her work as a Vatican archaeologist. Most striking was her emerald green eyes. He feigned a slight nod of approval toward Cappelli and then looked back at the Sister. "It is a great pleasure to meet you Sister," Justin said with a look of surprise not knowing what role the Sister was to play, if any, regarding his summoning to the Vatican. "Sister Mary Francis prompted the memorandum you received," Capelli continued. "My pleasure, your Eminence," she replied politely. Justin was still unsure of the details of the meeting about to take place and chose to limit any discussion until privacy was assured. Being in the presence of a Cardinal, intimidating to most did not faze Mary Frances. Perhaps it was because her work allowed an intermingling with people outside her faith. Wearing a traditional Nun's habit was the exception rather than the rule. Her eye for detail honed over the years as she brushed away specs of earth looking for clues to ancient relics extended to a keen observance of people. Justin's black hair with slight streams of gray gave him a very distinguished look that did not go unnoticed by Mary Frances.

The nun was a product of the southwest desert of Arizona. Born in 1965 in a small farming community named Casa Grande, near Phoenix. Her first job out of high school was as a tour guide at the Casa Grande ruins at Coolidge, Arizona. The 'Big House' as it was called, was one of the largest and mysterious prehistoric structures ever built in North America.

It was here at America's first archeological preserve she became intrigued with becoming an archeologist. A scholarship to the University of Arizona was the first step in her quest.

Her thesis on the Akimel O'Otham or the Hohokam, 'those who are gone' is still a text book study of the ancient people who inhabited the 'Casa Grande'. She could not remember exactly when she received the 'calling' to the Catholic Church, but her post graduate work at Notre Dame University and her close relationship with a Mother Superior of a local Indiana convent was a contributing factor in her decision.

Now after twenty plus years in her field, with experiences in exotic places such as Yemen, Ethiopia, South America, Turkey and the African continent, her crowing glory of discovery was at hand with her participation in the search for the Cross of Jesus of Nazareth.

"Come now my friends, we have a private room reserved next to the Papal Study. Please follow me," Capelli announced with an air of excitement. Justin and Mary Frances followed Capelli to the room adjoining the Papal Study.

Entry to this room was by invitation only with the Pope the sole person who could issue the invitation. Justin had never been in this room before, a testament to the importance of what would be discussed. They seated themselves around the conference table upon which was a fourteenth century, ornate sterling silver tray, engraved by the finest Italian artisans, depicting doves of peace flying up to touch the outstretched hand of God. A variety of cakes made fresh that morning by Vatican bakers were arranged on the silver service in an artistic shape of a cross. Apples, oranges, pears, and pomegranates outlined the perimeter. Matching tea and coffee service was placed next to the tray.

"Please, help yourselves to some refreshments," Capelli motioned. "If you would like something more substantial, please tell me and it will be ordered." Capelli didn't hesitate to fill his plate with a large sampling of everything available. His five foot-five inch frame supported about two hundred eighty-five pounds, mostly centered on his waist, and coupled with his smile, gave him a rather pleasantly portly look.

"May I pour you some coffee?" Justin asked the Sister.

"Please," she responded. Justin poured the coffee.

"As you may have surmised, Sister Mary Francis discovered the object that brings us together today," Capelli said as he walked to the door closing it to the outside world anticipating that the conversation was about to begin.

Privacy secured, Justin did not hesitate to inquire about this mystery that had been designated "Classified". "Would you be so kind as to start at the beginning and tell me of your find?"

Mary Frances began. "I was part of an expedition exploring some of the oldest monasteries in Russia. One, in particular, that we came upon was in Darbestand. I was left alone and made my way to the catacombs. The rest of the expedition concentrated on the historical significance of the architectural design of the church itself.

I lit a torch and entered the pitch-black caves trying to stay in the center of the pathway. As I continued, I came across another torch placed about six feet high fastened to the catacomb walls. I lit this torch with the fire from the torch I was carrying to gain more light and continued, finding two more torches fixed to the cave walls along the main passageway at about ten foot intervals. These torches were the only means of light. The church elders strictly forbade artificial lighting such as flashlights. It had something to do with their belief that only natural God given resources could be utilized in this ancient burial chamber. Man-made objects, consisting of anything that would not return to the earth embodying the principles of dust to dust and ashes to ashes, were considered unholy. I lit each torch as I proceeded deeper into the caves. The light from the previous torch barely illuminated the pathway leading to the next one. About forty feet into the catacombs I came upon the fourth torch. But, it was placed about nine feet high against the wall and I could not reach it. There was nothing to stand on and I thought of going back. Then my curiosity got the better of me. Why was this torch placed beyond man's reach? It was as if someone decided that no one was allowed to proceed beyond the third torch.

I continued into the caves. The main passageway curved eliminating all light from behind. I slowly moved my torch from side to side allowing the light to bounce off the walls as I continued walking. I looked to my left and saw cobwebs covering the cave wall in one particular spot. I stopped and went over for a closer look. As I approached I extended my arm to gain additional light and the fire from my torch ignited the veil of cobwebs. I backed away watching the threads sizzle as they were consumed by the fire. Then, I saw that the centuries of cobwebs did not cover a solid portion of the cave wall. Instead, the cobwebs concealed an opening that led to a side chamber. I walked through the remnants of the cobwebs and saw a wood casket that was placed in a carved out portion of the chamber wall. Closer examination revealed that wood pegs secured the burial lid, as was the custom of Jews over the centuries using the oldest renewable resource known to man to bury the dead. I knew that Jewish tradition forbade metal objects to be used on wood caskets as fasteners because they would not return to the earth as dust over time. The fact that this was a wood casket was a clue that the body inside was probably someone of Jewish descent, although this did not reconcile with the final resting place being in the catacombs of a monastery.

I reached out to touch the casket and must have pushed the lid a little too hard. The pressure of my touch was enough to cause parts of the wood pegs attaching the lid to loosen. The pegs had disintegrated over the years and wood dust from the pegs fell against the side of the casket freeing the lid from its body. I thought of stopping at that point, wishing not to disturb the remains, but my instinct told me to go forward. I slid off the lid of the coffin and saw the remains of a person dressed in priestly garments. I noticed a bulge under the cloak covering the body and lifted the garment. A small clay urn was nestled under the shoulder bones of the skeleton as if the urn was being cradled. I reached for the urn and took it from its resting place to examine it further. A stopper in the top of the urn secured whatever contents were inside. I put the urn on a ledge and balanced my torch against the sidewall to free my hands. As I turned the urn in my hands I noticed what appeared to be ancient Aramaic writing encrypted around the body of the urn, although it was foreign to any Aramaic writing I had seen before. The word 'Mark', which I did recognize, was written in large letters at the end of the writing. This could have meant many things, but due to the age of the vessel and the fact that the casket was hidden in a manner indicating it should never be found, my heart began racing with excitement. I knew then I had to take the urn with me so I could look at its' contents privately.

I picked up my torch and carried the urn retracing my steps and extinguishing the fire from each of the wall torches as I made my way back toward the entrance. My heart was still racing but this time for fear of being caught stealing a sacred object from the church. When I reached the entryway I took off my jacket and wrapped it around the urn tying the sleeves around it to make sure it was properly concealed. I then cradled it under my arm, inadvertently mimicking its last resting place. After carefully looking all around and not seeing anyone, I left the monastery and returned to my hotel room. I locked the door." She paused momentarily, as if to catch her breath, and continued.

"Convinced of security, I took the urn and placed it on the side table hoping I could translate the encryption with the benefit of better lighting, but I couldn't. I had to look inside. I removed the stopper and the ancient air inside escaped emitting an unexpected strange pleasant scent as if to beckon me to reach for its contents. Inside were three parchments that I removed, unrolled, and placed on the side table next to the urn. The parchments were made from the skin of goats or sheep. Writing in the same strange language as the encryption on the outside of the urn spilled over from the first parchment to the next as if they were all intended to be read in a specific order. A Cross was prominently centered at the top of each of the three parchments. Each Cross was red...unlike the dark ink used in the body of the writings. I had the feeling that I found something of importance. I carefully returned the parchments to the urn and called Monsignor Capelli reporting what I had found. Then I went back to the monastery to avoid suspicion, and joined the others."

"Of course I advised the good Sister not to reveal the find or its contents until it could be studied, having you in mind Eminence," Capelli interjected. "I arranged for the Sister to return immediately to the Vatican. The contents were shown only to me, and Pope Alphonse. Capelli continued, "We have indeed identified the writing as a form of Aramaic used around the time of Jesus, but it was unlike any we had previously studied. We were unable to recognize most of the words".

"I applaud your foresight in the handling of this matter, Monsignor," Justin said as he smiled at Capelli. He then addressed Mary Frances, "and to you Sister, the Church is grateful for your curiosity as well as your ability to recognize what may turn out to be a most significant find, and of course, your understanding of the secrecy that must be maintained."

"The few words we were able to decipher gives us hope that these parchments might be the three missing pages of the Book of Mark," she said, her voice projecting obvious excitement, "I pray this is so...I must confess, I feel immersed in a web of deception and guilt. Am I wrong for what I did your Eminence? I took what was not mine to take."

"Do not be too eager to judge yourself," Justin said, attempting to assuage her guilt. "Deception for the good of mankind is to be rewarded not condemned. Remember, only four of us know about this and we will keep it that way for the time being."

"Now, may I see the parchments," Justin asked, dismissing her concerns without further mention as if they were not worth noting given the possible significance of the find. Capelli nodded and walked to the framed painting of the Madonna at the west wall of the room. He pushed a concealed button installed under the frame and the painting slid to the right revealing a wall safe. He turned the dial on the combination safe listening for the tumblers to fall into place. He opened the safe, removed the clay urn and brought it to the table.

"I will remove the stopper for you Eminence," Capelli offered.

"That will not be necessary," Justin countered as he removed cotton gloves from his pocket and quickly inserted his hands. "Simply a precautionary measure to avoid the oils of my skin from touching the parchments," he added. Capelli then handed the urn to Justin. Cautiously, but without hesitation, Justin removed the parchments from the urn and placed the rolled pages on the conference table. He held the top end as he unrolled them. Unlike paper, the animal skin, once spread, remained flat without snapping back in place. He carefully reached for the first parchment and lifted it from the others placing it on the conference table. He adjusted his reading glasses and had his first look at the writing. The word "Mark" and a red cross were visible as if written yesterday just as Mary Frances had described. Many of the other letters were faint and some not even visible. The ink, or whatever was used to print the letters in the body of the manuscript, seemed to be of two or three different consistencies. Mary Frances saw the look of disappointment in his face as his eyes were fixed on the parchment as if he were held hostage.

"I noticed the missing letters also," she said anticipating his concern.

Justin looked up at her. "This will be no easy task. I cannot be sure that even after translation of the visible words that an accurate understanding of the message contained will be forthcoming."

Capelli shook his head in disgust as if he thought he had won the lottery only to discover he misread one of the winning numbers.

"The first thing we must do is to get a chemical analysis of the medium used in the writing. I also want DNA samples, especially of the material used in drawing the red cross." Justin's curiosity and determination were evident. "Also, let's do a carbon dating analysis on a small sample."

"Your Eminence," Mary Frances interrupted. "May I suggest a radical approach that might help?"

"And...what might that be," Capelli inserted before Justin could respond.

"Three years ago I was working with the Pompeii urns discovered in Herculium. The ash from Mount Vesuvius had buried the library under thirty feet of volcanic ash. The parchments in the vessels were charred and lumped together from the intense heat. We devoted the next few months with tweezers and micro-scopes meticulously attempting to fit together bits of writings as if putting together a puzzle. We were not successful. Then one day Professor Fritz from Cambridge came up with the idea of using ultra violet light cameras under intense magnification. It was a long shot but it worked. Over eighty percent of the faded letters came alive under the process."

Justin smiled. "If you can do the restoration, I will decipher the words. Monsignor, please see that the Sister has all the resources she needs to give this a fair shot."

"I will attend to her every wish, your Eminence." Capelli nodded as he spoke acknowledging his obedience.

"Is it possible to do all lab testing in a secure environment? We do not wish to contaminate or reveal our work."

"Yes, Sister," Justin responded. "The DNA testing will be under my supervision exclusively. I will collect the samples from the parchments personally. The lab technicians will not know what they are testing." Mary Frances was quick to grasp the sig-nificance of the DNA testing but said nothing. Would the results show that what appeared to be blood was human, animal, or from another world?

The papal conference room became their workplace. A small area of the corner of the room was enclosed by glass walls and acted as a "clean room" simulating laboratory conditions to avoid contamination. Justin took a deep breath as he bent over the first parchment, scalpel in hand. Mary Frances and Capelli watched from the outside the glass walls. Feeling both excitement and fear Justin's hand began to tremor as approached the area selected for taking of the samples. Being watched did not contribute to his comfort. Capelli's nose was nearly touching the glass enclosure as he strained to see what Justin was doing inside the clean room. His involuntary heavy breathing began to fog the outside of the glass partition. A snore-like sound, as if his nasal passages were partially blocked, permeated the glass causing a droning sound inside the clean room. Justin withdrew his hand at the last moment unwilling to risk a fatal error in scraping caused by the distractions. He exited the clean room and addressed his two associates.

"You know," Justin said looking at both of them, "Perhaps it might be better if I could be left alone for a few minutes."

"I know it's me," Capelli offered, "I just cannot contain my excitement. Of course we will wait outside."

"I thank you for your understanding, Monsignor. We wouldn't want to jeopardize the integrity of the parchment as a result of my nervousness," Justin said politely, attempting to shoulder the blame for an action that could otherwise be taken as rude.

Alone, Justin directed his scalpel to the very bottom of the red cross where the upright beam began. He carefully turned his hand exposing the inner edge of the blade and touched it to the red marking scraping a minute amount of the red substance from the bottom of the cross. He then dropped the red material into a Petri dish and sealed it. He picked up a second scalpel and returned to the ancient writing cutting one of the most legible letters from the bottom of the parchment and placing it in a second Petri dish and covering it as before. He marked the first dish "DNA". The second dish was marked "ink analysis". A third scalpel was used to extract a small piece of the parchment, which he placed in a glassine envelope marking it "carbon dating sample". Emotionally drained for the moment, he sat down and stared at his work before exiting the clean room hoping the results would confirm authentication of the find.

CHAPTER TWO

$\mathcal{S}$wiss guards accompanied the deliveryman wheeling a hand-truck with boxes marked "fragile" and addressed: "Vatican, attention: Sister Mary Frances". The boxes were placed on carts in a staging area and immediately hand-carried to the conference room by Vatican security police.

Justin delivered the parchment samples to Dr. Maxine Turek of the Turek Institute. Dr. Turek, an expert in scientific testing for age, composition, and DNA analysis, used the most advanced techniques in Europe including an accelerator for C14 carbon dating. Her laboratory was conveniently located in the heart of Rome. He was careful to select a laboratory independent of the Church in order to avoid skepticism and bias regarding the validity of the results.

"It is a pleasure to meet you, Cardinal Kennedy. I am pleased to be working for you and on behalf of the Holy Father." The call from Monsignor Capelli setting up the meeting gave her a little background on what would be required. Dr. Turek, a tall woman in her early fifties, had striking Scandinavian features of piercing blue eyes, long blond eyelashes, and clear milky skin inherited from her mother. She had a small beauty mark on her left cheek and blond hair pulled back into a ponytail that fell to her shoulders. Dark rimmed glasses, accented her high cheekbones as the only clue aside from her lab coat, that she might be a doctor. Her father was a Count of Polish descent, affording her the opportunity of attending the finest schools in Europe. "Why don't we go into my office and discuss the details of your requests?"

"Thank you Doctor. I'm just the messenger today but I do play a minor role in the research of the project," he said modestly. Inside the doctor's office Justin took the samples from his leather briefcase and set them on the desk. Still standing he continued, "I know your time is valuable and I have taken the opportunity to mark each sample to indicate the type of testing we want."

"Please, sit a moment," she responded. "Let's talk about the testing procedures so you can be assured that what we do will be sufficient for your needs. First, I want you to understand that carbon dating analysis is not a precise science." She picked up the glassine envelope and looked at the sample that was visible through the clear plastic. "Do you know the type of material in the envelope marked for carbon dating?"

"We believe it is animal material, possibly sheepskin," he answered.

"Do you wish to test the age of the sheepskin or the markings on it?" she asked.

"Good question. I didn't think about that."

"Let me tell you the variation possibilities without getting too technical. The sun's magnetic field, which varies over time, affects the amount of C-14 carbon in the atmosphere. Natural things take up the carbon directly or indirectly from the atmosphere when they are alive. But, exposure to carbon in other ways can influence the results. Now, we might determine the age of the animal at the time of death, but we would not know how long after death the marking was made unless we test for it. Having said that, I would caution you that even with our advanced equipment we couldn't pinpoint the exact age of either object. My best guess is that we could date to 200 years plus or minus. If we are lucky and get very good measurements of isotope ratios...we might get an accuracy of plus or minus 10 to 15 years."

"I see. Well then, let's test for both," Justin said with conviction.

"Now, your chemical analysis and DNA testing requests will be almost 100 percent accurate," she offered.

"How long until I see the results?"

"Carbon dating will require sample preparation and then about two hours for the actual testing using our accelerator dating process. We'll need about forty-eight hours for the other testing. We're fitting you in between other work scheduled as a favor to the Church."

"Thank you for your consideration," Justin replied. "I will pick up the results personally in two days time. Naturally, all results are to be kept confidential, correct?"

"Of course," the doctor replied. With that, Justin returned to the Vatican and to the work that awaited him.

Empty boxes still in the hallway greeted Justin when he returned to the conference room. He opened the door and saw that drapes had been placed over the glass walls of the clean room blocking out all light. Capelli, seated next to a window, looked up from his Vatican newspaper when he saw the Cardinal enter.

"I see changes are being made, Monsignor," Justin said looking toward the draped room.

"Yes, your Eminence. Our very own Vatican detective is busy at work inside our "laboratory" constructed by Vatican carpenters as she requested.

"Is the 50 cent tour available?" Justin laughed.

"I'll see what can be arranged." Capelli walked to the clean room and knocked on the door. "His Eminence is back and requests an audience with you and the "clean room", he said jokingly.

"I'll be only a few minutes, just let me get to a completion point and I'll be right out." Mary Frances shouted. Capelli turned to Justin and offered him a glass of cold water, which was promptly accepted. A few moments later Mary Frances emerged from her sequestered enclave, eyes blinking as her pupils adjusted to the daylight.

"It works," she announced overjoyed. "I can do it. Come," she held her hand out to Justin. "You must see this for yourself." She led him back into the clean room and as an afterthought said, "Monsignor, you are welcome also, come quickly." She turned on the normal lights and asked the Monsignor to stand by the lights ready to turn them off when she gave the word. She then took one of the parchments and placed it under the microscope fitted with powerful magnification lenses and affixed to cameras that projected images onto a small light sensitive screen. She peered through the double eye scope and focused in on an area where letters of one of the words was completely missing.

"Your Eminence, look into the microscope and tell me what you see." Justin looked and responded, "I see nothing but a blank area."

"Do not lift your eyes," she directed. "Monsignor, please turn off the lights." She then switched on the ultra violet lights.

"Amazing...just amazing. The letters are faint but I can read them," Justin said with eyes transfixed to the eyepieces of the microscope.

"Now smile," Mary Frances joked as she snapped the picture of what Justin was seeing through the microscope. "Lights on, Monsignor, if you please."

Justin looked up as she handed him the instant photograph of what he had seen. "It will be a tedious process," she reminded him, "but it will be done."

The next forty-eight hours were intense. Justin, relying on his studies of Biblical translations for the past twenty years worked tirelessly. He had scrutinized the <u>Septuagint</u>, the most ancient translation of the Old Testament from Hebrew to Greek and the <u>Latin Vulgate Bible</u>. But it was the <u>Chaldee Targums,</u> Aramaic translations of the language used by the sacred writers in certain portions of the Old Testament, that proved to be the "Rosetta stone" for deciphering the ancient dialect found in the parchment writings. Letters became words as the agonizingly slow work progressed with Mary Frances feeding Justin the missing pieces of the puzzle as soon as she finished photographing a section.

At the end of the second day Justin place a call to Dr. Turek who advised the test results would be ready at 9:00 a.m. the next morning and that she would discuss them with him. Justin had progressed far enough in the translation to where he was almost sure the parchments were the lost three pages. But, certainty could only be assured once the translations were complete and confirmed by the laboratory tests. Justin opened his briefcase and took out a yellow legal pad and a pencil. Experience had taught him never to take the risk of a leaking pen when dealing with priceless manuscripts. He focused on continued translation of the first parchment, now with words complete, thanks to the photographic images. Mary Frances and Justin continued working through most of the night. Mary Frances, exhausted, finally left for her apartment escorted by a Swiss guard at 3:00 a.m. Capelli left early complaining that his stomach was growling unmercifully requiring that he have dinner as soon as possible before retiring for the night.

At sun up Cardinal Kennedy was in the Vatican Chapel joined by several other Cardinals serving mass. Aides had breakfast prepared in the dining room where the Cardinals gathered after mass was concluded. They then went about their daily routines, except for Cardinal Kennedy. His driver was waiting to transport him to his 9:00 a.m. meeting.

Justin arrived at the Turek Institute thirty minutes early. Dr. Turek's secretary announced the Cardinal's early arrival by intercom and was instructed to show him in immediately. She rose from her chair as the Cardinal entered.

"Your timing is perfect. I just finished reading the test results."

"Good morning to you doctor," Justin responded in an effort to downplay the importance of the tests by putting the results aside for the moment. She nodded her head acknowledging his greeting and responded in rote Catholic fashion, "and to you, your holiness." Although her mother was Protestant, her father had insisted on a Catholic upbringing. The pleasantries out of the way, Justin was ready to proceed. "And, the test results, were you able to reach satisfactory opinions based upon the scientific evidence?" he asked.

"Yes and no," she answered. "Let's go over the positives first and then we can tackle the perplexing area. First, the carbon dating proved more accurate than we had even hoped. The sample provided is from the skin of a sheep. We have determined both the animal skin and the marking dates to the same time period around 30 AD give or take fifteen or twenty years. It would be prudent to take another sampling from a different part of the object for verification."

"No, that will not be necessary," Justin responded knowing that he was satisfied with the answer given. The parchments were written just after the death of Jesus just as he had hoped. "Let's go to the chemical analysis next."

"Very well. This was a material composed of soot or lampblack. There were also traces of burnt shavings of ivory mixed with gum. And...there were traces of vegetable matter used as dyes around the time the markings were made."

"And the red scrapings? Was its DNA composition of Human origin?"

Dr. Turek hesitated as she looked down at her notes. "I don't know.

"You don't know? So, what are you saying?" Justin questioned.

"Each of us has a certain genetic makeup, which is the hereditary blueprint imparted to us by our parents and stored in DNA. Every single cell in our bodies contains DNA, the genetic material that programs how cells work. 99.9 percent of human DNA is the same in everyone, meaning that only 0.1 percent of our DNA is unique! In the case of our testing, the 99.9 percent of human DNA was present just like it is in every human. However, there was more than .1 percent of DNA that was unique. In other words, the DNA found exceeded 100 percent known to exist in humans. Naturally, we tested the sample twice, but the results did not differ. Human DNA holds vast amounts of information that is transmitted to cells. How the additional information got there, we do not know. We only know that from the beginning of time through evolution or divine inception, whichever you believe in, additional information was added."

"So... you cannot trace the origin of the DNA?" Justin asked as if interrogating the doctor.

"Not exactly, we were able to identify the female of the species as human, descended from an African woman who lived perhaps 150,000 years ago. Scientifically, she is known as "Eve" and all humans can be traced back to her through genetic material present in the female egg cell that lives intact from generation to generation. We cannot do the same for males. The counterpart of that genetic material in a male doesn't exist because it comes from the sperm cell that dies and therefore cannot be traced." Dr. Turek stood and handed the test results to the Cardinal. "Are there any other questions you wish to ask?"

"Just one, just to be clear, "Justin responded. "As to the DNA results, is it your professional opinion that the DNA is of some human origin mixed with another species?"

"If you mean did a human procreate with an animal, the answer is no. At least, no animal presently known to man," she answered.

"Thank you, doctor. You have been most generous with your time. I'll leave you to your work and return to the Vatican to begin mine."

Mary Frances had just finished the photography of the last parchment and had removed the drapes covering the clean room making sure everything was in order when Justin returned. He looked at Mary Frances but did not say a word. He knew she was anxious to hear the results of the tests but he wasn't sure what to say. After what seemed to be many minutes of silence he said, "you may have found what I have been searching for all these years. If so, you have opened the door to eternity and a fresh start for the Catholic Church." A broad smile came to her face but she said nothing. Justin opened his briefcase and removed the written report of Dr. Turek but instead of reading from it, he put his own spin on the conclusions. "The manuscripts were definitely written at or about the time of the crucifixion. The red mark of the Cross is not an ink. It is blood. Possibly mixed with gold to retain its color. It is not animal blood. It is a mixture of human blood and something else." Mary Frances looked puzzled.

"If my suspicions are correct, it could be the blood of Jesus." At this point that possibility cannot be refuted." Justin continued. "The reddish tint to some of the letters is most likely to be plant or other material used as an ink mixed with gold. This was a practice known only to High Priests. There you have it in a nutshell. Confirmation must be made in the translation of the parchments."

Mary Frances handed him the last of the photographs produced under the ultra violet lights. "If any of the letters are too faint to decipher, let me know. I haven't broken down the equipment and we can try some adjustments bring them into better focus."

"Good thinking," Justin responded, "but so far I'm having no problems. A few more hours and I will have some preliminary information for you as to my progress with the translations. Why don't you have some lunch and meet me here at 3:00 this afternoon with Monsignor Capelli?"

"I hope I have the stomach to eat. I'm so nervous."

"Well then, why don't you lunch with the Monsignor, he has never been known to refuse a meal and maybe he can stimulate your appetite," Justin said sarcastically.

"We'll see you at 3:00," Mary Frances said with a smile and left the room.

Justin spent his time filling in the missing letters of all three of the parchments re-writing the words to his yellow legal pad before he started the final translations. His mind drifted back to the DNA results and he wondered if his interpretation of the manuscripts might be biased because he wanted them to be. Could he be objective or would he inadvertently, or by design, create religious history. Surely, no one could seriously challenge his expertise in this ancient dialect. He was in total control of the meaning of the words. He decided to let God direct his conscious and remove himself from the problem. Meanwhile, he had pieced together the first important segment of the puzzle. The symbols near the edge of the first parchment tied in with the symbols found in the ancient manuscripts of Mark! He reported his success to Mary Frances and Capelli at the afternoon meeting.

"Now the real task begins, word for word translation," Justin told them. We shall begin to decipher all three parchments tomorrow. For now, I need some rest."

"I am at your disposal Eminence," Mary Frances volunteered blushing from her feeling of humility after having made such a find, her face masking the building excitement of her participation.

"This is to be shouted from the rooftops." Capelli said.

Justin looked at him sternly. "Total secrecy must be maintained Monsignor."

"I did not mean to imply..." Capelli stammered, "I was just offering the thought that this will be such a monumental moment in the history of the Catholic Church that it will be difficult for anyone to keep reserve." He shrugged, "You are correct, of course."

"Patience my trusted friend, let's reserve judgment until I have had an opportunity to translate all three manuscripts." Justin said. "The first parchment seems to be a continuation of the Book of Mark, but I cannot be certain.

The group was destined to spend the next three days together. They had very little sleep and took meals only as their bodies demanded not wishing to be interrupted from their work. They now confirmed beyond doubt that the three pages of lost verses of the Book of Mark existed. They were on the verge of solving the meaning of the lost parchments. Justin spearheaded the painstaking research and translation. Sister Mary Frances' help in this endeavor did not go unnoticed by Justin. He knew he would be the only man in history who would be able to use the clues that these parchments might reveal. He never imagined that accumulation of such knowledge would one day bring him face to face with the Cross of Jesus Christ.

"Blessed Mother of God," Justin said as he saw the final words written by some ancient servant of God. He began reading aloud in a firm voice. "And to the north of the ruins stands the Temple of Joppa, and from this point towards the sea lays the Great Column; at one hundred and seven paces from the point of the Column at a depth of six cubits reposes the cross on which our beloved Savior was crucified. The rock lined crypt shall be the repository for this evil instrument until the Son of God comes again and from which he shall fashion the staff of redemption from its wood." "God is showering us with His glory this day" Justin said as they embraced each other.

"God grant that this be true. What a horrible trick if these parchments are bogus," Capelli said uneasily.

"So, the Cross is buried in Israel," Mary Frances said. Sure in her knowledge God would never play a trick on them.

"If it is so, then it is God's will and your reward for many years of faithful service to our Lord." Capelli bowed slightly to Justin.

"We will be extremely fortunate to discover the Cross was saved, let alone preserved in any measurable form," Justin said, trying to downplay their exuberance, at least until more facts could be established. It had been almost eighteen hours without sleep laboring over the parchments. Fatigue was becoming more evident. "Let's take a few hours break." Justin suggested, "Lord knows we can use it." The others nodded in agreement.

The parchments secured, the American Cardinal blessed Sister Mary Frances and his friend Monsignor Capelli. Capelli turned the lights off in the room and locked the door behind them. They then returned to their respective apartments.

Justin walked the short distance through the gardens of Vatican City alone. A full moon framed the great dome of Saint Peter's. The palaces stood mute. He felt full of his beliefs, sustained and elevated by the power of his purpose, armed with the knowledge, which would unlock the secret location of the Cross of Jesus. Entering the courtyard he nodded to the Vatican Swiss Guard who remained, as always, at attention. Justin entered his apartment suite, advanced to the small altar and knelt in front of the alabaster statue of the Blessed Virgin. Tonight his prayer was different from the usual rote. He gave thanks for the honor of taking part in the most remarkable discovery since the beginning of Christianity.

Justin was elated but very tired. His pride would not permit him to slow down to rest, not while many men in the Vatican, thirty years his senior, were still performing duties which would be best left to younger men. His only real physical complaint was migraine headaches that had recently surfaced. He had suffered the excruciating pain thirty years earlier resulting from a horrible automobile accident that left him in a coma. His mother made a solemn promise to God that if He spared Justin's life and cured him, she would raise Justin to carry on the work of the Church. Her pledge was accepted when Justin emerged from the coma eight weeks later. The migraines disappeared six months later when he entered seminary school. After washing and preparing for bed he slid beneath the sheets pulling the goose down comforter up to his neck. A twilight sleep finally overcame the dull pain in his head as he dozed off into a world full of dreams he could never remember the next morning.

CHAPTER THREE

$\mathcal{A}$t 5 a.m. the next morning, Justin was awakened by his aide's quiet voice and the sound of drapes being opened. "Cardinal— Cardinal Kennedy—it is time." The aide bowed politely and quickly left the room. Justin blinked his eyes as the change from darkness to light initiated the biological processes within his body beginning the natural circadian cycle once again.

Within the hour, Justin, Capelli, and Mary Frances met. The group worked in earnest for six more hours as Vatican waiters delivered coffee and breakfast croissants to the Vatican guard stationed outside the private room. The guard would then contact Capelli by beeper announcing the food was ready to take into the private room in order to maintain the strictest security. The trio was now very close to completion of the translation. Mary Frances suddenly laid her head on the table as Justin and Capelli looked at each other puzzled.

"Did you not rest last night Sister?" Capelli asked as he patted her shoulder.

Mary Frances lifted her head and sat upright in her chair replying, "No, I tried, but couldn't. Too many thoughts were going through my mind wondering what words would come next" she told them. Justin scanned the final parchment, seeing the outline of the words "Jesus King of the Jews..." Justin felt the emotion of the moment as his eyes teared. He felt both humbled and elated that his God had chosen him above all others to be the catalyst of this great discovery. Sister Mary Frances laid her hand on Justin's shoulder; he placed his hand upon hers and patted it as he turned toward her and gazed into her eyes. She felt a kinship of spirit. Justin felt satisfaction and at peace by her touch. The translation of the missing pages of the Book of Mark was completed.

With pride, Justin told the others of what would happen next. "Tomorrow we will make our presentation at the special conclave in the Hall of Broken Bones. The project will be revealed for the first time to the select few handpicked by Pope Alphonse. By that time, a preliminary plan to retrieve the Cross will have been conceived. We may have a great deal of difficulty locating the Cross, if it exists at all, let alone removing it. The trip to Israel and then back to Rome must be clothed in secrecy. Can you possibly imagine the uproar if we are caught in the act of smuggling one of the world's greatest artifacts from its country of origin?" Justin asked, not expecting an answer.

"Only from the non-Christian world," Cappelli replied.

"No... we will have our critics within and without the Church," Justin cautioned. "There is jealousy within the Church hoping for our failure. There will be jealousy from all three of the great faiths. Jealousy can be as dangerous as a spurned mistress. We must prepare carefully and carry out our mission flawlessly, if... we receive the Pope's blessing."

CHAPTER FOUR

$\mathcal{T}$he morning rays of the sun glinted off the dome of St. Peters Basilica as Vatican City began another fateful day.

"Your breakfast, sir." Justin's aide announced.

"Thank you, Antonio," Justin replied, "it is good of you to take such care of me. The past few days I doubt if I would have eaten at all if it was not for you."

"And your gratitude has been received in many ways by me and my family, your Eminence," he responded.

"Peace and love be with you, my son". Justin blessed the man as he left.

The tray had two poached eggs, a bran muffin, a pot of American brand coffee, the Vatican newspaper, and the single cigarette he allowed himself each morning.

Justin drank the last of the coffee, and stubbed the cigarette into an ashtray having taken only a few puffs. He began making preparations for his audience with Pope Alphonse and the synod, fully aware of the mixed emotions running through his mind as he combed his hair and placed the cardinal cap on his head.

Pope Alphonse was a closet liberal whose policies regarding reformation of the Church were kept stifled for political reasons within the Curia. Nevertheless, Justin knew the Pope's views on abolishing celibacy and admission of women to the priesthood was similar to his own, creating an unpublished bonding between the two. But, Pope Alphonse was weak, not just physically from the cancer that had metastasized, but also in failing to deal with critical issues affecting the very life of the Church. He refused to deal candidly with sexual abuse of altar boys and other indiscretions involving a multitude of priests. Catholics throughout the world were confused, deeply concerned and angry at the Vatican.

Justin could not accept the lack of action but he remained silent recognizing that Alphonse was one of the few allies that shared his views for the future reformation of the Catholic Church.

The issues being ignored would not go away simply by failing to address them. Lawsuits, filed in the United States, were numerous. They not only named the priests as defendants but also their Diocese. Financial responsibility became the burden of the only entities with "deep pockets", the respective Diocese, and now the Vatican.

Under the provisions of the insurance policies, if a priest was found liable one time, the insurance carriers did not have to pay damages to any other victim claimed to have suffered injury at the hands of that same priest. Those priests accused more than once were immediately retired. However, aggressive plaintiffs' lawyers were attacking the Church retirement funds, administered by each Diocese. Not only was the Church now a self-insurer having to pay the victims, but also had to support renegade priests who had no money to support themselves, no retirement benefits, and no means of earning an income. Alphonse, before being named Pope, refused to admit the Church's ineptness at containing the scandalous activities. Justin believed the Church needed a more forthright Pope attuned to the realities of life.

The American Cardinal left his residence and walked to the Hall of Broken Bones, aptly named as it had once been the storeroom for broken statues and was well suited for the events that were about to occur.

He entered the room and seated himself among those already present. The synod opened promptly on signal as the Papal secretary rang the bell. Pope Alphonse sat at the center chair of the U-shaped table. The frescoed room was chilled as usual. It was here that the hierarchy of the Church could discuss its many problems outside of public scrutiny. Also, it was the only place that all invitees could speak their minds without any direct threat to their positions. Even Il papa could be questioned without the rule of papal infallibility being in force. This was the one time that decisions already decided by the Pope could be debated and a "post mortem" of their affect, good or bad, was allowed in the hopes that future mistakes might be avoided. It was this same room where the now famous debate on priestly celibacy and birth control had been held. Today the discussions were to be limited to two issues; first, the translation of the three parchments by Cardinal Justin Kennedy and second, the direction the Church would take with the discovery.

As was the custom, a spiritual exhortation before the first order of business would take place. This was an honor falling to the oldest Cardinal priest in attendance. Eighty-four year old Paulo Galvenieto lifted shakily from his chair as all others bowed their heads in respect. Like the others, Justin knew that the words forthcoming from the doddering old man would be a jumbled version of prayer and selected passages of liturgy he was still able to remember, all thrown into a religious stew of half intelligible vowels and verbs... remnants of his recent stroke. Once accomplished, a collective sigh of relief broke the silence. The synod came to order.

His Holiness, Pope Alphonse was robed magnificently in white. He slowly rose from his chair and made eye contact with the nine others in attendance carefully avoiding any show of favoritism. To his right sat the traditionalists of the group; lantern jawed Wilhelm from Germany; cherub-faced Pleaschack from Poland; Sun Yet from Korea who always seemed to have a smile on his face; Rachmand from Argentina and Fitzgerald from Dublin. To his left sat Secretary General of the Vatican, Bishop Jacob Lattimer, and a black-robed priest of such youthful age that he appeared out of place. By the time the Pontiff got to Paulo Galvenieto, the old man was fast asleep.

"My Lord Cardinals and servants of Christ," the Pontiff began, his voice gentle yet firm, "we are assembled today to make decisions that will affect all of mankind. The Mother Church stands on the threshold of the most monumental time in history. The decisions made here will indeed change the face of the Roman Catholic Church." He turned and nodded to Justin, a signal for him to begin.

No less than four Vatican guards secured the large conference room. The select Catholic leaders, primed in advance by Monsignor Capelli, were awaiting Cardinal Kennedy's revelation of the location of the Cross and his plan to retrieve it. However, the decision had been made not to reveal the exact location of the Cross or the method the Cardinal and his staff would employ to accomplish the task.

Justin rose, cleared his throat, made the sign of the cross, and began. "The journey has just begun my friends" Justin said. "We are embarking on an odyssey which could change the course of mankind. I will now read aloud only the last page of the parchment. His Holiness has directed that the parchment pages revealing the exact location of the Cross be known only to me, my two associates, and the Holy Father." The American Cardinal began the recitation in a reverent tone of voice tinged with a degree of nervousness; his hands trembled slightly as he intoned the deciphered page.

"And Joseph of Arimathea and Nicodimas, having bribed the soldiers on Calvary for the body of Jesus, returned to the site of Golgatha wherein they met with Gaius Cassius, who was compelled to confide in them of the miraculous restoration of his failing eyesight. It was he, the official representative of the Pro Counsel Pilate who had prevented the legion officers from breaking the legs and crushing the skull of the man from Galilee. Gaius Cassius watched with disgust as the soldiers carried out their orders on the two thieves who were crucified with the Nazarene. Through his failing eyesight, Gaius Cassius approached the man on the cross and to prevent the soldiers from perpetrating further abuse on the body of Jesus, he did take his spear and pierce the side of the silent figure nailed on the cross. This he did to determine that the man was dead, local custom declared that all crucified must expire by dusk if they were of the Hebrew faith. As blood and water spewed lifelessly from the deep wound, Gaius Cassius lifted his lance and spear to the dark and menacing sky. Droplets of the blood of the slain Christ splattered into his eyes and his sight was restored in an instant as the lightning and thunder rent the air. So great was the power of the dead Jesus that Gaius Cassius did accept the man as the true Son of God; and so great was the forgiveness of Jesus that his final act was to perform yet another miracle. And Gaius Cassius did not only delivered the body of Jesus the Christ unto Joseph, but he also directed Simon the Cyrenian to again take the task of laboring the Cross on his shoulders and to deliver it also unto the house of Joseph of Arimathea. From the house of Joseph, they made haste to secret the bloodstained cross, the dreaded spikes, and the crude sign, to the Jaffa gate and thence to Emmaus. From this place to the river Akhdar, a perilous journey unto the ruins of Caesarea. With pitch and tar which they secured from a rich sea merchant who believed in the Christ, they preserved the Cross of Calvary."

A hush came over the room as Justin finished reading; Pope Alphonse soon broke the silence. "This could be the new beginning the Church has been searching for to renew the faith," Pope Alphonse declared. "We must seize this opportunity to call attention to something other than the sexual abuse of which our clergy has been charged. I have given the matter much prayer and thought. If we are to find the Cross, we may need to employ a little sleight of hand." Murmurs permeated the room as the others tried to understand what the Pope intended. Lattimer was the first to raise his hand to be acknowledged and with a nod from the Pope his request was granted.

"Need I remind all here, we are clergy, not magicians. Sleight of hand rings of deceit. I would pray that his holiness has nothing of the kind in mind." Lattimer said.

"Are we not magicians of a sort?" the Pope responded. "We must all remember that the growth of our Church has been made upon decisions which had dangers, real and perceived. Faith has been our watchword and what we ask of our followers. Faith gives us shelter when we are asked to explain miracles. I now ask you to have faith. If, in our judgment, things need to be done we might otherwise find objectionable, is it not worth doing in order to secure the Cross? You must believe we have weighed the risk and the reward. You must look away for the future of the Church."

Cardinal Wilhelm cleared his throat. "We have before us a simple choice. It is only a matter of time before our discovery is known. Shall we, who have made it possible, be the ones to step aside and allow the other religions to step in and profit? Shall we let others increase their memberships by millions because we are timid?" As always, the German Cardinal pulled on his left ear lobe as if to demand an answer. He decided the time was right to posture for a leadership role, covering all the bases in the event the Cross would be recovered.

"This is too serious a matter to decide now," Lattimer interrupted trying to buy time to make sense of the import of the

Pope's words not believing he was the only one hearing the Pope admit to not being above utilizing a less than honorable tactic. "We must go slowly in the situation."

"Slowly . . . .Did I hear you say slowly?" Cardinal Fitzgerald exploded. "This is the very thing that is wrong with our Church! We sit in conclave and debate while the world around us changes almost daily. Did we not debate the fate of Galileo? How long did it take us to admit that the sun did not revolve around the earth? John Paul Second finally got the Curia to decide Galileo's innocence... in 1982. This after 350 years!"

"Brothers, brothers." The Pope raised his voice a few decibels higher than usual. When the murmurs did not subside, the Pope rang the bell of obedience. Immediately, silence dropped on the room.

The Pope's eyes encompassed each face. "We have knowledge that the Cross of Christ can be found. Now, understand what this means. We are not here to debate the 'how' of the situation," his voice was firm.

"We cannot disregard world opinion," Secretary General Lattimer insisted, his gray eyes intense.

"The diplomacy we will leave to you, my dear Jacob. It is our right, our heritage," Cardinal Rachmand suggested, a benevolent smile fixed on his lips.

"We have no right to steal a world treasure from a foreign country!" Lattimer shouted. "Can you imagine the outrage if an Israeli commando group swooped down on the Vatican and stole the Pieta?" Cardinal Rachmand answered Lattimer by showing the folly of the analogy.

"And tell us my dear Secretary General, of what interest would the Israelis have in stealing the Pieta? Certainly, you don't suggest they wish to display Christian art in their synagogues, do you?" The group laughed at the thought as Lattimer's face turned a light shade of red.

Cardinal Fitzgerald added. "First of all, if it were not for the labors of brother Kennedy, the world never would have had this opportunity to . . ."

Lattimer interrupted him in mid-sentence. "Your observations are damnable and border on heresy!" he shouted and pounded the table. At the sound of the thumping, the aged Cardinal Paulo Galvenieto awoke, and as if to signal his presence, expelled a report of gas. The interruption went almost unnoticed except for the blush on the cheeks of the young priest.

"We must proceed quickly, . . .at a time when the vitality of the Church is ebbing seriously, we need this cultural injection. The true Cross of our beloved Jesus must be revealed to the world and we must be the ones to do it," Cardinal Pleaschack said, breaking his silence. Justin knew his words weighed on the group, for many felt the Polish Cardinal was already heir apparent to the Chair of Peter.

"You are correct, my dear brother. Many of our members are straying from the traditional doctrine and teachings. The Cross of Christ will bring them back to the flock by the millions". Fitzgerald said.

"Then it is agreed that we proceed?" the Pope looked about the room.

In unison they responded with one word, "agreed", except for Lattimer who, knowing he was outvoted, was compelled to make a record.

"I must insist, Your Holiness, that all precautions be made to anticipate the adverse reaction of anything that may give even the appearance of impropriety," the Secretary General of the Vatican replied.

"This task I will leave in your capable hands, Camerlengo," Pope Alphonse commanded. The position of Camerlengo, administrator of all fees and revenues belonging to the College of Cardinals, might be very useful in the quest. Pope Alphonse was attempting to appease Lattimer knowing he was a critical piece of the puzzle. Money for the expedition would have to come from an untraceable source to distance the Church if the effort failed. The Pope also knew Lattimer would not be made privy to the methods used to accomplish the result beyond the general plan of engaging a task force of trusted Vatican members posing as an archeological team to enter Israel to carry out the project.

"We must assume the true Cross exists and that we be the first to retrieve this holiest of all artifacts." Alphonse said.

"And what if we fail? Suppose the Cross is non-existent—what then?" Wilhelm injected, again playing both sides so that if the Cross were not found, the others would remember it was he who questioned the propriety of the risk. Justin winced noticeably; he could not bring himself to the realization that the Cross would not be found. He felt his voice must be heard.

"The Cross does exist! It is in God's plan for us to return it to Christianity as a new reminder of our Redeemer," Justin said as a hush settled over the group.

"The rumors concerning the existence of the Cross have been with us for decades. Was it not last year when that American television evangelist began raising funds for the search?" Pleaschack asked. All assembled were aware of the efforts of Orlo Thompson and his organization.

"A flamboyant huckster, only interested in relieving gullible pensioners of their wallets," Fitzgerald said.

"Do not underestimate the man—I would venture the guess he has eyes and ears even in the Vatican," Rachmand responded.

"Come now my brethren. The vision of the true Cross ensconced in some prayer tower in America is too repulsive to contemplate," Cardinal Sun Yet spoke.

"Or the sale of splinters at $5,000.00 a copy," Bishop Lattimer said to perplexed faces.

"We have the upper hand at the moment, . . . it is within our province to expedite the search for we have the alleged location," Pope Alphonse said assuredly. "God grant us this secrecy".

All assembled nodded in agreement except Cardinal Kurt Wilhelm. His mind formulating avenues in which he could turn this momentous occasion into his own personal glory. Wilhelm now attempted to modify his initial objection to the expenditure of Vatican funds, which he had pompously labeled a waste of time chasing an elusive dream. Few knew of the Cardinal's new interest in seizing this opportunity for his own gain. Justin Kennedy confided his suspicions about Wilhelm with Monsignor Capelli when he had likened the German to a weasel, which could never be caught asleep.

All now focused their attention on Pope Alphonse as he began to speak.

"I have also assigned Father Peter to be liaison with the Holy See," Pope Alphonse announced almost as an afterthought. Justin Kennedy looked directly at the youthful priest as the announcement was made. The man did not react; he was stoic. They all knew the young priest was out of his element. Yet no one dared question the Pope's command. It would not bode well to bring up the fact that Alphonse's interest in Father Peter had a direct correlation to the amount of monies and property donated to the Church by Father Peter's parents. The priest's vow of poverty added his share of the family fortune to the Vatican coffers, built from wartime profits gained from the family's Doxell Munitions Corporation. Justin accepted the Pope's decision with quiet resignation as he met the gaze of Father Peter, a man with a fair Dutch complexion and deep blue eyes that never seemed to blink.

"I'm sure Father Peter's expertise will be of immense help to you, Cardinal Kennedy," the Pope offered.

"I believe we all issue our esteemed brother our heart-felt thanks and blessings for a successful journey," Cardinal Sun Yet added.

"Yes, and with you, my brother the destiny of the Mother Church rests," Pope Alphonse said looking in the direction of Justin. "Succeed and you will be honored among men. Fail, and we shall be forced to disavow any knowledge of your unlawful entry and involvement on foreign soil." Pope Alphonse rose, as the Secretary of the conclave sounded the papal bell. Alphonse extended his hand to Justin, who obediently kissed the ring of Peter. The task was established, the Vicar of Christ, a participant. The gamble was worth the risk. The reward for the Mother Church was incalculable. The group disbanded, silently disappearing into the throngs of Catholic pilgrims swarming into Saint Peter's Square.

The dignified German, Cardinal Kurt Wilhelm, was unmindful of the polite bows and respectful looks directed toward him as he walked the hallowed square. Under normal circumstances he would have relished the moments of recognition, the fearful way the people would fall back, the respect in their faces, this unabashed adulation welcomed and coveted. Wilhelm was oblivious to the sounds and bustle of the huge square until a scattering of pigeons broke his unusual virgate style of walking.

He pondered the developments of the hour, his facility of abstract thinking enabling him to encapsulate the possibilities of his expanding power base, a base which he had painstakingly built over the decades, brick by brick, in an unrelenting effort to pave the final mile to the Chair of Peter and the ultimate power of the Papacy. Indeed, he thought, the American Kennedy would be a formidable foe and would have to be dealt with.

Wilhelm produced a pipe and tobacco pouch from his frock. The German Cardinal paused as he filled the pipe with the aromatic blend from Malta. He inhaled as the flame touched the bowl; the moment of anticipation was quickly marred as the nicotine juice siphoned into his mouth. He looked very undignified for the moment as he spat onto the Square of Saint Peter's. Indifferent to his actions, his thoughts returned to his formidable foe Justin Kennedy, and the Cross of Jesus of Nazareth.

The German Cardinal hurried to his apartment, quickly secured the door, and placed a call on his private telephone line.

Within minutes a secret meeting was established with a confidant. Wilhelm next contemplated how he would orchestrate his moves to receive credit for the elusive Cross, realizing he would not be first to procure it.

Father Peter entered Cardinal Wilhelm's apartment promptly on schedule. His fear of the German was deeply rooted. His attraction to his superior was something he could not control. He was no stranger to homosexuality. Father Peter was an active participant in a pornographic web site from America called "Kids in Christ". He was unaware that the site was owned and promoted by the famous television evangelist, Orlo Thompson, a fact Thompson managed to conceal from his adoring flock. Thompson was rumored to be a billionaire. He profited handsomely from his purchase of the alleged table of the "Last Supper." A purchase arranged by none other than Hosni Khatabi. Thompson's followers willingly paid the viewing price of $1000 dollars to look at the fake artifact and receive a blessing.

Hosani Khatabi was no stranger to the world's intelligence community. As the premier arms dealer in the mid-east, his exploits were almost legendary. He brokered the deal with a Russian company to supply missile-jamming devises to Iraq during the Iraqi war in 2003. He arranged with the United States CIA to alter the electronic codes, which rendered the devices harmless, he was paid by Russia, Iraq and the CIA.

Recently he expanded into gold bullion, diamonds, masterpiece art and religious artifacts. World peace put a major crimp in his arms brokering. A son of Bedouins and the product of the hard scrabble desert near Cairo. His mastery of five languages along with superior intellect propelled him to a position of power and major wealth.

A two-year stint in the Egyptian army as a twenty-year old weapons specialist opened the door to his new found career. A Chance meeting with an Israeli intelligence operative convinced him to provide Israel with Egyptian weapon documents for a princely sum of one thousand dollars. From that start he brokered thousands of arms deals from Bosnia to Afghanistan to Jakarta. All the while under the watchful eyes of the CIA, Interpol, Massad and M5. His tentacles reaching into most of the major capitals of the world. His fortune of one half billion dollars secured him financially. The 'game' as he called it was all that mattered to him now.

His appetite for women and jewelry almost matched that of food. His girth expanding as he entered his forties. It was also when he met the one woman who could satisfy his sexual proclivities. The Countess Marcella De La Sant. Extremely jealous, he had his operative's spy on her immediately upon their marriage in 1992. One hapless man who complemented her beauty was beaten severely within hours of the encounter in the market place. Now divorced and looking for a new 'deal' or 'scam' to perpetrate.

The possibility of the existence of the Cross, and its potential priceless value was to become his latest quest.

Marcella Costanzo was born July 6, 1964 to a prosperous family in the city of Valletta, Capital of the Island of Malta. A family of devout Catholics, having one son in the priesthood and Marcella enrolled in a convent school for her formal education. Not surprising for the inhabitants of the Mediterranean Island who were ninety eight percent Catholic.

Marcella was a beautiful teenager with full ripe lips and curvaceous body. Her Catholic uniform could not quite hide her large breasts. Her luxurious black hair cascading down her creamy shoulders. An innocent smile always upon her face set off with perfect teeth.

At age fifteen walking to her home in the darkness, she was accosted by four drunken British sailors, dragged into an alley and gang raped.

The next day, April 1st, 1979, all British troops left Malta after 179 years of military presence and no one was ever prosecuted for the terrible crime.

Over the next five years, Marcella was withdrawn and reclusive until her father arranged a job with the Department of defense as a stenographer. She was assigned to a position with the Prime Minister and within two years, was promoted to a post with the Prime Ministers office.

At age 25 she became a modern liberated woman with many suitors, none of who had any money.

Her goals were established money and power was all that mattered. If she had to sleep with a man with these attributes, she considered it part of her plan.

The day she met Hosni Khatabi was one destined to change her life, his charm and money was overwhelming and within days they were married.

Her bedroom attributes convinced the Arab that Marcella was the only one able to slake his thirst for unusual sex. Her family disowned her almost immediately. Their shame outweighed their love for their only daughter.

The marriage lasted less than a year, as the two temperaments clashed daily. The only truce was in the bedroom. The settlement from Khatabi was one million dollars, which she managed to spend in two years.

Marcella now set her sights on a Spanish Count, reported to be a distant cousin of King Emanuel. She seduced him the first night they were introduced. The Count De La Sant was sixty years old, almost thirty five years her senior, but was a free spending jet setter who needed a trophy wife and Marcella fit the mold exactly.

After the Counts death by a heart attack, some said it was in the throes of passion with Marcella, she again sought out Khatabi for financial help. The only asset left in the count's estate was his title.

Khatabi's proposition was for her to seduce a Cardinal of the Catholic Church in a blackmail scheme. The Cardinal Kurt Wilhelm, heir apparent to the Papacy, would become a willing participant upon discovery of her sexual charms. Now solidly ensconced in her villa provided by the Arab arms dealer, she would continue to play the game for power and money.

Thompson began the blackmail of Father Peter when, during a lengthy connection to the website, the priest answered too many questions revealing a homosexual profile. His wealthy parents had forced Father Peter into the priesthood after they discovered his sexual involvement with little boys as a teenager. It was prison or priesthood, with a handsome monetary payment to the victims and their families to keep quiet. The parents dutifully paid the extraordinarily expensive monthly website fees without question, believing the billing was for educational purposes to further his advancement in the Church. The additional vows of obedience and chastity required of Father Peter as a priest of the Franciscan order were apparently overlooked, or unknown by church officials, when agreeing to accept him on special assignment to the Vatican. It wasn't difficult for Thompson's computer hackers to discover that Peter Doxell, with a Rome Internet address located within the Vatican walls, was a Roman Catholic priest. Thompson now had his connection to Vatican politics, a subscribing pedophile. Soon thereafter, Father Peter was contacted directly by Thompson. Thompson demanded Father Peter keep him informed as to the happenings in the Vatican or face exposure of his secret. Over time, Father Peter told him of his involvement with Cardinal Wilhelm.

"Come in my dear boy" Wilhelm told Father Peter.

Father Peter kneeled in front of the Cardinal and kissed his ring; at the same time Wilhelm unzipped his fly.

Later in the day, Thompson was informed of the search for the Cross by Father Peter and made a phone call to a contact in Egypt to arrange a hasty meeting with... Hosni Khatabi.

CHAPTER FIVE

$\mathcal{S}$ tanding as an ageless sentinel, the port city of Valleta guarded its position as the most sparkling jewel in the crown of Malta.

Seasoned fishermen, still smelling from the days catch, swapped lies, smoked Turkish cigarettes, and guzzled liquor as they refreshed themselves at the local tavern. They took little notice of the pair who entered the smoke filled tavern. A closer inspection would have revealed a swarthy Mid-Eastern type sporting a bushy black mustache. The second of the duo, a tall American wearing silver reflective sunglasses, was Orlo Thompson, known worldwide as king of the evangelical infomercial. It was said that the net profit from his sales of "made in China" religious trinkets topped six hundred million dollars per year. His hairstyle appeared as if it required a construction permit. A brown leather briefcase was handcuffed to his left wrist. The mustachioed one led the way to the small private room at the rear of the tavern.

Hosni Khatabi was seated at a small table facing the door. "Ah, my cousin, it is good to see you again." Khatabi stood grasping the right hand of his cousin. The two Egyptians each placed his left hand on the other's right shoulder exchanging kisses on each cheek. Khatabi then extended his right hand to the American in the traditional manner of westernized Egyptian businessmen. Khatabi bid his cousin to leave then motioned the American to sit close to him so that when seated they were separated by only inches. The American, finding the distance between them cramping his personal space, scooted his chair back...a rude gesture and personal affront to Khatabi. This attempt to distance himself from Khatabi was perceived as finding Khatabi's physical presence distasteful.

"I must have it," Orlo Thompson said with unquestioned determination. He took a key from his right pocket and unlocked the handcuffs. He then put the briefcase on the table. Khatabi focused his eyes on the hands of his guest, which still seemed welded to the handle of the briefcase. Thompson took out another key from his pocket and inserted it into the keyhole of the briefcase disengaging the locking mechanism. He then pushed the buttons unlocking the briefcase but hesitated before opening it. He wanted to tease him just a little before the bargaining began. He looked at Khatabi's eyes which remained fixed on the briefcase. Thompson slowly opened the briefcase and turned it towards Khatabi. Stacks of money bound in wrappers imprinted with the words "one thousand dollar" filled the case.

"I would estimate a mere two million dollars... and the balance?" the Arab questioned as his eyes shuttered as quickly as a camera lens and his face contorted into a half grin. He was negotiating for something he didn't have and would keep the two million whether he delivered or not.

"Cost is of no consequence . . . within reason of course, please take this as a token of good faith, a deposit of sorts" Thompson quickly added attempting to appeal to Khatabi's greed by giving him financial encouragement.

"Secrecy and results are most expensive in this part of the world," Khatabi admonished as he reached across the table spreading the fingers of his right hand over the stacks of money. The Arab's fat ring-laden fingers displayed a huge ten-karat diamond on his middle finger. Orlo Thompson quickly placed his hand on top of Khatabi's, patting it gently as if to offer little resistance, should the Arab desire to claim the money for himself.

"And what might the balance be on delivery?" Khatabi said baiting him to come up with the first number.

"Compensation is relative to results. I would say... forty-eight million more sounds like a fair number." Thompson smiled benevolently as he pushed the briefcase toward his host.

Khatabi knew of the American evangelist's ability to mesmerize people and knew he could be assured of prompt payment when the goods were delivered. The preacher's "war chest" in Atlanta awaited only Thompson's signature to release hundreds of millions of dollars to a pre-arranged offshore bank account under Khatabi's control.

"Then it is settled" Khatabi said, grinning as brightly as a neon cat in a cellophane bag having no intention of honoring the agreed amount.

"Do not fail in this endeavor," Thompson said as he stood his full six foot four inches towering above the short rotund Arab.

"Have I ever failed you?" Khatabi said alluding to the prior transaction between them regarding the table of The Last Supper, upon which was allegedly served the Passover meal. The authenticity of the artifact was always in dispute, but it catapulted Thompson into the national limelight and poured millions into his coffers

"I must have authentication . . . and I don't mean a leper claiming to be cured when given three choices. The Cross must be mine," Thompson said.

"Rest assured my friend, we shall succeed and you shall have your prize," Khatabi stood and bowed toward Thompson and gracefully issued the Arabic gesture of goodbye. "As the hammer strikes the anvil, things not apparent begin to take shape,"

Khatabi muttered to himself as he left the room, robes asunder as if he was being propelled across the floor on a magic carpet.

Khatabi knew of the Vatican's impending trip to Israel through his informant, a former wife dependent upon his generosity to maintain her lifestyle as a Countess. She was now the mistress of Cardinal Kurt Wilhelm. The Countess Marcella de la Sent was financially captive to Khatabi. He could stop the funds now flowing to her bank account with a phone call. He could render her a pauper in a matter of days and evict her from the Roman villa where she resided. His recent demands to illicit more details regarding Vatican activities and Cardinal Kennedy seemed more urgent than most of his inquiries, more direct and threatening. Her lover, Cardinal Kurt Wilhelm, was more bemused than suspicious regarding Marcella's newly found interest in the happenings at the Vatican. Her questions only served to boost his already immense ego.

CHAPTER SIX

*I*t was after two weeks of feverish, secret preparation for the venture into Israel when Mary Frances visited Justin at his apartment. It was late afternoon.

"Do I pass the test, Your Eminence?" Mary Frances asked.

Justin, seated at his desk, looked up from his work into her sparkling green eyes not recognizing her at first.

He stood up and stared at Sister Mary Frances, transformed from a Roman Catholic nun into a charming and beguiling woman. "I must say you do," Justin replied. It was as if he met her for the first time. She was wearing a collared white blouse with the top button opened and an emerald green skirt that came just below the knee. Her long red hair, previously concealed under her religious dress, fell to below her shoulders. She appeared much taller than he remembered, but then she wasn't wearing high heels when in her religious garb. Her face was spared of an abundance of freckles associated with a person with red hair and fair complexion. She did have a few on her cheeks that seemed to have been drawn by a master artist, which in a sense was true. Her nose could not have been more perfect than if designed by Michelangelo.

Mary Frances pirouetted in the room holding the edges of her skirt as she twirled moving the air, which carried the scent of jasmine from her hair. Her shapely body was a testament to God's perfection. Justin's eyes were glued on her every move, and she recognized that he appreciated what he saw. Justin had to remind himself he was a man of the cloth. This was no time to discover lust in his heart. He'd learned to sublimate desires very well.

"I guess it's my turn to ask some questions," she said, smiling.

"Were you not briefed by Mother Superior?" Justin asked.

"I was instructed to remove all traces of my vocation, put on civilian clothes, and report to you," she replied.

"You were told nothing else?" Justin questioned.

"Only that you would answer any questions that may concern me," she replied. Justin's eyes followed her gaze as she looked around the apartment furnished with ornate appointments, which seemed out of place considering Justin's penchant for controlled moderation and humility.

"And that satisfied you?" he asked her, his question targeted as a test of obedience rather than one of inquisition.

"I am sure you are aware we never question orders. If it is not God's will, then it is the will of our Order," she said, her head tilted upward almost in defiance.

"You don't seem the least bit intimidated by me," Justin said.

She met his gaze with steady eyes. "I am a servant of the Holy Church, as you are, your Eminence. As oxen hooked to the same yoke, we should work together for the good of all. If we pull in different directions, we become adversaries and will get nowhere. There is no room for vanity or intimidation."

Justin laughed aloud. "Good grief, I have been called an ox, and the day is not yet over." He watched the color rise in her cheeks.

"Your Eminence, I do not mean disrespect. But I think that you should know from the beginning, I am not just a subservient secretary who will fetch your coffee. However, if it appears to me that you would enjoy a cup of coffee, I would be more than happy to get it, and I would hope you would do the same for me."

Spirit, that's what she has, Justin Kennedy thought as he motioned her to sit on the leather couch. At least this is one they did not break when she took her final vows. He sat down on his matching leather rocking chair facing the couch. They were separated by an ornate glass coffee table. He reached for the file on the coffee table. The file was labeled 'Sister Mary Francis'. He opened it and began reading.

"May I bring you a cup of coffee?" she asked in a conciliatory manner as she watched Justin study the computer data in her file.

"That would be kind of you, sister," Justin said with a smile, there is coffee brewing in the kitchen." She smiled as she stood and walked to the kitchen, took two cups from the cabinet above the counter and poured the coffee. She looked into the refrigerator and took out the half pint of cream and enriched one of the coffees with two teaspoons of the cream, returning the half pint to the refrigerator.

"I see you're from Phoenix, Arizona," Justin spoke loudly unaware that Mary Frances was already back in the living room carrying the coffees.

"Actually, it's a smaller place near there called Casa Grande. It's a lot easier to tell people that you come from a larger city just to avoid the obvious question of just where Casa Grande is," she said as she placed the coffees on the table in front of them. Justin's eyes remained glued on the contents in the file. "I see you attended the University of Arizona and received a doctorate in archaeology. Your thesis on religious rituals of the Hohokam Indians was published and is used as the authoritative college text on the subject. Quite impressive."

"The Hohokams were quite impressive," she said modestly. "The name means 'those who are gone'. We can make only an educated guess as to the true nature of their culture from the relics left behind."

Justin glanced up at her as she handed him a cup of coffee.

"I put a little cream in it."

"And how did you know that is the way I take it?" Justin questioned.

"Deductive reasoning," she replied.

"And may I be so bold as to ask you how you came to that conclusion?" he asked.

"I call it attention to detail. This is your private residence, and as I understand the rules, it is rare that any meetings are ever held here. The cream has to be for one person, the occupant."

Justin smiled nodding his head. "Your file tells me nothing of your motivation to become a nun. What was your reason?"

"This is not the time to delve into my inconsequential past," she said deflecting his question for the moment. "There are more important issues at hand than the story of my life."

"Very well. We'll save the answer for another day, maybe when there is less on our minds." Experience taught him restraint when he sensed he was touching on delicate matters. He quickly switched the subject.

"What I am about to tell you will challenge all your intuitive skills, and could possibly change your life." She sat quietly waiting to hear more. For a person so attentive to detail Justin wondered why she did not pay more attention to her skirt, which had inched up above her knees when she sat innocently revealing her very shapely legs. He quickly realized that the longer habit of the Magdalene Order made it unnecessary for her to be concerned about such things having been programmed for ten years with the secure knowledge that she had no danger from any man of the cloth. She had none now, he told himself sternly. "As you know, we are planning the trip to Israel and it is my wish that you be part of the team I am assembling." Justin said.

"I was hoping you would invite me. It will be a great honor." she replied excitedly.

"Then it is done." Justin replied.

"When do we begin, your Eminence?" she asked. The straightforward question solidified Justin's confidence in his choice.

"First of all, you must from this moment on call me Justin. We cannot reveal ourselves, or our true vocations, to anyone. We will pose as members of a visiting archeological team under assumed names. In fact, some of us are archaeologists, so there is some truth in that," he paused looking at her closely. "We must break our habits even if it means to temporarily forego our teachings and beliefs. We cannot appear to be reverent people; further, our prayers must be in silence," he said. "If others swear and curse we must appear to accept it. To do otherwise might cast suspicion upon us."

"Justin . . ." she hesitated over his name, then went on, "I am honored you have chosen me. I've always believed that I have a higher mission. I became a nun because it seemed the thing I needed to do, but I must confess there have been times when I would have changed vocations, had it not been for an inner calling that somehow kept me in my sacred vows." Justin returned her steady gaze. He admired her candor. She would do well.

"One other small matter," he said. "It has been suggested we must maintain the highest degree of secrecy to ensure no unauthorized person has knowledge that we represent the Catholic Church. To do this we are instructed to . . .act as a married couple." Justin waited for a reply, studying her face.

"The fact that we are already married to the Church will not make our affair an adulterous one will it?" She laughed aloud and brushed back a lock of red hair. Justin laughed. Her sense of humor was the icing on the cake, he thought. The task of obtaining the Cross was dangerous at the very least, and the tensions that were to build would need an outlet.

"Well Mary Frances, the journey has begun. This is an odyssey that will, if we are successful, leave its imprint on mankind for the rest of time. God has chosen us for this mission, and with His help we shall succeed."

"You have been chosen by God, and I have been chosen by fate. I trust your confidence in me will not go wanting, your Em—Justin," she stammered.

"Good. You are indeed a quick learner. It will come easier." Justin said.

"It is difficult to change ones habits," Mary Frances said blushing at the double entendre.

"It is your training and respect for my position. I know it's not easy," Justin replied, recognizing her humor but restraining himself from further comment. He again took note of the color in her cheeks. It was a refreshing bit of femininity that he had not recognized for many years. "We leave in three days," he said.

"And I shall be ready." She started to kiss his ring as she prepared to leave. He withdrew his hand.

"That is one thing we must forego. As husband and wife, there may even be occasions when we must kiss each other, to keep up appearances only, of course." He felt his own face flush.

"You may be assured that we shall keep up appearances," she said, her eyes suddenly bright.

The Swiss Guard did not blink as she passed him in the hallway. Justin remained in his apartment thinking about the charade he had agreed to take part in...an assault to his vows and to the vows of the nun. The light scent of her perfume lingered about the couch where she was sitting, an added reminder of the deception. He sublimated his thoughts immediately, transferring his energy into the work of planning every detail of the expedition.

Logistics fell into place rapidly. Almost everything was ready the day before they were scheduled to leave. Only a directive from Pope Alphonse remained. This was essential in order to cut through bureaucratic red tape. Justin knew the guise of entering Israel, as an archeological team would fit perfectly with a recent request by Italy for help in restoring some of the ancient monuments in Rome. Six months earlier, Italy's Minister of Culture and Communication had met with Israeli officials regarding sharing data on erosion problems that was causing deterioration of some of Rome's ancient artifacts. Twentieth Century pollution and acid rain had seriously eroded some of the Doric columns near the Arch of Constantine in Rome, once the official entrance to the city. The Italian government authorized $285,550 euro, a little more than $250,000 US dollars, for Italian experts to search for columns rumored to be buried near the ancient city of Caesarea, once the capital of the Roman province of Judea. The Israeli government had consented to the accommodation. Although never intended at the time of the request, this was the perfect solution to the clandestine trip by Justin and his associates. Lattimer, as Camerlengo, would be prevailed upon to advance additional funds not subsidized by the Italian government, if and when needed.

Justin reviewed each detail of the project with his assistant, Mary Frances. He commended her on the "nothing short of brilliant idea" she suggested. The idea of smuggling a Roman column into Israel disguised as a lever to be used with a fulcrum as part of the archeological equipment. Vatican artists were instructed to fill in the column grooves and form ninety-degree angles on the sides with plaster making the round column take on a rectangular appearance. They then painted it a shade of industrial green, and attached fake rivets to perfect the deception. A sand blaster was included as part of the archaeological equipment and packed into one of the crates to serve its purpose later. The plan required time to locate the Cross using the pretext of searching for a Roman column. They could not risk coming up empty handed. By bringing their own Roman column into Israel they could "find it", if and when circumstances required.

Justin had undertaken the task of hand picking the rest of his team. Each member was required to have expertise either as a Vatican engineer or a Vatican archaeologist. The expeditionary force totaled ten, including Justin, Mary Frances, and Father Peter. Pope Alphonse who then blessed them and dismissed them to attend to last minute details of the expedition swore them all to secrecy. They were to leave the next day.

CHAPTER SEVEN

$\mathcal{B}$oeing AliItalia flight 171 from Rome to Tel Aviv arrived on schedule at 3:00 p.m. Israeli time. Justin and Mary Frances handed Customs Officials their forged United States passports identifying them as Justin Templeton and Mary Frances Templeton. Their passports were stamped and Justin led his archeological team to the baggage claim area. Several porters helped load the baggage on carts and directed the group to customs. After each piece of baggage was thoroughly searched, the team was directed to an aircraft hanger where the packing crates housing the archeological equipment had been unloaded. Israeli soldiers were stationed around the crates. Customs officials requested two from the party accompany them as witnesses to their inspection of the equipment. Justin and Mary Frances followed the officials who began opening each crate. Mary Frances held her breath as the nails were pried open on the wooden box housing the fulcrum and lever.

"And what is this," one of the inspector's asked.

Playing dumb, Justin responded, "Let's see...is there a number on the box?"

"Number 36" replied the inspector.

"May I see the manifest," Justin said as he walked over to box 36.

He ran his finger down the manifest arranged in chronological order with the description of each piece of equipment listed opposite its number. Number 36 was missing. Beads of sweat began forming on his forehead as he thought of what to say next.

"May I look at it," Mary Frances interjected. The inspector handed her the clipboard. She quickly verified that Number 36 was indeed absent. She continued the search until she came to item numbered 63 identifying the contents of the box as a hydraulic fulcrum and lever combination for lifting. A search of all the crates showed there was no box numbered 63. "A reversal of the order of the numbers on the manifest," she said to the inspector. The box is marked correctly but is listed as number 63 on the manifest."

"Yes, you are quite right," Justin chimed in as corroborating support. The equipment passed without further incident. All permits were in order and the customs officials authorized clearance. The Italian government had prearranged transportation for the archaeological team and the equipment from Tel Aviv to Caesarea.

The archaeological equipment was loaded into a Dodge extended bed pickup. One of the engineers rode with the driver. Justin, Mary Frances, and the rest of the team followed in two Defender 90 Land Rovers. Caesarea was originally a Phoenician settlement conquered by the Romans and rebuilt by Herod the Great in the 1st century BC. As the team approached their destination, Justin looked over the barren landscape thinking how desolate it was and wondering why this was the area chosen to bury the Cross of Jesus. The Dodge stopped just outside the city to allow the driver an opportunity to relieve himself by the side of the road. The Land Rovers, following in tandem, pulled up behind the Dodge. Justin and Father Peter took this opportunity to get out and stretch their legs. The slightly built Dutch priest definitely leaned toward the effeminate. He was spared of any significant amount of facial hair and his movements were of a gentle nature.

"Indeed . . . a fitting place for a prophet to wander. A place where the wind blows and each shrub becomes a miniature oasis attempting to anchor the soil against the forces of nature," Justin remarked.

"Can you imagine we are walking on the same land where our biblical fathers once traveled?" Father Peter said.

"Yes . . . it's hard to fathom, isn't it?" Justin replied as he crouched down and picked up a handful of dirt and then let it sift through his fingers as he stood back up. The driver, having finished his business, got back in the Dodge and motioned the others to follow. The caravan started up again and drove the last few miles to the hotel where the group would be staying. Tired from the long days journey, they were looking forward to a hot shower and a good nights sleep. The members followed Justin and Mary Frances into the hotel to the makeshift registration counter, a wood board supported by two sawhorse type wooden braces. There were a number of newspapers in Arabic and Hebrew neatly stacked on top of the counter as if to draw attention away from what appeared to be an otherwise half finished room. Justin flipped through the newspapers noticing the dates on some of them were as much as a week old. A clerk stood behind the desk. The band of his fez was encrusted with whitish salts from sweat. "Yes, please to register," the clerk offered in broken English accented with an Arabic dialect. Justin stepped forward and registered for all of them signing himself and Mary Frances in as husband and wife. "Please to follow me," said the clerk as he walked the cement floors leading to the rooms carrying a small cardboard box containing the room keys. One by one the clerk gave the team members a room key. Each key was attached to a pocket sized rock by a small rope threaded through a hole drilled through the rock. The clerk pointed the way to the rooms...holding back the key for Justin and Mary Frances. Recognizing Justin as the leader, the clerk wanted to personally escort him and Mary Frances to their room. The clerk inserted the key into the lock unlatching it as the rock bounced against the door. He then opened the door and with humble pride bowing his head slightly said, "I am sorry, Madam, it is the best that we have to offer," addressing Mary Frances as he wiped his greasy hands on a stained apron. Mary Frances smiled politely as she viewed a double bed in the sparse room. The clerk then turned and left.

"These keys must be very valuable," Mary Francis said jokingly as she took the key out of the lock and handed it to Justin, along with the oversized rock attached. The joke was a welcome icebreaker buying a little time for both of them to figure out just what was going to be said next regarding the double bed.

Justin dropped his duffel bag on the floor next to the bed. "Rather close quarters," he said eyeing the small space between the bed and the wall.

"Yes," she responded nervously... "This place is so small you have to walk outside to change your mind," They both laughed at her humor, which broke the tension for the moment.

"Why God chose this place to send us His Son, I will never know. Look at the desolation of the desert," Justin said, wanting to change the subject.

"Well, I think I'll wash up and get ready for bed," Mary Frances said still feeling somewhat uncomfortable and not being able to erase the double bed from her mind. She walked over to a closed door thinking it was the bathroom and opened it. She laughed when she realized she had opened a small closet with a half shelf containing two army blankets and two extra sheets. "They really know how to disguise bathrooms in this part of the world," initiating a laugh from Justin also.

"I believe you'll find the spa and bathroom facilities down the hall, madam," he said doing his best to imitate an English butler. "Why thank you... you may be excused, Jeeves," she replied in her best impression of an English noblewoman. Their laughs continued as Mary Frances gathered a few things and headed to the communal bathroom down the hall. Meanwhile, Justin unpacked his duffle bag waiting for Mary Frances to return.

After about ten minutes she returned to the room wearing a full robe and said, "O.K. it's your turn to be pampered by the facilities". He laughed, grabbed his toiletry kit, and wrapped some things in a towel then walked out to the bathroom down the hall. Mary Frances hung up a few of her things in the closet and put away her undergarments in the drawers of the small dresser by the window. She was hesitant to get into bed.

When Justin returned he was wearing sweat pants, and a light blue Mickey Mouse T-shirt. The shirt was a Christmas gift from his aid's six-year-old handicapped son. Justin went to the closet, took out the extra blankets and placed them on the floor between the bed and the wall. His duffle bag would serve as a pillow with one of the sheets as his cover.

Mary Frances took off her robe and hung it up on a nail sticking out of the closet door. She was wearing cotton lavender pajamas that brought out the color of her eyes and accented her red hair. She pulled back the top sheet and climbed into bed. They wished each other good night. The day's travel left them both tired. Justin turned off the light by the door and made his way back to the blankets, which he used as a mattress. He proceeded to lie down on his back and then covered himself with the sheet. They silently said their prayers, their lips mouthing the words. Justin, eyes open, looked up to the ceiling reliving the events of the day but found himself distracted by the fragrant scent of jasmine that he was now getting used to each time he was in close quarters with Mary Frances. He turned away from Mary Frances, his back toward the bed. He rationalized that it was best to remove all thoughts from his mind except for the mission at hand.

That was easier said than done. Justin felt his migraine take hold with unbearable intensity as he swallowed his medication, unmindful he had already taken his daily dose a few hours earlier. He became dizzy almost immediately as the room spun around him. Justin's dream state again encapsulated him once more.

The tomb of Joseph of Arimathea nestled in a garden near where Jesus of Nazareth was crucified. The outcropping of boulders was a natural place for a sepulcher befitting Joseph's wealth. The place was strangely silent as if the world was holding its breath for some universal occurrence to take place.

Judas Iscariot approached the tomb, impelled by some strange force to seek out this place. He noted that a series of stones had been placed in the entrance, as was the custom when a burial had taken place. The stones had been designed to keep out the predators, both man and beast. There was total silence enveloping Judas as he stepped closer; even his heavy breathing became soundless as if he had been struck deaf. Not a leaf stirred as all creatures about stilled themselves. Judas felt the unmistakable power of something beyond his comprehension. He had entered another dimension, a time compression that was to be experienced only once in the history of man. He was strangely captured in a spell of peace and serenity, his conflict and guilt washed away.

A small butterfly appeared at the entrance to the sepulcher, the body of the creature dazzling crimson with strange white markings on its gossamer wings. He watched it flit from one stone to another, as if to seek an entrance to the holy place. A small opening at the top of the tomb's face allowed the butterfly to enter effortlessly.

Judas felt a soft breeze over his left shoulder, just as the leaves of the brush began to rustle slightly; he was unaware of a huge cloud in the azure sky that began to block out the sun. In a matter of seconds, the area turned to twilight, almost as if an eclipse of the sun had occurred. A chill shuddered through his body, even as perspiration ran down his face into his beard. Judas looked to the strange sky and his peripheral vision caught the attention of a small stone tumbling out of the tomb, then a second and third as if some invisible hand was tearing down the seal. The top half of the sepulcher was now clear as a brilliant light emanated from within the deep confines, a light bright enough to blind his eyes and numb his brain. He fell to the ground, then raised his right hand as the light dimmed in intensity. He saw the butterfly leave the place and fly toward him. Instinctively, Judas held out his hand and the beautiful creature alighted on his palm, he saw the strange markings on the crimson red wings were white crosses. Judas was bewildered as he studied the marvel of nature. In an instant, it flew to the front of the tomb. Judas felt the liquid on his palm, his heart beating in terror as he attempted to wipe it away. The blood staining his palm, resisting all efforts to remove it.

The light returned with even more intensity as the butterfly grew larger and larger until it filled the entrance of the tomb. Its wings now took on the appearance of a linen shroud. The metamorphosis continued as Judas again fell to the ground.

"I call you out of darkness to take my hand and follow me!" A voice commanded.

"Is this the miracle of which you foretold?" Judas screamed out.

"A miracle is an event which creates faith; ye have witnessed the lightning bolt of my presence so that the future of people of the world shall know me." He was told.

"How can this be? My Lord is dead...at my hands which have on them the blood of the lamb," Judas cried.

"There is death before death...and life after a life as my God has gifted us."

"I have killed you!" Judas screamed.

"I have died so that you may live...even if thou are the only person in the world, my destiny would have been the same. My stripes have paid for all the sins of mankind before and now after."

"They shall believe...thou art the Christ who has come alive! Shall I be the one to spread the good news?" Judas asked.

"There will be doubts even among my disciples. For they have seen the power of God and yet remain in remorse, even though I have commanded them to rejoice in my resurrection. Mortals cannot believe that I have come from the dead to lead for all eternity. They shall, before this day is out, come to the throne of God and take my hand."

"I take thy hand now, Lord," Judas said as he reached for Him. He looked into the face of Jesus and saw the beauty of the transformation.

"Touch me not, Seed of Kerioth. I have yet to ascend to my Father in heaven," Jesus spoke.

I beg forgiveness of the dark deed of my treachery," Judas said.

"The salvation event was predestined and I know whom my Father has chosen for this course. All men are forgiven, even thou, Judas Iscariot, for thou has fulfilled the Scriptural message," the Son of God said.

"Am I to follow you to the gates of paradise?" Judas begged, rather than questioned.

"Your fate is already sealed, ye shall fall down...the limb shall break and thou will be remembered for all time." The radiance intensified, brightness without heat, a marsh-fire flare of luminescence filled the tomb entrance and then diminished slowly.

* * * *

CHAPTER EIGHT

$\mathcal{T}$he morning came too soon. The first order of business was to meet with the local authorities, show them the permits for excavation, and select a campsite near an area where they suspected the Cross might be buried. Justin was concerned about the constant checking of documents at every turn by local officials. He was informed it would take hours before the officials could issue a clearance due to other commitments. The clerk in charge suggested that Justin, as leader of the group, wait so that when the official assigned to review the permit returned, the process could go forward. If Justin left and came back, the clerk told him he would have to start from scratch.

Mary Frances used the time prudently. She wandered the marketplace and came upon a shop with Hebrew and English signage that read "Antiquities." She entered the shop and was immediately greeted by the proprietor, an old man walking toward her with a white tipped cane. "Shalom" the old man said and introduced himself as Seymour. Mary Frances returned the Hebrew greeting. "Is there, something of particular interest you are looking for?" He asked. Mary Frances explained her mission as an archaeologist dispatched by the Italian government to locate ancient Roman columns that could be shipped to Rome and used to replace several columns that had deteriorated due to weathering. She asked for help in locating the Roman columns, rumored to have been buried somewhere near Caesarea. The old man reached for a large leather bound book, dusty from age and lack of use, and placed it on the counter. "The site you are looking for is recorded in this book," he said, opening it and straining his eyes to find the page that showed a hand drawn map. He continued speaking as he was searching. "The year was 1908. An Englishman dealing in Egyptian artifacts came across the Roman columns quite by accident during a dig. He sold a column to my grandfather not realizing the treasure he had found. My grandfather sold the column to an English museum. My grandfather, seeking more of the Roman columns asked the Englishman to bring him as many as he could find. But, the Englishman had no time for Roman columns when the wealth of Kings lay buried somewhere in the desert. The Englishman readily revealed the burial site when asked by my grandfather. He had no further interest in wasting his time looking for Roman columns. The proceeds of that sale started the business you see here today. My grandfather, told the story to my father, and my father told it to me, may they rest in peace."

"And what is the price for the book? Asked Mary Frances.

"Price?" replied the old man, "No, the book is not for sale."

"How about selling me the map?" she asked.

"I am sorry but there were no other Roman columns ever found. I would not wish you to pay good money for something of no value," the shopkeeper replied.

"But it has value to me" Mary Frances urged.

"It is not for sale," replied the shopkeeper, but you may look at the map

"How much to look at the map?" she asked expecting to bargain with the shopkeeper.

"To look there is no charge," the shopkeeper continued. "You may make a drawing of it if you wish."

"If I may just study it, I do not need to draw it," she said realizing that a drawing could find its way into the wrong hands and might jeopardize the mission.

"If you find a Roman column you may reward me by allowing me to broker it for you to a museum or one of my private collectors", added Seymour, the shopkeeper.

"Agreed" she said hardly able to contain her excitement. "We have a deal" and the two shook hands on it.

She knew that indiscriminate digging would provoke inquiry from the Israelis. Now, if questioned, a viable starting point for the excavation had been identified and could be verified by the shopkeeper if necessary. Mary Frances was exuberant. The team now had a valid reason for excavating in the area near where the Cross was believed to be buried. She returned to meet Justin and the others at the office of the local authorities. The hot desert sun was now directly overhead. He had been waiting four hours for the official in charge to show up. When the official finally showed, it took three minutes for him to affix the stamp of approval on the permit and send the team on their way.

Mary Frances pulled Justin aside and told him the story about Seymour the shopkeeper. "That gives us another arrow in the quiver if we need it," he said approvingly. He realized that if nothing were found within a few weeks the Israelis' would likely question their reasons for staying.

The group got into their vehicles and slowly drove toward the base camp Justin had previously mapped out. They would use the base camp during the day and return to the hotel in Caesarea at night.

The first few weeks of the excavation consisted of marking off certain areas using gridlines to prevent duplication of effort and making sure every inch of ground was thoroughly searched.

Night after night of sleeping on the cement floor was taking its toll on Justin. While he did not complain, Mary Frances could see his walk was stiff and his patience was wearing thin from lack of sleep.

That evening, after a light supper of humus and broiled lamb, she confronted him.

"I think it's time we exchanged sleeping arrangements. Your turn for the bed and I'll take the floor," she offered.

"I wouldn't think of it," he responded. " You'll stay right where you are." She couldn't help but admire his chivalry and concern, especially, since she knew he was struggling with terrible migraine headaches, which she diagnosed as emanating from back pain caused by sleeping on the hard cement.

"All right, we'll both sleep on the bed," she said with authority.

He looked at her rather dumbfounded, not knowing what to say.

"Don't worry," she continued, "everything will be fine. You need a good nights rest."

"I don't think this is the solution," Justin responded hoping she would persuade him otherwise.

"Tell you what, let's try it for tonight...just to see if you have a better nights sleep. If it doesn't work, I won't be offended that you would prefer to share a bed with the cockroaches on the floor than with me," she said smiling understanding his reluctance.

"Well, maybe for one night," he said, "but I may be tossing and turning all night to find a comfortable position, my lower back is killing me. You must promise to tell me if I shake the bed too much. If I do, I'm moving back to the floor." He was grateful for the hope of one nights sleep without pain.

After supper, Mary Frances excused herself and went alone to see the hotel clerk who was very accommodating in filling her request for two more pillows.

That night Mary Frances slipped under the covers on the left side of the bed and turned down the covers on the right side waiting for Justin to return from the bathroom. She had propped the two extra pillows on Justin's side of the bed figuring that if he felt really uncomfortable he would place the pillows between them. If not, he could use them to place under his legs to ease his back pain. Justin returned wearing his standard bedroom dress, his Mickey Mouse shirt and sweat pants. He smiled at Mary Frances and sat down on the edge of the bed hesitating for a moment. Then he gingerly dropped his shoulder to the mattress and gently lifted his legs onto the bed one at a time, trying to avoid any undue strain, his head now resting on the propped pillows. Mary Frances knew he was in pain and probably could not have handled one more night on the floor.

"Now," she said, "how do you feel?"

"Can I let you know in the morning?" Justin asked, "My lower back could use some support".

Mary Frances looked around the room and said, "Well, looks like we've used all the pillows and I don't think there's room in this bed for you, me, and the duffle bag. So...I don't want you to take this the wrong way, but there are only two choices...no back support... or me," she said surprising herself. Having said that, she turned on her left side and scooted toward him using her back to support his.

"You don't know how good this feels," Justin said as if his pain had gone away. Mary Frances said nothing in response, a slight smile of contentment on her face.

Their attraction for each other grew with each day almost to the point of wishing that finding the Cross could be postponed. They were now in their seventh week of excavation with no results. May brought the hot winds to the land. They wondered, like many before them, whether the Tower of Joppa ever existed. The blowing sand peppering their faces and the hot sun burning their skin made the search even more unbearable. The weather conditions coupled with the cautious eyes of the Israeli officials continued to unnerve Justin, as every lead turned to failure and his hopes began to diminish. The shopkeeper's excuse had been

used by the end of the fifth week. Now, however, the local officials were questioning Justin on an almost daily basis for
progress reports.

That night, as they lay next to each other in the double bed,
Justin told Mary Frances of a precautionary measure he took
when planning the expedition known only to the Pope, and now
Mary Frances. It was understood and agreed that what he was
about to do could not be revealed to the other team members.

The next morning Justin wandered away from the others at
the excavation site claiming he wanted to expand the search area.

After about an hour, he rushed back with an ancient gold coin
he claimed to find at another site he was exploring. He urged several of the others to return to where he found the gold coin and
help in a further search. They gathered up some of the equipment
and returned to the new dig. It didn't take long before one of the
members and then another each found a gold coin. The flat side
of one of the coins carried the veiled head of Pietas, the inscrip-
tion C Caesar Cos Ter, and A Hirtivs Pr, the name of the mint
master of Rome at the time. One of the archaeologists identified
the coins as being minted during the third term of Caesar. Pope
Alphonse had provided Justin with the gold coins so he could use
them as a "plant", to buy time for extension of the excavation
permits.

The coins served their purpose. They were immediately
brought to the attention of the local officials and used to convince them that the Roman column was likely to be found in
the vicinity. Justin, having persuaded the officials of the
authenticity of the coins, went one step further. He insisted that
the officials should have the three coins, which he relegated as
an unimportant by-product...the true purpose of the expedition
being to find the rumored Roman columns. In return, two
benign promises were asked of the officials. First, that there
was a tacit understanding to allow his team to search other
areas with their sophisticated sounding equipment; second, that

the officials would help in securing a flat bed trailer so that when found, the column could be safely transported. A gentlemen's agreement was safely in place. In Justin's mind, he equated this bribe of local officials with thirty pieces of silver. But, this was the real world and Justin was unaccustomed to dealing with people outside the Church. His inexperience would come back to haunt him.

CHAPTER NINE

$\mathcal{D}$ inner that evening found Mary Frances and Justin lifting and touching their glasses filled with sweet red wine from the region and reciting the Hebrew toast "le chaim" (to life) while recapping the days events. It was her suggestion to retrace the steps already taken in an effort to determine if they had overlooked anything.

"Perhaps we can arrange a computer model on middle-eastern weather patterns from the Vatican." Her words came out slowly and slightly slurred as the evidence of the wine took effect. Justin ordered another bottle and poured the remaining contents of the third bottle into her glass. "I admit it's a long shot, but it is possible."

"An excellent idea," Justin said in support. He was constantly amazed at her problem solving abilities and marveled at the way her mind worked even when slightly intoxicated.

"We know from the facts that the Tower of Joppa existed somewhere around here at one time. The problem is we no longer have any landmarks to go by. Plateaus are now mini-mountains, seacoasts have shifted their boundaries, and the sands have covered just about everything. A computer model of weather patterns prevailing in this area just might give us a clue to the shifts in the terrain. Would you see to it then?" she asked.

"I'll give it a try first thing tomorrow morning. I just hope the Santissimo Padre won't think we have suffered sun stroke...by the way, did we get any good readings today?"

Mary Frances responded in a disappointed tone, "Just one possible site, and a faint read on the magnetometer. It might only be a depression in the soil."

"I'll have the crew get started on it anyway. At least we can eliminate the site if nothing comes of it," Justin said. They finished the fourth bottle of wine. Mary Frances summoned the waiter by loosely raising her hand above her head unsuccessfully clicking her thumb and finger trying to attract his attention. "The ladies room is around the corner near the entrance," Justin said, anticipating her needs. She rose bracing herself against the chairback and standing there for a moment while she caught her balance giggling at her circumstances. Justin walked her to the ladies room arm in arm, and then paid the bill.

It was four blocks to the hotel. She rested her head on his shoulder looking up at the night sky. His arm was firmly around her waist steadying her steps as the effects of the wine became more apparent. This was a perfect time to find out more about this woman disguised as his wife. But, his thoughts strayed, prompted by the smells of the desert air and her hair. He visualized the hotel room and the bed, imagining that this time his back would not be turned towards her.

"You were going to tell me why you became a nun," he said nonchalantly.

"I have never told anyone the story. When asked, I would simply say I had a calling...and in a sense, I did."

Justin felt she was willing to talk about her inner secrets at this moment, although he was unsure whether it was because of her trust in him, or her lack of inhibition from the wine. He was curious and did not wait for the reason. "Your secret will be safe with me...I promise you. Let's sit," he said, leading her to a small-secluded area away from the sidewalk where there was a wooden bench.

"Very well," she said, not understanding why it mattered to him.

She looked up at the night sky and pointed to the North Star that far outshined the others. "There, you see that star?" She questioned.

"Yes."

"Well, it all began with that star." She paused, somewhat reluctant to continue.

"Go on. Tell me the significance of that star."

"I was twenty-two years old. It was a night similar to this night. Warm, a slight breeze blowing the smells of the desert air as I sat around a campfire in the desert with five other doctorial candidates...all men. I was finishing up my thesis and this was the last night of a dig that yielded numerous relics of the Hohokam people. Earlier that day, one of the men found what appeared to be a phallic symbol carved from wood adorned with markings that symbolized some type of religious ritual. We ate from a gourd filled with mashings of the peyote, a wooly cactus used in ancient Indian religious ceremonies. I knew it had intoxicating properties, but I didn't know to what extent. As it came my way for the third round, I found it to be like a sacrament, producing a sense of well-being. I saw richly colored visions that took me to a higher level of consciousness. Native Americans regard it as a divine "messenger" enabling the individual to communicate with God without the medium of a priest. It is an earthly representative of God. Indians claim that God told them to do good even before He sent Christ to the whites who killed him."

"What does the north star have to do with all this?" Justin asked, using the same psychological lead garnered from hearing thousands of confessions.

"It is the last thing I remember seeing that evening. I remember fondling the phallic symbol as it was passed among us. We rubbed it as one of our group told the story that it held mystical properties that we would absorb by touching it.

The beautiful intoxication lasted two days and then ceased. During that time I did not feel fear or hunger or thirst. I felt protected from all danger."

"Go on," he urged.

"About three weeks later I experienced stomach spasms that caused vomiting in the morning. I didn't know why. I saw a physician who diagnosed the impossible. He said I had all the signs of pregnancy. Yet, ultra-sound tests did not detect a fetus. Nevertheless, my body reacted as if I was pregnant. My thoughts were deluged with visions of Mary and the virgin birth. I questioned my reason for being. I truly believed that I had entered a higher spiritual level and was chosen by design to serve God. Nothing made logical sense. I didn't know what happened those two nights in the desert. To this day I look toward the North Star for an answer, I don't know why. Shortly thereafter, I decided to become a nun."

He stood and helped her up. She was amazingly sober as if her story had absorbed the intoxication from her body. She moistened her lips with her tongue and said softly, "ever since that time, a yearning within me cries out for help. Satisfaction has eluded me. Something is missing in my life. It may not be of a spiritual nature. I just don't know." They walked the final two blocks hand in hand in silence.

The next morning Justin slept longer than usual. Mary Francis was already hard at work. Realizing he overslept, he washed and dressed quickly, bypassed breakfast and joined his confederates within thirty minutes at the new dig site. After an hour, the work crew managed to dig to a depth of three feet when they heard the unmistakable sound of metal against metal as a pick head clinked against another object. Within minutes, they had cleared a small rectangular space. "It might be an abandoned cistern," someone said aloud. "Or a chest of gold, lads" another said sarcastically doing his best impression of a pirate.

"Let's get to it," Justin instructed, never expecting the site chosen to be the repository of the "planted" gold coins to actually contain something he didn't plant.

"Hold on for a minute," Mary Frances shouted as she stepped into the hole dropped to her knees and began gently brushing the dirt and sand away from the object. "Human bones!" She yelled excitedly as she sat up. The entire crew peered into the hole and saw the partially exposed skeleton. Justin Kennedy made the sign of the cross over the remains and directed the crew to back away so Mary Frances had the benefit of the sunlight to probe the grave. "I want this site extended to ten feet all around. Very carefully," she instructed.

Justin summoned two of the engineers and instructed them to construct a tent over the find.

It took less than one hour to erect the canvas tent over the dig, now measuring a ten by ten hole in the ground, three meters deep. Mary Frances stood in the center drenched with perspiration, with the sweat on the front of her cotton khaki shirt highlighting the lines of her breasts, and her shorts mottling with the dirt of the gravesite. She kneeled down again, brush in hand, only to feel a sharp pain in her knee as it made contact with what appeared to be an iron object concealed by a thin layer of dirt. But she was now in another world, the archaeologist's world where pain had no place and could not compete with the curiosity and anticipation of what might come next. She carefully brushed away the dirt all around the area paying no attention to her bleeding knee leaving the matter in the hands of God and the tetanus inoculation she received prior to leaving Rome. She had knelt on an edge of a soldier's mess tin. The pain was forgotten as she saw the word <u>ALBANUS</u> appear. She deftly brushed off the dirt of two thousand years and wiped away the green rust covering the ancient bronze with the handkerchief wrapped around her head as a bandana. Shaking her head in amazement, Mary Frances felt her heart almost stop as she saw the remains of the centurion's breastplate and apron terminals, the artifacts preserved well enough to reveal the faint traces of gilded decorations inlaid with black <u>NIELLO</u>. By late afternoon the grave had yielded not only the breastplate but the helmet and sword as well. The bones of the soldier had not faired as well, as some parts crumbled as soon as touched. The most remarkable find was a sealed leather dispatch roll. She saw the scroll cylinder still gripped in the skeletal remains of the left hand of the Roman soldier. "If the message he was carrying is still intact, we just might find out who he was or at least what unit he was assigned to," she said. "We must determine how to open this without injuring its contents."

Biting her lips, she carefully pulled the scroll from the skeletal hand making certain not to risk any damage to the skeletal remains or the scroll. Once freed, she took a deep breath, gripped the object with two hands and handed it to Justin. He held it in one hand and lent his other hand to Mary Frances as he helped her out of the hole.

"I'll secure the dig for the night. Alfredo will stay here for now. We'll have Thomaso relieve him at midnight," Justin said.

"I need a shower then off to work I go," Mary Frances said, rejuvenated by the discovery.

CHAPTER TEN

C ountess Marcella de la Sant paced back and forth like a caged animal, puffing on one cigarette and lighting another before finishing the first. Her chain smoking filled the room with a blue haze as sunlight shafted through the glass windows overlooking the grounds of the villa. She knew her lover was always late and yet she realized her tenuous position regarding an affair with a Cardinal of the Church. The middle aged, still attractive Countess chased the doubts from her mind, smoothing her gown and lighting another cigarette while contemplating a romantic interlude with her paramour. Her pulse quickened as she heard the sound of tires crunching the gravel in the villa's driveway. Her excitement was evident as her pear shaped breasts and nipples firmed with anticipation. She stubbed out the cigarette, placed a mint in her mouth, and opened the double door with a bright smile illustrating her face.

"Good evening," my dear Countess. Marcella suddenly felt the blood drain from her face as if she had been caught in a compromising position. She was looking into the eyes of Hosni Khatabi, her former husband. The Arab did not wait to be invited in. He stepped through the doorway past the startled Countess. She smelled the musky odor of Khatabi's cologne, a smell that brought back memories she would have sooner forgotten. Images of his perverted sexual habits flashed in her mind as she attempted to regain her composure. Her previous life with Khatabi refreshed her memory of the Arabic saying he repeated often... "when the camel sticks his nose in the tent, watch out! ...There is more to come." She was now face to face with the camel, not knowing what was in store for her.

"I have a task I wish you to undertake," Khatabi snapped his fingers at his driver who promptly retrieved two cases of equipment from the spacious trunk of the limousine. Countess De La Sant stood in the middle of the room as she looked at the photographic equipment in wonder. "This should bring back some memories. You now will have an opportunity to showcase your talents." The Arab smiled at the horrified Countess. "A small price to pay for a life of opulence, wouldn't you say?"

CHAPTER ELEVEN

𝒥t was after midnight when Justin returned to the hotel. He quietly entered the room thinking Mary Frances would be fast asleep. Instead he found Mary Frances immersed in her work writing the translation of the courier's scroll. The door banged against the casing as he shut it, but he was no longer concerned about being quiet. Mary Frances looked up when she heard the noise.

"I've been waiting for you. I started working on the scroll and forgot about everything except you," she beamed, her face flushed with excitement. "The parchment is in very bad shape. But we couldn't wait for a lab environment to find out what it said. I took care not to damage it. Here's what we have. First, we now know that Tiberius Caesar, Emperor of Rome at the time of the crucifixion found out that Gaius Cassius had stolen the Cross. Second, it is clear that Tiberius Caesar dispatched a courier to bring a message to Pontius Pilate, governor of Judea." Justin remained quiet. "Let me show you the key words I have deciphered from the scroll," she said as she handed Justin her notes.

Justin looked at the notepaper. Highlighted were the words
"NAZARENE, LOCATE, DESTROY, CRUCIFIXION, GAIUS
CASSIUS, TRAITOR."

"May I see the scroll?" Justin asked. "Certainly," she
answered. "Sit here and see for yourself".

"Dear God," Justin said studying the work. "It all makes
sense. The courier carried instructions for Pontius Pilate to
locate the Cross, have it destroyed, and have Gaius Cassius
killed as a traitor. Tiberius Caesar, had to destroy everything
associated with Jesus to stamp out any chance that the people
would make Jesus a martyr by perpetuating a belief that he was
a King or a God."

"But the courier never made it to Pilate." Mary Frances interjected. "He was killed just outside Caesarea, then the capital of
Judea governed by Pilate... but who killed him? Thieves would
have stripped him. He did not die in battle or he would have been
cremated by his comrades, as was the custom." Mary Frances
reasoned. "It had to be someone who knew the Cross was taken
and found out it was no longer a secret...possibly a disciple?
Mary Frances queried. "No," she said answering herself, "more
probably Gaius Cassius". He would have the most to loose... his
life...for betraying Pilate and challenging the authority of
Tiberius Caesar."

Her reasoning made sense Justin thought, but solving a crime
was not on the agenda. "The important thing is all evidence
points to one thing...the Cross still exists," Justin said.

"The scroll identifies the courier as Quintilius Caelius. I'll
contact the Vatican archives by phone and see what information
exists about the courier. I'll put a priority rush on it. I know it's
academic but who knows what we may find out?"

It was three days before the dispatch arrived from Rome.
Mary Francis could hardly contain herself as she tore at the manila envelope. She quickly studied the printout.

Quintilius Caelius

First cohort to General F. Cladius. Service record in Spain, Egypt and Caesarea.

Most Prominent assignment: Design and building fortifications for Caesarea (drawings enclosed)
Last Assignment: Special courier to Tiberius Caesar
Death: 33 AD Age 29 Presumed dead/ Body never found. Rapid promotion in Roman Legion indicated by direct intervention of uncle; Augustus Antonious, noble of the Roman Senate.

No more to follow—finis.
C.C. Kurt Cardinal Wilhelm
J. Victor
R.C.C.
Rome

Mary Frances studied the written report carefully. "Not much help," she said as she handed it to Justin who quickly scanned it.

"Let's look at the drawings," Justin requested. Mary Frances unrolled the drawings and put them on the table.

"God in Heaven, look!" she pointed to a small mark in the upper right hand corner of the drawings of the Caelius fortifications of Caesarea.

"The tower!" They said in unison. The meticulous engineers of Rome had clearly indicated the location of the tower of Joppa with a small footnote: T Joppa. They both knew the Roman draftsman's calculations would not be off by more than inches as they traced the triangulations to a perfect intersection of the tower's former location. The existence of ruins as a starting point would now show them the way to the Cross.

"Caelius died before he located the Cross but the fortifications of Caesarea that he designed reveal the critical location of the Tower identified in the lost pages of Mark," Justin remarked.

"We aren't the only ones to figure this out, Justin," Mary Francis said as if secrecy might not be intact, an obvious threat to the entire expedition. "Quite perceptive of you," Justin answered. "You noticed Cardinal Wilhelm was copied on the transmittal."

Neither of them suspected that it would be Father Peter who would alert Orlo Thompson to the contents of the dispatch.

CHAPTER TWELVE

$\mathcal{I}$t was four-thirty in the morning when Justin awoke. He quietly dressed so not to disturb Mary Frances and walked outside into the morning darkness, got into his Land Rover, and drove toward the site of the dig. He lowered the windows and took several deep breaths of the cool desert air knowing early morning was his only chance to do so. The fresh smells of the desert filled the car. He thought it ironic that such a peaceful setting was such a formidable adversary unwilling to give up its secrets easily. A greater adversary was struggling within him. He sensed his feelings for Mary Frances were fighting for recognition and that the sacred oath that bound him to the Church was being compromised in favor of human desire. Tagor's quotation floated into his mind as he recalled the words of the poet; "Faith is the bird that still sings while the dawn is still dark." He thought the quotation most appropriate because he realized only faith could lead him to victory against both adversaries.

Unbeknown to him, Mary Frances was also awake when Justin left the hotel room. She simply did not want him to know it for fear she could not trust her own feelings. After making her way to the small vanity table next to the chest of drawers she stared into the mirror. She laughed as she thought there was nothing to fear because the way she looked would send a man imprisoned for thirty years into retreat. Her lips were chapped from the hot desert sun and her long red hair seemed dry and brittle from the relentless heat, nothing a little lipstick and conditioner couldn't cure, she said to herself.

She knew the unfolding events would dramatically change her relationship with the Cardinal from America and yet she felt removed from it all. Not unlike the powerless Gods of Mount Epicurus, unable to alter that which was destined to be accomplished by mortals.

She also knew she had to fight to keep her emotions in check and not allow those inner thoughts to surface. She prayed for these feelings to cease coming in installments. She dreamed of soaking in a hot bath freshly scented with vials of special potions such as those used by Egyptian queens with bubbles surrounding her and maids in attendance. She settled for a hot shower at the end of the hall grateful for the small tube of shampoo she brought with her. She looked at her fingernails and decided they would have to wait for another day. She dressed and walked to a nearby open-air café ordering black coffee and a roll for breakfast. The proximity to the Mediterranean Sea offered little comfort for those destined for a day's toil. It was time to return to the dig and she was anxious to do so, both for the adventure about to begin anew, and to quench the desire burning within her that could only be satisfied by being near Justin.

The other members of the expedition arrived shortly after Justin, even before local herders released their sheep for grazing on the sparse terrain. Justin instructed his lead man, Antonio, to set up the engineering transit at the Southwest corner of the crumbling walls of the site. The triangulation and plotting necessary to locate the former resting place of the Joppa Tower went smoothly and culminated with the driving of a steel rod into the soil of the Holy Land. It was now mid-morning and the heat was already intense.

Perspiration ran down Justin's face as he began the last calculation of one hundred and seven paces toward the Sea. He stopped and wiped the sweat from his forehead then suddenly began to laugh hysterically. The crew arched their respective brows in an attempt to fathom the strange outburst from the Cardinal.

"What is it?" Mary Frances said as she gripped Justin's shoulders. He attempted to speak and again laughter came forth.

"Suppose," Justin managed to say. "Suppose the one hundred and seven paces were made by a dwarf." He began to laugh even louder as he looked into the face of Mary Frances who stood with her hands on her hips, a red bandanna wrapped around her forehead.

"I think we ought to get back to the job at hand or at least take a break." They all went over to the water barrel and used the dipper to pour water into their drinking cups. Mary Frances, feeling quite uninhibited, poured two dippers of water over her head sighing as the cool water ran down her face. "This feels so good," she remarked as she tilted her head back and flipped her long red hair over her head, her eyes closed as if in ecstasy.

Justin had previously decided not to mark off the last direction in order to preserve the crypt's exact location until they were assured of total secrecy. He was the first to notice the military vehicle approaching the site. He watched quietly with the others as the lone occupant emerged.

"Who is in charge here?" the Captain asked.

"That would be me," Justin Kennedy said as he walked toward the military man.

The Captain thrust an official looking document toward Justin. "Sign here," he directed.

"What is this about," Justin asked.

"You must leave at once. This is a cease and desist order from our government," the Captain responded, "your signature is only evidence that you have received it."

"This must be a mistake, our papers and permits are in perfect order," Justin protested as he walked to the base camp and retrieved his authorizations from a briefcase.

The Captain waved the folder away. "You have one hour." His words backed up by the arrival, as if on cue, of a truckload of military personnel; the men took up positions around the dig.

* * * *

Within the hour Justin returned to the hotel and placed a phone call to the Vatican in an effort to make sense of the happenings....

"We cannot at this point intercede in your dilemma," the Papal Secretary General advised.

"I do not need any lessons in parliamentary politics, Jacob, we may be within hours of our goal and now I'm told the Israeli government has declared the site a national monument," Justin retorted.

"I will make inquiry to the Italian Ambassador. But please understand, we cannot involve the Church at this juncture" . . . Jacob Lattimer attempted to explain.

"We are involved, Damn it". . . Justin swore, "I insist on speaking to the Holy Father immediately," he demanded.

"Dear Brother," Lattimer said. "I'm afraid your assignment has addled your senses. We are not about to disturb our ailing Vicar with a problem better left to the Diplomatic corps. We all understand the importance of your undertaking, but we cannot risk more suspicion. Furthermore, some of us still have serious reservations that this mission was ill conceived in the first place. Manifold doubts have arisen regarding the existence of a so-called crypt let alone a secret repository of some timbers, which may or may not have significant historical value. Even if the

Cross is found, how do we know it is the Cross of Jesus? It could be the cross of any number of thieves or innocents crucified during those days."

Justin took a deep breath and composed himself realizing that arguing with Lattimer regarding propriety of the mission would serve no purpose. Lattimer was always against the incursion into Israel to steal the Cross. Nevertheless, Justin could not back off entirely, too much was at stake. He knew that if Pope Alphonse declared the Cross was that of the Crucifixion, devout followers of the Church would take it on faith and convince others if need be. "The Holy Father must be told," Justin again insisted.

"Impossible!" " Pope Alphonse is resting at Castle Gandolfo and cannot be disturbed. Surely you are aware of his deteriorating medical condition," Lattimer intoned.

"Then I shall return to the Vatican at once." Justin said with little hesitation.

"Foolish notion, Justin." The Secretary General called him by his first name. "I would advise you to contact Cardinal Wilhelm for instructions. He has been appointed to be temporary liaison by Il papa during his incapacity."

Justin felt the Secretary General, assured that Kurt Wilhelm would thwart his every move unless the credit or glory would flow in the German's direction, had sandbagged him.

"Where is Cardinal Wilhelm" Justin asked.

"I'm afraid the Cardinal is not available at the moment, however I shall advise him of your inquiry," Jacob Lattimer said begrudgingly, turning and winking at the German Cardinal who nodded his head in agreement.

Justin hung up the telephone without a reply, knowing in his heart of the growing political conflict. He knew he could not use the intrinsic power of the Roman Catholic Church now involved in a clandestine operation on foreign soil and unwilling to raise even the appearance of impropriety for fear of upsetting the powerful Israelis.

The conversation strengthened Justin's belief that the
Secretary General was more an opportunist than a dedicated man
of God. His allegiance was to Wilhelm for personal reasons now
beginning to surface. Frustration began to swell in his chest as he
left the hotel in a rage. He instructed his driver to take him to the
local Military Director's office. In less than ten minutes the car
arrived at a rather non-descript two-story masonry building in the
downtown section of the city. There was no signage on the front
of the building identifying it as a military office. Probably for
security purposes Justin thought. He entered the office of gray
desks, tile floors, and pictures of government officials that was a
clone of any number of government offices he had visited in his
lifetime. A clerk in military garb was seated behind the metal
desk piled high with various papers. Justin requested to see the
Commander in charge. There was no stalling in this environment.
The clerk picked up his phone, rang the commander in the next
room, briefly said a few words in Hebrew, and immediately
showed Justin into the commander's office.

"Please sit down," the Israeli officer motioned to Justin.

Justin noticed the tank commander's battalion insignia on the
breast of the perfectly fitted shirt. He estimated the officer to be
in his late thirties, about six feet two inches, and very fit. He had
movie star good looks. Justin eyed the young officer, attempting
to determine a weakness. He knew it would be folly to rely on
youthfulness in this nation of patriots and heroes who had spent
their entire lifetimes with their backs against the sea.

"Coffee?" Justin was asked as he settled into an uncomfortable straight back chair in the sparse office. The officer adjusted
his cap tucked under the epaulet of his right shoulder nonchalantly drawing attention to the insignia above his right breast pocket
indicating his status as a Captain in the Israeli army.

"My name is Captain Gideon Lot. How may I help you?"
Gideon spoke through perfect teeth. His eagle sharp eyes signaled he would be happier exchanging ninety-millimeter shells in

a tank duel, rather than sitting behind a desk laden with a myriad of official looking documents. Justin quickly explained his situation as the officer listened politely. He offered the official permission papers and permits signed by both the Italian and Israeli governments as evidence of his right to excavate in the area. The Captain studied the documents and said, "I am well aware of your mission and your papers are indeed in order. . .however they have been canceled". The Captain opened an Israeli military transmittal pouch and handed Justin a letter from the district military office in Tel Aviv. Justin quickly scanned the letter, which, he noted, had been signed by a Lt. Colonel Moishe Steingard. "This is absurd. Can you explain why the military is involved in this?" Justin demanded as he tossed the letter onto the desk.

"It seems your work has attracted some national attention. The location of the Joppa Tower is of significant importance it appears. I can also assure you that the work will be permitted once we have our own people on site with your team," Gideon said. Justin felt the bones in his knees melt. He experienced the terrible feeling of failure that quickly turned again to anger.

"Just how can the military intercede in this matter?" Justin demanded.

"Please...in this part of the world, military and political reasoning must compliment each other. It is a matter of survival. I do not know this Lieutenant Colonel however, we must presume his instructions came from a higher authority," the tone of Gideon's voice indicated a degree of sympathy for Justin's situation. "There must be something that can be done," Justin countered, "perhaps a direct appeal to the Lt. Colonel himself. I'll make arrangements to go to Tel Aviv immediately." Neither of the men had any way of knowing that Lt. Colonel Moishe Steingard did not exist, but was created by none other than Hosni Khatabi who, by a rather elaborate mixture of bribery, forgery, and stolen Israeli documents managed to stop the excavation.

The impasse continued between Justin and Captain Gideon
Lot, until the ringing of the telephone interrupted the two.

Gideon reached for the phone in one deft movement. "Yes
Yosi, what is it?" he said to his clerk. After a few moments, the
Captain's face grew pale. He put the telephone down quickly and
looked to Justin. "Our meeting is at an end, perhaps another day
we can discuss a possible solution." Gideon quickly ushered
Justin out of the room leaving him puzzled until he heard the
unmistakable sounds of police and ambulance sirens. Justin
rushed outside and witnessed the frenzied activity in the street.
Palestinian extremists, explosives strapped to their bodies, blew
themselves up along with a number of children and teachers in
the American Christian School for Orphans run by American
missionaries, all in an effort to disrupt the Middle East peace
process from going forward.

Within twenty minutes Justin met Mary Frances at the hotel.
She breathlessly told him the military had abruptly left the dig
site leaving nobody to monitor their actions. Justin knew what he
had to do. "Have the crew assemble, we are going back to the
dig".

CHAPTER THIRTEEN

$\mathscr{J}$ustin quickly walked off the one hundred seven paces toward the sea and pointed to the ground. "This is the most sacred spot on earth, may God in His wisdom and mercy reward the world with the absolute reminder of His Son," Justin said aloud. Justin handed Mary Frances a small shovel. She began to outline the area about to be excavated.

The winds subsided almost on signal as an eerie silence enveloped the area. The digging proceeded methodically as Justin constantly looked around knowing any minute the Israeli military might return. He felt the tension building. After about an hour, a layer of top stones was reached. Each stone was quickly removed one by one and a small ladder was lowered into the dark hole of the hidden chamber. Mary Frances handed Justin a flashlight as he paused at the top rung, again making the sign of the Cross. He began the descent into the sacred resting place. He was sure he knew what the darkness would hide. The irregular opening beckoned him to enter. Justin's mind froze for an instant. What if it is empty?

His heart pounded in his chest as he descended at the urging of Mary Frances. Father Peter stood by anxiously awaiting first knowledge of any discovery. Justin felt the collective anticipation of the team and knew the moment was at hand when the world would possibly know if the Cross of Jesus Christ was found at last. He reached the bottom and moved the flashlight to circle the body of the cavern only to see dust particles reflected by the lights rays as he moved his feet. Minutes passed and the dust settled once more and ...there it was. His eyes focused on what appeared to be an upright beam, almost eighteen feet long. His mind reeled for an instant as he grappled with its size and the approximate nine-foot cross member lying next to it. His eyes made out what appeared to be a wooden sign covered with pitch. Slowly he reached out his hand and touched the Cross. He wanted to gain even further nearness to his Lord, yet he felt unworthy to look upon the Cross of Calgary. He walked back to the ladder and looked up to the top to tell Mary Francis, but began to choke as his feet disturbed the fine dust that covered the floor of the chamber. He struggled to breathe. He called out to be lifted from the place, and then called again, not from fear, but from some force within him telling him to leave. The sacred symbol of Christianity, adopted by the Emperor Constantine as his ensign after he had banned crucifixion, was about to be brought forth into the daylight of the twenty first century. The true Cross of Jesus Christ of Nazareth, now unearthed.

Justin felt himself being pulled roughly from the deep hole. His breathing labored. Sweat poured from his body as his associates gathered around him and offered him a glass of water. He fell exhausted against a large rock. Maybe the Cross was never supposed to be found. Maybe, he had no right to touch it.

"Give me a moment. I just feel a little faint." Justin took a deep breath. He saw Mary Frances' look of concern. The dizziness continued. He felt as if his head had been clamped in a vise. The choking did not stop as he attempted to stand. As he rose his eyes began to roll back in his head, his balance completely gone. His legs gave out from under him as he started to fall to the ancient ground.

"Catch him! He's fainted!" he heard Mary Frances shout, before he hit the ground and went limp.

"Heat prostration," Father Peter said. They lifted him quickly and placed him into the back of the pickup truck. Sister Mary Frances elevated his feet and wiped the perspiration from his face. Justin was unaware of everything about him. It was a blessing, for his subconscious took over, and once again his chronic dream returned.

"And thou art the one who will be despised among all men," the voice said. And the visions came. Judas walked along the water's edge, his sandals making perfect outlines in the sandy soil. The humidity triggering perspiration as the robe seemed to cling to his sweaty body. His gait became faster as trembling hands pushed away imaginary obstacles in his way. He broke out in a run as the midday sun beat down upon him. He did not know nor care where he was going as he attempted to flee some fearsome apparition.

"And he shall deliver up the Christ to the chief priests, and thirty pieces of silver shall be the exchange. The greatest debt of mankind will be settled for a small sum," the voice told him.

Justin had been unconscious for only a few minutes then came to as he felt the cool water on his forehead and the stong unpleasant odor, remembering nothing of the dream.

"My head feels like it was run over by a hundred camels," Justin said as he waved away the broken ampoule of smelling salts Mary Frances waved under his nostrils.

"Lie still, you passed out," she said. Pressing her hand against his chest, keeping him from rising.

"We better make that opening bigger," Justin grimaced. "The air down there is foul. The walls keep crumbling, dust all over the place."

"The men are seeing to it, just lie here for a few minutes," she said as she wiped his sweaty forehead with a damp cloth.

Justin looked into her eyes. "I saw it. I saw the Cross. It's bigger than life! I cannot describe the feeling!" "We must work quickly". "Yes, I know," Mary Francis responded.

"We will have to work all night, if necessary. We must remove the Cross before morning," Justin added, already formulating a plan. Looking toward Mary Frances Justin said, "It looks like the time has come to find a Roman column."

"I'll see to it that we get a flatbed trailer," Mary Frances said as if reading Justin's mind. "I'll see that the sandblaster and the lever join in holy union, she added with a half smile and a proud smirk. "Just stay put and rest. I'll take care of the details," she ordered. Justin was content at the moment to let her take over. She directed one of the engineers to convert the industrial green to the original color of the column and to remove the plaster filled in the grooves as well as the manufactured rivets. She then slipped out of camp for an unannounced meeting with the local officials. It was time for them to make good on their commitment, the quid pro quo for the gold coins. She wondered if the officials considered the gold coins a bribe, triggering the earlier problems that necessitated the meeting with Captain Gideon Lot...or, was she just being paranoid?

One hour had passed and it quickly became apparent that Justin felt no ill effects of his fainting spell as he issued orders to his crew to continue the task at hand. Justin was not in the chamber long enough to assess the time it would take to remove the Cross and bring it to the surface. The opening to the chamber was just too small. He knew it could not fit unless the cross beam was made vertical with the main beam. He could never allow that to happen. The Cross had to be removed intact or not at all. The team worked nonstop knowing this was their best and possibly only chance to remove the Cross. The opening was made larger but it took the crew into the night to shore the sides leading to the chamber. They no longer would have the benefit of daylight to aid in the recovery.

"There. Down there!" Father Peter shouted as a strong beam of light was focused on the object from the generator power source. The artificial light gave the Cross an almost supernatural appearance.

"Holy Mother Mary," someone whispered.

"Bring over the tackle. I'm going down," Justin said.

"I'll go," Father Peter insisted. Justin looked at the young priest nodded permission thankful for the reprieve. Justin thought he could best direct the exhuming from the surface rather than confront whatever it was that caused him to pass out from his earlier venture into the ancient storage vault.

Father Peter wrapped the Cross with shrouds of white cloth where the engineers would attach the lifting ropes. He had decided, in consultation with Justin, that only a priest should dare risk the ramifications that could result from another mortal making direct contact with the Cross. Unknowingly, Father Peter's left arm became entangled in one of the ropes as he gave the order to lift the treasure to the surface. He failed to notice the droplets of blood dripping onto the white cloth binding the Cross as it was being lifted. He yelled to the engineers to stop after he felt the rope tighten painfully around his wrist. Had his cry not been heard, his wrist could easily have been severed. The Cross was immediately lowered allowing the rope to slack. The engineers rushed to release Father Peter but were too late to prevent the ropes' rough fibers from piercing Father Peter's skin.

Father Peter climbed out of the hole, his face covered with grime and sweat. His shirt saturated as if someone had poured a bucket of water under each armpit; his hair caked in clumps of clay and debris and his wrist now bleeding profusely from a severe rope burn.

One of the engineers yelled for someone to get a first aid kit.

"No" Father Peter cried out, "I was close to the Lord, if protection is warranted He will provide it".

Justin paid little attention to Father Peter's wound, although he recognized its severity. His mind was focused elsewhere. "The board—did you see it?" Justin asked.

"No. I looked, but I couldn't see anything else," Father Peter responded.

"I saw it! It must be there," Justin cried out. "Maybe we buried it in the dirt when we disturbed the place," Father Peter responded. "We must find it!" Justin said.

"I'll go back for it," Father Peter volunteered as he descended the ladder before anyone could stop him.

Justin looked up to the heavens mouthing a prayer for Father Peter's success. As he brought his head down and opened his eyes he saw headlights on the horizon from a vehicle that appeared to be headed towards them. He yelled to Father Peter to hurry.

"I got it, I got it. It's here!" Father Peter shouted from the confines of the chamber.

"Blessed Jesus, thank you," Justin said aloud. The archaeologists lifted the cross and carried it fifty meters from the dig site and laid it carefully on the desert ground as instructed by Justin. The veil of total darkness was now the hiding place of the Cross as the archaeologists, flashlights guiding their way, returned to the base camp three hundred meters away. Justin personally hid the inscribed board, upon which Pilate proclaimed Jesus "King of the Jews". Justin instructed that the hole be backfilled with the dirt as fast as possible. The vehicle was dangerously close when Justin gave the orders for everyone to return to the base camp immediately. The backfilling was not yet complete. Evidence of haste was everywhere as shovels were scattered around the dig site hidden by the blackness of the night. A low cloud cover blanketed the desert blocking the light from the stars and the moon. Justin reasoned that the lights from the base camp would be more likely to invite an intruder than the darkness of the desert. He instructed the crew to wash the dirt from their faces and hands quickly and to change clothes. He did not want to risk having to explain why they were so filthy at this hour just before bedding down for the night. He watched anxiously as the vehicle, which appeared to be swaying and making jerk-like movements, approached. Three lights were now visible. A straying spotlight from the vehicle was searching the desert on each side of the main dirt road. The vehicle abruptly left the road and headed straight for the campsite lights. The wheels churned the off-road earth raising a cloud of dust, as if a team of horses were following the vehicle. The dust settled as the vehicle came to rest at the campsite. The driver's side door opened slowly. Mary Francis got out of the Dodge pickup, walked to the rear of the truck, and inspected the hitch of the flatbed trailer being pulled by the truck. The hitch was loose as she suspected, causing the erratic movement.

* * * *

There would be no sleep this night either. Justin and some of the crew immediately returned to retrieve the Cross and complete backfilling the hole. They carefully covered their tracks to wipe out all signs of activity. Justin mapped the exact location, mindful of the thought that it also would one day become a shrine. They then returned to the campsite with the Cross in the darkness, after having carefully wrapped it in Government Issue tarpaulins. The Cross was laid down about ten meters behind the campsite and placed on the earth of Israel. Father Peter took the first watch over the Cross. The crew dug a small firepit placing various sized rocks around the edge. Justin brought over a grill plate balancing it on top of the uneven rocks. He then lit a fire to warm Father Peter from the chill of the desert air. Mary Frances brought over a pot of coffee and placed it on the grill. Father Peter was then left alone. He was of little use other than to place blankets next to the fire and to sit, eyes wide open, keeping a careful watch on the treasure. He was exhausted from the physical activity of the night before and in pain. The rope burn had torn into his flesh, leaving an ugly deep gash in his left wrist still oozing bodily fluids. His blue eyes began to tear as the pain reassaulted his senses. He reached for the coffee hoping the caffeine would keep him awake and alert. But, that was not to be. His reflexes had slowed from lack of sleep and physical exertion. His mind was playing tricks on him. Father Peter rested his head on his good hand and fell asleep.

Dawn came slowly for a very tired American Roman Catholic Cardinal who was up all night. The crewmember assigned as camp cook made breakfast for the crew. Justin ate with his team, excused himself, and went to lie down. He quickly experienced a twilight sleep, feeling himself being pulled into a trance-like state of euphoria. Awake enough to experience, once again, the strange thoughts permeating his mind. Afraid of the magnetic hold his subconscious appeared to have established. His fear became more real as he attempted to hold back the visions and voices from the ancient past. Justin was still weak from his episode at the dig when the Cross was exhumed earlier. His headache grew in intensity as he and Mary Frances were preparing to retire for the night. He swallowed three tablets of the prescription Dr. Carlton had given him, unmindful of the three he had taken earlier. Justin glanced over to the bed and noticed her pouting nipples through her 't' shirt and suddenly felt his longing for her grow. They bid each other goodnight as Justin slouched into a chair. Mary Frances pulled the coverlet to her shoulders and lay with her back to him.

Justin's mind was reeling at the impact of the day's events, thoughts jig sawing through his brain. A cloud of euphoria came over him as the drugs took effect, thankful that peaceful sleep would soon overtake him. Everything appeared in a light fog and in slow motion as he saw her arise from the bed and slip off the

T-shirt, exposing exquisite breasts. He knew danger to be one of the greatest aphrodisiacs. Mary Frances hooked her thumbs into her sweat bottoms and dropped them to the floor. She looked longingly as she walked the few steps toward him.

She nuzzled her breast to his face as she cupped it to his mouth. A moan emanating from deep within her as Justin marbled her nipple with his lips. He reached to her panties and pulled them to the floor. Mary Frances stepped out of them as graceful as a thoroughbred horse jumping a low hurdle. She kneeled before him and took down his sweat pants, exposing his bulging member, her mouth, hot over the cloth of his shorts. Justin lifted her to the bed, her luxurious hair spilling over the pillows. "Love me" she whispered as Justin explored her body with his hands and mouth, his tongue finding her pulsing vee, the sweet scent of jasmine urging his tongue to violate her womanhood. She rolled over holding his head to her mound she held his arms down as she straddled his face in a rhythmic motion, arching her back with each thrust of his tongue. Her arm reaching around to grasp his hard, velvet manhood, stroking it in cadence with her own movement.

Justin pulled her down gently toward the now indescribable passion they were experiencing. He entered her effortlessly as her eyes widened and her head swaying from side to side. They loved each other with an intensity neither had ever experienced before.

Mary Frances' womanly instincts, now uninhibited, increased the intensity by deliberate thrusts each time Justin met her with ever deeper penetration and demand. Her mouth found his, as tongues explored, the moans growing more vocal until both knew the moment of climax was at hand.

Justin exploded in her as she let out a childlike cry. He shuddered as after eruptions muscled him. He felt the throbbing deep within her as she lay her face next to his.

"I love you" Justin said as he took her face in his hands. Then without warning a satanic smile crossed her face and then started to morphisize. Justin's senses frozen as if electrocuted. She took on the countenance and beauty of the Blessed Virgin Mary. She looked at him in sadness. Justin felt as if he was having a heart attack as he fought the ungodly vision.

His screams of terror awoke Mary Frances who jumped from the bed and rushed to his chair. Alarmed at the fear in his eyes, she took a wet towel and attempted to soothe him. His arms flailing in a fruitless attempt to push her away.

"Justin...Justin wake up you're having a nightmare." He began to awaken, the vision already fading, his heart pounding dangerously in his chest as he envisioned the flames of purgatory consuming his soul. Later they both surmised the over medication caused the hallucination. Justin, not relating the specifics of his dream nor the monumental guilt filling his mind.

He left the tent and walked the short distance to the Cross and saw the kneeling figure of Father Peter. He heard the prayers of the youthful priest as he approached. Justin coughed to announce his presence. Father Peter looked up with glazed eyes and saw Justin.

"My wrist! My wrist!" Father Peter said as he held both his arms out to Justin with his wrists pointing downward preventing Justin from looking at the wound that Father Peter was so anxious to show him.

"Let me give you something for the pain so it will not hurt so badly. When we get to the town, we will have the doctor look at it," Justin suggested.

"No, No, look at my wrist!" Father Peter said as he turned his wrists over to show Justin.

Justin reached for Father Peter's left hand to examine the wrist. Justin swore the priest had injured his left wrist. The wound was closed. There was only a slight red tinged line where the skin appeared to have come together and healed. Justin immediately reached for Father Peter's right hand, believing he had made a mistake in memory. There was no wound. This moment of disbelief gave way to the sudden realization that he was intertwined in a miracle.

"This cannot be! I saw the injury; it was a deep cut. I saw the blood and fluids oozing from the wound. You refused medical attention of any kind. I do not believe this. . .I. . .there must be some explanation", Justin's mind reeling with the magnitude of the happening.

"I was praying," the young priest whispered. "I felt for the Cross of our beloved Jesus. My hands were touching it as I thanked Him for giving us this symbol for His glorification. I felt blessed to be a part of this. I told our Lord that I rededicated my life to His service and asked Him to use me in any manner He willed. I...In an instant I felt the power of God go through me. My wrist burned as if it had been seared with a hot poker. And when I looked, the wound was healed. I don't know what to say. My Lord has taken my pain away. He has touched my heart." The young priest cried unashamedly as he looked at his wrist.

Justin scanned the area noting the campfire Father Peter had used to warm the cold air and heat the coffee. The grill was no longer balanced on the uneven rocks encircling the campfire. One end of the grill had fallen into the fire pit. The other end angled against the side of the rocks. The coffee pot was on its side, spout down, dripping coffee into the fire and making a sizzling sound as each drip hit the smoldering wood. He reached for the handle of the coffee pot not realizing how hot it was from direct contact with the fire. He barely touched it when he pulled his hand from the burning hot handle shaking it wildly as if to cool it. He then realized the metal was hot enough to cauterize a wound, but he didn't dare ask Father Peter what had happened. He felt it best to immortalize what Father Peter believed was a miracle. It was better to cast a blind eye toward explanations.

"Blessed Mother of Christ!" Justin cried. "The Cross...it has the power to cure, to take away pain! This is the final proof. This is truly the Cross of Jesus. A Cross of divine miracles." The two men knelt in the darkness, praying silently. Justin was already formulating the ramifications this miracle would create if announced to the world, and for the moment, disavowing the explanation running through his own mind of how the wound could have been cauterized, not wanting to destroy Father Peter's epiphany.

"Come, Brother Peter, walk with me for a moment. We must talk alone," Justin said as they went back to the tent where he picked up the first aid kit. They both then left the tent and walked into the desert.

"I'm still in a state of shock. I don't know if I can handle this," Father Peter said as he looked over the vast desert.

"That is why we must talk," Justin said softly. "I believe we should not speak of this until we return to the Vatican. I will be the authenticator when the time comes, but for the moment you must remain silent. We will bandage your wrist so the others remember only the condition of the wound when it happened." Justin did not know if scarring would occur and took the precaution of taking vitamin E from the medical kit and applying it to what remained of the wound. He quickly bandaged Peter's wrist while they were talking.

"I do not understand. I want to shout this from the highest hilltop. All will believe in this Cross, even the most hardened of sinners," Father Peter insisted.

"I am sorry...this you must not do. Your Cardinal not only requests your silence, it is demanded upon your sacred oath as a priest. You will not divulge what happened this night, including this conversation until you are released from this vow by me."

"But, this must be told!" Father Peter demanded.

Justin sensed the priest's turmoil and recognized his delicate state of mind. He knew Father Peter was aware of his high office of Cardinal, aware also the Prelate could, with a single signature on a piece of paper, effect excommunication.

"I know, my son, and it will be...at the right time and at the right place. We must ensure the safety of this mission and the conclusion of the task. Our first priority is to bring the Cross of Jesus to St. Peter's for all the world to glorify." Justin was solemn, even stern. "I want your holy promise."

Father Peter gave a sigh of resignation. He began to tremble. "I swear on my oath as a Catholic Priest and on the Bible that my mother gave me as a child," he said.

"And to you, my son, my thanks and my homage, for you have been chosen by our Lord, Jesus Christ, to manifest His miracles in this century. The world will soon know of the happenings of this place and I shall prevail upon the authenticators to bestow the title of miracle on this occasion in your life," Justin promised, fully aware that the Church could take fifty years before it might judge the matter, if at all. Justin now had witnesses in place able to attest to the severity of the wound. The healing would be a miracle Justin would authenticate. He was the only one who saw Father Peter's wrist after the "miracle" occurred. There need be no other explanation and the Cardinal would not be questioned. Father Peter was in no condition mentally, to raise an issue.

CHAPTER FOURTEEN

*M*ary Frances and Justin walked to the tent to inspect the Roman column now restored by the engineers who used the sandblasting equipment she had the foresight to bring on the expedition. Alone, they could discuss the plan for getting the Cross past Israeli customs. Justin was now questioning the original plan.

"We must stick to the plan or risk getting caught," she said.

"To separate the timbers of the Cross would be to defile it," Justin told her.

"The Cross can be repaired. You've seen first hand the skill of the Vatican restoration teams. The public will never be able to tell," she retorted. "We have no choice now. We must get the Cross back to the Vatican." Justin saw that there would be no compromise and that she was right. His morality was corroding his reason.

"Let's bring the Cross into the tent and separate the cross beam. Then we'll place the larger of the two pieces on the ground next to the column and use rope tackle to lift the marble," She instructed. "We'll put the cross beam on top of the column using the wood of the Cross to sandwich the column." It will appear we are simply using timbers to protect and transport the column."

"I'll get the engineers." Mary Frances was taking charge of this part of the operation. She knew Justin found it too distasteful to endure. He offered no objections to her actions.

The engineers returned with the Cross and placed it on the tent floor next to the column. They carefully detached the crossbeam. They secured both ends of the column using slings, and lifted it. The main beam of the Cross was wrapped with heavy cloth where ropes would bind it to the column. They slid the beam under the column and lowered the slings. Justin winced as he watched the weight of the column push the Cross into the canvas floor of the tent. He gritted his teeth in dismay as the rough edges of the column splintered off small pieces of the beam on impact. Mary Francis kneeled and picked up the splintered pieces and placed them in a small sack she took from her pocket. Next, the cross member was wrapped with cloth for protection and placed on top of the column. They covered the disassembled Cross and the column with tarpaulins binding them together with heavy rope. The sacred package was loaded onto the flatbed trailer.

They quickly broke camp and backed the pickup truck up to the flatbed and secured the hitch. The first order of business would be to contact the Vatican advising the Holy See of the status of the expedition. This was accomplished by portable satellite communication. The location for the transmission was atop a mountain in a desolate region deemed secure during the planning stages prior to commencement of the trip. It was sufficiently far from the Tel Aviv airport to avoid the threat of governmental eavesdropping through the normal airwave channels. As an added precaution, two prearranged code words in Aramaic were to be used indicating success or failure. Once the connection was made, Justin spoke the word "Necx Ano" the Aramaic word for victory. That would be the extent of the communication. Even if someone intercepted the communiqué, the gist of the one word message would not be understood.

"Now we must make it through Israeli Customs," Justin said as he looked at Mary Frances.

They arrived at the airport within two hours. A cargo plane from the Italian Air Force awaited them. Justin showed the export documents to the Israeli official in charge of customs who studied them carefully.

"Very well, the documents appear to be in order," the official stated. "We will need to examine the cargo."

Justin was confident that the Cross was sufficiently camouflaged even though in full view. The wooden sign, still fastened to the underside of the trailer, gave the appearance it was acting as additional support for the column.

"Of course, let me help you remove the tarps," Justin offered.

"Thank you, but that will not be necessary. Our men will take care of it," replied the official.

"You must be very careful, the column represents over three months of work," Mary Frances cautioned.

"We simply need to have the exact measurements of the artifact to determine its pedigree," the customs official added. Justin and Mary Frances could do nothing more. Their fate was in higher hands. Either their plot would be uncovered or it wouldn't.

The next thirty minutes seemed like hours. Finally, the official announced, "You may proceed, everything is in order. Your cargo jet is located at terminal three."

They quickly located the terminal and backed the flatbed trailer up to the yawning rear hatch of the Italian Air Force cargo craft. The loading went smoothly as they locked the flatbed trailer into place inside the hold of the giant aircraft. Justin and the other team members walked down the cargo ramp to the tarmac and proceeded to the side of the plane where Justin signaled the pilot to raise the cargo hatch. The noise of the hydraulic lifting mechanism was music to his ears. Then, out of nowhere, Justin heard the blasting sirens of two speeding airport police vehicles as they raced to the plane. The vehicles skidded to a halt thirty feet in front of the craft, effectively pro-hibiting a take-off.

Four Israeli Army personnel exited from each of the marked sedans and approached the tired looking, non-threatening archae-ological team. A muscular Israeli with jet-black hair and carrying a sidearm broke from the group as the others formed a not-too-discrete semi-circle around the plane. He walked cautiously toward Justin. Justin estimated his age at about twenty-eight but saw that his demeanor was that of a much older man. Battle ages one quickly, Justin thought to himself. He was not about to chal-lenge this experienced soldier. This Israeli was definitely in com-mand. The others had Uzi's at the ready.

"I believe you have somehow gotten past customs with something that belongs to the government of Israel," he said in a firm but soft voice exuding confidence.

"I do not understand," Justin protested. "Our papers are in order. Your customs have given us clearance."

"Yes, clearance for removal of a marble column from Caesarea, nothing else," the soldier replied. Justin's mind raced at the possibility that the game was over. They were so close. How did someone find out about the Cross?

"I still do not understand," Justin said, playing dumb.

"Perhaps if you open the aircraft, we will be able to enlighten you," the officer said with a head nod towards the aircraft cargo hatch. "Why don't we talk with the pilot so you may issue him instructions." They walked to the front of the cargo plane. Justin signaled the pilot to open the side window so they could speak. The Italian pilot was unaware that Justin was a Cardinal of the Roman Catholic Church, but did understand that he was the man in charge of the operation and that his authority was not to be questioned.

"I shall lodge a strong protest with your government," Justin warned.

"Because of attempted theft? I doubt that the Italian Government would appreciate becoming involved." The officer motioned to his associates and glanced at the aircraft pilot, his look indicating that the rear lift gate had best be coming down in a matter of seconds. Justin gave the approval, feeling somehow that stalling was not an option.

Justin, led by the soldiers, walked up the ramp of the rear cargo hold and went directly to the flatbed trailer. One of the soldiers, who appeared to be an officer, dropped to the floor of the cargo hold and began to search the underside of the trailer. Justin prayed silently that the one under the trailer would not locate the wooden sign secured to the underside of the flatbed. The sign supported nothing. Justin now realized it was a mistake to suggest that it did. Any idiot could tell it was tied only to the iron beams of the flatbed. On the other hand, he reasoned silently, who would suspect it to be anything of value?

"I got it! No question about it. It matched the description," the voice from under the trailer remarked. His voice sounding as excited as a bloodhound's bark.

"I believe you had best come with me." The soldier ordered.

"Am I under arrest?" Justin questioned.

"That is not my decision." He turned to the crew. "I must advise you, however, that this craft is quarantined for the moment. You will all remain here until further notice." The remaining Israelis' directed their "hostages" to one of the aircraft hangers and placed them under guard.

Justin was quickly ushered into the rear seat of a police vehicle between two of the soldiers. He heard the radio transmission in Hebrew and caught part of the conversation. The words, "theft from Netanya," did not make sense to him as he pondered his dilemma. What if he was found out to be a Cardinal? Worse, a renegade Cardinal entering Israel under a forged passport, stealing what rightfully belonged to Israel, lying about all of it, a total disgrace to the Catholic Church which would have no choice but to excommunicate him! These thoughts rocketed through his mind.

Justin was escorted into the security office, a sparsely appointed room with a small desk and three chairs making up the bulk of the furnishings.

"Please sit here," he was instructed.

"I still do not understand why I am here," Justin protested once again.

An army-clad official entered the room and stood quietly for more than two minutes allowing the silence to fill the room with fear and uncertainty. After the room filled with just the right amount of tension, he eyeballed Justin and spoke, "We do not wish to make an international incident out of this unfortunate situation. We are well attuned to political discretion, however, no one is exempt from the law."

"And what laws have we broken?" Justin said, wanting to make sure that if caught, he could plead ignorance. Sweat began beading on his forehead. It was easily noticed by his interrogator, trained to look for any chink in the armor, recognizing such physical betrayal as a sign of guilt and providing an opening for further pointed questioning.

"The theft of any national asset is dealt with harshly, and we must advise you that your cooperation is vital for your survival," the officer replied, still not quoting the line and verse of the law. Justin was no novice at psychological profiling. Many times his skills were employed to quickly analyze opponent's positions and adjust his arguments accordingly to persuade adoption of his view of a matter.

"I still insist that you are making a grave mistake," Justin said, his nervousness turning into an attempt to reason logically, hiding the internal anger brought about by his failure to complete the most important mission of his life. He now decided that the best defense was a strong offense. The Army official adjusted his horn-rimmed glasses. He wore a military cap, a green fatigue shirt on his back, and...Justin suspected, a very large chip on his shoulder. Justin was confident in his ability to match wits with this man, although he knew he was dealing from a position of extreme weakness.

"And now to the problem at hand. The facts are clear, the serial numbers match perfectly. There is no doubt that the trailer is from the city of <u>Netanya</u>. It has been reported stolen for the past week. Perhaps you would like to explain?" the officer said, giving Justin an opportunity to plead his case. The man's solemn face did not change expression as Justin broke out in a loud laugh. It was not the Cross! It was the trailer, sold to them by the local Israeli officials whom Justin attempted to bribe with the gold coins! The officials had stolen it!

Justin carefully explained how they had purchased the trailer and suggested that contact be made with the officials in Caesarea for verification. A nod by the officer to his aide started the process as the aide left the room.

"We would, of course, be happy to sign for the trailer or make absolute guarantee of its safe return," Justin added, trying to keep from smiling so as not to offend his involuntary "host". This was not so easy given the relief Justin was now experiencing.

The ringing of the single telephone in the office broke the now reduced level of tension. The officer lifted the phone to his ear. The short conversation ended with a polite, "Yes, sir," to whomever was on the calling end of the message.

"Excuse me for a moment," the officer said as he left the room leaving Justin alone to ponder what would come next. The officer returned momentarily.

"It seems you have been duped. Nevertheless, payment for the trailer must be made. You may handle the payment details with my aide before you leave. Is that satisfactory?" Asked the officer.

"We will take care of it. So... the trailer cost us twice the price we agreed to pay." Justin remarked.

"Maybe, you are too trusting," replied the officer. No mention of an apology was forthcoming.

CHAPTER FIFTEEN

$\mathcal{T}$he jet was cleared for takeoff in a matter of minutes. No one said anything until the lumbering craft lifted off the runway and gained altitude. Justin was seated next to a window, his eyes fixed on the slate gray of the Mediterranean watching as it dropped away as the jet zeroed in on a Northwest vector heading to Crete and from there, to Rome. Father Peter, his insecurity becoming more and more apparent, would not leave Justin's side, and sat in the aisle seat.

"Your Eminence, may I ask a question of you?" Father Peter said as he reached for Justin's arm. Justin's thoughts interrupted, he turned away from the window and toward Father Peter.

"Speak freely, ask any question you like," Justin responded.

"Do you believe in reincarnation?" The simple question with the difficult answers came as a surprise to Justin. He knew the official position of the Church on the matter and was aware that Father Peter was not as well versed in the subject as he.

"I believe in our Church's decree," Justin said as he saw the sincerity in the blue eyes of Father Peter.

"Did you ever question that position...I mean, have you ever tried to grapple with a Church dictate? One that you could not quite reconcile in your own mind?" Peter continued.

Justin nodded. "Of course. We all have at one time or another. As you grow older, you will find it much easier to comply with those things with which you are not comfortable. There are some of us who would counsel that you must have faith in the edicts of the Church and not question those matters with which you are not equipped to struggle," Justin said, not really believing his own words. More than once, he had sought answers to his mind's dilemma and had come away wanting.

"Why is the subject so taboo, so cloaked in secrecy, almost swept under the rug?" Father Peter persisted.

"It is a subject which has never been addressed during these modern times. The laity is confused enough without the possibility of reincarnation hanging around their necks," Justin explained.

"Why then, if the majority of the world believes in reincarnation as a basic fact of their lives, do we as Catholics pretend that it is not possible?" Father Peter asked. The sincerity of his question was obvious in his face as Justin realized that logic rather than absolute faith was invading Father Peter's conscious. Father Peter was in no condition to think for himself or to question the beliefs of the Catholic Church. Justin had to do exactly what Paul did when he reinterpreted the Hebrew bible for his own purposes in order to attract followers in the time of Jesus. Justin had to give Father Peter an explanation that appeared logical to quell further questions. He would do so for his own purposes and the future of the Catholic Church so that the "miracle" he had just witnessed would be preserved.

Justin hesitated..."Somewhere in the vastness of the Himalayas in desolate lamaseries, there are those manuscripts which have been kept secret for thousands of years." He looked at the beauty of the distant mountains in the morning light, and then turned back to the young priest. The Church cannot accept the possibility that we keep coming back to this world in some sort of Karma," Justin replied.

"Do you believe modern man is ready to accept reincarnation?" Father Peter asked, his face imploring an answer. Suddenly Justin became weary of the pointed questions.

"Why are you so insistent? What bothers you, my son?" Justin asked.

"I just don't know. I felt something tonight that I cannot comprehend. At that instant when my God and I were in perfect union a strange feeling came over me. I...I felt that I had been at the Cross, a spectator or a witness on Calvary. I know it sounds ludicrous, but I did have this vision of myself at the foot of the Cross when Jesus died."

The two men were silent. Justin knew he could not reveal his own questionings and strange dreams on this delicate subject. "It is the time, the place, and what we are all about. You have experienced what few men have experienced. Your mind has been touched by the glory of God, and it is possible that during that state of grace, your mind was taken to another dimension," Justin attempted to explain, hesitating to be totally candid with him.

Justin Kennedy was one of the very few privy to the secret documents hidden in the Vatican archives which clearly indicated that the subject of reincarnation was at one time an integral part of the doctrine of the Catholic Church. He was only twenty-six years of age when he first read the documents, the result of an error made by his superiors. The words directed the Catholic Church from early on to keep the subject of reincarnation a closely held secret in order to promote the state of purgatory on its followers. Justin believed his elusive dreams and mental flashbacks could be the manifestation of a form of reincarnation. Many had likened reincarnation as the missing link of Christianity. The book was closed on the subject by the decrees of the Fifth General Council proclaiming that if anyone asserts the pre-existence of souls, and the monstrous restoration that follows from it, he should be excommunicated.

"We are both tired and under a lot of pressure, Father Peter, we had best leave this subject for the moment. We will talk again on the matter, I promise you." Father Peter looked to his now bandaged wrist and began grappling with unanswerable questions.

"I will leave you to rest now. I have some business to discuss with some of our team while we still have the privacy afforded by the flight". Justin unbuckled his seatbelt and excused himself leaving Father Peter to wrestle with his own angel for answers, much like Jacob did in the Bible.

Justin was exhausted. He walked to the rear of the aircraft, found Mary Francis, and settled down in the aisle seat next to her. At least she would have his company for the remainder of the flight. She felt comfortable with Justin next to her. She adjusted the pillow wedged between her seatback and the window and laid her head on it as she looked out the window catching a glimpse of the last rays of daylight. The drone of the aircraft's engines made her drowsy. Justin was in a state of mixed euphoria and thought. The others, too, were probably lost in private meditation, possibly thinking of the holy relic strapped indecently to the trailer that was bolted securely to the base of the cavernous hold of the cargo plane.

Justin glanced at Father Peter. He was still staring at his bandaged wrist, trance-like, as he fingered his rosary beads as gingerly as a blind man reading speed-Braille. Justin felt as if a holy parasite was twisting inside his stomach. He was using the priest and he knew it.

Mary Frances was almost in full repose. Her eyes were closed yet her mind was awake and fomenting. Would her God forgive her for having feelings for Justin that rivaled her oath to the Church? What role was she destined to play in the continuing scenario? Would she silently slip back into her role as a Catholic nun and accept its dictates? She knew she wanted Justin to the exclusion of everyone and everything else. Her desires were safe as long as they did not leave her memory. She was now awakened to the fact that there was much more to life than the Church. She opened her eyes and turned toward Justin. The aircraft lumbered forward toward its destination. It was now night. The aircraft descended below the clouds making it as dark as a curtained cave. Everyone else in the cabin was asleep.

"Would you get me a blanket," she asked. Justin reached up to the overhead compartment and handed her one of the red blankets. She placed the blanket over both their laps and shifted her position so her head was resting next to his shoulder. Her right hand found a resting place on top of his thigh, concealed under the blanket. He lifted her face cradling it with both his hands. He brought her head toward him and touched his lips to her forehead. He gently placed her head to his shoulder, his left arm pulling her closer. They both felt an unaccustomed, but comfortable, contentment. Justin felt his heartbeat quickening as he put his head against the headrest and looked up toward the ceiling of the plane. His soul was begging for direction as he whispered to her, "this is not the time". She looked up at him with silent understanding as a tear ran down her cheek.

* * *

Once it was known that the Cross-had been found in Israel and smuggled out of the country protests were sure to follow.It would now be Justin's task to deal with it and render the escapade harmless, yet momentous, for the good of mankind. His wishes to bring the Mother Church the glory it deserved were weighted with the practical notion that the world might in fact receive the benefit of a lethal dose of Catholicism for the Church's clandestine foray into the land of Israel. Soon the huge jet approached the city of Romulus and Remus. The distant prisms of light flickered and appeared as if the earth had decided

to grow diamonds instead of trees. The terse landing announcement over the intercom was accompanied by the always familiar
yet still unnerving sound of the ponderous landing gear lowering. The pilot illuminated the interior lights of the plane. The
passengers all returned their seats to the upright position in
preparation for landing. The craft shuddered as the whine of the
hydraulics forced the twenty-four wheels down and locked to
await contact with the abrasive concrete of the tarmac. The passengers eyed each other nervously as the jet appeared as though
it had stopped dead in the sky in some terrible defiance of
Newton's Law of gravity.

Now Justin saw the approaching runway, the powerful direc-
tional strobes blinking a code of welcome. Rows of emergency
fire and rescue vehicles lined up on both sides of the tarmac. Their
flashing lights implied neither a salute nor salutation of welcome.
He craned his neck to see out the window as the jet settled on a
direct aim for the runway. Justin wondered if the appearance of
the emergency vehicles was for contingency purposes. If a rescue
was needed would the inhabitants or the Cross be the first to be
evacuated? The weird thought left him as the plane touched down
as gracefully as a swan landing on a Florida lake. The thunderous
roaring down the runway of the Air Goliath produced smiles from
everyone. The plane taxied to a hangar and was secured for the
night out of view of all but security personnel.

Promptly at 4:30 a.m. the next morning, Justin returned to the
hangar to supervise the unloading of their precious cargo. He felt
the pride of the moment as he watched Vatican security people
removing the Cross of Calvary from the cargo jet. He was acute-
ly aware that he had obtained another prize, more valuable, more
intrinsic. He felt he had found his soul, measured his worth and
discovered that mortal life was not one of awaiting death one day
at a time, or the inevitable dust to dust and ashes to ashes finality of the human race. Justin was no longer sure if the path his religion directed him to take could fulfill his needs. His heart and

soul dictated a different path. His recent experience had given him a new found confidence in his ability to tap heretofore-unknown resources of his spirit to overcome any earthly obstacle including the sexual desire for Mary Frances burning within him. He now questioned if that was against the laws of nature for a man who was merely mortal.

The appearance of a flatbed trailer traversing the streets of Rome in the early morning hours attracted little attention in spite of the flashing lights of the lead vehicle of the convoy. The eternal city had not yet begun another day. Very few people were to be found on the city streets. They soon entered the Vatican through a little used gate near Triangle Court, then down Garden Avenue, past the heating plant and Sacristy Court. The slow route continued to Mosaic Street, and then finally to the place pre-designated, a small, nondescript building near the Arcade of <u>Pier Luigi da Palestrina</u>.

Monsignor Enrique Capelli was the first to greet the returning heroes. A broad smile radiating across his face. "Welcome home, my brother, welcome!" Capelli embraced Justin, his eyes furtively darting to the holy relic under the tarpaulins.

Justin grinned. "And it is good to be home. At times we felt like a speeding boat full of holes. If we kept going, all was well; if we slowed, we would have surely sunk."

A Vatican car pulled up and Mary Frances stepped out of the passenger side and closed the door before the driver could get around to open the door for her. She thanked the driver and sent him on his way. Then she walked toward Justin.

"Good morning, your Eminence," she said as she bowed and kissed his ring. "And to you also, Monsignor," she added addressing Capelli.

"Ah... Sister, our love and affection to you also," Capelli said, noting for the hundredth time the strange enchantment of her beauty now concealed in part by her habit. Sister Mary Frances bowed slightly and kissed the hand of the church official.

Capelli smiled and spoke to Justin, "We have nothing but jubilation since receiving your message. His Holiness has been in prayer and meditation for the past twelve hours. Even canceled his audiences for today."

"Is the plan to place the Cross temporarily in the museum still in effect?" Justin asked, looking concerned.

"Yes, we must hide the relic at once. I have arranged everything." Capelli's tone indicating that he was now in charge of the entire operation.

Justin watched as the tarpaulin was removed. The ropes were cut with haste. The huge marble column was removed from the upright member of the Cross with little regard of its own value. Two pieces of the Cross were placed on a baggage cart borrowed from the Vatican railway station. The group pushed the pieces toward the Vatican museum where restoration of the Cross to its original configuration would occur. The first rays of the morning sun reflected off the golden dome of St. Peter's as Sister Mary Frances remained behind and began picking up tiny splinters of wood that had flaked off during the journey. Her mind lost in intense thought.

Pope Alphonse and his entourage were standing under the Bramante portico as Justin and the others approached. They maneuvered around the courtyard fountain with deliberate movements, as if to soften the shock on the Cross as the baggage cart click-clacked across the bricked pavement. Pope Alphonse was dressed in his Papal regalia. A white pontifical cap secure on his head, symbolizing the powers over heaven and earth as defined by the Catholic Church. Pope Alphonse spoke, "Benedicat vos, Omnipotens Deus, Pater, et Filius, et Spiritus Sanctus," then said, "The Cross exists because it is the work of God. It will survive all the attempts of man to destroy it." His voice was now wavering. "In our world everything changes. Generations die one after another in the orderly scheme of things. But let the day come when the world destroys itself in flame. This Cross will burn the longest and the glow of the embers will become a tiny beacon for the next universe to guide upon."

The Pontiff's words thudded in Justin's ears. This strange pronouncement from the Fisherman was not expected at a monumental time such as this. Justin felt suddenly afraid. The very real threat of nuclear incineration still prevailed throughout the world in spite of non-proliferation of weapons and arms treaties.

Justin followed the Cross as it was wheeled into the museum with reverent care. Few were permitted to actually touch the Holy Relic and then not without white gloves. This was an order issued by the Pope, as if the slightest fingerprint would somehow take away some of the Cross's mystique. The spikes and the sign were brought forward. The group eagerly craned to see them.

"A committee has been established to begin restoration. Monsignor Capelli has been appointed to head this sacred task," Pope Alphonse announced. He blessed the group and left the museum. It was an exit, made only after Alphonse's secretary discreetly passed a note to Justin.

Justin deduced that the note was a personal letter of praise for the successful completion of the mission. His error in judgment was duly noted when he stepped to the museum courtyard and read the message in the early morning light. "Please join me in my private residence, ten o'clock this morning. Most important." The handwritten note was impressed with the wax papal seal at the bottom, a large letter "A" embossed in the wax. Justin looked at his watch. It was just past 7:30 a.m. Just time enough to return to his apartment and freshen up.

Justin reached into the kitchen cabinet and retrieved a bottle of Aspirin. He swallowed three aspirins in an effort to relieve his head of a torturous migraine that was building. He showered then drew the window shades to block out all light. He lay quietly on the couch in the darkened room, his mind still wide-awake as the physical body fought for rest. He closed is eyes succumbing to a trance-like sleep... and the dream continued.

*Ragged and dirty, his feet blistered, Judas Iscariot limped
along the rough stone road. He noticed the familiar landscape of
his home in the distance.*

*The scene at the Cross, was burned into his brain, an offen-
sive symbol destined to remind the world forever of the condemnation. It would remain so forever to tell all that they were sinners and the blood of propitiation would remain with mankind for
all time.*

*"I beg a mortal death... contrition is in my heart. I beg thee
to release me from this torture of body and soul," Judas pleaded.*

A shrill cry of a sand partridge broke the silence as it fluttered
in fright from an acacia tree. The place where he had disgraced
his blood, befouling his own nest with his treachery, had changed
over the years. The clean home was now in disrepair, the water
well was dry, and its cyprus bucket rotted through. An inner force
was prodding him to continue his trek. The desperate hope in sad
memories propelled his weak legs to inch forward and recapture
his happy youth. Judas knew that his effort to look back could
produce more than he wanted to understand. The confrontation,
more than a memory, whatever its shape or premise, loomed
large. The scene at the Cross, was burned into his brain, an offensive symbol destined to remind the world forever of the condemnation. It would remain so forever to tell all that they were sinners and the blood of propitiation would remain with mankind for
all time. Judas came abruptly upon an old woman. Her weathered
features and ragged clothing completed the specter of an ancient
hag, scratching a living from the barren land.

"Hail woman.. where hath the family of Simon gone?" Judas
whispered through parched lips.

"Iscariot?... the name is linked with the dung of the cattle pen."
The old hag spat and began laughing through a toothless mouth.

"What blaspheme dost thou speakest... where are they?"
Judas demanded.

"Look to hell for that is the only place that would have them," she replied as she wiped the spittle from her face. Judas looked into the dull eyes of the old woman; a spark of remembrance seared his heart. The form in front of him was his mother! He fathomed the sweet smell of her hair as she had once cuddled him to sleep when a babe. The warmth of her bosom on cold nights filled his being as he struggled with the words.

"Mother?" He asked, as tears welled in his eyes.

"What madness dost thou speak? Be gone from this place!" She shrilled.

"Thou art my mother.... It is I, Judas, your son."

"I have no son... this Judas thou proclaim is the son of a she-bitch who fornicated with the devil and suckled on black milk," she screamed.

"Thou cannot deny thy seed...It is I who suckled at your breast." Judas implored.

"Be gone from this place... I have misery enough without the wild imaginations of your mouth," she answered.

"I speak the truth Yohannah bar Iscariot," Judas continued to plead.

"Thou art as mad as the prophet from Galilee...the one who called himself the Son of God." The woman's insanity was in complete control as she cackled.

"Do not deny me, mother of my youth... can thou not see the torment of my soul? Will thou cast me aside as a rotten morsel of putrefied food?" Judas fell to his knees. The woman backing away in disgust. "My heart is longing for thy touch, thy embrace for the one who is lost in the maelstrom of time," Judas cried as he reached for her ragged garments.

"Touch me not... I will have the dogs take thee for their supper if thou persists." She waved a menacing stick in his direction, her eyes wild with anger, her face contorted like a beast in mortal pain.

Judas felt the bones of his legs melt as he attempted to rise from the dirt. This final rebuke was more than he could bear.

"My God, why hast thou give me this cup? I cannot endure the pain of her denial... release me from this torment. Take this sinner to his death for I am even unworthy to breathe the air," Judas pleaded.

"Thou art destined to live forever, Seed of Kerioth." The voice emanating from a patch of brambles set aflame.

"What voice is this?" Judas screamed.

"I am who I am." The burning bush flamed higher but the brush was not consumed.

"It is the madness of my mind which speaks...I cannot fathom this which thou proclaim," Judas covering his eyes in an attempt to make the apparition disappear.

"In the time of man thou shalt live many lives. The future generations of the world shall know thee Judas lest they forget the deed which has blackened the heart of their God," the voice intoned.

"I beg a mortal death... contrition is in my heart. I beg thee to release me from this torture of body and soul," Judas pleaded.

"Thy pleas will be answered and the flesh of thy body shall be food for the jackals. But thou whom are despised shall carry the cross of the betrayal across the millennium, for in each generation thou shalt appear and remember," the voice admonished.

"Can this not pass over me?... I beg of thee," Judas cried out.

"Only when the true Cross of my Son is restored, and thy paths are joined, shall the Seed of Kerioth find mercy in the eyes of your God." The bramble bush burned in intensity with this promise. The phenomenon faded and disappeared leaving the bush intact.

"Be gone from here, madman," the old woman screamed.

"Did thou not hear the words?" Judas questioned in reply.

"I hear only the voice of one who has addled brains talking to a bush," she screeched, and pointed a bony finger at him in disgust.

"Do not deny me, my mother... I speak to you as thy son who has come home," Judas implored.

"I have no son," she said as she turned and left him standing alone.

* * * *

Justin awakened startled by the appearance of his aide, Antonio. The migraine headache was still bombarding his brain.

"I'm sorry, Your Eminence, I was just collecting your laundry from the trip. I am sorry for disturbing you," Antonio apologized.

"I'm glad you did," Justin said looking at the clock that read 9:15 a.m. The aide noted the soiled Mickey Mouse T-shirt as a smile spread across his face. "You may stay and assist me in dressing," Justin said.

Justin put on his robe and red cassock that he had not worn since leaving Rome, the longest period of time since becoming a member of the Sacred College. He felt his demeanor change as quickly as his clothes. He sensed a change in attitude cloaked in the power of the Church, the mystique of the high office and attendant respect of the Catholic followers recognizing the power of his role. He ordered Antonio to depart and again assumed the role of Cardinal of the Roman Catholic Church.

Justin did not enjoy the sensation of dominion over his fellow man. Yet the consuming human nature of it all fed the ego with heavy doses of something akin to arrogance in weaker moments. He looked to the mirror and noted the suntanned face staring back at him, his red skull cap placed upon his gray streaked hair. A quick smile brought him back to reality, as he announced aloud, "Let's not take ourselves too seriously, old boy." He grinned, his mind already on the impending audience with his Pontiff.

He was well aware the Roman Catholic Church was a fearful master and yet his steps were purposeful as he entered the Papal office.

Justin was ushered into the private study of the Pope, past sparse furnishings, which rested on a very large ornate woven rug on a cold floor. The room, measuring twenty by twenty meters, made the appointments appear scant. A large mural depicting the Last Supper covered the west wall. A squat oak desk holding scattered memorabilia occupied the center of the room. Heavy damask drapes, still drawn, allowed only the slightest hint of daylight to enter. A large crucifix hung on the east wall, a small spotlight beam focused on it, a modern touch that made the miniature Savior nailed to a Cross look somewhat surreal as the light reflected from his forehead.

Pope Alphonse entered through a side door at the far end of the room. Justin walked to him, genuflected, kissed his ring, then rose and looked at his Pontiff.

"Come, my brother, sit with me," Pope Alphonse motioned. They sat next to an ornate marble table, which held the Triple Crown of the papal throne.

Alphonse picked up the crown and handed it to Justin. Justin was taken aback as he felt its weight, wondering how the frail old man in his eighties could support it on his head.

"It is the symbol of your office and our symbol of obedience to your Holiness," Justin replied.

"It is much more than that, my son. It is a responsibility thrust at the man who is chosen to become the heir of Peter. They tell us in Latin to take this crown and know that you are the father of princes and leader of kings of the world, the Vicar of our Savior, Jesus Christ."

"And that is as it should be, your Holiness," Justin answered.

"Yes, all of my life I have been told that it is the will of God and all that has happened is as is should be," Alphonse said, rubbing his arm.

"Do I detect sorrow in your voice, my Father?" Justin asked.

The Pope nodded. "I would suppose it is sorrow of a sort. Sorrow that I will never see my dreams of reformation so needed by the Church accomplished in my lifetime."

"But you have become the Pope of the people. A leader when the world needs leadership," Justin said.

"The problem is that we always elect old and tired men to the Chair of Peter. About the time the logistics of his office are completed and the politics of the entire Church hierarchy fall into place, the petty bickering and squabbling is over, the Pope is too old or too weary to provide the youthful exuberance and style needed in this era of fast change," Alphonse said in his soft-spoken manner.

"But we have entered a new era," Justin protested. "The Cross of Jesus is in our hands. The symbol of our Lord and Savior will be shown to the world. The true religion of the world will become inspired once again."

"You are one of my Uomini de Fiducia, Justin, a man of trust. And I love you, my son, as dearly as I have loved any man. This may come as a surprise to you, but I have always admired your intelligence and natural wisdom. Your counsel did not go unnoticed when you gave it during the trying times of our debates concerning the weighty questions of our administration."

"And I am honored to serve you, your Holiness," Justin replied, attempting to fathom the dialogue between them.

"I am quite ill—seriously ill," The Pope said quietly. The words echoed off the barren walls of the room. Justin heard the utterance and yet his mind could not quite accept the pronouncement. Alphonse nodded as if to give more proof to the sentence.

"Illness can be treated with prayer as well as medicine," Justin said, his throat suddenly cracked dry.

"It is so and we cannot deny the truth. They tell me that I have very little time left." Alphonse walked to the window and parted the drape. "The cancer has spread to my lymph glands. They want to remove several lymph nodes but that will only result in a slow and agonizing death. An operation at my age would never succeed," Alphonse said, now a little more relaxed as the words were uttered.

"Why are you telling me this, my Father?" Justin asked, the whirlpool of words still not penetrating his mind.

"The Chinese symbol for crisis is the same as for opportunity and this opportunity in which we have to speak to each other will not come again. I know your heart speaks to you, dear brother, but we must discuss more important things concerning Church affairs."

"What can be more important than you, Holy Father?" Justin pressed.

"The Church and its destiny" the Pope replied. We are the rock on which the world can cling. The Vicar of Christ must be more than a padre to his flocks," Alphonse said, looking into Justin's eyes. Justin returned the gaze, noticing for the first time the turbulent gray eyes of Il papa that never seemed to settle in the wise face. "The single most important aspect of my tenure in office has been to help reconcile the differences with our brothers of the Former Soviet Union and the United States," the Pope said.

"This has concerned every Pope since John... I would think that your health would be of immediate concern," Justin replied. He marveled at his own brashness.

"The role of the Mother Church is not dependent on a single man. We, who have been chosen, are supposed to see further and do more, and yet..." The Pope's words trailed off momentarily. "...And yet, we see further only because we stand on the shoulders of our predecessors and not because of some divine revelations to whom the scepter has been passed."

"This resignation in your voice... am I to believe that your Holiness is defeated? The man who has done more to bring our people together than any other Pope in modern history?" Justin asked.

"Your words favor me, my son... but only history will record whether this heir of Peter was worthy of the task. But enough of this... I have glad tidings which I wish to impart," Pope Alphonse announced as a smile lit his cherub face, which did not quite hide the peasant cunning, which had served him well over the years.

Justin Kennedy sat quietly, still attempting to comprehend this remarkable audience with his Pope.

"I have just signed the document in which you have been named as a Cardinal Bishop. The formalities of bypassing your rank from Cardinal Deacon to Bishop has been handled by a little used cannon law which I have invoked," Alphonse said.

"Cardinal Bishop?" The words came out of Justin's mouth as a two-word question mark. He was mindful that his tenure as a Cardinal Deacon was not nearly long enough to be promoted to Cardinal Priest let alone the highest post of Cardinal Bishop—a double appointment unheard of in the recent history of the Church.

"Yes... for your magnificent task of securing the Cross of our Savior," Alphonse explained.

"My Father... I do not know what to say... my mind tells me that my faith is not strong enough," Justin said. "I am unworthy of this honor."

"It is a necessary step in the scheme of things," Alphonse said.

"How may I serve your Holiness?" Justin asked, still not grasping the enormity of the situation.

"When the announcement is made that we have found the Cross of our Savior, you shall become better known than the President who had the same surname as yours. You will be both revered and reviled. I am hopeful that you will not suffer the dark moods of the Irish when fame changes your life," Il papa grinned.

"I do not seek this fame. I want only to serve my Lord," Justin responded.

"The Irish temper will serve you well. I only wish I could see the verbal contests between you and the Prefect of Armaugh. Now that is one Irishman who is worthy of verbal combat." Pope Alphonse laughed and shook his head.

"The glory belongs to the Catholic Church, not me," Justin said humbly.

"The Catholic Church has all the honor it needs... what it really needs is the understanding to grow and prosper. We are at that critical juncture when the traditionalists are chipping away at the foundations of the ecumenical movement that had us pointed in the right direction. We can no longer bring ourselves to accept the silencing of our more moderate brothers." The Pope walked over to the papal crown, fingered its jewel-encrusted surface for a moment. "The fear which pervades all of our Curia meetings must be dispelled. More and more, these conclaves are taking on the semblance of inquisitions. The real leadership of the Church must untie the knots of inflexibility in matters such as priestly marriage, ordination of women, and birth control. We need a leader, a well-known leader of our Church to become the vanguard of a new movement toward a unification of all churches, be they Catholic or Protestant. I perceive that you are this leader."

"I am not equipped for this task... the conclave would never accept this even from Il papa himself," Justin acknowledged.

"I must make my plans now... there is so little time left," Alphonse said as he grew weary.

"And I will refuse to accept this... this finality of yours!" Justin whispered.

"You will accept, my son". Alphonse commanded.

"There is nothing more important to me than your life, dear Holiness," Justin insisted.

"Nothing is more important now than the Chair of Peter." Alphonse replied.

"I do not understand," Justin replied, his heart thumping.

"The world still believes that we select our Pope behind closed doors and only after deliberation. The traditions are kept alive with the burning of the white ballots and the straw. We both understand that the choice for the Pope of this age cannot be left to chance or to politics. The selection is already made. I have chosen you. You, my son, will be the next Pope. Prepare yourself as best you can for it shall be done. And once done, remember that the sacred truth is that there is <u>no</u> sacred truth. Only the ability to adapt assures survival. I must go now my son," Alphonse sighed and left Justin Kennedy alone to ponder the startling pronouncement that would change his life forever

PART TWO

CHAPTER SIXTEEN

$\mathcal{T}$he sound of a priceless vase smashing through a portico window in the Mediterranean villa of Hosni Khatabi was his answer when informed that the Cross had reached the Vatican.

"Someone will pay dearly!" he vowed to an associate standing discreetly at the rear of the library. The associate knew of the wrath of his employer, who once ordered the severance of four fingers of a servant's right hand for stealing a loaf of bread from his master's kitchen. The wealthy Arab grimaced and knocked his knuckles on the mahogany desk as he contemplated his next move.

"Advise the Countess she will put into effect our little agreement," Khatabi instructed, still seething at the inept actions of his confederates in Israel. Khatabi had gone to great expense in "creating" the fictitious Lt. Colonel Moishe Steingard by bribing certain officials in order to stop the excavation. The only task his servants in crime had to carry out was to steal the Cross. "How difficult could this be!" he screamed. "The Cross was found. It was taken from its chamber! It was lying on the ground! The

Israeli's effectively quarantined the entire team while interrogating them! Nobody was guarding the Cross! Where were my men?" he shouted to a now empty room. His mind began conjuring up the excuses he would make to Orlo Thompson.

* * * *

Justin Kennedy was ending two days of much needed rest at a small villa on the outskirts of Rome owned by the Vatican, and one of several made available to select guests, when the phone rang interrupting his solitude. It was Monsignor Capelli requesting an audience, a request that was quickly granted. Justin's two day escape did no more than to identify, with brutal clarity, the three major conflicts he was now facing; ascension to the throne of Peter; his feelings for Mary Frances; and, the consequences of his theft of the Cross. It was late afternoon when the Monsignor arrived at the papal villa. Capelli entered breathlessly as if the devil himself were chasing him.

"What is it?" Justin asked, as he reached for his friend's arm and directed him to a chair. "Have you not heard?" Capelli said with a look of surprise.

Justin had no idea what he was talking about. "Concerning?"

"Il papa... he's dying," Capelli's voice spoke the name as if the air was being forced from his lungs.

"It is the talk of the halls. They..." Capelli stopped in mid-sentence interrupted by Justin.

"Ah... it is the select group, the all-encompassing they again... the sacred College of Cardinals, am I not correct?" Justin questioned.

"You are...but are you not concerned?" Capelli was startled at the impudence of his question that came forth without thought. He fell quickly to his knees. "Forgive me, your Eminence... I am overcome with grief. I allowed my friendship to interject a dreadful question... please forgive me."

"There is nothing to forgive, Enrique... I understand your hasty speech. And as to my concern, yes... I am concerned only if the information, which is by now crossing Saint Peter's Square, is of some truth," Justin said as he bid the Monsignor to rise from the floor.

"It is said that his heart is failing... a matter of days and His Holiness may be dead," Capelli said. Justin speculated that the Monsignor had picked up the information at the Vatican pharmacy. He knew of the refined hypochondria of Capelli's nature. Some even ventured to say in jest that he never went anywhere without his thermometer, umbrella, and jumbo bottle of vitamin C. His imagined ills were the talk of the papal back rooms. If he read it in the "Readers Digest", he somehow contracted it by osmosis. Unfortunately, this time Justin knew Capelli's information was correct. Pope Alphonse had already made Justin privy to the terminal nature of his medical condition.

"I would suggest that you give no further credibility to this rumor, Enrique," Justin advised. "It is best left unsaid until, or unless, the facts of the matter have become known."

"Are we to wait until the news is printed across the front page of the L'Observatore Romano?" Capelli asked.

"Perhaps the Secretary General will shed some light on the matter," Justin said in an effort to stall any further comment on the subject.

"You must be joking. Lattimer? He is the last one Pope Alphonse would trust in his inner circle. Certainly, he would not be a confident to the personal medical condition of his holiness. He is tolerated simply because he holds the position of Camerlengo responsible to untie the Vatican purse strings when requested by Alphonse, a position he does not deserve. Were it not for his rank of office he would have been ridden out of Rome on a rail as an incompetent "yes" man. That is one man that would never be on my council should I ever become the Pope," Capelli said.

"But, he serves his purpose," Justin was aware of the ill feelings between the Monsignor and the Secretary General. It was the Secretary General's written missive to the College that had eliminated any chance for the well-qualified Italian Monsignor to be elected a Cardinal Deacon during the most recent nominations.

"To his credit," Capelli continued, "Pope Alphonse has not tried to make a "silk purse" out of this sow's ear. But never, would he be one of my advisors".

"So, it is you who would be the Pope. Even before the Pope Alphonse is struck on the forehead with the silver hammer," Justin said. His smile at the humor hid the very real sorrow in his mind.

"The post is always up for debate. Even you would have a chance at the Chair of Peter," Capelli offered in mock seriousness. "However, you are right, of course. We must remain in prayer for the health of our pontiff." The Monsignor crossed himself.

"And if the news is true, who would you support for the Throne of Peter?" Justin asked.

"It is not my place. Although God knows that I am qualified to sit in judgment. The two-thirds plus one vote of the Scared College will make the decision. This means the fate of our Church rests with one hundred twenty-seven men in red," Capelli said. Justin knew the monsignor's calculation would not be off by more than a few since those over the age of eighty and those who were infirm were not permitted to vote. The final count would bring the total electorate eligible to vote to no more than one hundred ninety.

"But, I must sit in judgment and I need the counsel of my trusted friend," Justin said.

"You are now implying that the rumor is true... A few moments ago I was being admonished for my haste." Capelli's face expressed hurt feelings.

"My dear brother, if the Pontiff is not terminal, then it is only a matter of time until the throne is vacant. Should we not share this moment in which to express our views to each other?" Justin waited, hoping to obtain a reading on who Capelli thought would be contenders if the election was imminent.

"I am indeed flattered by your confidence in my opinions. I do, however, have some rather strong comments regarding members of the College and I pray forgiveness for what I am about to say. May I have your dispensation to speak my mind?" the Monsignor asked.

"In the privacy of this villa you may speak whatever is in your heart, I know your words are not delivered in anger but in contrition, your love of the Church is not questioned."

"First of all, the group from Germany will be the strongest force in the selection of a new Pope. Wilhelm and his colleagues are experts at politics. It would not surprise me if the quest has already begun. He is the leader of the group attempting to hand over the Church to the Vatican core theologians. He would become a King in his own mind. He has carefully orchestrated a power structure to do his bidding," Capelli said as he sat down.

"I see that you have made notice of the happenings in the College," Justin replied.

"I'll wager Wilhelm and his group are already conniving plans to take advantage of the news that the Cross of our beloved Jesus has been found," Capelli said.

"And what of the Pole, Pleaschack? Would he not also throw his red cap into the ring?" Justin asked, delving into the thoughts of the monsignor.

"Jealousy will reign supreme between them, of this you may be certain," Capelli said in response.

Justin smiled. "Jealousy, someone once said, is the tribute that mediocrity pays to genius. In this case, it seems either each thinks the other is a genius, or mediocrity rules supreme."

Capelli laughed, and then became more serious. "None the less, the battle lines will be drawn quickly. The weapons will not be quill pens or verbal niceties. Indeed... I have the distinct feeling that vicious innuendo will be only the tip of the iceberg. The power blocks will begin to build. The winner is not likely to be the best choice, but merely the most devious and resourceful."

"You must have faith, my brother. After the battle is waged and the body count is made, the selection will be one which the Church will accept," Justin said.

"Selection imports a fairness of choice. No... victory may go to he who nurtures to the needs of others. Others who crave power and are duped into relying on promises that will never be kept. It is akin to a man who will say anything during the heat of passion in order to fulfill his desires. I dare say that the blood-letting will begin even before the <u>moto propio</u> is over," Capelli replied.

"As history has taught us... and if we have learned anything, we know that in the same instant that the words <u>Habemus Papam</u> are spoken, and the crowds in the Square begin to cheer, the battle is over," Justin said.

"I remember well when John Paul was named the <u>Summum Pontificem</u>. The four or five seconds before the crowds began to shout their approval were the longest in my life. I relived these moments many times and often wondered if a Papal election could be overthrown if the masses rejected the wisdom of the Sacred College." Capelli said, shaking his head.

"The crowds will always respond. I would be willing to wager even Billy Graham would be cheered should he be named Pope," Justin smiled.

"A ludicrous suggestion, Eminence. That bit of rhetoric brings dishonor on the Cardinalship," Capelli admonished his superior, mindful that a freewheeling discussion was still in effect.

"Lighten up, my friend," Justin said with a smile. "My point is to make you aware that the election of a pontiff is not the stuff that is made in heaven. The process has undergone many changes over the years, changes that may not sit well in your heart, or the hearts of devout Catholics. The pomp and ceremony is expected. The mystic is a necessary ingredient to give the aura and respectability to the ceremony. The rituals must be followed to the letter. Our followers demand rituals. It makes us better in the eyes of the world. At least that's what most Catholics want to believe."

"If only you were older," Capelli said suddenly injecting his spur of the moment thoughts into the conversation.

"I beg your pardon?" Justin said.

"You... an American Pope. If you were twenty years older and had the necessary experience... you would make a viable candidate," Capelli replied.

"I think our thought processes are being tortured by hunger Monsignor. It is well past the supper hour and I would suggest we dine together and continue the discussion over some fine pasta from Senora Delores' kitchen." Capelli nodded his head in agreement. Justin wanted to take advantage of the wise counsel of his associate. He knew that should he become Pope, the close personal relationship would change as a result of the office.

Within the hour, the meal was served. The first course was steamy minestrone for Capelli and an antipasto salad for Justin.

A forkful of the salad laden with a heavy dose of mozzarella cheese pleased Justin's taste buds. The main course of broiled lamb was a bit undercooked as expected. The Monsignor met Justin's preference for rare lamb with chagrin. Capelli had once experienced trichinosis from undercooked meat and never forgot the illness he endured.

"The secret is to taste the spinach-filled ravioli first. It is a fine complement to the lamb. A hint of lemon will clear the palate from that horrendous minestrone you gulped down." Justin laughed heartily as he reached for a bottle of <u>Lacrima d'Arno</u> wine, then held the label for Monsignor Capelli to accept or demure. Enrique shrugged his shoulders indifferently.

"Come now my brother, drink. . . be happy", Justin urged.

"And if you were to choose between Wilhelm and Pleaschack?" Capelli asked pointedly between bites of his meal.

Justin remained quiet for a full minute before answering the direct question of his friend.

"As Talleyrand once said, when asked to choose between Robespierre and Voltaire; when I think of one, I prefer the other," Justin smiled.

"The election process has produced some terrible flukes in the past. Deadlocks and prolonged debates have provided us with Popes ill-equipped to deal with even the most mundane duties of the Chair of Peter," Capelli offered as he sipped the sweet wine.

"The election process can be parliamentary prostitution, even mental incest to some of the membership. But I believe that God shall always have his hands in the final decision," Justin replied.

"Nonetheless, in geometry there are certain known rules or axioms which must be accepted in order to get the correct answers. The rules must be applied in order to have God answer our prayers," Capelli said. "Perhaps God has answered us by rewarding us with His Cross of Calvary." Capelli's statement was the first serious mention that Justin, having found the Cross, might be a candidate for the highest office.

Justin looked at him not wanting to discourage the possibility, but not wanting to appear anxious either. "It is understood we stand on the threshold of a new beginning for the Mother Church, it is agreed the Cross shall play an important part in any new administration," Capelli said. Justin kept silent but acknowledged the suggestion with a confident smile.

After dinner they retired to a small study, the dialogue between the pair destined to continue far into the night. Opinions were bantered back and forth for hours. The stage was set, scenery in place. The players selected. Only the omniscient author knew the beginning, the middle and the end. The Cross of Jesus, the future of the Roman Catholic Church, and even the fate of the world would be held captive amidst the happenings at the Vatican during the coming weeks.

CHAPTER SEVENTEEN

$\mathcal{U}$atican tongues were set wagging by the announcement naming Justin Kennedy a Cardinal Bishop, the recipient of a remarkable double promotion. This, adding to rumor and speculation, had given new energy to the mystique of the Cross, the Pontiff's health, and the politics of ambition. The summer was heating to a historic flame.

Monsignor Enrique Capelli quickly moved to consolidate his power base. The appointment of Capelli by Pope Alphonse to head the team responsible to restore the Cross of Jesus was an opportunity filled with great potential. Capelli knew his hypochondria must take a backseat to this new challenge. Capelli was aware a successful conclusion to the restoration would lead to an appointment as a Cardinal Priest. The Pope had something else in mind. He summoned Capelli to his private chambers.

"You have done well in your duties for the Church," Pope Alphonse began. "I would like to hear your views on various subjects of interest to me regarding the future of our religious doctrine."

"I am honored your Holiness. But of what importance are my opinions? I am simply a Monsignor doing his best to serve the Church in a subservient way dictated by my position." Capelli chose his words carefully. He wished to convey his desire to be elevated in the Church ranks in a subtle manner.

"Yes," Alphonse replied, "I agree your present position may not sit well with your abilities. However, to me, loyalty is even more important. If I am to trust your opinions and bring you into my inner circle, I must be sure that your ideas are aligned with mine. If they are not, it is not fatal for your advancement. You may still proceed through the normal channels to reach higher office, although the process will indeed be a long one."

"Of what subjects do you desire my comment, your Eminence?" Capelli knew that by asking the question he would be prepared to give the answers expected and was willing to do so. After all, he knew the main issues regarding reformation of the Church and even if he did not totally agree with the thoughts of the Pope, he could surely bend a little with a modicum of encouragement.

They spoke on various matters for over an hour. At the conclusion, Alphonse looked pleased at having attained what he desired.

"Then, I can count on you to act as my emissary to the various factions in the Curia to ferret out their positions on who shall be my successor?"

"Yes, your Eminence," Capelli replied. "And as promised, I will suggest to them that it will be Cardinal Justin Kennedy as the one deserving of the Chair of Peter, just as you have requested. I will report back to you with the answers you are seeking."

"I am pleased at your acceptance of my proposition. I will arrange for my personal aide to meet secretly with you for the fitting of your new garments. Naturally, you will have to wait until my announcement of your new position until you may wear them. And that...shall remain private between you and me."

"I understand, your Holiness, and am grateful for this audience and your trust in me." Capelli bowed and kissed the ring of his new mentor and left the chambers.

The Cross was located in a secret room west of the main corridor to the rear of the Vatican museum. Large double locks on the heavy doors, as well as security guards posted around the clock, only added mystery to the place. A large plywood partition cordoning off the Cross from the main room protected the Cross from view. There was great speculation in the Vatican halls regarding the happenings in the room of intrigue as restoration experts probed the secrets of the Cross. An elaborate alarm system was installed as electricians complained about the overtime for which they would not receive compensation. Even the priceless Pieta did not have the security that was bestowed upon this room; this fact only heightened the mounting speculation.

"I want the solvent tested on something else before you touch the Cross," Capelli instructed a subordinate.

"I doubt any solvent will clean the pitch and tar off... that substance is almost petrified... bonded deeply into the wood," Father Byron Callahan, a Vatican restoration expert advised. Callahan had been around so long, no one would doubt that as a little boy, he climbed the tree from which the Cross was cut.

"All the same, I do not want any testing started until we are absolutely certain that damage will not result. Is that clearly understood?" Capelli asked.

"Yes, Eminence, quite fully understood," Father Callahan answered.

Capelli seemed to forget for the moment that Father Callahan was the most talented expert on the Vatican restoration staff, and that he had played the leading role in salvaging a priceless fresco by Michelangelo that had been slashed by a crazed visitor in 1989.

"Has Father Kleinschmidt finished the drawings yet?" Father Callahan asked.

"He finished them this morning. They are in the safe. I'll get them." Capelli walked to the safe, opened it, and retrieved the drawings that he placed on the drafting table. A broad smile spreading across his face as he looked at the renderings. The drawings depicted the enshrined Cross between the twisted Bramante columns above the main altar in the Basilica. The huge Cross dominated the space between the four massive columns. Thin, almost invisible wires would hold the Cross as if in neutral gravity, suspended twenty feet above the altar; it was a ghostly specter. Pinpoint beams of light focused on the four outermost points of the Cross, would give the completed placement an even more glowing rapture. Father Kleinschmidt's renderings depicted a golden-hued beam of light directed at the wooden sign.

"Magnificent! Absolutely magnificent! Truly an inspired work," Capelli said, elated.

"It has been suggested that we have the spikes encased in glass and placed at the foot of the altar," Father Callahan added.

"Preposterous! They will be nailed on the Cross in the very same holes. Whose idiotic suggestion is this?" Capelli demanded.

"The suggestions came from his Holiness as I understand it," Father Callahan answered, his face not betraying his glee of satisfaction at the reaction of the Monsignor.

"Well," Capelli stammered at his faux pas, "I must seek an audience with Il papa to go over this particular aspect of restoration."

Capelli blanched as he attempted to regain his composure, fully aware that when two Catholic prelates got together there would always be three opinions.

"May I suggest, Eminence, that we arrange a meeting with Father Kleinschmidt as soon as possible," Father Callahan said.

"Yes, I want to congratulate him again on these marvelous drawings. Please have him consult with me this afternoon," Capelli's power base was expanding as wide as his stomach.

"It is indeed fitting that the Cross of our beloved Jesus should find its way home at last," Callahan said.

"Home? I dare say... the Israeli government would take umbrage at that statement. I hope our Vatican diplomats are working as hard as we are towards an explanation of why we stole the Cross from them in the first place." A grin now spreading across Capelli's face.

"I only meant to say that we above all in the Christian community have been blessed to place the Cross in such a holy place for the entire world to hold dear. But what about the Israelis? Do they look upon the Cross as an embarrassment?

"My dear brother, your craftsmanship and dedication, I hold in high esteem, but I must bring to your attention a few theological points which are salient. First of all, the Jewish state and its people do not attempt to hide the fact that Jesus was crucified or that he was a Jew. Most of them believe that He was one of the greatest prophets to ever come from the house of David. Secondly, Jews as well as Catholics know that various political factions and the Romans were to blame for the death of Jesus. The Hebrew faith is steeped in tradition and the first to preserve historic artifacts.

"You are correct, of course, but my heart tells me that our faith and prayers have been somehow answered. I am also aware that world attention will be focused on the Roman Catholic Church. Well deserved attention of a positive nature, I might add," Callahan said.

"It is fitting that the final resting place for the Cross of Jesus should be the very place where Simon Peter gave his life. As the flames from two thousand Christians who were torched and crucified upside down in the classical sign of Satan, so shall the Cross of our Lord light up the nights for all the people of the world for all time to come. Out of this light shall come the true redemption," Enrique Capelli said.

"Eminence, would you come with me, I wish to show you something? "I am sure my calculations are correct, and yet I hesitate to make a judgment. Please walk with me and I'll show you my concern." Father Callahan directed Monsignor Capelli to the horizontal piece of the Cross.

"Look at the nail holes on the Cross," Callahan said, pointing to the defined indentations. "The holes are not where they should be."

"What do you mean?" Capelli asked.

"I mean that Jesus was not nailed to this Cross through his hands!" responded Callahan.

"This cannot be!" Capelli said.

"Well," Callahan continued, "unless our Lord has extremely short arms, it is impossible for his body to have hung in the center and been nailed through the hands on the crossbeam. The distance from the middle of an average man's palm to his wrist is seventy millimeters. That is precisely where the nail holes on the crossbeam are positioned.

Capelli demurred in his protestations, and then finally spoke out. "How can this be?"

"Eminence, it is my considered opinion that our beloved Jesus was fastened to this Cross with spikes through his wrists, not his hands!" Callahan, the respected restorer waited for Capelli's reaction.

"Do you realize the implications of your statement, the ramifications of this thought, Blessed Jesus! We cannot, we dare not even think of such a possibility!" Capelli shouted. "You are betrayed by your own words, you said an "average man". Are you suggesting that Jesus was merely average? The tradition of the Stigmata and its miracles have been formulated by the Roman Catholic Church over the centuries and were ingrained in the minds of Catholics. Either the Scriptures are incorrect or, the placement of the nails as reported is incorrect. Is that it? Is that what you are telling me?"

"There is one other possibility," Callahan responded, "This may not be the Cross of Jesus."

"That is not a possibility," Capelli quickly asserted. "I suggest you keep that opinion to yourself. Are we clear on that point?"

"Perfectly clear," Callahan said as his eyes cowered away from Capelli. "I did not mean to offend you. But, I have a duty to discuss with you my findings even if you determine I am incorrect, which I apparently am in this case. Please let me explain the logical aspect of what I incorrectly suspected."

"If it will put an end to this nonsense, you may proceed with an overview. Let's not spend a great deal of time investigating a blind alley," Capelli insisted.

"To be clear, my reference to "average" dealt solely with the human form. Consider our Jesus was of average height and weight. Body tissue and bone structure of the hand would not permit his weight to hang for long before the flesh and bones would tear apart." Callahan's voice sounded very scientific.

"We must not make any hasty judgment," Capelli said. He was aware that any profound announcement of this sort could bring discredit on the authenticity of the Cross and thus create a tidal wave of disbelief that could wash away any chance he had for fame and could negatively impact the deal made with Pope Alphonse. He would have to nip this thinking in the bud or risk loosing the cherished Cardinalship.

"I believe we best seek a medical opinion on this, Eminence," suggested Callahan.

Capelli dismissed the suggestion out of hand not wanting to know if Callahan was correct or not, "What good would that do?"

"If it is the truth we seek, the truth must come out," Father Callahan replied. "Doctors could give us a scientific opinion on this situation," he added.

"Would you place a doctor's opinion above the faith of the Pope?" he said in an intimidating tone. "Are we back to evolution vs. religious faith?" Capelli reached into his cassock, removed two suspicious-looking pills and held them in his hand. "Are you asking the medical fraternity to locate a cadaver and impale it on a cross to prove your point? And, then, who is to say how long a lifeless body should be left hanging on the cross? What if the body is riddled with sickness that caused the flesh to deteriorate? Would you compare mortal man to the Son of God?" This, he could not let happen. The truth would be what the Church wanted it to be. Capelli continued challenging Father Callahan as if it was an inquisition.

"Have you ever questioned the medical opinion of a doctor?" Capelli challenged. "For every medical doctor with an opinion, there are other doctors willing to stake their reputations to the contrary. So, who is to say which expert is correct? We will never get the truth from medical doctors because they will never agree. We will be opening a can of worms for a fishing expedition. The Church has decided what the truth is and that is that!" he said emphatically as he reached for a glass of water, put the pills in his mouth, and swallowed.

* * * *

The two men who were conjuring plans that would affect Justin's future as a force in the political schemes of the Vatican strolled the neatly swept walkways of the Vatican gardens. The well-manicured lawns and magnificent flora of the gardens were a paradox of serenity as the two plotted a scenario of politics and intrigue.

Secretary General Lattimer walked side by side with Cardinal Kurt Wilhelm as late morning sun filtered through the thick foliage. Wilhelm walked with his usual slow, deliberate pace, his hands clasped behind his back. Lattimer, sixteen years his junior, found it difficult to maintain the slow pace of the walk and the fast pace of the dialogue.

"As you are aware, my dear brother, I keep my opinions to myself, and for good reason. I correctly surmised that if Cardinal Kennedy's mission were successful we would have a new power bloc with which to contend. Kennedy and Capelli are now formidable personages. Their strength will grow by leaps and bounds as the day nears for the announcement of the finding of the Cross," Cardinal Wilhelm surmised.

"Capelli is a fool! His dream of becoming a Cardinal is a foolish fantasy. It would not surprise me if he even had designs on the Chair of Peter," the Secretary General said laughing.

"It is Kennedy I fear. His American heritage will push him to further heights of accomplishments. I sense something about him that disturbs me. His natural intellect only needs a spark to ignite the flame of power in his mind... yes, Kennedy is the one whom we must be wary," Wilhelm predicted.

"And what do you read into the announcement that Kennedy has been named as a Cardinal Bishop? He now holds the same rank and prestige as you." Lattimer could not disguise the jealousy in his voice.

"I perceive this double promotion has more meaning than just a reward for finding the Cross. Much more..." Wilhelm paused as he reached down to the walkway and retrieved a feather that had blown from a nest set precariously between a small fork in a branch. He fingered the feather for a moment and continued his discussion. "A bird cannot navigate without its feathers. I suggest we pluck that key tail feather from the American eagle," Wilhelm said as he placed the object in his red cassock.

"And just how is this to be accomplished?" Lattimer asked.

"We will use the fact that he is an American to our advantage. It is the United States that has brought shame upon the Church. This business with unbridled priests has cost the Church millions and we have not seen the end of it. All we need is to plant a seed questioning whether it would be wise to detach the Catholic movement in the United States from the rest of the Catholic world. Let them fend for themselves and suffer from the ills of their own depravity." Wilhelm smirked.

"It will never happen."

"It doesn't need to happen, my friend. The mere thought that our brethren are thinking about the possibility is enough to eliminate Kennedy. The workings of the College are considered very mysterious and yet it is quite simply a matter of alliances. You scratch my back and I shall do likewise for you. The plan I have in mind will remain secret for the moment," Wilhelm said.

"I trust that you will consider me as part of this alliance," Lattimer said as he placed his hand on the shoulder of the Cardinal.

"Trust... that is the common denominator between us, Jacob. I must be able to trust you implicitly," Wilhelm said, setting his lantern jaw.

"Was it not I who gave you the first word concerning Alphonse's health?" Lattimer insisted.

"Among others, yes." Wilhelm's words giving weight to the fact that he had his spies in other high places.

"I will do whatever you wish, Eminence," Jacob Lattimer said.

"Your position as Secretary is of vital import. You not only have the ear of the Pope, but are in a post which gives you access to the financial dealings of the Church, dealings that are the touchstone of Roman Catholic power, the one privy to these dealings has the knowledge to help one gain the throne," Wilhelm said.

"And should the quest be successful, I trust his Eminence would be leaning toward my appointment as a Cardinal Deacon?" Lattimer phrased the request as an oblique question.

"It is much too premature to discuss these things, but I believe you see the picture," Wilhelm said encouragingly. "We have much to do, consolidations to effect. Many have attempted this journey but few have made it. The failure rate is astronomical. The one who makes the least mistakes will be the victor," Wilhelm said.

"It is usually someone else's fault that the truly great men are never elected. We must be suspicious of those who place themselves between us and the throne," Lattimer said in a further effort to consolidate his bonds with the red-capped German.

"Alas, dear Brutus, the fault is not in the stars, it is in ourselves..." Wilhelm countered as he paraphrased Cassius.

"You may depend upon me, Eminence," The Secretary General said as he bent to kiss the Cardinal's ring.

"Remember, we must stick to the high road and keep our true feelings and ambitions to ourselves," Wilhelm cautioned. Tomorrow we attend the International conference of Catholic Bishops in Milan. Various Cardinals will also be in attendance. We will have an opportunity to shore up alliances in private. Kennedy will not be attending. I have been asked to give the keynote address. I intend to use the opportunity to "our" best advantage".

"What about Capelli? Will he be in attendance?" Lattimer asked as if Capelli might be a fly in the ointment.

"Of course, Capelli is in charge of the entire conference. It was Capelli who asked me to speak. The man has cut the legs off his favorite candidate and doesn't know it. The damn fool!"

Lattimer laughed, "Why on earth would he be so naïve?"

"Reason and politics do not necessarily go hand in hand my brother." Wilhelm retorted. "I will meet you tomorrow and we will perform our magic at the conference." They parted company and Wilhelm walked alone towards St. Damascus court on the edge of the gardens thinking of the speech he had carefully planned to deliver the next day. Wilhelm smiled and began to fill his pipe. His plans were falling neatly into place, his mind envisioning actions for the future.

On the flight to Milan, Wilhelm struggled with mixed emotions regarding the news of the Pontiff's failing health, his love for the Vicar of Christ ingrained with his resolute and uncompromising drive toward the papacy. The German's demeanor and outward appearance of always being correct discouraged others from challenging him. This served well to hide his secret inner thoughts... thoughts that gave him a green light to do what had to be done, right or wrong, to accomplish what he set out to do. Given the proper reason, he would become a modern age sorcerer's apprentice using every device available, even if it meant consorting with the devil himself, to obtain his goals. He knew this would be the final opportunity for his election as Pope and he was now pressured to put into action the plans that were meticulously crafted over the past two decades waiting for the moment at hand.

The Vatican limousine waited for the German Cardinal at the Milan airport and took him through the countryside to the gated resort chosen for the Bishops conference. Wilhelm used the time to go over his speech and to make a mental tally of his supporters. His relationship with the banking community of West Germany assured him of powerful financial support in his quest for the Chair of Peter. A German Pope would be quite a feather in the cap of the political elite. The Germans knew this and forged powerful relationships with the Catholic Cardinals in bordering countries. Funding was made freely available at low interest rates to await repayment not in kind, but in the favor of pontifical support when the time was right. The limousine approached the gates of the resort and the driver lowered his window and presented the Vatican guards with the papers required for entry. The guards, for security purposes, requested the rear window be lowered to verify that it was Cardinal Wilhelm who was entering the grounds and it was done.

It was a beautiful day and many of the Bishops were outside on the steps of the resort conversing and waiting for the conference to be called to order. The setting was perfect for Wilhelm. The limousine pulled up to the steps and the driver walked to the rear of the car and opened the door. Cardinal Wilhelm, adorned in vestments befitting one who had reached his stature in the Church, stepped out and was immediately greeted by admiring clergy awaiting his arrival. In orderly fashion, ranked by importance of each Bishop's perceived prestige, each approached the Cardinal and kissed his ring welcoming him to the conference. Wilhelm was careful to pay particular attention to each one as if he was the only Bishop in attendance. Invited Cardinals looked on as Wilhelm displayed the humility expected of a Pope.

The conference was called to order and Wilhelm was introduced as the keynote speaker selected for his tireless work in
combating the worst man made obstacle to life, world hunger.
After the applause subsided, Wilhelm spoke.

"My dear Bishops, Cardinals, and invited guests, " he began
purposely addressing the lower ranked Bishops first in recognition that it was their conference. The invited guests were
reporters from the media whom Capelli had insisted on attending
and Wilhelm viewed as another opportunity to spread the word of
his achievements allowing others to do his bidding.

"Welcome, and thank you to Monsignor Capelli for selecting
me as your keynote speaker to open this international conference." He paused and nodded toward Capelli waiting for his
audience to finish clapping their hands.

"For those of you whom I have not had the chance to become
acquainted with on a personal level, I will begin by giving you a
brief background of how I became involved in attempting to eradicate world hunger and then suggest to you what role you may
play in working with me in achieving this most important goal."
Wilhelm's oratory skills were well known. He chose to bring all
those present into his fold by limiting his importance and stress-
ing a cooperative effort in which all would join him in his crusade.
The Cardinals present, most of whom were favorable to his views
and supportive of his ascension to the Throne of Peter, still had a
few fence sitters. The conversion was about to begin.

"My first parish when I became a father was working at "Our
Mother of the Angels" church in Addis Ababa, Ethiopia. The
Catholic population of the country was slightly more than one percent. Malaria and tuberculosis were major endemic diseases; also
health problems from parasitic and gastroenteritis infections, lep-
rosy, venereal diseases, typhus, typhoid, trachoma, conjunctivitis,
and childhood diseases. All complicated by insufficient health
facilities, shortage of medical personnel and unsanitary practices.
The greatest factor in early death was nutritional deficiencies. Life

expectancy for males was fifty years and for females, fifty-three years." He continued knowing his audience was hanging on his every word.

"Is there anyone here who did not eat a hearty supper last night or a bountiful breakfast this morning?" Like a good lawyer he never asked a question if he did not already know the answer.

"Of course you did. I wish you could say the same for the Ethiopian children whose stomachs are distended from lack of food, who go to bed hungry every night, who await the mercy of a partner with a sickle in hand. I looked into the eyes of mothers unable to suckle their offspring because of malnutrition. Mothers were so weak with despair and hopelessness that even begging was beyond their ability. We are talking about a country that cannot feed its people. Inaccessibility, water shortages, and infestations of disease-causing insects, mainly mosquitoes, prevent the use of large parcels of potentially productive land. Of Ethiopia's total land area of 1,221,480 square kilometers, maybe 15 percent is under cultivation." He waited for the numbers to sink in as he looked around noting the concerned look on the faces of the religious leaders.

"I knew my calling. I knew what I had to do. I knew that if I could rescue one child from the grip of a tortuous death it would be a start." He continued... "You have all taken a vow of poverty voluntarily. The children I am speaking of had no such choice. In order to eradicate hunger, I must make you all rich. If I could do that without compromising your vow to the church, would you all be with me?" The meeting hall shook with the strength of their approval. Capelli clapped halfheartedly as he recognized the avalanche of support for the German.

"Then I will share my plan with you. Together we will start a new institution, "The Pope's Bank", an international food bank funded by the one billion Catholics worldwide. We do not ask for money, we ask for food to feed the poor. Riches like you have never experienced will find a path to your door. You have a chance at spiritual wealth every minute of every day. The more you bank, the richer you will get. We will cut through the red tape and put the food where it belongs, in the mouths of the hungry based upon need, not religious beliefs. Our story will be carried from the newspapers, the television reporters, and other media all the way to the heavens...and you will be truly blessed. Are you with me?" Screams of "yes" resounded against the walls. "Do you believe in my plan?" Another "yes" was their response even louder. " Will you move forward for the good of the world?" All stood up this time, applauding louder and louder until Wilhelm extended his arms like a college quarterback to quiet the fans. Wilhelm had them right where he wanted them. The press conference scheduled at the conclusion of the meeting would add further fuel to the fire of respect he was experiencing. Even Pope Alphonse admired his work and believed Wilhelm would make an excellent Pope, if he would change his conservative views. Of course, few knew of Wilhelm's private life. He knew another aspect of his life had to be dealt with, swiftly and without compromise. His involvement with Marcella had to be regrettably terminated, quietly and without trace.

Capelli acted swiftly and on his own knowing he had to throw cold water on the popularity of the German Cardinal brought about the oratorical skills that created nothing short of a frenzy. He had expected what he had just witnessed but he was not the fool Wilhelm and Lattimer thought he was. The reporters invited to the conference were not invited by accident. They were hand-picked by Capelli. Now the pre-rehearsed questions would begin. Capelli was counting on his new adversary not faring as well as he did before a favorable crowd.

The first question from CNN set the stage. "Your Eminence, is the Pope's Bank your idea or someone else's?"

"It is mine alone. I have thought about it for the past several years," proudly came the response.

"Then why do you call it "The Pope's Bank"? The world is suffering along with a gravely ill Pope Alphonse. Are you playing

Vatican politics and making a play for the Chair of Peter even before the Pope passes?" Wilhelm bristled at the direct question. He realized he was too quick to claim sole possession of the idea and could not think quickly enough on his feet to formulate a proper answer.

"I am here on behalf of the needy!"

"Then, you have no aspirations for the Chair of Peter? You are simply a humble servant of the Church trying to do good? Is that correct?" came the next flurry of questions.

"I will serve the Church as I am requested," Wilhelm said succinctly. "Next question," he announced attempting to change the subject and the reporter. "Yes, you sir, in the tweed suit."

"Then, your Eminence are we to understand from your last answer that you are throwing your red cap into the ring?"

Wilhelm regained his composure and stated, "I am surprised by your questions. Pope Alphonse is alive. Why are you dwelling on his death. You should be more concerned about keeping children of the world alive and my food bank program!"

"A follow up question your Eminence," the first reported yelled.

"If it is the Pope's food bank and your food bank program, are you not saying that you soon will be the Pope?"

Capelli had successfully dampened the propriety of the eloquent Cardinal's use of words. Newspapers the next day seized upon the impropriety of the statements rather than the good to be promoted by the potential success of Wilhelm's plan. Headlines read,

"German Cardinal Positions Himself As Next Pope In Light of Pope Alphonse's Failing Health."
"Order The Sauerkraut, The New Pope Will Be German"
"Cardinal Wilhelm Claims He Will Be The Next Pope"

The body of the stories almost ignored the good intentions to eradicate worldwide hunger. Instead, the arrogance and

audacity of a Cardinal bidding for the highest position in the
Catholic Church and...doing so in public, was the focus. The
spin, although not to the point of libel nor taken completely out
of context, could nevertheless be damaging if taken the wrong
way by the Cardinals eligible to vote upon the Pope's death.
Capelli had bent the rules for his personal advancement, but he
chalked that up to trying to achieve a result desired by his Pope
and therefore acceptable. Wilhelm's time for shoring up the
weaknesses was now, given the fact that Alphonse was deteriorating rapidly.

* * * *

The countess Marcella de la Sant, twice divorced, once widowed,
was well aware of the possible dissolution of the affair and yet
she maintained the romantic notion that her Kurt would somehow
choose her, as the Prince of Wales had chosen Wallace Simpson
over the throne of England. Wilhelm, however, harbored no such
thoughts. He would, of course, continue financial assistance to
the Countess, the monies to secure her accustomed station in life,
as well as payment to assure her total silence. Sometimes in
moments of self-examination, he had given consideration to the
way he felt about the Countess and the way he masterfully generated the discrete clandestine trysts concealing disclosure from
all, not realizing for even a moment that the Countess may have
been a willing accomplice for reasons other than love. He cursed
the frailties of the human condition that thrust him into the compromise of his Catholic faith. If, this love affair was found out, it
could not only destroy him, but would bring total dishonor upon
the Mother Church.

He had to be extremely cautious in the termination of the
affair. His role as private confessor to the Countess, once the
proper excuse for the frequent visits to her villa, would be dis-
continued. The expected tears would be dealt with. He had a

self-assured trust in his ability to write a finish to the affair. He stepped from the limousine and took in the surroundings of the villa, twelve kilometers from Rome. The circular driveway was swept clean of the expected leaves for this time of year, the arbors trimmed to perfection, a replica of Francesco Messina's sculpture of <u>Gian Battista</u> set in a water fount and back dropped with a wooden crucifix.

The villa's gardener raced breathlessly to the Cardinal, hat in hand, genuflected quickly, and then reached for the Cardinal's ring. Wilhelm allowed the workman to embrace his hand and kiss the symbol of his office. A hand blessing and benign smile signaled the man to back away, the ritual completed.

Wilheims attention was drawn to the Countess standing under the archway at the entrance. Queen like, she smiled a welcome. A handsome woman resplendent in the latest fashion, hair coifed to perfection, a trifle more jewelry than necessary for the afternoon hour, nonetheless she was a striking picture of femininity. The sight of her drew his mind away from the task at hand. Thoughts of engaging in hours of foreplay and then mounting her one last time caused his heart to beat faster and the blood to rush to his loins engorging what was rumored to be an exceptionally large penis. He imagined her mouth once again kissing his now throbbing private part. She had the unusual talent of using her tongue in a circular fashion to bring him just to the point of emission and then take it whole in her mouth causing him to thrash his head side to side on the pillow, his groin lurching upward in spasms until all was released inside her mouth. He believed she must have studied the Kama Sutra to give such intense pleasure. He never asked, preferring to believe his own ability to make love spurred her on. He never knew that her accomplishments were the result of demands made by her former husband Hosni Khatabi, which over time, she came to accept and even crave.

It was a simple choice, the Countess or the Chair of Peter. But who was to say he could not have both, he thought. The Chair of Peter had to come first, and then maybe he could partake in the charms of the lovely Marcella de la Sant. He immediately switched gears knowing his first priority was straightforward. Now was the time to control his emotions and gird his loins for the impending drama.

The Countess Marcella was an authoritarian female, the type most men instantly disliked and yet under the efficient exterior loomed a charming and passionate woman, very feminine and extremely intelligent. She extended her hand in greeting. Once joined, she kneeled to receive the Cardinal's blessing. The gardener, hovering in the distance, smiled in satisfaction as she bade the Cardinal to enter. Once safely secured behind the massive doors, the Countess embraced him. Wilhelm stiffened as his gaze took in the anterooms and foyer to assure himself they were alone; once satisfied, he kissed her gently on the cheek, desperately trying to make sure his earlier thoughts did not play out, at least not now.

Seeing his concern, she laughed. "I have dismissed the servants for the afternoon, all except Georgio," she told him.

"It is as well... we have much to discuss," he answered her. They walked quietly to the study, a room filled with seemingly thousands of books lining the old mahogany cases, books having pages which had not seen the light of day or eyes of a reader for decades. It was a literary wasteland giving an ostentatious trapping to the room.

"Sherry?" She offered. He shook his head in the negative, knowing he could not afford to dull his faculties if he was to match words with his mistress.

"You seem pensive today, my love," she said as she draped herself on an ornate Victorian couch.

"Perplexed. I'm afraid," he said.

"Affairs of State?" she asked.

"Yes," he said, "Of the highest magnitude."

She smiled. "Are you not the most masterful negotiator in the Vatican?"

"There is no compromise in this situation. I have been summoned by God for a greater calling," he said, focusing his eyes directly on hers. The Countess Marcella's brow furrowed as she listened intently.

"Your faith must be strong..." he began, "the hour of destiny has cast its shadow on the two of us."

"Very eloquent, my dear Kurt... yet I fail to comprehend what could possibly be of so much import... unless..." she hesitated, "my God... it's the papacy!" She whispered the title as if in terror. The truth was evident as she looked to his face. She began to tremble and retreated to a window overlooking the grounds, her face changing colors from a frightful pale to angry red almost as a reflection of the autumn leaves of deciduous trees in the near distance. The Countess drew a deep breath and regained her composure. She turned to face him, her brown pupils almost blotting out the whites of her eyes.

"I think I'll have that sherry now," Wilhelm said as he walked to the bar and poured vintage sherry into a crystal goblet that acted like a prism reflecting rays of light across the room that fell to her breast.

"We must face this dilemma with intelligence," he said.

"Am I to be exiled to Malta... never to see you again?" The tears began and he saw she could no longer control herself. He closed the distance between them. She felt the strength of his arms, which had held her after the many passionate episodes of lovemaking. The security of his touch was like a blanket of soothing music. Limp, she fell into his arms as he took her to the bedroom suite.

The Countess quickly regained her composure. She then excused herself and entered a dressing room to the left of the master bedroom. She looked to the mirror and saw the streaking mascara running down her flushed checks. She took a deep breath and vowed to herself "If I cannot have him, no one will! Not even the Catholic Church."

He made love to the Countess with abandoned passion. Perhaps, he told himself, as a final gesture to her genuine love for him. A camera recorded every second of his uninhibited libido.

CHAPTER EIGHTEEN

$\mathcal{D}$r. Sansone was in his office seated behind his mahogany desk. His coal black beard and youthful face belied his age of sixty-five. The office walls were lined with advanced medical degrees from the most prestigious universities in the world. His expertise as a cardio-vascular surgeon was well known as was his work in genetic engineering. He was the first to develop a commercial treatment termed angiogenesis, used for combating cardiovascular disease by isolating a specific protein that would induce new blood vessel growth to circumvent blocked arteries. Across from him sat his newest patient, Cardinal Justin Kennedy.

"I can find nothing in your tests to indicate any reason for your headaches," Doctor Sansone said peering over his glasses, his voice soft but bearing a definite Sicilian intonation. "I first checked for a tumor, which is the most common suspect for migraines of your magnitude. There was no tumor. We have ruled out a brain aneurysm and subdural hematoma. Sometimes bright light provokes a severe headache of vascular origin but your tests were negative showing no constriction in the vessels. I cannot find one single physiological reason for your migraines."

"They seem to be more frequent and the severity lasts longer. Is this something which I must live with?" Justin asked.

"Well, you need not live with the pain. At least not to the degree you have experienced in the past. I will give you a pain medication but, it is not without some risk," Dr. Sansone warned as he opened his desk drawer, retrieved some pharmaceutical samples of the drug and handed the vial to Justin. "This will last sixty days. Take one in the morning and one in the evening with meals. I believe it best not to write you a prescription. The Vatican pharmacy seems to be the main communication center for the ills of our clergy. When you run out, you must come to me for more. "I am sorry, Eminence, medical science can only do so much. However, your complaints concerning strange dreams and nightmares may have underlying psychological significance. I could, if you wish, arrange for Dr. Carlton to see you," Sansone said fixing his eyes on the medical report he held in his hands knowing Justin knew that Dr. Carlton was a psychiatrist, American trained who, while in residency at Long Island Jewish Hospital, was already recognized by the top doctors in this specialty as the most promising newcomer to enter the field of psychiatry.

"I do not know what to say," Justin said. "The thought of having my mind turned inside out by a stranger could be dangerous for a man in my position."

"I highly recommend Dr. Carlton. He is one of the most learned men in his field. You should seek his counsel. Let me arrange an appointment for you," Dr. Sansone offered.

Sansone's insistence on an appointment with the Swiss doctor was of great influence. "Can this be accomplished in strict confidence?" Justin inquired without making a commitment.

"The confidentiality goes without saying." Sansone softly replied... the doctor/patient privilege is kept at the highest standard Eminence," reassuring Justin that the secret would be between the two of them, except for Dr. Carlton should Justin agree to the consult.

"Having said that, I must inform you that there is a young priest, Father Peter, already in counsel with Dr. Carlton. Since he is on your staff it is only appropriate that you know that, although the details of his problem are alien to me. All I know is that his mind is a bit mixed up over something that occurred recently while he was in your charge." The doctor knew he was approaching as close to the edge as he ethically could in mentioning Father Peter. Justin immediately saw a red flag. He mentally made plans to speak to Father Peter to reassure him that knowledge of his treatment would never be mentioned outside a medical environment protected by the doctor/patient privilege, and only then if requested by the doctor.

Dr. Sansone, sensing Justin's discomfort, quickly added, "I would not mention this to your Eminence but for the fact that you should be privy to the needs of Father Peter since his affliction occurred on your watch and I know you wish to help him."

"Your confidence is safe with me" Justin said, understanding that the mere revelation that Father Peter was being treated would, under normal circumstances, never be disclosed by the good doctor. Justin rose from his seat and walked toward the window, focusing again on his own problem. "I know I am not crazy, yet these headaches are going to drive me there," Justin said as he slowly turned and faced the doctor.

"My examination of your medical history indicates your migraines are not genetic or environmental; the further fact that you do not have the typical profile of a migraine sufferer leads me to seek other sources for your discomfort, therefore, I believe a visit with Dr. Carlton is in order."

"It appears my choices are few. I will accede to your professional judgment. Please make the necessary arrangements," Justin said in resignation. He left the medical office with a degree of doubt in his mind. If his seeing a psychiatrist were ever to be found out, it would end any possibility for his ascension to the Throne of Peter. He realized it was too late now to put the genie back in the bottle.

The balance of the day passed swiftly. When darkness came, Justin retired. The emotional strains mixed with the powerful drug he took at the evening meal exacted payment from his body. Justin felt the pain behind his eyes begin to relent as the pain medication took hold and his body began to relax. His brain began to let up from its insistence for sleep, now that its demands were being met.

Strange thoughts filtered in and out of his mind as Justin struggled with the desire to sleep. The possibility of becoming Pope, the implication of the Cross, his thoughts of Sister Mary Frances and her absence from his daily life continued to wage an internal battle fighting acceptance of the drug until his mind closed its doors on reality, the medication being the victor. Once again he was in a twilight sleep.

* * * *

The telephone rang repeatedly as Justin struggled to awaken. He reached toward the sound even before his eyes focused.

"I must see you, tonight if at all possible," he heard a voice insist.

"What hour is it?" Justin asked his caller, straining his eyes in the darkness to stare at the luminous digital clock.

"It is urgent we talk, I must see you," the words repeated.

"Very well—twenty minutes," Justin agreed, he hung up the telephone, his mind racing as to the reason for the frantic request from Mary Frances.

She arrived at Justin Kennedy's private apartment within one-half hour of her call. Her request for entrance met with protestations from the Swiss guard who duly noted the time at 2:30 a.m. in his logbook. The guard insisting he call his superior before allowing her to disturb the Cardinal. Justin, hearing the commotion, opened the door and broke the impasse with his words of welcome. "Please come in, Sister, we have been expecting you." Justin's use of the Cardinal "we" instigated a shrug of the shoulders by the guard at the door.

"I am sorry for the urgency. I had to see you Justin. I have been debating for hours with myself whether to seek an audience here," Mary Frances apologized.

"And how may I help you?" Justin asked as he once again felt a kinship with the nun.

"I really don't know how to begin. My heart is troubled, and I have no one I can turn to. It is also very embarrassing for me to involve you in my situation," she attempted to explain.

"Ah... we have a situation. I am sure that there is a solution for all situations. I am flattered you feel comfortable to seek my counsel," Justin said.

"Since we have returned from Israel," she began, her face a mixture of frustration and anxiety, "I have this building resentment against returning to my duties at the Vatican. My happiest days were when I was practicing my vocation of archeological investigations. I have petitioned Mother Superior that I be permitted to become involved outside these walls, which have suddenly closed in on me. My requests have been denied and I do not know why," she explained, her face showing her helplessness.

"And you wish me to intercede on your behalf?" Justin asked.

"Yes," she said quietly, lowering her eyes.

"I can readily understand your dilemma," Justin said softly, "but we in the college try to stay at arm's length with the various orders and for good reason, I might add."

"Out of harm's way?" She blurted out.

"Not exactly," he tried to explain, " you are aware of the foolish notion that many people believe every prelate from the local parish priest to the Cardinalship is having secret assignations with the nuns at our disposal," he was dead serious.

"I am aware of that as well as the thought that a lot of people believe that some nuns have affairs with other nuns," she said.

"And unfortunately some priests are pedophiles", Justin said sadly.

"Do you also know that you are one of the people who will be propelled into fame once the secret of the Cross is know to the world?" Justin asked.

Mary Frances blushed. "I do not care for honor or glory. I seek fulfillment in my life."

"I also seek that elusive commodity, and yet I know that our lives will be altered dramatically in the weeks ahead". Justin commented gravely, his mind envisioning the Triple Crown being placed upon his head.

"Am I to understand that you will not help me?" she said questioning him.

"It is not a matter of helping you. There are happenings over which we have no control. I share your frustration and I am sorry to see your spirit being subjected to this situation," Justin said, knowing it was he who requested of the Magdalen Order that Sister Mary Frances be denied any request for an outside assignment.

"Then I have no other choice except to renounce my vows," she replied.

"No, I will not hear of it!" Justin shouted, surprised at the emotion in his own voice.

"I have other sins more grievous than that of personal ambitions. My sins are those of the mind, and of the soul, and of the heart, all linked by a common thread...my earthly desire for you which brings on the greatest sin...that of the flesh. My heart cries out for confession," she told him.

"Am I not guilty of the same offenses? And, if I am, who is to say they are sins? And suppose, just suppose, I was elected to the Throne of Peter. How do you reconcile these "sins" of mine with the edict of infallibility of the Pope? Am I given special dispensation and if so, by whom? There is only one higher than that position. If it is confession you seek, who is better to hear you out than the one who is your accomplice? I will oblige you in this private setting if you think it necessary."

"I am filled with revulsion for my sins," she started crying, tears streaming down her cheeks.

"We shall seek absolution together—come let us talk," Justin said calming her for the moment.

Mary Frances kneeled before Justin, her head bowed, hands in prayerful repose and began:

"In Israel, I committed sins of human nature, sins against man and God."

"What we did was not sinful" Justin said quietly. "Life, my precious one, is a balancing act. Sins of commission and sins of omission may be treated the same, but they are not of equal weight. The sins of which you speak are only sins in your mind. We are only mortal with human desires we have learned to repress. Basic instincts are difficult to cast aside. Our bodies need natural expression just as our minds need to be free to practice the faith. So even if you have transgressed, and I do not say you did, you must put it in context to what you have delivered to mankind. Finding the Cross and securing it tilts the scale so far to one side, there are not enough sins that could be committed on this earth to balance the scale. Christ has already absolved you. In the scheme of life, The Cross, in exchange for your perceived sins, should elevate you to sainthood, not penitence." Justin lifted her to her feet and continued, "no sin is so great that our Lord will not forgive. It is the touchstone of our beliefs. God in His mercy has already forgiven you."

"And you? Do you forgive me?" She said looking imploringly into his face.

"If God forgives, am I not able to do the same? All of us have the sins of the heart and mind. It is the nature of man and woman," he said.

They talked a long time. Her head cradled by his hands and brought into his chest. The smell of her hair brought back memories he longed for again. Finally, he could do no more.

"You must seek patience," Justin said, tilting her head back so he could look into her eyes. He knew his words were no more than a pseudo-panacea so often used by clergy. "Our lives are at this very moment being molded by the hands of an unseen potter. Man who has been given the power of choice molds the shape of the future guided by an unseen hand. Events will decide our destiny and we, who are caught up in the drama, will have little to say in the matter."

"And this patience which I must seek, is it to be laced with thoughts of faith lost, dreams dashed and hopelessness?" Mary Frances said, looking longingly into his eyes and begging for the answer she desired.

"Of course not. I understand your feelings," he told her.

"Understand!" Her eyes met his and he saw the anguish in them. "How could you possibly understand how I feel! How can any man know how a woman really feels!" she said in desperation.

He reached to touch her trembling hand. "I only mean to console you," Justin explained. "The understanding of which I speak is to the human conditions we all must face."

"How could you know of the hidden fears of a woman, the flights from reality, the torments of her body and the frustrations she must continually battle as her body tells her one thing and the mind fights back in retaliation?" She began to cry in earnest as she buried her face once again in his chest, the spasms of emotion shaking her shoulders. Justin wrapped his arms around her trying to give her comfort. Justin felt her relax in his arms as they stood in the middle of the room, motionless, locked in a familiar microcosm of humanity and drawing strength from each other.'

She was the first to break the silence. "Please forgive me, Justin, I have no right to burden you."

"The burden does not exist, my dear. It is my joy that you have sought me out with your problems." Justin responded.

"I am ashamed of myself," she said, as she wiped the tears from her face and stood away. "My mind is so confused," she started again. "I do not fathom myself as a German guide girl trying to convert Munich prostitutes, nor a nun willing to be raped and killed in San Salvadore. I only want to be a person who has her life in order," she added.

"You are a nun who is a person, not a person who is a nun," Justin said in reply. "Your life is intertwined with Christ's. The greater calling of our Church must overwhelm your personal guilt, and when that peace comes over you, you will understand what the Saints must have felt."

"I only know how I feel; degraded and...alone," she said in a low voice.

"You are never alone. That was our Lord's promise: 'I am with you always,'" Justin said, attempting to console her.

"I have believed that all my life," she said. "But now, I have these doubts. My faith is being tested at every turn. I need to believe again."

"Remember the old story about the nun who walked the sands of the pristine beach praying to God asking why He had forsaken her?" Justin asked gently. "God replied that He walked with her day and night. When she asked God why only one pair of footprints marked the sand where she walked, God replied, 'Because I have been carrying you my child.'" Justin saw a sense of relief in her face.

A slight smile emerged, dimples appeared in her cheeks, her eyes widened, and she laughed through her tears... the tension broken by the tale they both had heard so many times before.

"Often, laughter is like a soothing balm in these periods of despair," he said.

"Yes, of course. And yet I feel idiotic standing here in the middle of the night laughing and carrying on like a teenager." She smiled, shaking her head.

"But you do feel better, don't you?" He asked.

"Yes, and I must thank you for your patience and understanding.

I'll not bother you any longer," she said, walking toward the door.

"And I shall see what I can do about your request. I cannot promise you any quick results, or even any results at all, but I'll make some discreet inquiries," Justin promised.

"And that is all that I can ask of you." She gratefully replied.

"Good. Let us now see to it that you get safely back to the convent. I'll have the guard call an escort for you."

She left without further comment, her footsteps echoing across polished floors until they faded away. Justin looked to his bedroom door knowing sleep would be elusive that night. He picked up H.G. Wells' Outline of History locating the place at which he had inserted the bookmark some week's prior.

He began to read the story concerning Constantine the Great and his role in the rise of Christianity, quite unaware that the name Constantine would play an important part in the rest of his natural life.

CHAPTER NINETEEN

$\mathcal{T}$he rising sun was beginning to highlight the Vatican as fruit and vegetable markets of the independent state began to open. Papal entrepreneurs made haste to place their wares on their carts and roll them onto the sidewalks to be sold to the influx of tourists waiting to glimpse the magnificent grounds and buildings of Vatican City. Life on the streets was beginning to surge with activity.

Justin looked into the mirror as he combed his hair. The tan from his days in the hot desert sun in Caesarea was beginning to fade.

He sat at his writing desk and composed a note to Father Peter telling him that a driver would pick him up in the afternoon and bring him back to the Cardinal's apartment. Justin handed the note to one of the Swiss Guards and instructed the guard to deliver the note to Father Peter at the hospital where he was now under the care of Dr. Carlton. Justin then made his way to the secret room where the Cross was located.

Father Peter was pacing the floor of his hospital room, when the note was delivered. His confinement, on top of his psychiatric

problems, triggered a new fear of claustrophobia. He was captive
to the eight by ten foot hospital room and could no longer stand
it. His senses told him he had to get out. He opened the door to
his room and seeing nobody in sight, simply walked out the front
door, not waiting for Justin's driver. He made his way to Cardinal
Kennedy's private apartment. He passed the guard and went
directly to Justin's apartment. Father Peter reached for the door-
knob, his hands trembling, and eyes wild in some hidden fear that
seemed to smother him. The door was locked.

"I must see him! I must!" He yelled. The guard, alerted by the
commotion rushed to see what was happening. He found Father
Peter on his knees crying and pounding the floor with his fists in
frustration. Upon seeing the guard, the priest stood up and
grabbed him by the tunic. The guard stepped back, holding the
priest at arm's length.

"The Cardinal is not in his apartment, he's at the museum.
Hold on, sir!" the guard said trying to calm Peter. "Let me help
you.

"You don't understand! You would never understand. Never!
I must see him."

"I'd better get you some help, Father. He reached for his
phone to make the call to Central security but before he finished
dialing, Father Peter was gone.

The priest walked toward the museum, slowly at first, then in
a trot. An inner force propelling him to gather even more speed
as he began to run across the courtyard, heart pounding, past
astonished nuns, priests, and tourists roaming the Vatican
grounds. His lungs begged for oxygen and his legs stiffened into
knots of spasms. Finally he reached the Museum grounds. The
guard, under strict orders from Enrique Capelli to admit no one,
brought his pike to port arms positioning it diagonally across his
body with the sharp point sloping toward his left shoulder as he
watched the disheveled priest approach. Father Peter now
exhausted, showed the guard the note from Justin. The guard read

the message carefully noting the meeting place was the Cardinal's apartment, not the museum. Father Peter explained that it was of urgent importance that he sees Cardinal Kennedy immediately. The guard, who knew Father Peter, unlatched the bolt and twisted the huge brass knob opening the Museum door allowing the distraught priest to enter without further questioning. Father Peter was in a daze as he walked past the statues of Saints lining the entryway, all of whom he believed were staring at him. The huge sculpture of the "Cnidian Aphrodite" loomed as an apparition, while the torso "Belvedere of Hercules" gleamed in the semi-darkness. Approximately one hundred feet in front of him he saw the huge floor to ceiling plywood partition that cut the width of the museum in half protecting the Cross from the eyes of those not yet permitted to see it. A doorway was cut in the middle of the partition for access to the construction workers and the select clergy, but it was closed. As he made his way toward the partition in his quest to find Justin, hundreds of crucifixes filled his sight, blending with icons from ancient times. His stomach was still churning. He spotted the lavatory to his right and made it to the commode as vomit spewed from his mouth. Spasm after spasm convulsed his insides as his body reacted to the call to rid itself of the bile in his system. The young priest was fighting to regain consciousness as the room spun around him. The porcelain of the toilet felt cool to his head. It didn't take much for him to collapse from exhaustion.

The men on the other side of the plywood partition were building an exact replica of how the Cross would be exhibited when enshrined in the Basilica testing every guy wire, viewing lights, and protective devices. They were unaware of Father Peter's intrusion. Workers standing high on ladders were installing the last of the spotlights and making final adjustments so the light from the spots was directed precisely to the points of the Cross as desired by Cardinal Callahan. The workers were ordered down from the ladders. Callahan then gave the instruction to activate the lighting circuit and one of the workers pushed up on the lever of the electrical panel. A series of "popping" sounds like machine gun fire was heard and the room immediately plunged into darkness. "Nobody move," Callahan said. "Next to the electrical panel is a flashlight. Turn it on," he ordered the workman who had just thrown the switch. "Bring it to me." The workman walked toward Callahan and handed him the flashlight. The others remained in place as ordered looking like mirror images of the statues lining the inside of the main museum. "Now, everyone, follow me, do not panic. We are going to exit the museum until the lighting is repaired." Callahan shined the flashlight around the room so everyone could get a bearing and then focused it on the door in the plywood partition. As he walked to the door he slowly began swinging the flashlight forward to focus on the pathway in front of him and than backward so those in his charge could follow the light. He opened the door and they made their way to the main door of the museum, which they opened, flooding the museum with the natural light of the outdoors.

"Must have been fuses," Capelli commented on the obvious. "Cardinal Callahan, please be good enough to contact electrical and see if we can get the power restored on a top priority basis. Also, it might be wise to provide more than one flashlight in case this should occur again," he said, perturbed by a lack of attention to detail even though the blackout was not foreseeable. They decided to congregate in the courtyard and simply wait for the electrical problems to be fixed and the all clear signal given so they could re-enter. An ornate fountain sporting four statues designed by Bramante looked down upon them with disinterest while they discussed scheduling of the different trades necessary to complete their work as fast as possible.

Meanwhile, Father Peter, alone and in the darkness of the lavatory, crawled toward the door and pushed it open groping his way along the wall until he stumbled into the plywood barrier. In his confused mind, he thought he was heading toward the museum entrance. Sweat was pouring from his body. He was still shaking in spasms and cried out in his dementia, "Eminence... Eminence... where are you?"

He felt his way along the plywood toward the midpoint of the partition. He reached into his robe for his handkerchief to wipe the sweat that was now burning his eyes and felt his cigarette lighter. He wiped the sweat from his forehead with his handkerchief and sniffed an alcoholic type smell emanating from the handkerchief. The lighter fluid had leaked from his lighter soaking his handkerchief. He was not in the presence of mind to recognize the possible danger he was in. He flicked the hammer of his lighter. He flicked it again and again but couldn't bring it to a flame. The room took on the look of an old time picture as the flicker acted as a strobe and he saw the upright Cross through the door left open by the restoration team when they hastily left the building. At that instant, the Cross took on an eerie vision mesmerizing him as he kept hitting the hammer of the lighter faster and faster until the spark caught the fuel shooting a flame into the air. Now, he saw the Cross suspended from the wires for the first time. The sight transfixed him. His hands were trembling. He was unaware that the flame followed the fluid that spread to the outside of the lighter down to his handkerchief, which had now caught fire. He lighter fluid ignited in a flash as felt the burning of his skin and opened his hand dropping the handkerchief and the lighter to the floor. The handkerchief landed at the base of the doorway, the casing acting as it's new source of fuel and rapidly spreading the fire to the plywood partition. Flames began shooting along the bottom of the plywood and racing upward. The sprinkler system activated popping the heads and spewing water everywhere. Frantically, the priest beat on the fire with his hands, but to no avail. The fire shocked him to some semblance of clarity as to what was really happening. He pulled the cord of his robe and struggled to get his arms out of the sleeves. Once released, he flailed the robe at the fire, hitting the plywood partition again and again. The water from the sprinklers flooded the smoldering wood, which was the last barrier of protection for the Cross. The smoke inhalation burned his lungs and the flames singed his eyes until they were swollen shut. The fire was out, but the psychological burning in his mind was intensified. The Cross was intact having somehow been untouched by flame, water, or smoke damage. Father Peter wandered in a semi-conscious state until he reached the front door of the museum and somehow managed to get the door open.

Capelli, Lattimer, Callahan and Justin were startled to hear the fire alarm followed by an inebriated looking figure stumbling from the entrance of the museum and then collapsing to the cobblestone pavement.

The figure, dressed in civilian clothes, must be one of the restoration experts who couldn't get out in time, Justin thought. He rushed to the man lying face down on the cobblestones and yelled for someone to call the Vatican emergency medical team.

"Don't move him," Capelli screamed. "He might have a spinal injury."

"He needs air," Justin said as he ignored Capelli's instructions and rolled the figure over. "God in heaven, it's Father Peter!"

"Is he breathing? Capelli said. "Stand aside, I'll start CPR," his excitement was overtaking rational reasoning.

"He is breathing!" Justin answered.

"I hear the sirens," Capelli said. "Thank God for the emergency medical team." The EMT's took over placing the priest on a gurney and transporting him to the Vatican hospital by ambulance. Justin rushed to the hospital by private car. After about an hour, the physician in charge opened the door to the waiting room and gave Justin the prognosis. The priest's burns were not life threatening, but the lung damage was severe. Justin's thoughts concerning Father Peter were intermingled with the happenings in Israel. Could the incidents surrounding the Cross be the wrath of God being visited upon the Catholic Church or was the accident just an unfortunate happening?

Several days passed. Father Peter was only now coming around due to the heavy sedatives administered to ease the pain of breathing. His eyes were partially open. He was sitting on the edge of his bed, hands to his face as Justin entered the hospital room. Justin did not know if the young priest was in prayer or pain.

"Good morning Father, I pray you are feeling better" Justin said quietly.

Father Peter looked up, through slit like eyes. His hair was disheveled and his hands were trembling. "Eminence-hear my confession" Father Peter implored as his outstretched arms directed to Justin Kennedy.

"Of course my son" Justin walked toward Father Peter, his hands making the sign of the cross.

Father Peter looked to his Cardinal who saw in his eyes the truly remorseful look of the priest, a requirement for absolution of sins.

"Oh my God!" "I am heartily sorry for having offended Thee. I detest all my sins because I dread the loss of heaven and the pains of hell. But most of all because they offend Thee, my God, who art all good and deserving of all my love. I firmly resolve, with the help of thy grace, to confess my sins and to do penance and amend my life".

Justin replied, "to return to communication with God after having sinned is the process we Catholics use as a gift from the all mighty."

"Forgive me Father for I have sinned."

"Please go on my son, confess your sins great and small, you must be humble, sincere and entire."

"My sins are of great enormity Father, I have cast my soul to the devil and cannot retreat" Father Peter said.

"No sin is so great that God will not forgive you" Justin said.

"I am a homosexual and more grievous, a pedophile for the past ten years" Father Peter blurted out.

Justin's face masked the shock of the pronouncement as he bit his lips. "Go on my son," Justin urged.

Father Peter told Justin of his treachery to the Church, his involvement with Cardinal Wilhelm and his blackmail by an American evangelist named Orlo Thompson involved in pedophilia. The young priest gave Justin the details of the pornographic web site and admitted that he apprised Thompson as to what happened every step of the way during the expedition for the Cross. Father Peter told of the liaison set up in Amsterdam where he first met Orlo Thompson and recognized him as the television evangelist from America. The "blackmail" was then initiated, but the priest did not know it. Thompson made a "gift" to Father Peter to bring him into his confidence and prey on his sickness. The "gift" was a boy, thirteen years old and a runaway. The "blackmail" would be the video tape of Father Peter having his way with the boy, knowing it would garner hundreds of thousands of dollars on the web site, especially with the priest depicted in his clerical garb.

"I am destined to spend eternity in purgatory – I cannot help myself, this sickness is burned in my soul." Father Peter began sobbing loudly, his shoulders shaking. Justin knew the sanctity of confession and reeled at the implications of the priest's words. He also knew that knowledge of an ongoing commission of a crime by a priest destroyed the privilege of a confidential communication. In past years the confidentiality remained inviolate, but the laws were reformed after the numerous accusations against priests for sexual misbehavior involving members of the congregation.

"Have you not thought of reporting Thompson to the authorities?" Justin asked.

"I would be implicated myself...I do not want to be ex- communicated or taken to prison for my crimes" Father Peter sobbed.

"This man, Thompson, must be stopped immediately. Either you must report him or I am obligated to do so. If you lay the burden on my shoulders, I will take care of it. But, you will be the sole witness, and you must be prepared to testify against him in a court of law. This will necessitate bearing your soul of the sins you have committed before a jury."

"Forgive me Father, are my sins of great enormity that I shall burn in hell?" Father Peter asked.

"As a Cardinal I have the authority to absolve you of sins committed without full consent or understanding of their seriousness such as minor offenses. Such sins do not deprive the soul of divine grace. A mortal sin such as murder or other serious offense willfully committed, is beyond my power of absolution. There are issues in your case of mental capacity that could diminish your culpability. However, that is better left to the civil courts to decide. It is not for me to pass judgment on your state of mind. Therefore, there is no penance known to me that I could ask of you. No priest, Cardinal or Pope, however pious or learned, has power to forgive you for mortal sins. Such power belongs to God alone. Therefore my son, I absolve you of all your sins for which I am capable. Go and sin no more," Justin said in finality without specifying which sins were absolved and which were not.

"You will rest now and give me your answer tomorrow afternoon as to the path you choose to travel regarding the evangelist, Thompson," Justin ordered. "I will be here at 2:00 p.m." Father Peter wept openly and loudly as if a great anchor had been lifted from him. Justin had already scheduled a meeting with Dr. Carlton in the morning hoping that a candid revelation of what happened to Father Peter during the expedition might help in his treatment. He would be careful to avoid the delicate portions of the confessional he had just heard. Thoughts of the revelations were still reeling in Justin's mind. He was very aware that homosexuality and pedophilia was a real threat to the Church. He knew the vast majority of the clergy abhorred the sordid actions of a few of its members. Nonetheless, the priest's confession brought the issue up close and very personal to Justin. He left the priest to contemplate in the confines of his hospital room and hurried to his apartment to meet with Mary Frances.

CHAPTER TWENTY

$\mathcal{W}$e are born wet, hungry and naked and It only gets better." Justin said as he held Mary Frances' hand in the privacy of his apartment.

"For some and not others" she told him as she placed his hand over her heart. Justin could feel the firmness of her breast as she pushed down on his hand.

"Can you feel my heart beating?" she asked.

Justin managed to nod affirmatively and made no effort to withdraw his trembling hand.

"We have been on a journey which has no ending I'm afraid," Mary Frances said as she approached the couch in Justin's private apartment.

"Only God knows what is in store for us. It is out of our hands now." Justin said walking to the couch. He smelled the familiar womanly scent, which again stirred his senses. Justin put his arms around Mary Frances and felt her melt into his embrace.

Justin knew his spiritual soul was in jeopardy, but millions of years of man-woman attraction was boiling in his blood.

Mary Frances innocently placed her hand on Justin's thigh. Within seconds he felt an arousal beginning and gently moved her hand away.

"I'm sorry Justin...I can no longer hide my love for you. I know in your heart you have the same feelings," she said quietly.

"Why has God cast this upon us? Are we not mortal?" Justin exclaimed.

"We are indeed mortal, why else would we be involved. Our bodies cry out for each other while these vestments that clothe us act as a knights armor" she said.

"I too have a firestorm of emotions Mary Frances", Justin explained as he looked into her emerald eyes, seeing the longing of her soul.

"God help me...I love you so much" she managed to say.

"Can this be happening?" Justin whispered in her ear. Her right hand pressed hard against his back not wanting to release him from the embrace. "Love me Justin," she moaned almost inaudibly as she rested her head to his chest.

Mary Frances knew Justin was as much aroused as she was and also knew that a woman was supposed to control the demanding sexual urge for both of them. Something deep within her soul told her this was not the time.

They talked far into the night, discussing what had just taken place and trying to come to grips with their emotions and what to do.

The Swiss Guard duly noted the time at 5:30 am, when Sister Mary Frances left the apartment. The Guard was under the thumb of Cardinal Wilhelm who promised a promotion if every detail regarding activities between the nun and his American adversary were reported to him.

* * * *

Justin entered the private office of Dr. Carlton, fifteen minutes late for his appointment. He noticed a gold chain hanging from

Carlton's pocket watch that appeared to encircle the doctor's stomach. A hunched posture destroyed the lines of the expensive three-piece suit the psychiatrist wore.

"How may I be of service, Eminence?" The doctor asked, greeting Justin at the door.

"I wish you to assume psychological responsibility for Father Peter. As I told you on the telephone, I have information that may possibly be germane to his treatment," Justin said, his directness cutting through the layers of pretentious posturing inherent in this first meeting.

"Any information that you have would be helpful. Thus far, this has been a very difficult case study. Unfortunately, since his accident, he will not give me any information." Carlton looked thoughtful as his eyes met Justin's. Justin nodded.

"I will tell you everything that I can. The story that I am about to relate must be governed by the privilege of strict confidentiality between a patient and his doctor. That privilege overlaps in this instance so that the confidentiality between a Cardinal and his parishioner is preserved. The information you will receive has far-reaching consequences, and total secrecy must be maintained. The very foundation of the Catholic Church will be split asunder if we are not deliberate in our plans," Justin said slowly.

Dr. Carlton nodded in assent. "Please," Justin said to him, "your consent must be audible. Do you agree to the strict confidentiality? Yes or No?"

"Yes, I do," responded Carlton. Justin then proceeded to relate the story in narrative form beginning with the search of the Cross and ending with the miraculous cure of Father Peter's wrists.

"Good Lord!...This story borders on fiction! It is of no wonder that the Father had a nervous breakdown," the Swiss-born doctor said as the truth took hold in his mind. "You have told me that we have the Cross in the Vatican museum at this very moment! Certainly, you recognize the danger if the Israeli's find out about it! What will they do?"

"We are aware of the ramifications, of course, yet the risks had to be taken. It has been a long time since a miracle has been authenticated," Justin said.

"You may rest assured that the secret of the Cross is safe with me. But, what about those restoring the Cross, and others who have been made privy to its capture? How long do you think it will be before the Israelis' find out and raise an international incident?"

"That is not your concern nor is it mine. It is a political matter and will be dealt with at that level." Justin knew Carlton was right and only hoped that Pope Alphonse had not underestimated the Israelis'. Neither he, nor anyone else, was aware of the political alliance Pope Alphonse secretly made to ensure success of the retrieval and the future of the Catholic Church.

"I did not intend to make it my concern, your Eminence. My mind is trained to anticipate future conduct. You can be sure I will stick only to medicine and not invade territory better left to others. In that vain, only Father Peter's illness is the issue for our discussion. I can tell you that time is the healer in most cases of post traumatic stress disorder." Dr. Carlton said, re-focusing the subject of the conversation to Father Peter, after realizing that the political matter was none of his business. Carlton was still unaware of the priest's other sickness.

Justin felt a sense of relief flood over him. "Thank you for your consideration and involvement," he said. "My own life is filled with immense pressures, and I must react to these problems and still maintain control."

"Dr. Sansone has already spoken to me," Carlton volunteered. "I'm surprised that the Vatican medical fraternity has moved so efficiently," Justin responded.

"Come now, you must admit, Eminence, your rank would tend to speed things along. In fact, if you have the time now, we can discuss your case and determine if I can be of assistance," Carlton said trying to accommodate Justin's schedule.

"I'm afraid this will take more time than I have to spare at the moment. In fact, I promised Father Peter I would visit him in the hospital this afternoon. I think it best to postpone our appointment regarding my situation until a later date."

"I appreciate your understanding of the importance of giving me your undivided attention when we begin. But, let's not wait too long for your appointment," Dr. Carlton said with a smile.

"I promise, I will not disappoint you," Justin said as he rose from his chair, shook the doctor's hand, and left the office.

He had two hours before his scheduled meeting with Father Peter and took advantage of the time to enjoy lunch at an outdoor café not far from the hospital. This was two hours he later would wish he could take back.

The priest, alone in his hospital room, walked to the lavatory and looked at his reflection in the mirror. Haunted eyes stared back at him as if belonging to another person. His unkempt face showing no emotion as he felt he was looking at a stranger. The shaving kit was unzipped very slowly, almost as if the priest was afraid of the contents. He deftly lifted out the throw away razor and turned on the warm water in the basin. A bar of soap with an unknown pedigree was lathered in his hands. His mind was retreating further from reality as he imagined he was Pontius Pilate cleansing himself from the guilt of the death of Jesus Christ. Without hesitation, he took the razor and twisted it into the spout of the faucet. The plastic gave way with ease, the metal blade dropping into the sink. He felt blindly for the two-inch object within the depths of the soapy water. Then he walked back to the bed and seated himself. His eyes were fixed on the large wooden crucifix on the wall as if it mesmerized him. "Why me, Lord...why hast Thou chosen me?" He sobbed. The room spun around him, his senses astray, the past and the present merging. "I know that You performed the miracle. My wrists were cut badly and Thy hand of healing entered into me and made me whole. They will not believe in Your power and Your glory. They must know the truth, and I shall be Your instrument. Dear God, heal my burns, cleanse my spirit." At this, Father Peter arched his wrists and with a motion as exacting as a skilled surgeon he cut deeply into the flesh. He was in no condition to realize he made the fatal mistake of bringing his fist toward his body, thus allowing the large artery, normally buried deeply in the wrist, to come to the surface. He performed the same function on his right wrist as bright red blood spurted onto his clothing. He walked to the large crucifix and placed each wrist on the white wall, one on each side of the Cross. "I pray again to my Lord, heal my wounds again. Let the world know of your presence," the priest moaning softly as his blood splattered against the wall with each pulse beat, its grotesque patterns tracing a path to the floor.

They found him 30 minutes later, the whiteness of his skin a testament to the excellent bloodletting technique he had used. The obscene tracks of blood on the wall his final epitaph.

The surprised look on Father Peter's face was something that no one would understand. Would God in his mercy accept Peter's mortal soul into heaven? Was his confession enough to grant him a stay from purgatory? Justin did not know the answers. What he did know was that the material witness to Thompson's evil transgressions was dead.

CHAPTER TWENTY-ONE

$\mathcal{I}$t was night and Rome's Via Veneto sprang to life, as bands of street urchins rummaged through garbage cans behind the swanky restaurants on Piazza Navona. Young pickpockets, and child prostitutes with heavy make-up awkwardly strolling the side streets in high heels, were plying their trade. The street of dreams was the setting of another drama unfolding in a small café.

"It is good to see you my cousin" Khatabi kissed Moustapha on both cheeks.

"You have business to discuss?" Moustapha looked at Khatabi with steel gray eyes.

Khatabi's eyes narrowed to slits as he began to speak to his cousin.

"But of course, our arrangements have always been fruitful for both of us have they not?" Khatabi sipped an expresso, the demitasse cup appearing even smaller as he tried to handle the tiny vessel with his fat fingers.

Moustapha eyed the huge diamond on his cousin's finger, proceeds from a swindle Moustapha had orchestrated with a

Rome jeweler. Moustapha had done the dirty work and Khatabi took the spoils.

Khatabi did not trust his cousin, but knew for a price he could carry out any assignment, including murder. He was known in the underworld as "Moustapha the Assassin".

"I wish to find information regarding an American Cardinal and a Catholic nun, Khatabi told him.

"Lovers?" Moustapha inquired, raising his eyebrows and smiling at the thought.

"I'm not sure, but I have a client who would pay handsomely for "dirt" that could be used against the Cardinal."

"Consider it done my cousin" Moustapha said with a grin. "One cannot keep the stallion in the stall when it comes to lust".

"One more thing...although we have, in the past, been very successful, my camel is still thirsty. I have great expenses and must insist on greater participation in the spoils," Moustapha said quietly.

Khatabi looked at his cousin's face, a large scar running down his left cheek made him appear more ominous in the dimly lit café.

"Yes...yes, it will be arranged," Khatabi lied with a straight face. He was aware the man was utterly ruthless and cruel and thrived on torture and murder, with money only a secondary matter.

Even by Khatabi's standards, Moustapha's brutality knew no bounds. His warped and completely unpredictable sense of fairness was well known. Once he had a woman's hand cut off for absentmindedly placing a small trinket into her apron while cleaning his desk. A surveillance camera recorded the theft.

Keeping her in his employ, rather than killing her showed his benevolence. A year later she was overheard exchanging house gossip with another woman in the market place, which was reported to Moustapha. He took offense, and had her tongue removed. The going wager was what would come first, dismemberment of her remaining body parts or a knife in the throat because she could no longer perform the physical work demanded, having the use of only one hand.

* * * *

Justin scheduled his appointment with Dr. Carlton, as promised. The guilt he felt, after the gruesome death of Father Peter, was one more trip he did not need. He could now tell Dr. Carlton what the priest had confessed, but realized it was no longer relevant. Justin entered the doctor's office through a private door leading to Dr. Carlton's study, all pre-arranged to protect him from being seen. Within moments the doctor entered the room and shook the Cardinal's hand.

"I see you are truly a man of your word. I was afraid you would change your mind in light of Father Peter's death."

"It hasn't yet sunk into my mind. I am still stunned and deeply saddened," Justin said softly.

"We will deal with it when the time is right. Let's first get to your concerns and the reason for your visit."

"This is new to me. Do you want me to lie down on the couch?" Justin asked.

"The couch increases my fee substantially, so of course, feel free to lie down." Justin smiled at the reference to cost, the doctor having done well in breaking the tension. They both knew that no finances would be involved. He began to feel at ease with Doctor Carlton.

"So, let us begin," Dr. Carlton said. He motioned Justin to the couch.

Dr. Carlton was a master of recognizing cues displayed by his patients and used his abilities to gain their confidence. He knew Justin was not completely comfortable with this appointment and that was expected.

"Don't let the couch intimidate you. It's only a method to get you to relax. Sit wherever you are most comfortable, even the floor if you prefer. Although, the couch is a bit more gracious to your derriere." Carlton said in an appeasing manner.

"When do you start with the thick accent to lull me to sleep?" Justin quipped, still a little apprehensive as he reclined on the couch.

"Please, I'm embarrassed enough with the accent I already have," Carlton replied. He drew a chair close to the couch, picked up a clipboard and leaned forward, eyes intent, and spoke seriously. "Let me first tell you some of the methods I use with my patients. Therapy may consist of hypnotic trances or drugs such as scopolamine. Sometimes, I administer combinations of scopolamine with other drugs such as morphine, if inducement of twilight sleep becomes necessary, or if the patient is extremely agitated. I do not know at this time just how we'll proceed in your case. If at any time you have any questions, stop me, and allow me to answer them."

"All I would like to know is how to lessen these attacks. They seem to occur at the most inopportune times," Justin said, now realizing a migraine was beginning.

"Some physicians describe a person with a 'migraine personality' as someone who is rigid, competitive and generally an overachiever. You may or may not fit that description—however, I think I can help you."

"You have a plan?" asked Justin.

"The treatment usually develops as we go along. We ask basic questions looking for clues we can utilize in treatment. I would like to try age regression in your particular instance," Carlton advised.

"Age regression?" Justin asked. He knew that scopolamine's effect on the central nervous system also made it useful as a truth serum by means of which uncooperative persons might be forced to answer questions. In light of the strange nightmares, Justin felt he might be very vulnerable, if he allowed the doctor to treat him as suggested.

"Do not allow the words 'age regression' to offend you. It is now a defined therapeutic science and more than that, a valuable tool for our profession. We have discovered that many ills which cannot be explained on the surface can be pried from the subconscious." The doctor adjusted the bridge of his eyeglasses on his nose, and then looked closely at Justin. "I have had one case where an occurrence at age two was sublimated for forty years. The woman never knew why her fear of water was so deeply rooted. During age regression therapy she recalled an instant when she almost drowned in a bathtub—she was one year old! The mind reacted to this occurrence and built in a defense mechanism for a possible recurrence. After she became aware of the reason for her fear, it simply went away."

Justin returned the doctor's gaze. "And do you believe that something happened during my childhood which could be causing my migraines?"

"That is impossible to tell at this point. I have had some patients go back beyond the time of birth." Carlton seemed to weigh the words carefully as he measured Justin's response.

"Beyond? This borders on the occult!" Justin responded.

"Perhaps" said Carlton, "but you as well as I know that this is an area which has not been fully explored."

"Are we talking reincarnation doctor?" Justin questioned.

Doctor Carlton nodded affirmatively. "I prefer to call it memory transference. I believe memory cells are passed from one generation to another in basically the same manner as blue eyes, long fingers, and so forth are passed from parent to child."

"Am I to believe that whatever is causing my migraines may be the fault of some distant relative?" Justin asked.

"Again, perhaps... and then again, perhaps not," Carlton replied evasively.

"How is this accomplished?" Justin asked, now becoming interested. His migraine was getting worse by the minute.

"We have the patient relax, then a small amount of scopolamine is injected into the bloodstream to depress the central nervous system. It acts as a sedative to bring on a state of relaxation. The mind tends to give up its secrets and we can then formulate a plan leading to recovery."

"Is this procedure dangerous?" Justin questioned.

"It can be extremely dangerous if administered incorrectly, especially in combination with morphine. However, it has been proven effective for a variety of disorders from motion sickness, delirium tremens, psychosis, mania, and Parkinson's disease. Not to worry, I'll be in complete charge. I haven't lost a patient yet." He said smiling confidently. "Monitors control all bodily functions. If you seem to be in an area of distress, I can move you forward or backward in time in a few seconds," he added. "Naturally, I would encourage you to seek a second opinion, as I do with all my patients I believe would benefit from this type of treatment."

"You know that is not possible in my case. If you're the best, and this treatment is at the cutting edge of medical science anyway, why should I waste the time on a second opinion even if I could seek one?" Justin's temples began to pulsate with the beat of his heart throbbing to the point where he knew something had to be done, and quickly. "I'm ready to begin?" Justin ordered.

"I must say, you do not waste time." Carlton seemed surprised.

"I do not have the time to waste," Justin replied. "I have many duties and responsibilities as Cardinal Bishop. This added pressure might influence my migraines. If they do, I must know now!" He knew he could not deceive the Church if his duties were compromised because of physical or mental ailments, regardless of Pope Alphonse's wishes. Justin's mental state would have been eased considerably had he been aware of the happenings at the secret meeting being held in Tel Aviv at this very moment.

"Very well. Please remove your robe and I'll attach the monitors to your chest and legs." Carlton ordered.

Once disrobed, the doctor inserted thin acupuncture type needle monitors under his skin. Justin was relieved that medicine had advanced to the point where the cold, gelatinous circular patches that always fell off causing the entire procedure to be repeated, were no longer used as monitoring devices.

"Your left arm please," the doctor said as he constricted Justin's arm with rubber tubing in order to expose a vein so he could administer the sedative.

Justin barely felt the needle enter his skin. Within seconds the room lights appeared to dim. His body began to feel the euphoria of escape from reality.

"How do you feel?" The doctor's voice sounded far off.

"Fine." Justin responded.

"I want you to imagine that I have placed a heavy log on your legs. You cannot lift your legs because you are pinned down. There is no pain, just a feeling that you cannot lift up." Carlton said in a soothing voice. "Now try to lift your legs."

Justin commanded his brain to signal his legs to lift and felt surprised that they would not. He strained and grunted and yet the invisible log had him securely pinned. The euphoria kept him from feeling any concern.

"That is fine, just fine. I want you to relax completely." Doctor Carlton paused, and then went on. "You are in an elevator—alone. You see before you a row of buttons. The green one in the middle is marked 'backward,' the blue one on the top is marked 'forward.' The red one on the bottom is 'stop.' You will control this trip with these three buttons. The control is absolute and your safety is assured. Do you understand?" Carlton's voice was soothing and reassuring.

"Yes, I understand." Justin's words slightly slurred.

"Good, very good. We now begin our journey. I want you to push the green colored button. We will now start our journey. I want you to feel yourself going back in time. One year... three years... ten years... twenty five years. Go back at a pace that is comfortable. You will now see your life as if watching videotape played in reverse. I want you to press the red button when you arrive at age three."

Justin's mind spun as he saw the years reverse. There were flashing images of his family, his ordination as a priest, his college days at Notre Dame University, his teen years, and his infatuation with a high school sweetheart. He also saw himself playing with a brown puppy he had received at Christmas when he was ten. Again, he felt the dread of his visit to a dentist for an impacted tooth when he was only eight years old. Next flashed the memory of his first day in kindergarten not understanding why another child threw sand in his face while playing in the sandbox. He reached an imaginary hand to the red button and heard himself moan softly as his eyelids began to flutter.

Doctor Carlton's voice jarred into his consciousness. "We are now at that point when we want to break the barrier of time. We are going to go back, back beyond birth into another time and another place. This barrier has been removed." Justin listened as the voice droned on.

"You may enter this new dimension at will. I want you to now push the green button again. Allow yourself to go back... back... back in time. Only stop when you feel the need. Have no fear, your mind is traveling to the place of your dreams," Carlton's voice soft and compelling.

Justin felt the green button depress under his touch. Then the elevator dropped suddenly, picking up speed as it hurtled down the deep abyss of time. Justin felt his head spin as flashes of strange places and time penetrated his mind. He slowly reached out and pushed the red stop button.

The elevator doors opened and he stepped into the dawn of an ancient land. The place was strange, yet familiar. Odd smells permeating the air. His clothes were foreign, yet comfortable.

"Can you tell me what is happening?" the doctor's voice seemingly distant.

"I do not know," Justin replied softly. "It is a strange place. I see purple hills in the distance. People are running. Many are shouting." His voice grew louder. "They are carrying me along with the throng. I am compelled to follow! I have fear, yet I know that this is the place I should be." The doctor noted Justin's hands curled into fists.

"And where are you now?" Dr. Carlton asked.

Justin fought the annoyance at having to answer the doctor when there was so much to experience. "I see myself in a house, a large house, many people, many sounds. It is the house of <u>Annas</u>. They have brought in a criminal. This is a gathering of the <u>Junto</u> and <u>Sanhedrin</u>. They are furious..." He stopped, watching the crowd surging like a boiling sea of angry faces.

"And what do you feel? Where are you exactly?" the doctor urged.

"I feel... ashamed. I am next to a high wall. This confusing noise is overpowering; a riot of words are pelting my ears." Justin felt his hands cover his ears yet the sound continued to roar on.

"I want you to tell me what is going on. Allow your mind to take over your words," Carlton commanded.

"It is early morning, cocks crowing their signal to the dawn, as they dragged Jesus through the streets. The mob approached the headquarters of the governor and stopped short at the gates. The mob aware no Hebrew could enter lest they become defiled and be denied the Passover meal. Pilate heard the commotion and came out to them; "What is going on here?" he demanded. "We have brought Jesus," someone shouted. "What charge has been pressed against him?" the pro-counsel of Rome shouted above the noise.

"He claims to be a King. He is a criminal! We have brought him here for justice," someone shouted. The mob was turning

ugly. I hear Pilate saying, "Do not bother me with this." I see Pilate re-entering the doorway leading to his headquarters but stopped by an aide who began whispering in his ear. I can hear the aide speak to him. "Would it not be proper to question the Jew in order to calm the crowd?" the aide counseled. Pilate nods in approval and orders Jesus to be brought to him. "Are you the King of the Jews?" Pilate demanded.

"Has someone suggested it to you?" Jesus shot back defiantly, his anger barely contained. Pilate is shouting and I see him stalking around the room. What? You dare question my authority? I bid you hold your tongue, Rabbi. Is it not enough to have your own nation and chief priests against you? Do you not fear the lash of Rome?"

Jesus speaks to Pilate; "My kingdom is not of this world, for if it were, my followers would fight to save me from your evil designs."

Pilate shakes his fist at Jesus. "I cannot believe this! Have you no fear? Are you not of a sound mind that you can comprehend that your own words are condemning you?"

"I fear my God and nothing else, for my kingdom is not of this place or of this time," Jesus replied. "So, you are a King. Is this not right?" the aide to Pilate, now enters the debate.

"King is your word, not mine! I only wish to bear witness to the truth," Jesus answered. "And just what is this truth?" Pilate asks.

"I was born for this, I came into this world for this, and all who are not deaf to the truth of what I say will listen to me," Jesus said.

I see Pilate now clearly agitated. He has met his match in the ensuing verbal combat and has come away with, at best, a tie. He returns to the outside and addresses the mob. "I find no fault with this man. I have not a case against him. I leave this to you. What is your decision in this matter?" he questions the mob, a mass of misfits supporting the criminal Barabbas.

"Kill him! They shout. The gathering is now raging out of control. The instigators are followers of a local insurgent, a man whose crimes against the state confine him to the Judean jail. They know if they riot, they can break into the jail and release their leader, Barabbas. Pilate is advised that the unruly crowd is growing in numbers. A dangerous situation will develop unless he acts in the matter.

"Very well, I shall question him further, and if the words are not forthcoming, I shall have him taste the caress of the whip," Pilate promises the mob. "Do you not hear the demands for your death? What laws have you so grievously broken to pit this mob against you?" Pilate questions.

"I have not broken God's law, that is my answer." Jesus responded.

Pilate responds, "I grow weary of your half statements. A clever man with words is also a very dangerous one. You have tried my patience, interrupted my sleep and I do not care to debate any longer. Take him and have him flogged," Pilate ordered.

A woven wreath of thorns is crushed upon Jesus' head; a red covering is wrapped around his shoulders after he has been beaten. The blood from his back, seeping through, turned the robe dark red. The guards struck him time and time again, angry that the Jew had dared to mock their leader.

"Hail, King! Hail, King!" They are mocking him and dancing around him. As they taunted him, one grabs at the wreath of thorns on Jesus' head and forces it down savagely. A large needle pierces the Nazarene's ear. Blood spurts from his temple where another of the spines of the acanthus bush punctures a pulsing blood vessel.

"Enough of this! Take him outside," Pilate says in sudden disgust.

The Roman guards are disappointed that their demonic fun is halted. They obey the Governor of Judea. Once again, Pilate addresses the mob: "Here is this man, Jesus. You see that I have had him punished, a severe punishment for one against whom I find no case except impertinence against Rome. And Tiberius, behold this man whom I return to you," Pilate said as if to end the matter.

"Crucify him! Crucify him!" they shout in unison.

Justin heard his voice as it cried out in his sleep state. The cry was not in terror or fear, but as a small child, whimpering.

"What is it?" Dr. Carlton asked gently.

"I have done this to him," Justin whispered.

"Who are you? What is your name?" Dr. Carlton asked, as the disc recorder continued to imprint Justin's words.

"My name is... Judas. Judas Iscariot." The voice came from Justin's mouth.

The words alarmingly filtered into the ears of the doctor. Carlton felt the furrows of his brow deepen as the name Judas Iscariot, echoed in his mind. Justin moaned and turned on the couch in Dr. Carlton's office. His face was twisting in torment, his arms flailing around. Dr. Carlton saw the immediate distress and began to speak.

"You are not in danger... everything is all right... no harm will come to you. Relax...listen to my voice."

"It is so large...so heavy... it's so pitiful!" Justin moaned again and continues, "The cross... they are making him carry it. His back is bloody, still bleeding... he is being forced up the hill."

"What hill?" Carlton asks.

"Golgotha... the place of the skull!" Justin said, his words barely audible.

"I cannot understand you. Please speak up," Carlton urged as he raised the input volume on the disc recorder.

"I cannot watch this... I must flee this place! I cannot... I cannot..." Justin began, strangling on the words.

Dr. Carlton saw that Justin's heart rate was climbing, and the EKG monitor began to spike in an atypical manner. "I will bring you back now...now your mind sees only a gray fog. You have no pain or remembrance as we journey to the present. Return to the elevator ...close the door and push the blue button. You will return quickly as the elevator speeds up. You will not remember where you have been and you will have no unpleasant feelings. You will feel relaxed and rested. Push the blue button... now." Justin felt himself return to reality, the hazy dream state dissipating as he once again became aware of where he was.

"Now, Eminence... that was not so difficult," Dr. Carlton said, checking the pulse rate and blood pressure of his patient.

"So, when do we begin?" Justin asked, suddenly aware that his migraine was gone.

"We have begun, Eminence. We have taken a journey to a strange place," the doctor replied.

"And what can you tell me?" Justin questioned.

Carlton responded, "I do not know. I must study the tapes and then we shall meet again."

Justin noticed that the demeanor of the doctor had changed. "Am I to believe that nothing of consequence happened?" Justin asked.

"We have had a positive reaction... you are a good candidate for regression therapy. I believe that we can soon get to the bottom of the problem," he said, as he removed the monitoring connections.

"Very well, if the cloak of secrecy has fallen on the mysterious science of applied psychiatry, then I must be patient." Justin began to get to his feet. Once dressed, he turned to the doctor. "You are aware that patience is not my strong suit, doctor," he said.

"And I wish to assure you, Eminence, that we shall make progress and you shall be fully informed as to this progress."

"Then it is time for me to leave... I have much to do and so very little time to do it." Justin shook hands with the doctor and left the office, strangely refreshed. At last he was coming to grips with his medical problem and a new zeal was beginning to permeate his soul.

Doctor Carlton looked at the disc still resting in the machine. His own mind was not yet fully aware of the awesome ramifications of what he had unlocked from the fertile brain of Justin Kennedy, Cardinal Bishop of the Roman Catholic Church. Dr. Carlton placed his notes and the disk in a file folder marked simply JK. He affixed a label reading "extremely confidential" on the front of the folder, opened the storage vault where all of the session disks were kept, and filed it under J.

CHAPTER TWENTY-TWO

$\mathcal{A}$ secure satellite video telephone was centered on the conference table in the office of the Prime Minister of Israel. The Prime Minister and the President of Israel were the only ones present waiting for the call. Precisely at 11:00 p.m. Rome time, the pre-arranged phone call came through. The video screen captured the image of Pope Alphonse seated behind his desk at the Vatican. He was alone. Pope Alphonse spoke first.

"Good evening to you Prime Minister Gold and President Hershel."

"Good evening," the President said returning the greeting. "It is nice to see you again your Eminence," added Prime Minister Gold, "how are things progressing?"

"That is why I requested this phone call, to bring you up to date on the status of our plan and enlist your aid to begin the second part of our agreement," the Pope responded.

"First things, first," Gold interrupted. "How is your health?"

"Deteriorating faster than I expected. My body is frail, as you can see, but I still have possession of my mind and the power of this office."

"You are too candid. That was not what we wanted to hear," Gold said saddened by the revelation that he knew was true. "I remember your first phone call to us, after you knew the Cross was found but had not yet left Israeli soil. We were together then, and we will be together now to complete our part of the bargain."

"I had to be sure Cardinal Wilhelm with his Nazi leanings could never ascend to the Throne of Peter. Cardinal Kennedy was the man whom I hand picked to succeed me. I did what I could to position him to be a contender. The double promotion to Cardinal Bishop was the first step. But, without your help in allowing the Cross to be removed from Israeli soil without a major incident, and doing so without the knowledge of those on the expedition, was critical. That had to be accomplished to elevate him in the eyes of his brothers who would vote...upon my death."

"As always, I will be frank with you," Gold said. "We did it for selfish reasons your Holiness. It was to our advantage to promote a Catholic revival, which we expect the Cross to generate. Restoration of a religious balance in the world is necessary. Normally, we would not care how many Muslims or Catholics there are in the world. Converting others to Judaism is not what we are about. We are few in number by comparison. The religions of Islam and Catholicism are both good. Both teach strong moral codes. It is the radical factions of each that terrorize the world. We can deal with renegade priests and the radical Jewish element...but we cannot live with Muslim terrorists. Also, as you pointed out in our first conversation, an American Pope would strengthen our alliance with the United States even more. Together, we can have our own "trinity" against the Muslim extremists. This alliance is our best chance of stopping the terrorism. The fear of death is always on the back burner. Let's not replace it with the fear of living. The bonding of Israel, the United States, and the Vatican is needed to stamp out terrorist threats.

"You need not justify your reasons to me, I understand completely. It is good to know we have come together in our efforts this time. I have concerns that require implementation of your security forces as soon as possible," the Pope said, his continued serious tone coming through loud and clear. "Did you receive the clothing I sent you?"

"Yes, we examined them and they will do fine. A nice shade of "priestly brown" I might add. I believe eighteen robes will be sufficient. Chai in Hebrew means eighteen. That's our lucky number, you know."

"Yes, I know," replied the Pontiff. "It's one of the first things I learned in seminary school when we studied Hebrew. Of course, I remember it for other reasons. 'La Chaim....To Life' went very well with our prayers over wine. I said it more times than I can remember," he laughed, breaking the tense conversation for the moment.

"Your concerns for faster implementation of our security forces, ...what is the urgency?" Gold questioned.

"You will recall that about seven years ago a fresco was removed from the San Petronio Basilica in the northern city of Bologna. It was a 15th century fresco, depicting a mid-evil crucifix on the main alter as if to ward off and protect the faithful from the evil of Mohammed and other demons. Five Muslims were arrested in Bologna. One of them was a Moroccan national who was caught video taping the fresco on display and making disparaging remarks. The Muslims were insulted by the painting, as they should be. The Church was intolerant of other religions during the time period when that painting was conceived. We have made great progress since that time, but I do not intend to defend the Church for its insensitivity. I ordered the fresco removed from public view and had it shipped here, under guard, to the Vatican. It is a work of art and I believe it should be preserved. Although an embarrassment, it is still history of our persecution of those who did not accept Catholicism, and that cannot be denied. The fresco is hidden in a room adjacent to the altar of Saint Peter. A massive tapestry covers the entrance to the room concealing it from inquiring eyes. That room houses Catholic art treasures of a similar nature as the fresco, treasures that would be found distasteful in this day and age. I won't go into that but I'm sure you recognize that the problems we currently have with some of the priests did not emerge suddenly, we were successful in suppressing them over the years.

We have been provided information from a reliable source that there is a security breach from within the Church. We do not know the name of our modern day Judas. Those who wish to destroy the fresco as an affront to their religious beliefs now know of the existence of the repository. It is only a matter of time before Muslim extremists with explosives strapped to their bodies, will storm the Vatican. If that occurs, we surely will know first hand what you, our brothers, have been living with on a daily basis in Israel. The extremists are angry and they seek revenge." Gold said nothing for a few seconds. He looked at the Pontiff, who's face filled the television screen, and pondered the words of the holy man whom expressed genuine fear.

"Yes...we will take care of the matter." There was no reason to expound on the method. The parties had already conceived a plan and only waited for the right time to proceed. It appeared that now was the time. "Have you other concerns we should discuss at the moment?" Gold asked, confident there was nothing more that needed to be said regarding the security matter.

"No, nothing right now. Only your aid to protect us."

"Do not worry. Anger makes them stupid. Those who seek revenge should first remember to dig two graves. Retaliation, of course, is a different matter. We will be in touch, your holiness." With that, the conversation ended.

CHAPTER TWENTY-THREE

S ister Mary Frances arrived at the private office of Enrique Capelli and was immediately escorted into the room. She was clothed in the traditional nun's habit, her awkward looking shoes peering from beneath her black dress, which dropped to just below her ankles. She noticed various vials of medication rimming the clutter upon the ornate desk, a tribute to his hypochondria.

"Ah, my dear Sister. It is so very good to see you again." Capelli smiled as he motioned her to be seated.

"It is my honor to be here, Monsignor," she replied.

"Honor indeed... it is I who am honored with your presence. Your name shall be enshrined in the Vatican archives for all time for your participation in the return of the Cross of our beloved Jesus," he said.

The nun cast her eyes down at the compliment, a pink flush of modesty spread across her face.

"I have asked you here at the request of Pope Alphonse," he asserted. "Your archaeological work in discovering the lost pages of Mark and help in procuring the Cross is to be rewarded. You are being assigned to a new project in the ancient land of Ethiopia. I cannot now tell you the details, but it does concern another biblical treasure, the Ark of the Covenant!"

She appeared stunned by Capelli's words. This was something she never anticipated and certainly did not want. "The Ark is sacred to the Hebrews. Why does the Church seek its discovery when there is much more to do now with the Cross, which we already have in hand?" she said looking perplexed.

"I will be straightforward with you," Capelli continued, "It has been decided that a trade might have to be arranged to appease the Israelis' for the Cross which, to put it bluntly, you helped steal from their land. We have nothing to trade. We need a bargaining chip." The Pope had been clever and successful in keeping the knowledge of his "Israeli connection" from anyone else. He readily acceded to the wishes of his hoped for successor when asked by Justin to reassign Mary Francis. The Pope knew Justin had his reasons and thought it best not to question his Cardinal.

"I have no wish to be reassigned," she blurted out.

"Come now my child....It is not of your making or of mine for that matter. As I told you, this assignment comes from the Holy Father himself," Capelli said.

"I do not understand," she said.

"It is not our vocation to understand... it is to obey and trust in the wisdom of the Vicar." He reminded her.

"I did not mean to be impertinent," Mary Frances said. I am only asking why the Pontiff would take such an interest in a nun."

The thought of the Pope instigating the reassignment made no sense to her. Immediately she felt the pang of guilt. The inner battle began again. Was she somehow a danger that had to be driven away?

"You are to report in two weeks to the Vatican Ministry of Religious Antiquities. Call to determine the time of your appointment with Secretary General Lattimer. He will be your contact and will issue you instructions on how and when to proceed with the assignment...which you cannot refuse."

Mary Frances knew his words were true. No one dared to refuse an assignment from the Pope. She left the Monsignor's office with a troubled heart, but aware that he was only a messenger. A last glance back toward Capelli saw him gulping a swallow of <u>Maalox</u>, evidently he had a troubled stomach, probably the result of having to do the Vatican dirty work, she thought.

Mary Frances entered her apartment, welcoming its quietude.

She needed time to contemplate her frustration and to wonder whether Justin played the major role in the scenario. If he did, then Justin had made a choice and she came in second, not that she thought it would ever be otherwise.

The Church was preoccupied with life after death and yet she was attempting to deal with life after birth. She knew that she was not alone. Millions of women around the world were as perplexed about their roles in life as she was. Ever since she joined the Catholic Church she was taught that her sensual responses had be limited; and yet, she still harbored the notion that this ancient rule forced upon women could indeed be the root reason that the world had yet to discover a female equivalent to Michelangelo or Beethoven or Rembrandt.

She took out a hairbrush and began to stroke her long, red hair. A nun, she was taught, had to be prim and proper and above all innocent, and yet she was worldly enough to know this was just another way of saying dull, unresponsive, and unquestioning.

She remembered the weeks in Israel when she and Justin talked for hours on every subject imaginable; his words came tumbling back; "Do not confuse sensuality with sexuality," he had told her in a moment of quiet reflection. She realized then, in the darkness of the desert, that to touch another's face in tenderness, to hold hands, to express warmth and affection, did not necessarily mean sex. She also realized her confusion between sensuality and sexuality had kept them apart more than any other condition.

Her new understanding of the finite difference was the giant step toward ending her isolation not only from Justin Kennedy but also from all of God's creatures.

She showered for a long time, feeling the suds of the soap in the washcloth caress her body. She felt the senses of her being screaming for attention as a knowing smile came to her mouth.

She would deal with her relationship with Justin Kennedy not as a nun but as a woman.

* * * *

Another woman was attempting to deal with her emotions concerning a relationship with a Cardinal. The Countess Marcella De La Sant had not slept for two days as her repeated messages to the German Wilhelm remained unanswered. She chain-smoked her way through the day and ingested Valium tablets on the hour. She could not and would not believe her lover would desert her and she further deluded herself into believing his absence was due to affairs of state. As if he read her mind, Cardinal Wilhelm was at her door, ostensibly to offer her confession, they both knew better.

The Countess looked forward to a frenzied sexual interlude with Cardinal Wilhelm. She also knew if Wilhelm became Pope, she would be assured of continued financial support, more than enough for her to rid herself of Khatabi. It was Countess Marcella who devised the plan to discredit Justin Kennedy.

The German Cardinal gave Marcella a perfunctory kiss on her cheek and sat on an ornate couch. He began filling his pipe with tobacco from his pouch, unconcerned that an equal quantity fell on the Persian rug. "If Kennedy receives sole credit for finding the Cross, we are out of contention for the Papacy."

"We will see that he fails" Marcella said solemnly.

"But how?" Wilhelm questioned.

"You told me of the rumors concerning the nun did you not?" she smiled wickedly.

"It is rumors, always rumors. Now a new story is circulating. It is said the American is seeing a psychiatrist for some mental problems," Wilhelm added.

"And, would you happen to know the doctor's name, the one treating him," she said.

"For what purpose?"

"I think I will need some psychiatric help and it is time to make an appointment to see the good doctor," she said coyly.

"His name is Dr. Otto Carlton. What's your plan? To seduce him for information?"

"Nothing as sophomoric as that, my dear Kurt, there are things best left to me that you need not be bothered with at this time. It may involve "sticky" fingers and I wouldn't want a Cardinal to be implicated. Records of psychiatric sessions are kept, are they not?"

"Well, nothing is kept in writing. The danger of information of a delicate nature getting into the wrong hands requires precautions. Now, all psychiatric notes taken by Vatican doctors are immediately shredded. We learned our lessons well. Attorneys have a nasty habit of requesting information during the pendency of lawsuits. Rather than risk exposure and contempt for spoliation of evidence, the Vatican has issued instructions to minimize the chances of wrongful photocopying. Of course, tapes or disks of sessions are still used, only because they do not pose the same vulnerability. They are not so easily copied. If you come up with any brilliant schemes, you know how to reach me." With that, Wilhelm left the villa, not wanting to be singed by the hellish deeds his lady friend might conjure up. Marcella, dampened her libido, was disappointed that her lover did not take her sexually but she was also keenly aware more important tasks were at hand.

Marcella was shrewd and worldly; she needed to balance her checkbook between her lover and her ex-husband. The all-consuming desire to be wealthy never left her mindset. It would be one paramour or the other, unless of course, she could secure the benefits of both.

That afternoon, she made her way to the bank and produced one of two keys to a safety deposit box. "He should get his rocks off on this stuff," she said to herself. She would continue to light both ends of the candle for her own protection knowing Khatabi would expect business as usual, which required her to deposit the videotapes of her previous sexual encounter with the Cardinal from Bremerhaven. Marcella and Khatabi had joint access to the safety deposit box. He was made aware of each time she visited the vault without him, a privilege reserved for he alone, as the man who controlled the loyalty of the president of the bank. He had something on everyone. A practice he honed with great skill having "worked" Middle Eastern officials for years. Marcella never took anything from the safety deposit box for fear it would be reported to her ex-husband, if discovered. Khatabi knew with certainty his former wife would never violate his trust. Her death would be the penalty.

Khatabi would use the tapes if Wilhelm was named Pope. Marcella would use the tapes if Wilhelm tried to sever their relationship, a perfect blackmail scheme. In either case, the money flow would continue to her. But there were other tapes foremost in her mind. Without them, Wilhelm would never ascend to the position he craved. If she had her preference, she would choose Wilhelm. The power she envisioned for herself, if he were to become Pope, was much more appealing than the money from her ex-husband. With Wilhelm, she could have both.

* * * *

Marcella's appointment with Dr. Carlton was set for 9:00 am the next morning. She arrived promptly at the appointed time and dressed to perfection. A Georgio LaMonte dress with a plunging neckline framed the gold chain and crucifix, which drew the eye to her cleavage, the Christ nestled indecently between her breasts. Her exotic perfume permeated the room. She related her reason for seeking his advise; the story not far from the truth as she explained her sexual problems including fantasies, and the thoughts she was the reincarnation of Cleopatra.

Carlton listened intently memorizing her words rather than taking notes. He could always refer to the recording disks if he failed to remember anything.

Marcella played her role as the consummate actress. Tears flowed freely on demand as she related her dreams to Carlton over the next hour.

"I have a number of patients who I have been treating for this manifestation," he told her.

"I am almost at my wits end, all I think about is sex." Marcella crossed her legs revealing a creamy thigh almost to her pantyless crotch.

"Do not despair my dear, we have taken the first step." Carlton's eyes darted to her thigh for just a second longer than professional decorum would dictate.

"When may I see you again?" she asked as she uncrossed her legs and exposed her femininity for a split second.

"Please schedule your next appointment with my secretary as you leave."

She watched as the doctor retrieved the small disk from his recorder, placed it in a manila folder, sealed it and put "De La Sant, M." on the front.

"Doctor, I am very concerned where you keep this information".

Do not worry Countess, all my most confidential files are placed in a secure vault.

"Where?" she asked coyly.

"Come I will show you." He took her by the arm, attempting to assuage her concerns, and walked to an adjacent room and opened the door.

Dr. Carlton pointed to the vault with a smile of satisfaction.

It was seven feet high, three feet wide and appeared impregnable, a solid mass of steel with an electronic keypad activating the combination.

"I do not wish to be a bother, but I would like to see my file put away".

"Of course, it is no trouble." Carlton was careful to shield the keypad from view as he punched the numbers of the access code to the vault. A distinctive beep could be heard as each number on the keypad was pressed. An electronic device, hidden in Marcella's purse, that converted sounds to numbers, recorded the beeps. He filed her records in the cabinet marked "D" for De La Sant and locked the vault.

"Thank you, doctor," Marcella said bidding him farewell for the moment.

"Goodbye," he said, "I will see you soon."

Marcella went straight to her apartment, opened her purse, took out the device and saw the numerical translation of the electronic sounds on her machine.

"Looks like his birthday numbers," she said aloud to herself. "5251950, some people have no imagination." Curious as to her own intuitive instincts, Marcella went to the Internet and looked up biographical data on Dr. Carlton. Within minutes she had the information she sought. "Bingo" date of birth; May 25, 1950" she smiled smugly at her own inventiveness. Her next move was to get back into Carlton's office to access the disks stored in the adjacent room and find the disk devoted to Justin Kennedy, if it existed.

CHAPTER TWENTY-FOUR

$\mathcal{Y}$ou do not argue with one who buys their printing ink by the carload," Wilhelm said smiling at Lattimer in obvious reference to the lead editorial in the Monday edition of L'Observatore Romano.

"It is indeed gratifying to see the paper reporting a groundswell of support for your candidacy should our Pontiff be called to his reward. You are indeed <u>Papable</u>, Eminence" the Secretary General fawned. The fiasco at the Bishops' conference now took second seat to the good deeds of Wilhelm and success of the "Pope's Bank" of food for the needy.

"The early front runner is usually last in the race only because he expends his energy early, we shall not make that mistake. I shall conserve our resources for the final lap," Wilhelm promised.

"The gossip in the halls are touting Pleaschack as a potential candidate," Lattimer offered.

"Is it possible to teach a noodle to dance?" Wilhelm said in a derogatory reference to Pleaschack.

"Pleaschack's power base is expanding every day as death draws near for our Holy Father," Lattimer commented.

"Your thoughts have no nutritional value, Jacob—as I have told you. Kennedy is the one to watch. The Cross will propel him across the sky as a shooting star; power is heady."

"And also corrupting," Lattimer volunteered.

"He must have a weakness—everyone does," Wilhelm countered.

"Perhaps the rumors concerning Kennedy and the nun have some validity," Lattimer suggested.

"I have also heard this speculation and if true we may have found a chink in his armor", Wilhelm smiled.

"If we only had photos of them engaging in sex," Lattimer sneered.

"I believe our esteemed colleague from America is more careful regarding any liaison with the nun," Wilhelm snorted as he privately thought of his own secret sex life with the Countess.

"I will make arrangements with our papal guard at his apartment to keep his eyes and ears open." Bishop Lattimer offered.

"Yes, by all means but you must be discreet.

"It shall be done."

"By the way," Wilhelm inquired, "I wish to read up on some medical issues and would like access to the reference room of the Vatican medical library. Would it be possible to do so? I do not wish others to know of the content of my research."

"Of course. As Camerlengo I have a master key to most of the Vatican offices. Since it is you, Eminence, I could loan it to you for this purpose. Of course, you understand I should not let it out of my possession."

"Yes, I understand. I will use it after hours and return it to you this evening if that is acceptable."

Lattimer took the key from his key ring and handed it to Wilhelm, "that will be fine...just return it to me before 10:00 p.m. this evening if that is convenient." Lattimer saw this favor as an opportunity to cement his relationship with the German whom he was betting would be the next Pope. The closer he got to Wilhelm, the greater the possibility of a promotion to Cardinal Bishop. Delivery of the master key to Wilhelm's co-conspirator would now allow access to the private vault of Dr. Carlton and nobody else would know about it.

Marcella De La Sant was unrecognizable dressed as a cleaning woman pushing her cleaning cart laden with a mop, a bucket, and an assortment of rags and brushes. The Vatican library was on the third floor in the same building as Dr. Carlton's office. It was 7:30 p.m. and the building appeared empty except for the cleaning crew and Cardinal Wilhelm. Others, who might still be in the building, were either working late in their offices, or catching up on their reading or research in the medical library. Wilhelm inserted the master key into the lock and opened the door to the Vatican medical library. He then propped his foot between the door and the casing to hold it open while he deftly placed the key on the sand of the freestanding ashtray just outside the library door and with a single movement of his fingers covered it with sand. He entered the library and to his dismay saw several other doctors reading. He had hoped that the lateness of the hour would render the building empty of the medical academics. He would just have to be more careful.

As planned, Marcella wheeled her cart to the door of the medical library. She looked around and saw that she was alone in the hallway. Under the pretext of cleaning the ashtray of its cigarette butts, she took out the insert in the ashtray and searchingly felt for the key as she ran her fingers through the sand. Her perfectly manicured fingernails would betray her newfound occupation were she to be caught. The key gravitated to her hand as if the inanimate object expected a sexual reward. She quickly returned the insert to its holder relieved that the real cleaning crew had not yet reached the third floor. She pushed her cart down the hall and stopped in front of the office marked 303. The sign on the door read, "Dr. Otto Carlton, M.D., Ph.D. How fortuitous, she thought, that the Vatican doctors all occupied the same building that housed the medical library. She unlocked the door with the master key and pushed her cart inside closing the door behind her. She went directly to the adjacent room where the session disks were stored, unlocked the door, and walked over to the vault. "Open Sesame," she said aloud as she punched in the numbers 5251950 on the keypad and swung open the vault. She found the cabinet marked "K" and rifled through it quickly for the Kennedy folder. It wasn't there. She looked through the cabinet again to make sure she hadn't overlooked it this time using her finger as she flipped back the tab of each file while searching for the name. She realized there was little time to spare before the cleaning crew would reach the third floor and find their way to office number 303. "Where would he have filed it?" she said to herself. "Sure, "C" for Cardinal." She went to the cabinet marked "C" and found thirty or more files of various Cardinals whom sought help from the psychiatrist, but Kennedy was not among them. Time was running out. "Could he have filed it under the name Justin?" she again said to herself. The files were in alphabetical order so she reached for the files starting with "Ju" in the cabinet. There were several files but nothing with the name "Justin". "Maybe there was no file and the Vatican rumor mill was wrong again regarding psychiatric treatment for the American Cardinal," she thought. Marcella began to walk out of the vault, then hesitated, and returned to the "J's". She would make one final pass starting at the beginning. Then she saw it. A file marked "JK". She removed it and saw the words 'extremely confidential' written on the outside. She opened the file and looked at the patient intake sheet made out in the name of Cardinal Justin Kennedy. She took the disk, replaced the file, closed the vault and hurriedly left the disk storage room.

The cleaning cart would be used as her "exit vehicle", at least for the present purposes. Marcella held the key up to her lips, kissed it, and reached in her pocket for a small tin of special molding clay. She pressed the master key into the clay making an imprint. She opened the office door and wheeled the cart back toward the medical library pausing just long enough to return the key to the freestanding ashtray where she buried it just under the top of the sand. She continued pushing her cart to the end of the hallway. Just as she reached the stairwell leading to the lobby level, the elevator door opened. The cleaning crew stepped off the elevator and began their nightly chores on the third floor going from office to office, knocking first to alert any office stragglers working late so they would not be alarmed.

Wilhelm looked at his watch, which showed thirty minutes had passed. It was time to leave. Either she found the disk or she didn't. In any event, he could not risk "loosing" the master key to the cleaning crew. At that instant a worker knocked on the door of the Vatican medical library and opened it announcing, "cleaning crew". The worker, not used to a response, was startled as Wilhelm, his pipe perched in the corner of his mouth, said, "thank you for holding the door."

"Forgive me your Eminence, I didn't know anyone was here." Wilhelm saw one of the cleaning ladies reaching toward the sand filled cigarette canister getting ready to empty it, but frozen in place upon seeing the Cardinal.

"Wait, one moment please," Wilhelm ordered as the cleaning woman stepped back. Wilhelm, a master at personality changes, adopted a regal camouflage and addressed the cleaning lady.

"With your permission, I would like to empty the ashes from my pipe before you clean the canister," he said as if not to alarm her.

"Pardon me your Eminence," she said and put the insert back into the receptacle for the Cardinal's use. Wilhelm took the pipe from his mouth and tapped it on the edge of the ashtray. Feigning a hot ash touching his hand, he dropped the pipe into the receptacle. For the first time his clumsiness was contrived.

"Let me help you, your holiness," said the cleaning woman as she reached out to retrieve his pipe.

"No, thank you I'll get it." He reached for the pipe and probed the sand beneath finding the key and lifting both from the ashtray as the sand sifted through his fingers falling onto the tiled floor. The cleaning woman grabbed one of her rags and fell to her knees to wipe up the loose sand as the Cardinal walked past her.

The Cardinal left the building and walked around the Vatican grounds biding his time until the courtyard clock read 9:45 p.m. He could not afford to arrive earlier than 10:00 p.m. since an early arrival might activate the curious mind of the Secretary General. He did not want to be questioned about the nature of his "medical research", which would be sure to occur if it only took a short time at the library to accomplish.

He rang the bell to the Camerlengo's apartment and was invited in by Lattimer who was expecting the visit. "I have expresso and biscotti for us in the study."

"Very thoughtful of you, my friend. It's just what the doctor ordered," Wilhelm said appreciating the gesture.

"Hope everything went well."

"Thank you, Jacob. Things went very well. Two hours in the library and I started thinking of entering medical school. You know, it was a possibility when I was young, but then I received the calling for a different kind of healing," Wilhelm smiled non-chalantly as he returned the master key to Lattimer.

"We do not have much time, Alphonse is all but dead and yet he still shows a vitalita as our Italian friends call it. It would not surprise me if he were already plotting a strategy for his successor.

"He is a fool, he should resign and not wait for the reaper to visit the Vatican," Lattimer suggested.

"When a Pope dies, we have the emotional factor to deal with. Electors who were harmed by Alphonse in some way tend to forget and elevate him to sainthood. Others in his camp will most certainly follow the lead of Sun Yet, we all know he is the

Pontiff's favorite, also one of the last of the true spiritual teachers. He is prudent of words and calm in demeanor. Such traits also make him our adversary," Cardinal Wilhelm reasoned as he purposely included Lattimer as a seasoned disciple.

"Perhaps we are overstating Kennedy's influence and should concentrate on Sun Yets popularity."

"No...it is Kennedy. We need to turn him into a thorn bird and watch him impale himself with some foolish mistake."

"Mistakes cut both ways eminence. We must insulate you from harms way. I have already begun to gather the flock of Cardinals who will support you. Some already with out stretched palms!"

"I dare say at this juncture we can promise them our good wishes – if the time comes for rewards it will be done". Tell our dear brothers we ask for their prayers and support". The German Cardinal began filling his pipe with tobacco and his mind with thoughts of the American, Justin Kennedy.

CHAPTER TWENTY-FIVE

$\mathcal{S}$ister Mary Frances felt at home in the Vatican Ministry of Religious Antiquities. She was given a difficult assignment to research a relatively obscure biblical quotation concerning the Ark of the Covenant. It was a task that encompassed a visit to the Vatican catacombs relating to ancient Jewish artifacts.

She was seated at a reading table in the stillness of the Archives when she felt the presence of another person looming over her.

"I'm sorry if I startled you," he apologized.

Flustered, she rose from her seat and then kneeled to kiss the Cardinal's ring.

"Please, my dear sister, allow us to dispense with the expected protocol. We are quite alone with the words of centuries." Sister Mary Frances looked upon the face of the Oriental Cardinal and noticed his penetrating eyes, which seemed to be not of this earth, the slanted features giving his face the look of wisdom and gentleness. She immediately felt at ease with the soft-spoken Cardinal Sun Yet.

"I am glad to have this opportunity to speak to you privately, my child," he said. Again she flushed and glanced away,
embarrassed.

"I have wanted to congratulate you for your part in securing
the Cross for the Mother Church. In all the excitement many have
already forgotten the peril and courage it took to accomplish this
magnificent feat," he took her hands and held them.

"I also have a perception of things... no, please do not allude
this to my Oriental heritage as most people are wont to do. It is
my perception as a man of the world, not of the cloth," he began.

"I am not sure of what you are trying to say, Your Eminence,"
Mary Frances said quizzically. Sun Yet smiled and nodded knowingly, taking in the loveliness of her presence and the sister's
emerald eyes, an unknown feature in his own country.

The Church is rapidly moving to a new direction; new faces
and new structures of power will be manifest in the future. This
new direction, out of necessity, will affect you personally," the
Cardinal intimated.

"But...how? I do not understand," Mary Frances asked.

Sun Yet continued, "I know you are struggling with your calling. I also know of your emotional battle with your feelings
regarding Cardinal Kennedy."

Sister Mary Frances remained silent for a moment, uneasy at
this private intrusion. "And upon what basis do you say such
things," she said challenging him.

"Now, do not despair, my child; I come as a friend of Justin
and of you. I cannot stand the torment which I see in your eyes,
nor can I stand by and watch you destroy yourself with self-pity
and doubts."

Again she started to object to his intrusion into her personal
world. He squeezed her hands tightly in an effort to give her a
sense of safety and assuage her fears. Sun Yet looked at her with
compassion, "our dear Justin, whom we both love deeply, is destined to play the role God has determined. I have watched his

progress over the years and this latest accomplishment has sealed his fate. There is no doubt in my mind that he shall be the next Pope."

The words felt as if a thousand knives where thrown at her mid-section.

"Unrequited love is the most powerful pain issued upon humanity. It does not allow for reasoning or the frailties of the human condition. The pain continues forever and yet God has mercy on His children," he said softly.

"What am I to do?"... She said as tears began to well in her eyes.

"You will do what you must, my child. The future of the Catholic Church rests in your hands. At this moment you are as important to the Church as the blessed Mother of Jesus. And as Mary was forced to sacrifice her only begotten son, you also are forced to make a sacrifice for the good of the Church."

She covered her face with her hands as his words took hold. Flashes of memories with Justin flooded her mind in a wild collage of scenes.

"In my country it is said that a woman's sexual power is so great, it must require great restrictions on its use," Sun Yet said.

"I am fighting these thoughts but I cannot help what I feel in my heart; I am confused. I don't know what to do," she pleaded.

"I know, daughter, and I shall help you cross the bridge if you allow this old man of the East to be your friend."

"I am afraid but I don't know why!" she exclaimed.

"Courage and faith will overcome this fear. They are your weapons. Your choice has been made for you. It has been made for Justin. But do not be concerned, because your search for this elusive love will find you, but at a higher level than mere mortals ever experience." She looked into his kindly eyes. The wisdom was imparted, as a loving father would talk to his child.

"But I am only a mere mortal, not a Saint. Am I to just walk away living with pain in my body and soul? By what strength do

I count on to write the final chapter of my feelings without endur-ing suffering for him and for me?" she asked.

"Most people do not have a fear of death, but everyone has the fear of pain. But, it is the emotional pain which is most dam-aging; it lasts longer than bodily pain. The problem we face over and over again is trying to live our lives devoid of pain of any nature. Sometimes in the scheme of life, one must hurt someone a little to help someone a lot." He looked deeply into her eyes. "It is important to obey the eleventh commandment, my child." She felt surprised at Sun Yet's words. "It may be Oriental in its phi-losophy, yet it is germane to this hour," he began. "<u>Thou shalt hurt no one, including thyself</u>. There is one more thing you must remember, he will no longer belong to you or to me... he will belong to God." The words of Sun Yet trailed off as he gave Mary Frances a hand blessing and departed as swiftly as he appeared.

She was left alone among the works of the ancient scribes. Before her, in the dusty shelves, lay the past of Christianity. In her heart lay the future of the Roman Catholic Church.

PART THREE

CHAPTER TWENTY-SIX

$\mathcal{A}$ n Arab Christian is forgiven... an Arab Muslim is to be scorned." This pronouncement was stamped with the official seal of Pope Alphonse. Ten years of unrelenting suicide bombings condemned the entire Muslim world. Even those who followed the righteous teachings of Mohammad were tainted with misinterpretations of the Koran taught by Hamas, Islamic Jihad, and other terrorist factions vowing to take over the world and killing all non-believers. The plan was simple. For the past fifteen years Muslim children were taught to hate the Israeli's, the Americans, and all who did not accept the beliefs espoused by the Muslim terrorist organizations. Military terrorist training films replaced respect for the sanctity of life, all in the name of religion. Children were taught to shoot AK-47's and fire surface to air missiles. They were promised a bevy of virgins in the afterlife if they would strap explosives to their bodies and detonate them in civilian hotels, marketplaces, restaurants, and public buildings around the world. Indoctrination began when they were six years old. Not surprisingly, leaders of these factions never sacrificed their own lives as human bombs. Retaliation only fueled Muslim resolve to continue the death march. Yet, retaliation was the only choice of the free world. No nation had come up with a diplomatic solution to end the escalation.

The ancient code written by Hammurabi for the Babylonians in 2285BC was still the law of the day, "an eye for an eye, and a tooth for a tooth". Could it be that when God promised Abraham he would be the father of a "multitude of nations" the intent was to pit each nation against the other until only the killing capacity would determine which was to survive? Relations between the Arabs and the Catholic Church were always strained, needing only a spark to ignite the tinder in the forest. Many felt the edict from Vatican City was more than a spark, it was as if lightning had struck. The terrorist trained children were now young adults ready to accept death in the name of Allah and looking for their reward in the afterlife based only upon faith in their cowardly teachers, whom had no compunction in using them as part of a military arsenal to promote personal political interests. The Catholic Church was their next target.

A bold headline in a leading Middle-Eastern newspaper read: **"Painting Of Mohammad As Devil Moved To Vatican".**
This was all it took to incite the masses. The lead-in paragraph continued with,

"In an unprecedented display of hubris, the Vatican has moved the fresco depicting Mohammad as the devil, from the San Petronio Basilica to the Vatican, apparently believing that relocation can hide the evil sins of the past, as it attempted to do when it transferred sexually abusive priests from one parish to another. It did not work then, and we must not allow it to work now! It is time to take the infidels to task!"

The Vatican retaliated that same afternoon by exhuming the oldest and most powerful censorship force in the world: the Roman

Catholic <u>Index Librorum Prohibitorum.</u> The Sacred Congregation for the Doctrine of the Faith added the newspaper to its list of writings to be avoided which were considered dangerous to faith and morals. The lack of ecclesiastical law enforcing the <u>Admonitum</u> only served to increase the circulation of the newspaper.

The newspaper retorted with a late evening issue designed to feed more oxygen to the spreading wildfire—an editorial denouncing the ancient <u>Constitutum Constantini</u>, the so-called "gift" of Constantine, the first Roman emperor to become a Christian. The "gift" was under attack as illegal. The Roman Catholic Church used the edicts of the <u>Constitutum Constantini</u> as its legal right to rule spiritually over all of the world, and for the Holy See of Rome to be empowered with secular authority over all of Europe. More importantly, the attack by the newspaper was designed to raise doubts as to the legality of the Roman Catholic Church to occupy the one hundred plus acres of Vatican City. The fourteen hundred year old Leonine walls surrounding the womb of Catholicism was now under direct frontal attack for the first time in history. Orchestration of the headlines and stories were conducted behind the scenes by Hosni Khatabi as a diversion to his real purpose...dominion over The Cross.

The world's media picked up the newspaper's front page denouncement of the Catholic Church. Fence sitters in the broiling controversy defected to different sides as the battle was joined. Hundreds grew to thousands, as the Square of Saint Peter became the focal point of the gathering storm, a mixture of Catholics, Muslims, and eighteen Jews dressed as Jesuit priests in brown robes. Vatican officials scurried ant-like throughout the great halls, each looking to the other for direction and guidance.

Capelli rushed into the office of Cardinal Kennedy. "<u>United Press International</u> and the <u>Associated Press</u> are asking for a statement. <u>Reuters</u> has been ringing the phone off the hook since five this morning!" Capelli said, adding to the growing dilemma.

"I have asked Secretary General Lattimer to draft a statement from His Holiness," Justin advised, thinking in terms of a preemptive strike at the next headline he expected the newspaper to spew. "He has already informed Alphonse and as I understand it, the Pontiff is very distressed." He frowned. "So much so, the doctors are extremely concerned." The buzz of the intercom interrupted their conversation. Justin picked up the phone, "Yes," he answered, and then listened to his aide on the other end of the phone. "You may assure the Pontiff I will be there in thirty minutes time," Justin responded after hearing that Pope Alphonse requested an emergency meeting with him alone. Justin dismissed Capelli and hurried to the private apartment of Pope Alphonse.

Upon arrival, the American Cardinal was asked to be seated in the anteroom by a Papal aide, who explained that Vatican doctors were with Alphonse and his meeting would be slightly delayed. The tone of voice used by the aide sent a chill through Justin as he recalled his previous meeting with the Roman Catholic leader in which he was designated heir apparent.

Only ten minutes passed when Justin was ushered into Alphonse's study on the third floor of the Apostolic palace. The Pope remained seated. It appeared to Justin that the man had shrunk two sizes since their last meeting and his skin took on the gray pallor of impending death. The eyes of his Pontiff appeared sunken in the sockets. Alphonse was holding his left arm across his chest, the frail wrist showing blue veins through the skin. He nodded to the grim-faced departing doctors, who bowed politely as they exited the room.

Justin approached Pope Alphonse and noticed the blue of the cuticles on the fingers as he knelt and kissed the ring of the fisherman on His Holiness' fourth finger of the right hand.

"It is so very good to see you, my son," Alphonse began, his voice soft and deliberate.

"And I pray God rests his hands on your shoulders, dear Father," Justin Kennedy said quietly.

"There are certain things I must tell you while I have the strength," Alphonse began. "I fully expect that revelation of the Cross soon to be enshrined in the Basilica will be exploited before we have a chance to reveal its existence ourselves. It will come as a follow-up story to the San Petronio fresco. The communication leak in the Vatican has not been found. There is a traitor within supplying information to that dreadful Middle-Eastern newspaper intent on fueling a religious war. The next headline will be, 'Vatican Steals Holy Cross From Israeli Soil', or words to that effect".

"That will raise a host of questions, your Holiness. Can we deny the truth of the statement and maintain any semblance of honesty? How do we react when the Israeli's come knocking at our door? No doubt the Muslim splinter groups would relish destruction of any relationship between Catholics and Jews."

"Yes, Justin, but there will be no destruction nor even a hint of a strained relationship. That is why I called you here. I have kept this a secret to prevent this "Judas" from capitalizing on our next moves. You will be the only Catholic, beside myself, who knows what has truly transpired.

"What do you mean your holiness," Justin said wondering what in the world he could be talking about.

"Finding the Cross was brought about by divine intervention. Bringing it back to Vatican City was a calculated decision made in concert with the President and Prime Minister of Israel for political as well as religious reasons." Justin looked dumbfounded, unable to comprehend what Alphonse was saying.

"The Church needs the Cross, Justin. You are well aware of the threats of bankruptcy by several of the dioceses' in the United States faced with major lawsuits and judgments in the millions of dollars. I have serious doubts as to whether judgments would be discharged even if bankruptcy were filed. Our lawyers have relayed their concerns advising that knowledge of priestly misconduct by the diocese and attempts to hide the truth from the parishioners and victims could easily be construed as misrepresentation and fraud. If so, bankruptcy solves none of their problems. Certain acts of conduct will not discharge obligations under the United States Federal Bankruptcy Code I am told. This may leave the Vatican coffers vulnerable to pay damage awards. Even if our lawyers can find a technicality to escape legal liability, do we not have a moral obligation?"

"This is indeed a serious concern, your Eminence," Justin said as he continued to listen to the sobering truth of his mentor.

The Pope continued, "The Catholic religion could be hit with tens of thousands of parishioners leaving the Church. The Church could be left in a financial condition so dire that it would not have the 'staying power' to negotiate acceptable settlement arrangements with the victims."

As if reading the Pope's mind Justin added, "And, the Muslim extremists would not be sleeping during our misery. They would denounce Catholicism as an untrue religion being punished for its evil. The theft of the Cross would be a fundamental breach of the Ten Commandments. And I was the prime instrument of the theft," Justin said ashamedly.

"But you were not," responded Alphonse. "The Cross was never stolen. Our Israeli friends understood the ramifications completely. Prime Minister Gold and President Hershel stand ready to announce to the world that the discovery of the Cross was a joint effort between Israel and the Vatican to preserve a sacred religious relic recognized by Jews to be the cornerstone of the Christian faith. When you called me from Israel and told me in one word of your success, I immediately placed a call to the Prime Minister of Israel. Together, we thought this through just like the "end game" in a chess match and obtained the endorsement of our plan from President Hershel. The Israeli's advised total silence must be kept".

"The Prime Minister anticipated the Muslim strategy once informed by me of the existence of the Vatican traitor. We knew that the enemy had knowledge that the Cross was secreted safely in the Basilica. We decided to keep the information of Israel's participation in the expedition in total secrecy anticipating that at some point the Muslim extremists would accuse the Catholic Church of thievery. Israel would then destroy any Muslim credibility with the might of their words rather than the strength of their weapons by announcing the joint effort."

"It seems the pen is still mightier than the sword," Justin commented with a grin. "Of course, the final chapter is not yet written."

"That's one of the things I like about you my son, you never jump to conclusions. But, we fully expect the Muslims to fall into the abyss waiting for them," the Pope replied. "There is something else. I called you here for another reason."

"After what you have just told me, what else could possibly be of any importance?" Justin asked.

"Words cannot always take the place of swords, Justin. It is in the interest of the Israeli government that the Vatican and its antiquities be protected. They have offered their assistance and I have accepted," Alphonse announced. "The details must be saved for a later time. I am very tired now and must beg your indulgence for my weakened condition."

"Of course, your Holiness. It is the desire and prayers of the College that you cancel all further audiences and leave for the tranquility of Castle Gandolfo. The Alban Hills are cool and peaceful at this time of year," Justin said.

"The chains of office do hang heavy at times. But I must settle this business before..."

Again, Justin felt the lump grow in his throat. His heart pounded so loudly he felt sure the Pope could hear it.

The Pope became frighteningly quiet, almost as if he had ceased breathing. In a few moments he coughed lightly and continued, "I am sorry, my son." The Pontiff's eyes met Justin's once again. "I seemed to be daydreaming. You must forgive me for my breech of manners. Go with God, dear Justin, for in you lies the greatness of our Church." The smile was a stark contrast to the pain Justin knew was in the Pope's ailing body.

Justin left the Pope and walked to the square. Throngs of Catholic pilgrims were gathered waiting for a response from Pope Alphonse to the newspaper articles attacking the Church.

A fog of excitement began in the giant square. Great bells of Saint Peter's were tolling in the background, as nuns from various orders scurried to and fro. Citizens of the world were asking questions of black robed priests as if their Catholic dress made them privy to a mystery.

Justin walked past the brass markers in the pavement where his predecessor Cardinals had trod for centuries before him, wondering if they were smiling or frowning from beyond the grave. For the thousandth time Justin was awed as he walked up the stone steps of the Basilica to view the installation of the Cross that had just been transported the three hundred yards from the museum to the Basilica under cover of darkness. He felt his life was coming to an apex; his pride increasing as each step took him down the long aisle of Saint Peter's, the years of labor in the name of his God being rewarded. He thought of his mother, his ordination, Mary Frances, and then of Father Peter.

Once again Justin felt the immensity of the place; the coolness of the Basilica felt chilly after the warmth of the piazza. He continued walking the center aisle, past the Papal altar foursquared with the twisted bronze columns of Bernini. It seemed to him almost impossible for pillars to hold up the thousands of kilos of weight from the Baldachino structure. Justin looked at the symbolic chair of San Pietro, set high in the wall, then took a deep breath as he approached the awaiting assembly of men. Father Byron Callahan was there as was Enrique Capelli. The Monsignor sucked in his breath as he looked at the massive scaffolding erected on the altar. A gray canvas covering all traces of the appointments on the main floor. Only the four massive, twisted bronze pillars gave any indication that he was standing in front of the most revered place in Catholicism.

"Shall we begin?" Justin inquired, "God grant us the wisdom of our deeds." Justin exchanged glances with Capelli. A hush fell over the place as a large platform cloaked in royal silk was wheeled into the hall. Father Callahan hovered over his architectural drawings, confirming the measurements of the guy wires designed to hold the Cross in suspension. Large eye-hooks were screwed into the four columns. Justin cringed at the act of defacing the sacred pillars, as he heard the electric drills boring away. Monsignor Capelli lifted the covering from the Cross, as all work halted. An electrician high on the scaffold held his breath and made the sign of the Cross. The men on the floor of the Basilica knelt in unison as Justin prepared to say a blessing. He looked at the group. All the members of the expedition, sans Father Peter, were there. Sister Mary Frances was the lone female.

"Heavenly Father," Justin began, "we ask both for forgiveness and guidance for this act of love and contrition. Knowing that your blood was shed upon this wood for all of mankind, we assemble here to consecrate this time and place in the holy memory of Jesus of Nazareth. And we pray God that we have done thy will." Each of the assembled knew the significance of the moment and would live their lives a bit differently because of their participation in the event.

Justin was relieved that the installation proceeded quickly. The fine wires of steel were attached to the Cross, as a hoist began to lift the Christian emblem into position exactly 21 feet above the altar. It swayed dangerously for a few moments while the wires were carefully pulled taut. Once secured, the scaffolding was removed. Finally the area around the altar of Saint Peter was cleaned and vacuumed. Mary Frances again gathered up the small splinters to add to her collection of the relic, the only person thoughtful enough to do so. The rays of the late afternoon sun shafted through the stain-glassed windows and cast golden light onto the scene. Justin looked up to the Cross. "My God!" It's beautiful!" was all he could manage to say, his body trembling.

After the installation, they all departed and the Basilica doors were locked. Justin walked over to Mary Frances. The troubled expression he'd noticed when he last saw her was still there. But the sparkle seemed to have left her eyes as if she had accepted her situation and was powerless to change it. They walked side by side down the steps of the Basilica, while bright sunlight reflected off the dome of San Pietro.

"It was not very political of you to invite me, Justin," she said as a group of tourists stepped to the side and bowed politely. Her eyes were grave as she looked into his face.

"You, above all, have the right to be here," Justin said softly.

"What will be the ramifications of this glorious day... will the flocks gather? Will the Cross of Jesus become the beacon we all have prayed for?" she asked as they continued to walk.

"Questions... I have not the answers. The forces of heaven are at work today and only God has the answers," he said humbly.

"Shall we ever know for certain if it is the true Cross?" she asked.

"And if we could know the answer, would it matter? Perception,...that is what is important. If one wants to believe, then it is so," Justin answered.

They walked in silence, then Justin said, "And you, my dear, are balm for the soul of this poor servant of Christ," Justin touched his lips to her cheek. For a moment they were unmindful of the people's curious glances. Then, suddenly aware of the stares, they walked to the center of the Piazza. The area around the Center Obelisk was crowded even for this particular time of day.

"Shall we count the columns?" Mary Frances joked. Justin grinned at her reference to the three hundred seventy Doric columns that formed the graceful half oval of the Piazza. He glanced up at the statues of Christ, Saint John the Baptist and the Apostles looking down on the pair as they continued along. The golden brown and ochre facade of the Piazza was emanating warmth.

"It's such a fine day it makes one wish to be left to one's own devises to visit the shops on the Via Veneto," Mary Frances said wistfully as she gazed down the wide Via della Concilazione towards the rounded tomb of Hadrian and the eternal city of Rome.

Justin took this as an opportunity to volunteer, "I would be delighted to go with you. I know of a little cafe in the Piazzo Barberini that serves delicious melon and prosciutto! It would excite even a gormandizer. It's across from the fountain with the triton and sea shell."

"I know the place!" she said excitedly.

"Shall we?" Justin asked.

"Why not?" A devilish sparkle suddenly returned to her green eyes.

Justin hailed a taxi, and they were off. Justin began to relax, glad to be away from the stares of the tourists and priests. He knew his rank of Cardinal and his distinctive attire made him stand out almost like the bird of the same name in a green forest. Still they were not alone. The driver's stained-tooth grin reflected in rear view mirror as the taxi crowned the Quirinal hill, past the spectacular Trevi fountains. Justin and Mary Frances smiled at the tourists tossing their coins in the pool.

"If Neptune and the other deities holding court in the Trevi could speak, they would most certainly laugh at the folly,' Justin remarked with a wry grin.

"As long as there is a wish, there is hope, and therefore a chance it will come to be," she said wanting to believe the words would apply to her.

The Via Veneto was crowded as usual; the wide avenue with its hotels, shops and sidewalk cafes seemed alive as the tourists, eager to lighten their wallets, scurried in and out of the colorful shops. Digital cameras were strung about their necks like visual passports announcing they were on holiday. Justin instructed the driver to pull up at <u>Rafelles</u> and paid the cab fare, leaving the driver a generous tip.

Justin and Mary Frances were directed to a table near the sidewalk fronting the Veneto. An obese waiter immediately delivered Pelegrino mineral water, not waiting for it to be ordered, and bowed with respect for the rank of his customers.

"Welcome, Eminence... and Sister, I am honored with your presence." The waiter hovered over the pair like a mother hen.

"And we are pleased to be here," Sister Mary Frances replied, and quickly turned toward Justin when the waiter stared for just an extra second.

"We would like a bottle of the white Frascati, prosciutto and melon," Justin said.

"Excellent...Eminence. It will not be but a moment," he promised.

"I feel almost guilty enjoying myself so much," Mary Frances said quietly as she reached for Justin's hand under the auspices of studying the ring of the Cardinal.

"I hope it's not just the calm before the storm for both of us," Justin replied, knowing that the announcement respecting the Cross was not far off. Another storm was brewing in the mind of Mary Frances. Her expression suddenly changed as if she was contemplating something of great importance. Justin noticed the change in an instant.

"I didn't mean to cast a dark cloud over our afternoon," he said.

"May I speak freely?" she asked.

"Of course," Justin replied.

"If only I could expunge that desperate something within me which is struggling to flee from Rome... from the Church. I know what it is...but I cannot face it," she paused then continued, "It is the fear of the pain that is sure to come of our relationship? If I could not feel, I would be safe, out of harm's way. No matter how much I try, I still cannot stem the rising tide of devotion I feel for you. It cannot be denied," she confessed.

The words of Mary Frances duplicated his thoughts. Only she had the courage to say what he could not. Her words were sincere, longing, emotional, and they struck the center of his heart.

"I understand more than you know," he said smiling at her.

Again the flush came to her cheeks. Wonderful the way red-haired people could turn rosy faced in an instant, Justin thought.

"Are you to be my <u>Anna</u> and I, the <u>King of Siam</u>?" he managed to say.

"I do not know what I am to become... my Church has called me to do its bidding, a task which I have committed my life to do. And yet... my feelings for you have made me question my vows, which have never given me the happiness you have allowed me to experience."

Justin could only stare at her in silence, groping for words, but he found none were forthcoming. The appearance of the waiter eased his pain.

"<u>Buono appetito,</u>" the waiter announced as the wine was poured and the thinly sliced prosciutto was served.

She barely touched her food, her mind seemed to be in a far off place totally oblivious to the noise and bustle of the Via Veneto.

"Come now... is the melon so bad?" Justin asked, attempting to bring levity back to the conversation. She smiled but remained silent.

They sat and looked at the passing parade of humanity: the Americans with their flamboyant sports coats; the Orientals, multiple cameras at the ready; the Europeans with conservative clothing and good manners, all jelling into a stew of humanity. Happy couples embracing each other as they strolled along the avenue.

"It is getting late and I promised to be back in time for a late supper," she said breaking the silence. Justin wanted to speak words of understanding, but felt the time and place were wrong. Worse, he knew they could never be right.

"It has been enjoyable even if all too short," he said as he left money on the table. They walked to the corner, Justin holding her by the arm.

Impulsively, she turned and hugged him quickly. "Thank you for a lovely time!" Her face was radiant. Justin felt the love well up within him. It was Mary Frances who noticed the photographer. As she stepped back in surprise, the blatantly intrusive paparazzi continued to click his shutter. He danced around as if on a puppet's string, a court jester performing for his sovereign.

"Grazie..." the man smiled as he raced from the scene.

"I'm sorry, Justin, I beg your forgiveness for my mistake," she said as she held her hand to her cheek.

"Don't be foolish... it's not as if we were making love on the steps of the Basilica. Please... don't worry." They both noticed the press vehicle departing the Veneto. The unmistakable logo of the most notorious scandal tabloid in Rome was painted on its side panel.

"I must not be late for the meeting at the Synod room in the Nervi," Justin said as he looked to his watch.

"We had best be going back," she replied as she glanced over her left shoulder looking for another photographer.

The ride back to the Vatican was made in virtual silence, each with personal thoughts of their impossible attraction for each other. The taxi pulled into the Square. Justin told the driver to stop at the west fountain, then paid the man and helped Mary Frances out of the cab. She faced him, eyes steady.

"It's been a wonderful afternoon, Justin," she said softly.

He took her hand and held it tightly. "It has been much more... much more. I must leave you now," he said almost apologetically.

He watched her turn and walk towards the Magdalene Apartments. Each step added to his growing feeling of an impossible love for her.

CHAPTER TWENTY-SEVEN

$\mathcal{J}$ustin entered the Nervi, a strange trapezoidal edifice with the main doors of the building facing eastward. The architectural genius of Pier Luigi Nervi was evident upon stepping into the great hall. Justin had been told the famous man employed the same avant-garde architecture when he designed the Roman Catholic Cathedral in San Francisco. The undulating roof of the place gave Justin a sense of entering another dimension. Along the two walls of the main hall, there were oval stained glass windows that appeared as if they were portholes. Underneath it was the largest bronze sculpture in the world, commissioned by Pope Paul and created by Pericle Fazzine; it held dominion over the raised dais holding the Papal throne. He was aware the past three Popes had been selected in the Nervi and also aware of the growing sentiment to have future elections held in the Sistine as they had been since the beginning of the Roman Catholic Church. Justin took a deep breath as he eyed the staircase leading to the Synod, secreted high above the main hall, known as the "Upper Room" due to its proximity to the roof of the Nervi.

Justin elected to take the steps rather than the elevator to reach the Synod room. His mind was still on the Cross of Jesus, now secured in Saint Peter's Basilica. Cardinal Wilhelm had called for the meeting of the most influential dozen clerics from the Curia. The reason for the urgent request was obscured for the moment as the remaining attendees entered the place.

"It is not by chance that I have selected this place to meet in secret conclave, nor the fact that there are twelve of us involved..." Wilhelm began. "We can no longer ignore the fact that our Vicar and beloved Pope Alphonse is dying. Therefore, it is not too soon to begin the task of looking for a successor and planning for the procedural details in preparation for the selection of the new ruler of eight hundred million Catholics." Wilhelm's well -modulated voice, with just a hint of his Germanic accent, began to cast a spell on the clerics. It was apparent that he was approaching his goal to succeed Alphonse with the care of generals planning a battle.

"Is it not the General Policy which must be formulated... not the selection of the Pope?" Cardinal Sun Yet questioned. "The General Policy will be followed by whoever is Pope... It appears you have your priorities out of order, Eminence." A few nods of agreement gave validity to the Oriental's words.

"You are correct, dear Brother," Wilhelm said condescendingly, realizing this was not the time to alienate his brothers. "Contrary to popular belief, the Pope is not the bearer of the master keys to the Kingdom of Heaven... the General Policy must be adopted... all of us must know the state of the Catholic Church. We have current updates on conditions and developments, in not only the state of Roman Catholicism, but on the non-Catholic Christian community as well. Political and economic conditions throughout the world also must be analyzed and studied for us to delineate the General Policy," Wilhelm adding, backing off for the moment, searching for his pipe.

Justin Kennedy winced at Wilhelm's use of the word, non-Catholic. He intentionally made his displeasure evident as he began to speak.

"Are we to sit here and make this policy without the consensus of the Curia? Can we not wait until the Holy Father is called to his reward?" Justin's hand thumped the table to accent his words.

"Brothers... dear Brothers... I perceive both sides to this situation," Cardinal Avenel said. "We all know the time of death grows near for our Pope for he is all but incapacitated. Important decisions go undecided, questions remain unanswered and yet the world goes on. It is rumored he cannot attend the blessing of the Cross in the morning. I also believe my Lord Cardinal Wilhelm is correct." Cardinal Avenel turned to the German Cardinal, who was pulling on his earlobe, an old habit when he felt he was prevailing on any issue. "We must begin preliminary discussion regarding the eventuality we shall face with the death of Alphonse. We cannot leave the selection of the Pope to chance."

Cardinal Blackmore cleared his throat. "If we do not begin to think along these lines, we shall be under attack the moment Alphonse dies. We know Father Claude Monel, some call him the 'Black Priest,' he continues inciting Parisian Catholics with rhetoric unbecoming his calling." He paused, and then continued. "His support is growing, according to recent reports from the wine regions of France. In any vacuum created by the death of the Pope, Monel will certainly take advantage of the situation by spearheading a movement away from Rome and our edicts simply because of a snub of the French Catholic leadership by Pope Alphonse last year."

Justin looked at the assembled men. "I agree that in volatile times a schism could occur," he said. "But I do not believe that our Church is so weak that we cannot stand the searchlight of inquiry." Justin's knowledge, and new found direction adding to his stature as a leader among his peers.

Cardinal Sun yet coughed lightly, a polite maneuver to garner the attention of his associates. "We are all aware," he began in a soft voice; "that Papal electors belong to the world's most exclusive club. Each of us holds a gold-plated membership card which allows entry to the secret and mysterious arena of power—each must use this power judiciously and with the wisdom of Solomon."

"Then is it the consensus of all assembled that we must begin thinking along the lines of he who is best equipped to serve as the next Pope?" Wilhelm asked with a firm tone in his voice more like making a statement than asking a question.

"I will have no part of this back room agreement!" Cardinal Blackmore shouted. "It is the Curia, and only the Curia with the Cardinalship in vote, which will select the next Pope," he said, his voice cracking with emotion. "I beg your leave, Brothers, and pray God will soon show you the folly of this." Blackmore rose and walked toward the door.

"Even at the Last Supper, one of the twelve left on an errand..." Wilhelm said, pointing the stem of his pipe toward Cardinal Blackmore.

"And another spilled the salt, Brother Wilhelm," Justin said.

"Sometimes one is better off not knowing how Popes or sausages are made—I suggest we allow the normal course of events to take place... God will show us the way," Cardinal Sun Yet spoke to the remaining members.

CHAPTER TWENTY-EIGHT

$\mathcal{I}$t was a beautiful Saturday morning when Capelli entered the private chambers of Pope Alphonse.

"The time is growing near," Alphonse pronounced. "Have you secured the alliances needed to give our Church its first American Pope?"

"Your holiness, I have done what I can do. We are nineteen votes shy of the majority needed. Cardinal Wilhelm has lobbied using every trick in the book. Money, position, and favors have been pledged. There is one or two still sitting on the fence unwilling to commit to me, but neither is willing to commit to the German, at least that is what I am being told."

"I see." Alphonse took a moment to catch his breath and continued. "I have prepared a document under papal seal that is in my safe. Upon my death, you are to bring two Vatican guards with you and remove the document from my safe. The document shall be delivered by the Guards to Cardinal Wilhelm."

"When shall it be delivered, your Eminence?" Capelli stammered realizing that his dreams that the agreement with his Pope would not be honored because he had failed for his part of the bargain.

"It shall be deliver when it is called for by Cardinal Wilhelm.

Meanwhile, I would like you to arrange to bring twelve Cardinals to serve mass with me in tomorrow morning for the special blessing of the Cross. I do not want Cardinal Wilhelm or Cardinal Kennedy to be in attendance. You are to select Cardinals whom you deem to be independent and undecided, as well as those who support Wilhelm and Kennedy to make up the twelve requested. And, I want you to be in attendance as well."

"I will do as you ask, Eminence."

"Please, leave me now so I may rest. May God go with you my loyal friend," Alphonse whispered.

The Roman Catholic Church's blessing of the Cross of Jesus Christ began promptly at 8:00 a.m. in Saint Peter's Basilica, the hour chosen by Alphonse—it was Sunday. The Basilica was closed to all but the select group of clergy consisting of twelve Cardinals and Monsignor Capelli. The public was still unaware of the existence of the sacred antiquity. The mass was over quickly and Alphonse took thirty precious minutes of his life to address his brothers. He said what he had to say. He was attired in a gleaming cassock. His slippers white as a pair of snow geese and embroidered with gold crosses. A contrasting flaming red ceremonial rochet draped over his frail shoulders. His face pale under the whiteness of the mitered Papal cap. His voice straining, hands visibly shaking, he concluded his message.

"This Cross... " Alphonse lifted a shaky hand towards the high altar, "shall become the door. We must enter and begin a new resurrection for the Church. We cannot wait for a new generation to heed His call." Alphonse paused, looking slightly confused, then began again. "In this hour, I proclaim Introibo Ad Altare Dei, Ad Deum Qui La Etificat Juventutem Meam; I go unto the altar of God, to God who giveth joy to my youth. Let us in this hour ignite the spark of youth throughout the..."

Alphonse faltered momentarily; his body seemed to sway to the left as he reached for the lectern. His eyes widened, his face bewildered, as if some invisible hand had slapped him on the cheek. Every nerve ending in his body exploded into a gigantic cosmic event. At that instant, Alphonse, Vicar of Christ, Leader of the Roman Catholic Church, became one with his God as he fell to the floor, his eyes, fully open, fixated on the Cross holding dominion over him.

Confusion reigned. A semblance of order coming only after Vatican doctors declared him dead. Written instructions were swiftly delivered to Cardinal Wilhelm advising him that he had been named temporary <u>Camerlengo</u> of the Universal Church, the head of the interim government. His assigned task was to organize a caretaker government until the next Pope was elected. Wilhelm assigned Capelli to make arrangements to carry out the rituals covering the death of the Pope.

The body of Pope Alphonse had been hurriedly placed in the Pontifical bedroom. Capelli's first act was to select three Cardinals according to ancient ritual as well as numerous Vatican officials to watch over the body. Justin Kennedy was selected as one of the three. Representatives of the International Diplomatic Corps and the Italian government also assembled in the room.

Wilhelm was handed a small silver mallet and tapped Alphonse's forehead three times. Each time, he asked: "<u>Valdermer Baronoski, are you dead</u>?" Receiving no answer, Cardinal Wilhelm intoned the phrase: "Pope Alphonse is truly dead." The ritual continued as Wilhelm took the frail right hand of his Pope and removed the ring of the Fisherman from the fourth finger. He was then handed the official Pontifical seals of office. Wilhelm placed them and the ring on a marble tabletop and smashed them, an act designed to ensure that no one could use them to authenticate a falsified document.

The Papal Secretary, his face streaking with tears, handed Justin the official death certificate. Wilhelm ordered the private apartment sealed and appointed Cardinal Rachman, Cardinal Sun Yet, and Bishop Lattimer, as the committee to assume charge of Vatican affairs. Funeral preparations were assigned to Monsignor Capelli.

The fact that Alphonse was in very poor health had proven a blessing for this sad endeavor. Most of the arrangements had been settled week's prior. The call for a Conclave to name a new Pope was made even before the Pope's body was set with rigor mortis.

Within the hour, summonses were sent to each Cardinal elector throughout the world, announcing the death of Alphonse and establishing a date as the official opening, of Conclave eighty-six. It would begin on the 14th day after the death, August 30, well within the 20-day time frame required by Catholic Law.

Nine days of official mourning began immediately as the world was given the grievous news. Vatican flags already at half-staff. Five massive bells of Saint Peter's began a powerful and traditional mourning cadence, the tolling to continue day and night.

At the eighth hour after death, Alphonse was prepared for burial, his body washed and embalmed. It was to be placed in the nave of the Basilica on a bier trimmed in bright red. Papal guards in full Renaissance regalia, complete with pikes, would be positioned as a watch of honor.

Alphonse was to be ensconced in a triple coffin; cypress, lead-zinc, and elm, then be placed in a white marble sarcophagus with his name and dates on the top. He would be laid to rest with a white silk veil over his face, a velvet bag of coins and medals, his smashed pontifical ring, and a rosary in his hands. His body clad in liturgical vestments with a white miter cap on his head. A red leather bound book of scrolled parchments listing his accomplishments to be placed next to his body. The final resting place in the Basilica grotto just meters from Saint Peters tomb.

The Vatican post office removed Pope Alphonse photo and name from it's postage stamps and replaced it with a picture of Saint Peters Basilica with the Latin words <u>Sietus Vacantus</u> 'seat is vacant.' These stamps and newly minted coins destined to be sold at exorbitant prices to help offset the huge cost of the funeral.

A plea already issued to all world parishes to increase 'Peters Pence' required donations to the Vatican.

Ten's of thousands of sobbing Roman citizens filled the square almost immediately. Women knelt and kissed their rosaries; somber faced men made the sign of the Cross over and over, their faces expressing the anguish and deep grief as only the Italians could, at such a sad time in history. Justin was deeply sorrowed by the death of Alphonse, yet he plunged into the multitude of necessary details involved in the passing of the leader of the Catholic Church. He hardly noticed the absence of his grinding migraine headaches.

The mourning period, more traditionally referred to as <u>Motu proprio,</u> progressed unabated, events in the world taking a secondary position. Hundreds of millions were glued to their television sets as satellites beamed audio sound and video images around the world showing every minutia of detail of the Pope's funeral.

Multitudes of Catholics became closer to their church through the drama of the Papal death. Many who had opposed Alphonse's edicts and pronouncements a few days earlier, now elevated him to the status of Saint. It was an event that most Catholics would never forget. They would always recall with exacting detail where they were and what they were doing at that moment in history, much the same as people remembered an assassination in Dallas on November 22, 1963, or the World Trade Center attack on September 11, 2001.

In Africa, tom-toms beat out a requiem mass of death for their fallen leader. Hundreds of Yaqui Indians fell on their knees in front of Our Lady of Guadalupe near Phoenix, Arizona. Greek monks prayed silently on Mt. Athos. Millions of Catholics grieved for this man of God, the sorrow of the death cleansing them, tears washing away the doubts of their faith. The renewal began even as the Sanpatrini, the attendants at Saint Peter's, closed the three coffins. Gilt nails were used to confine the remains of the Pontiff. Wilhelm, in his continuing role as Camerlengo, sealed the last coffin and gave the signal to have it lowered by pulleys into the awaiting crypt beneath the polished marble floors of the Basilica. The triple coffin was placed inside a sarcophagus already carved with the dead Pope's name. Justin said a silent prayer for the man, noting the final resting place of Pope Alphonse was a few hundred meters away from the tomb of Simon Peter and the Cross of Jesus, a fitting memorial for the Polish prelate. Justin wept and remembered Alphonse as a man of the people who had never forgotten his peasant heritage. He stood silently wondering how the reforms so desperately needed by the Catholic Church would be fulfilled.

While the world community buzzed with dialogue about the death of Alphonse and the imminent papal election, others were busy formulating sinister plans to take advantage of the disruption in the Catholic Church. Mustapha, the assassin, under orders from Hosni Khatabi, was charged with making good on Khatabi's promise to deliver the Cross to the evangelist, Orlo Thompson.

CHAPTER TWENTY-NINE

$\mathcal{T}$he election of a new Pope quickly became the main business of the various power blocks of the Roman Catholic Church. Those concerned with the preservation of Romanita, the power of Rome, as the center of the Church, were most vocal in their efforts to ensure the election of a candidate from Italy. They were fully aware that with the election of Alphonse, an outlander from Poland, Rome had lost control of the Church. To the man, the Italian contingent was firm in their commitment to fight. The forthcoming conclave would not be as saintly as most outsiders perceived.

Other factions knew that the central theme upon which the four previous Popes had been selected would no longer suffice to gain the Chair of Peter. The perceived devil, in the form of Marxism, which had been used by previous winning candidates as the biggest threat to the Catholic Church, would no longer be a viable issue or weapon to the election process. They also knew Marxism capitulated because social injustice had been rejected. The cries of the oppressed and hungry of the world would drown out the pleas of unification emanating from the podiums of the rich and powerful Marxist community as well as those pleas from the pulpits of the wealthy and complacent Roman Catholic Church.

Even as the remaining Cardinals were arriving from distant parts of the world for the conclave, Vatican tailors were preparing three sets of vestments: small, medium and large. Within twenty-four hours the conclave would begin promptly on schedule.

As protocol required, all knew that the first order of business for the Cardinal Electors would be to take an oath to exclude all outside influences on their vote for the new Pope. The sacred oath would create a moral dilemma for a majority of Cardinals who had already pledged their votes. Those supporting Cardinal Kennedy would be mentally torn by their allegiance given to the now dead Pope Alphonse by way of Capelli's efforts, and the oath they were required to make at this moment. The same applied to loyalists of the German Cardinal. However, this division of loyalties, which otherwise could create a voting nightmare, was secure in Wilhelm's camp.The ominous threat of politics was now entering into the mix. The next twenty-four hours before assembly would also allow the gathering college to speak freely, some in secret meetings, others in open forums. The hastily called caucuses created more discussion and compromise candidates. The tree shaking would now begin and the weaker stems would break, their fruit falling to the ground.

Those oppressed cared little for either politics or religion. They would follow the one who filled their empty bellies. Full stomachs easily made minds all too eager for ideology of any persuasion.

Many thoughts ran through Justin's mind as he walked the polished floors of the Vatican. The words of his mother flooded over him as he recalled the day of his ordination into priesthood; "Within you is the hope for the poor. Go now and do that which you were born for." Was elevation to the highest of office of the Church the fate Kate Kennedy had known deep in her heart would eventually play out for her son?

The sisters from the various Orders dressed like bands of penguins as they blended into the scenery of the Vatican hallways. It was said that one could never move more than a few yards without catching a glimpse of one of the black-robed nuns accentuated with white head coverings, scurrying about always in a quiet or whispered hurry to go about God's business.

Mary Frances was also walking in the Vatican. She saw Justin coming from the opposite direction. He appeared to be lost in thought. Slowing her pace, she mouthed a silent prayer. She prayed he would notice her as he passed. Her heart was pounding as he approached, protocol demanding her to remain silent until and unless the Cardinal acknowledged her presence. She dared to steal a glance at him as her heartbeat quickened as the distance between them closed rapidly. He passed her without a glance. She forced herself to stare ahead as his footsteps echoed away, fighting the urge to call out his name, then took a deep breath of resignation and continued on her way when she heard his voice.

"Sister, excuse me," Justin called not realizing the nun was Mary Frances. Even before she dared to turn around, Justin was approaching her.

"The telephone, could you tell me where the nearest telephone is located? I must make a..." Justin stopping in mid-sentence. "Mary Frances! How very good to see you! Why didn't you stop me in the hall?" Justin knew the answer even before she gave him a perplexed smile. "So, some of the rules are not quite fair, but on occasion do we not transcend some of them?" he laughed and took her hand.

"Justin," she said whispering his name, "it is wonderful to see you," speaking to the only man in her life she had loved. "I pray you are well."

"Well enough, indeed, even with this heavy feeling, sharing the grief we all feel for our Church," Justin said.

"I, too, am filled with sorrow for our Pontiff. It's good that we have many things to keep us occupied during this time of mourning," she rationalized.

"Yes, work does help all of us through the times of trial. I also am quite busy; almost too busy for my own good, I'm afraid," Justin said.

"Too busy to walk in the garden with a good friend?" Mary Frances looked at him expectantly.

"Let's!" he said, taking her arm. The Vatican gardens were cool in their splendor and manicured to perfection. The botanical Sanpatrini, while mourning the death of the Pope, knew from experience that a Papal death was the signal for thousands of temporary workers to descend upon the Vatican to scrub, polish, and groom the base of Catholic power. The gardens had received special attention. Visitors and dignitaries from the four corners of the globe were arriving for the conclave. They would leave with a sense of perfection. In turn, they would tell the faithful at home about the loving care their Vatican was receiving. Justin walked Mary Frances to a small bench that was obscured from the main path. Thick foliage gave them a degree of privacy, except for the statue of the Madonna looking down upon them. A bubbling fountain a few meters to the left gave the place a sense of serenity.

"It is a sad time for all," Mary Frances began.

Justin nodded, turning to face her. "It is a time for renewal, a time for regeneration of both the body and soul. The spirit can be lifted even by death." He looked directly into her eyes as he spoke.

"My spirit is lifted just by being near you," Mary Frances replied, eyes bright.

"And I find your nearness does something to my own inner feelings." Justin reciprocated. Justin's gray eyes glinted in the sunlight as they both reminisced their time together in Israel.

"I would suppose if we continue this Romeo and Juliet meeting we might become the topic of conversation around here," she said, a longing and hope reflected in her eyes.

"I care not, my lady, thou art my heart's delight," Justin doffed his red cap and bowed in mock seriousness.

"Mother Superior would have cardiac arrest if she knew of this conversation," Mary Frances said with a smile.

Justin grimaced. "She may get the chance if the picture taken of us at the cafe hits the Tabloid tomorrow." Noticing the look of concern on Mary Frances' face, he grinned suddenly.

"Mother Superior will sit behind her desk and tap her finger for a few moments and then begin to debate whether she should send you packing or ask for the juicy details," Justin's voice mimicking Mother Superior's pompous tone. Mary Frances laughed at the parody and then tears ran down her cheeks. She held her sides as the laughter bubbled from deep inside her as easily as a giddy child playing tag.

Justin puffed his cheeks and placed his hands behind his back, stood, and walked duck-like, head bent, shoulders arched, shaking his head in mock anger as he parodied Mother Superior.

Mary Frances could not contain herself as she squealed in delight. The levity was a welcome reprieve from the sorrow of the past week although both of them felt an unspoken guilt for enjoying themselves.

"Is everything all right?" a voice asked. The pair was startled for a moment as they came face to face with an old gardener, hunched by years of selfless toil, aged by tenure to his flowers.

"Yes... everything is just fine," Justin replied. Mary Frances smothered another giggle, noting the old man peering at the jaunty angle of the Cardinal Kennedy's red cap of office.

"Sono bene accoppiati," the old man said as he quietly left.

"What did he say?" Mary Frances asked.

"He said we make a nice couple... I did not quite catch the inflection. He may have meant it sarcastically," Justin said. Then added, "Some days you're the pigeon and some days you're the statue."

"Or he may have meant it in love and understanding," she said, her voice now serious.

"Is love and understanding within our grasp?" Justin asked, and then continued to answer his own question. "Even the most confirmed, incurable romantic inside these walls would not understand that which we feel."

"It only matters what we feel... not what others feel or even think," she offered.

"Yet we must be aware of what people perceive... we are in a spotlight, the brightness and focus controlled by millions of Catholics who expect, and must believe, our love is reserved exclusively for the Church..."

"Because this is so... is it right?" she questioned.

"We have no rights... only to serve God," Justin reminded her.

"When I married the Church, I gave up my right to my body but not to my mind. I have in my heart the love for all of God's creatures... am I at fault for having a greater love for one particular creature?"

"The fault is not with you, dear Mary Frances... the fault is with the system. No one can ever imagine the thousands of our Catholic brothers and sisters of the cloth who have faced this same emotional battle. One day, perhaps not too distant, things will change. Priests will marry...maybe even to nuns... if not for love, perhaps for convenience."

"And I would not be surprised that it would become mandatory for priests to marry only nuns," she said wryly.

"At least the fathers would have some assurances of bedding virgins," Justin said, chuckling, almost pleased with his risqué remark.

Mary Frances looked back at him, smiled, and admonished him as a mother would a child, "You're being impossible."

"Impossible... because of this emotion, this sadness in my heart? Improbable? Why, because my fate has been intertwined with yours? Realistically, because I know that we cannot be together, I am unable to speak the words which are in me, I cannot command them to come forth," Justin said.

She glanced down at her hands quickly, and then spoke hesitantly, "Just a short while ago, I was sad for other reasons, and you gave me the strength to go forward, to search for an answer. I found I was feeling sorry for myself and burdened you with my feelings. It seems so childish now that I seem to have my priorities in better order.

"I am glad that you are content with your resolve, my dearest. I am afraid that events now taking place will preclude us having an opportunity such as the time we had in Israel, or even this meeting, to ever happen again. I'm glad we've had this chance to speak quietly and openly," Justin said. He picked a hibiscus from the branch and placed it in her hand. Then he re-seated himself beside her.

"And may I be so bold as to question why our relationship must end so abruptly?" She raised her voice, and just as quickly blushed.

"I see you still have absolutely no fear of me, you not only have a will of iron, but a whim of iron too," he smiled. "And you have coined the proper word. 'Bold" you are, but I love you for it." Justin looked back at her, feeling surprised at his words. They both became hushed.

"And I love you, Justin, in a way unknown to me, more than any man I have ever known. In you I see the good of man... the nobility of all mankind. I will always have a secret corner of my heart reserved for your friendship and love. You have filled me with your spirit and offered me your hand of compassion," Mary Frances said as tears welled in her eyes.

"And I share a kinship and bond with you that I'll never fully understand. I think I now know the love of a woman, my heart cries out for your touch, a feeling of contentment when we are near; still something within my mind draws me away to a greater calling. I don't know what fate has destined for me. The Cross of Jesus shadows everything I do. My life is no longer in my control. I am standing at the throne of God and He has yet to tell me what He has in store for me," Justin said quietly.

Can God in His infinite wisdom banish us from even a platonic relationship? Are we not brother and sister of the same family?" she appealed.

"Events are about us which are beyond our control, and we must transcend even our feelings for each other," Justin replied, not too sure if he believed his own words.

"Must I call upon the rage of angels to breech this closing door? Can I not interfere in the plans of man?" Mary Frances pleaded.

"The door to my heart is always open to you, dear Mary Frances. The days' ahead, place burdens upon us, and we'll be tested by God Himself. We dare not tempt these events for we have no control over them." He said with resign.

"And shall these events destroy the only human relationship with absolute meaning that I have ever had?" she asked.

He shook his head. "What we have shared can never be erased. We must draw upon our inner selves to remember with fondness the time that our Lord has allowed us to share with each other."

She hesitated, searching his face with tearful eyes. "I know of closer relationships between some sisters and priests. Even a few Cardinals have been known to entertain a relationship, within the grounds of propriety, of course," she beseeched.

"Mary Frances," he said, "this is impossible. Then again," he added, "perhaps I'll not be strong enough to accept what's in store for me."

Her expression suddenly turned to amazement. "Blessed Mary, can this be? Would they even dare have the courage to nominate an American?" Her shock seemed to increase.

"I must caution you that you do not have the situation in clear focus," Justin told her.

"That's it! They want you for Pope!" She caught her breath for a moment while the thought sank in.

"If it be the will of the conclave, then I must serve as I have always served God." Justin forced himself to speak in a matter-of-fact manner.

"If you shall be named Pope, I know in my heart that it is you who have the courage and capability to lead the church; your strength and compassion will unite the people."

"Human unity is an awesome power. If it ever could be accomplished, the world could be changed overnight. It is not so simple. The bottom equation is that Jesus is pitted against Satan, nothing more, the highest and lowest denominator. The good deeds of man are weighed against the evil deeds of man, each adding and subtracting in the course of human events. Human unity will never be accomplished as long as man lives without direction or without love. Only one former Pope came close to arriving at a solution. Giovanni Battista Montini, Pope Paul VI, lived by the theme of 'Witness by Service.'" Justin paused, then added, "unlike pompous CEO's of corporate America who live for stock options, signing bonuses, hefty salaries, and then they put the accountants and lawyers on the payroll. If the company looses money they don't worry because they already negotiated a retention bonus to turn the company around. They serve themselves at the expense of their shareholders."

"And shall we who serve have no benefits? Do we not also have the right to lead as we serve?" she asked, not really wanting to know.

"To be a servant of Christ is our benefit," Justin replied.

"Must the servants of Christ stay on their knees twenty-four hours a day?" she asked, "dismissed as shareholders without a say in the affairs of the Church?"

He looked at her knowing her sincerity and concern and said, "And should I become Pope, I shall put you in charge of all the sorrow in the world. Let us see if you can change that aspect of the human condition." He couldn't help but let out a slight laugh as he spoke, which was quickly stifled as Mary Frances responded.

"This task I would gladly take, as much for you as for God," she replied. Justin felt the flush on his face as her unyielding loyalty came forth confronting him.

"I joke with you and yet that haughty spirit which I greatly admire comes in waves upon me. Am I destined to have you by my side as counsel? If only it could be so. A woman behind the throne of Peter." He shook his head at the absurdity of it all.

"And why not? Was it not a woman who brought the Christ into the world?" she speculated as she watched his reaction.

"God grant me the wisdom to even dare to think of this...he paused then continued, "Shall you become my secret mistress? "Can we experience passion and remain chaste?"

"I will be at your side always if that is your will, for one who loves you as deeply as any woman has loved any man," she said.

"And can this love which you profess live without the spark of nearness which all men and women yearn for?" he whispered.

"I know in my heart that the greatest love is one which can never be totally satisfied. The exquisite hurt of unrequited passion of the mind does not transcend that which rests in the compartments of one's heart. I love my Christ in one manner, my family in another, and yet I cannot say that either of these loves is equal to this new found feeling I have for you," Mary Frances said.

"Fate has decided that we are to be caught up in a mysterious plan which will forever deny us that which our bodies may cry out for." He reached out to touch her as she turned from him in her frustration.

Once again, she retorted, "We'll not be as two ships that pass in the night. God will show us the way we can be near to each other. He'll give us the answers in due course, I'm sure of it."

"We'll be opposed at every turn. All eyes will be upon us. We cannot bring dishonor on our calling with clandestine meetings and hand holdings in the dark," Justin said.

"If they are without sin, let them cast the first stone for we shall know in our hearts that our love is pure and perfect," she argued.

"You are truly a wonder. You speak so openly, your trust so unique, and yet I am reluctant to reciprocate," Justin said.

"Speak only what is in your heart," she answered. "God understands our needs. He will not allow this to end with a noiseless thud, a soundless whimper and then oblivion. He is a compassionate God who watches over his children."

"We must seek His guidance. We must go to the altar of God and ask for His direction." Justin said.

"I already know in my heart His answer," Mary Frances said confidently.

"Unbelievable. Absolutely unbelievable, now you even have God in your corner. Such a woman should be at my side always," Justin said. He then held her gently. They remained silent in the solitude of the Vatican garden. He felt contentment for he had found that missing ingredient in his life. And he vowed that somehow he would find a way never to lose it. She in turn felt a new insight into the mystique of her own womanhood, at once delivered from the stifling protection of her Catholic calling. Mary Frances felt reborn, fresh and alive and now able to look with clear eyes toward the future.

CHAPTER THIRTY

A mid-afternoon mass of the Holy Spirit in the Pauline Chapel marked the formal opening of the election Conclave. The initial ritual was completed at 3:30 p.m. and the Sacred College along with various service personnel began assembling in the Sistine Chapel. The Cardinal Dean began reading Part Two of the special Constitution consisting of over 5,000 words established by Pope Paul VI in 1975. Each elector followed the script in his native language. After the Cardinal Dean completed his assignment, he began to read the formula for the solemn Conclave oath.

"Each and all of us Cardinal Electors gathered in this Conclave, promise, vow, and swear a solemn and sacred oath, that each of us and all of us will observe all prescriptions and laws that are contained in the Apostolic Constitution of the Supreme Pontiff, Paul VI, which was promulgated by him on October 1, 1975 and which begins with the words 'In Electing the Roman Pontiff...'"

After the words were spoken, the Cardinal Dean invited each Cardinal to stand and come forward to recite their acceptance.

Justin was the forty-first elector to step up to the high altar and in a clear voice he said: "And I, Justin Cardinal Kennedy, so vow and swear." He placed his hand on an ornate Bible and added: "So help me, God, and this Gospel of God, which I touch. Each of the Cardinals recited the same oath, their rank determining the order of roll call.

An exhortation ritual was the next order of business. Many Cardinals knew this could be a stepping-stone to the Chair of Peter if the sermon were of a spiritual leadership quality. Some in attendance compared it to a keynote address at an American political convention. Cardinal Kurt Wilhelm of Germany stepped to the podium and began the exhortation.

"Dear brothers in Christ" Wilhelm began, his voice booming over the hushed group of Cardinal electorates. "Welcome to a new era. First, I wish to congratulate Cardinal Kennedy for his effort in securing the Cross of Jesus and bringing it to all of us as the finest gift we can imagine. His work in that regard is over. Ours is just beginning. I call on you who have had the benefit of years of experience to join with me to carry the Cross to a higher level for the benefit of the Church. And, while we are raising the hopes and dreams of the parishioners for a new beginning, I ask that Cardinal Kennedy continue his work in searching for other religious relics and bring them to us for the betterment of the Church. When man works in the field where he excels above other men, he does the most good for the entire Church. Cardinal Kennedy has now proven himself as the best in the field of archeological recovery. I ask each of you, what is it in the universe of the Church that you do best? I have asked myself the question and the answer is always the same. I am a theologian first but also an administrator...a businessman... a man trained to solve difficult problems. There are some of you out there with similar backgrounds, perhaps younger and with less experience, but nevertheless having an aptitude to deal with people, problems, and ideas. You are the future of the Church. All you need is nurturing by someone willing to serve as your mentor. I will not dwell on the problems of the past...instead I invite you to solve them with me. There is no place in the Church for those who's physical desires outstrip them of understanding the difference between right and wrong. We all know that. We must be honest with ourselves, with our fellow clergymen, and our parishioners. We cannot condone, deny, or cover up sins that will bring dishonor and ruination on our heritage. Yes, we must cater to the hearts and souls of the people but, at the same time, we must not close our eyes to fiscal responsibility that is required of all businesses. You do not go to an electrician to operate on a tumor. You go to the man that is best for the job." He allowed his words to sink into the hearts and minds of the red caps as they broke out in applause. "We cannot deal with problems in fear. Fear is an emotional reaction to a difficult problem. It is an escape mechanism...the fight or flight syndrome. No...we must take a step back, analyze the situation, and act promptly and decisively once our business decision has been made." Confident glances were exchanged and papers shuffled as some of the Cardinals fingered through the copy of his exhortation previously supplied to all. "We must deal candidly with our past problems. Pedophilic clergy is assaulting us from with-in. We are being assailed from the outside by hoards of lawyers. And, I say that this too shall pass as long as we recognize that we cannot neglect our duties, we must deal with them. We need a new highway to travel. Open the gates and allow the glory of the Church to cleanse the minds and souls of our brethren. This new endeavor is not to be highlighted by symbols or relics from the past. We need action and we need it now!" he demanded as he pounded the lectern. "Leadership is the clarion call of the hour...decisive leadership to guide the ship of state to calm waters where once again the faithful can anchor their souls in a beloved union with God. I profess to love my Church and all it's glory. I have devoted my life to it and gladly give this life to save it". Wilhelm skirted the unwritten rule of the conclave not to promote or politic on behalf of one's self and seemed to have gotten away with it. "Many of our brothers here have publicly elevated me as the heir apparent and I have told them, it is in the hands of God, not mine. If this is your will, it is also God's will." Wilhelm paused, took a sip of water, cleared his throat and continued. "In these coming hours, as the ballots are placed in your capable hands, ask yourselves, 'are we courageous enough to cast aside our emotions in favor of what you and I know is really required to administer the Catholic Empire?' In this time and in this place we stare into the face of the future of our beloved church...we dare not fail?" The German Cardinal's voice ended as it started, with a powerful performance, as he bowed slightly and left the lectern thinking to himself that his speech effectively pigeon-holed Justin, taking him out of contention, just as he planned.

The Cardinals left the Sistine and began mingling together carefully discussing alliances with many commenting positively on Wilhelm's exhortation. Each ear was tuned for the bell, which would signal the official opening of the Conclave, the bell to sound only after the <u>Nervi</u> room, used for Papal Audiences and capable of receiving more than 10,000 people, was secured. Surveillance teams made certain that only authorized personnel were in attendance. The task was complete down to "sweeping" the areas with electronic units looking for any listening device to preclude any recurrence of a breech of security, which had occurred during Alphonse's election, when the media reported his nomination even before the final ballots were counted.

At exactly 5:15 p.m. the bell rang. Justin felt a chill run through his body. Many of the other Cardinals felt varied emotions. A few Prelates, who had experienced the election process before, walked reverently into the chapel; others were not sure of their emotions as mental drawbridges began to rise. The magnificent purple and white robes of the Cardinalship competed with the riot of colors used by Michelangelo when he created the inspiring works and frescoes on the chapel ceilings. The procession in the Sistine began. Various clerics, assisting in the Conclave, solemnly followed the Bishops and Arch Bishops, as the <u>Maestro di Cerionia</u> carried the Papal cross into the chapel. The strict protocol of rank followed to the letter as the first of the Cardinals entered. The Cardinal Bishops, the highest rank of the College, strode with restrained majesty. The Cardinal priests and Cardinal deacons, no less resplendent in dress and demeanor, followed. The magic of the moment seemed to have a physical life of its own as thunderous organ music, flooded the chapel high.

The Cardinal Dean approached the altar and began to recite the prayer, "<u>Deus Qui Cord Fidelium</u>." Once completed, the <u>Maestro di Cerimonia</u> intoned the message for all but the Cardinals to depart. The strong admonition echoed across the cavernous Sistine. "<u>Extra Omnes</u>" were the two words that signaled the business of electing a Pope was at hand. Murmurs settled upon the assembling Cardinals as they sought their respective seats on the two levels of the chapel. The kingly canopies over each position were designed to remind them of their princely duties and responsibilities. A grunt from Cardinal Botticelli echoed in the great room as he thumped his huge bulk down on a protesting wooden seat. Restrained babble continued as throats were cleared and looks exchanged.

Kurt Cardinal Wilhelm smiled benignly as he assumed his position, feeling his many years of waiting for the Papal throne were now bearing the fruits of his labors. A discourse was given on the sacred duties facing the Cardinalship. The key element was the building expectation of exciting debate with no holds barred.

The Marshall of the Conclave dressed in a Renaissance costume of magnificent colors, accepted the keys from Cardinal Wilhelm, assured that the area was cleared of cameras and other restricted items. He walked over to the huge doors, which was his duty to close to all outsiders, signifying the commencement of the election process. The Marshall pushed the first of the double doors to the threshold and reached for the second door to complete the sequestering of the Cardinals.

"Wait," Capelli cried out startling the Marshall who stopped dead in his tracks looking bewildered as he saw the vestments of the rank of Cardinal and red cap being worn by Capelli. Standing behind Capelli were twenty-one men each adorned with the familiar red cap and dressed as Cardinals. Capelli walked past the Marshall and entered the <u>Nervi</u> room followed by the twenty-one. The second door was then closed. The sound of the frame striking the metal latch reverberated throughout the hall and for a moment there was dead silence. The rest of the world was sealed off, with one exception, the communication allowed between the Cardinal Grand Penitentiary and the Tribunal of the Sacred Penitentiary. Emergency messages were permitted as the single link from behind the doors and allowed the priorities of God's mercy to take precedence over the election of the Pope.

Silence was fleeting as an undercurrent of muffled whispering began and Wilhelm and Lattimer rose from their seats and stood bewildered at what they just witnessed.

"Monsignor Capelli, can you explain what is going on here with you and your entourage of disciples?" Wilhelm shouted out as he looked around the room at the other Cardinals whose faces reflected similar surprise.

"What is the meaning of this?" Wilhelm demanded. "Why are these men dressed as Cardinals permitted entry in to this sacred chamber? I am the head of the interim hierarchy chosen by Alphonse himself to run the affairs of the Catholic Church until a successor is selected. I insist these men leave at once!" Wilhelm, uncertain of what was happening took the offensive recognizing that twenty-two new Cardinals might certainly tip the balance of power in the election of a new Pope.

Sun Yet responded to the verbal challenge. "These new Cardinals were selected by Pope Alphonse shortly before his death." They have all the rights and privileges to those of the same rank in the College of Cardinals." Wilhelm was well aware of the Pope's ability to elevate prelates to the College of Cardinals secretly by invoking the rule of "in pectore", a method used when the Pope believed a public announcement would be imprudent, usually for political reasons. "You are aware of the Pope's power of "in pectore," are you not?" Sun Yet knew the answer as Wilhelm prided himself on his knowledge of canon law and rules of the Church.

"Of course, my brother," Wilhelm said biting his tongue. "And you are certainly aware of the fact that a Cardinal named "in pectore" does not have the privileges of membership in the College of Cardinals until public announcement of his elevation."

"Yes, your Eminence. You are quite correct. Pope Alphonse left instructions to open his safe upon death and remove a sealed document written in his own hand and to provide you with it upon your request," Sun Yet offered in rebuttal.

"Then, by all means, bring it to me, now. Proceedings will be held up until the document can be examined," Wilhelm instructed.

"Your demand has been anticipated. Vatican guards just outside the chamber doors are guarding the document as instructed by our late Pope Alphonse. Cardinal Lattimer, would you be so kind as to open the door and receive the document for his Eminence Cardinal Wilhelm?" Lattimer accustomed to performing errand work for the German Cardinal opened the massive doors, requested receipt of the evidence, and presented it to Wilhelm.

"You will notice that the document is embossed with the Papal Seal, a tribute to its authenticity. And, of course on behalf of all of us present, you were selected to smash the ring of his Holiness upon his death, as security that a forgery could not occur." Sun Yet reminded him and then returned to his seat. Wilhelm opened the final missive written by the Pope breaking the seal of the envelope and studied the written words without looking up at Sun Yet as if to dismiss him.

After a moment, Wilhelm broke his silence. "I can verify the document is written in Pope Alphonse's hand. I can verify that except for Monsignor Capelli whom, by this document is presumably elevated to Cardinal Deacon, the remaining prelates have been designated as Cardinal Priests. I would be the first to welcome our new brethren if, under canon law, this document could be honored. But, I am sorry to say it cannot!" Wilhelm stated with finality. "You see my esteemed colleagues, even if a dying Pontiff leaves a written indication of the secret Cardinal's identity, his successor is not bound by that appointment unless it has been announced!" A broad smile came to Lattimer's face as he admired his friend's command of the legal intricacies of the Roman Catholic Church.

Sun Yet waited for the whispers of his brothers to subside then stood again and addressed Wilhelm. "Cardinal," he started. "Pope Alphonse was aware of the condition of which you speak. I ask those present who served the last mass with Pope Alphonse to please stand." As soon as the words left his mouth, a Cardinal rose from his seat followed by another and then another until twelve were standing in addition to Wilhelm and Lattimer.

"Look around you my brother. You will see twelve Cardinals to whom Pope Alphonse published his intentions of elevating these prelates to the rank of Cardinal at his final mass. Please notice that at least one third of those standing are confidants of yours. They will attest, if asked, to their oath of confidentiality given to Pope Alphonse promising that they would speak to the truth of this matter only at the time the doors to these chambers were closed. The requirement of public announcement has been satisfied!" Sun Yet said emphatically and sat down before Wilhelm could reply. Wilhelm held his tongue. He still had a war to win and this was one battle he would surely loose. His statesmanship would now take over.

"On behalf of all Cardinals present and as acting Camerlengo of the College of Cardinals, I welcome our new brothers and remind you that when casting your vote for our new Pope, you must disavow prior pledges, commitments, and promises all of which no longer bind you." Wilhelm attempted to repair the damage he had done and minimize any alienation that he might have projected against these additional voters.

The participants reserved the balance of the first day for rest and prayer. Within the first hours, however, consultations began. Small groups began to assemble. Some were meeting each other for the first time. Speculation undulated across the hall, as lesser-experienced Cardinals vied for tidbits of information fearful they would not be able to get on the train of the winning candidate before it left the station. Of particular interest was the elite gathering near the cell of the Cardinal from Germany. Wilhelm, was now holding court with five of the most powerful members of the college.

"I shall announce your name under the mode of 'Inspiration,'" Cardinal Avenel of Austria told Kurt Wilhelm.

"I believe we would be lost if we approached that mode. Never in modern history has a Pope been chosen because of 'Inspiration' by one of its members. It would take a dose of mass hysteria for every member here to shout 'Elezione...' The sentiment must be unanimous. No...We must be patient, choose our time," Cardinal Martin Cromwell said as he looked to his mentor, Kurt Wilhelm, for agreement.

"It is my judgment..." Cardinal Botticelli began, wiping perspiration from his drooping jowls, "that we press for selection under the second mode of 'Delegation.'" Botticelli and his confederates knew it would take a minimum of nine Cardinals to form a delegation and report back to the Cardinalship its selection. The uneven number had been established to ensure that a tie would not occur.

"I doubt..." Cardinal Wilhelm said, "if we could muster a sufficient number to ensure our candidacy by delegation. It must be by scrutiny...open forum is our best chance."

"I can assure you, Eminence, you shall pass the test... you shall become the Pope," Cardinal Avenel said.

"It depends on who is administering the litmus test...we have competition from that American," Cromwell added between clenched teeth.

"He is disliked...some would call it envy because of his relationship with Alphonse...however, his popularity is growing because of his involvement with the finding of the Cross...on the other hand, being an American is not in his favor," Avenel spat out the words, his opinions see-sawing back and forth.

"Everyone is disliked or even hated for many different reasons. I would venture that even in the remote jungle, the native is hated... perhaps by the lion, but hated nonetheless," Wilhelm said as he filled his pipe with an aromatic blend of tobacco.

"Then we must tar him with another brush. We must somehow lower his profile while still maintaining decorum," Cardinal Avenel suggested.

"My dear Charles... if you continue reversing your verbal engine, you may end up stripping your tongue," Wilhelm admonished. The red-faced Avenel did not reply to the reprimand.

The silence surrounding the group was as heavy as a coffin lid. It was a dilemma that had more questions than solutions.

For a time Justin remained alone. Then he began to walk, his gaze taking in the genius of Michelangelo. He felt finely tuned to the finger of God, which was reaching but not quite touching, the form of Adam, reaching to infuse him with life. Justin felt the finger of God near him, yet he did not know for certain whether it was a finger of papal direction or a finger pointed in accusation for the many shortcomings of his own life. The spell broke as Justin noticed once again that Michelangelo had given his Adam a navel. Perhaps it was a hint from the famous artist that he had some personal reservations about the authenticity of the creation of Adam from water and clay, he mused to himself. Justin lost himself in deeper thought under the magnificent scenes by Pergino,

Ghirlandaio and Rosselli. The paintings overshadowing an ornate marble floor so exquisite, it seemed a sacrilege to walk upon it. He felt a hand on his shoulder, and was startled for a moment. Then he recognized the smiling face of the Cardinal from the Netherlands.

"I am sorry for the intrusion into your thoughts, Eminence," Cardinal Helmut Aardweig said.

"It is no intrusion, dear friend...I was in fact admiring the paintings. They are a humbling factor when one considers the awesome responsibility we face in this most sacred of places," Justin replied.

"They are indeed inspiring for those of us favored to serve as Cardinals of the Church... I wondered if the view is different for the one who will sit upon the Chair of Peter before this conclave is completed," Aardweig's voice questioned.

"Is not the Pope supposed to see more clearly, feel more intently, react more swiftly?" Justin asked.

"The Pope is supposed to act, to lead and to explain," Aardweig said.

Suspicious glances were directed toward Justin and the Dutchman as a covey of Cardinals approached. Wilhelm intently watching the group embracing each other as he puffed contemplatively on his pipe.

"It appears the shepherd is gathering his flock," Cardinal Botticelli whispered to Wilhelm from his vantage point.

"You concern yourself with minor details... competition and politics are a necessary part of these matters. All must leave here with a feeling of accomplishment... fulfillment for their reverend duties. It is an unknown candidate which can create havoc," Wilhelm said.

"I believe it is a question on how to preserve already tainted bacon." Botticelli replied.

"And what is that to imply... are you privy to information you wish to share with me?" Wilhelm cocking his head, pipe smoke billowing around his face.

"I also have important friends in the Vatican... after all, it is a way of life for us," the Cardinal said, his face smug.

"Very well, my loyal brother, I have on occasion made alliances for matters which affect the Church. If—and I must underscore 'IF'—your information is beneficial, we shall see that you are properly rewarded," Wilhelm smiled benignly.

"It seems our American has had some consultations with Dr. Carlton... ostensibly for migraine headaches! Ah, I see by the look of surprise on your face you feel the same way I did when the information reached me... just why would anyone seek the aid of a psychiatrist for headaches? My inquiries..." Botticelli's eyes seemed to disappear under hooded lids as he continued, "have produced information that Kennedy is under mental duress and must have therapy." Botticelli's grin matched the girth of his face.

Wilhelm's expression did not change. Only he knew the direction of the computer-like thoughts pulsing through his brain. He tapped the ashes from his pipe and spoke, "Perhaps as Colleridge's <u>Ancient Mariner,</u> he is fatally wounded in his quest for the papacy." Wilhelm knew that while he had the session tapes retrieved by his mistress, he could not use them. He could never explain how they happened to come into his possession without incriminating himself. No...the tapes could only be revealed by someone else. And that would only occur as a last possible resort.

A dozen or more electors would meet anywhere from a few moments or for as long as an hour, throughout the first evening. The clan of Italian Cardinals seemed to be the most boisterous and vocal. The hand waving and urgent gestures punctuated their dialogue. One could not tell if they were talking about the weather or more important matters. The wary Italian contingent, fearful of losing another election, had already selected their candidate and made plans to announce their man by "inspiration," hoping the Cardinalship would be anxious to get on with the process and be done with the matter. Some of their heated dialogue was as salty as a deer lick. The night passed quickly.

Promptly at eight a.m., Cardinal Fitzgerald rang a silver bell to bring the conclave to order. Grim dispositions added to the off-key singing of "Veni, Creator Spiritus." The pace quickened as furtive glances were exchanged across the great hall. The assembly collectively held its breath in expectation and silence, realizing that one among them might rise and announce that he has just been inspired by God to announce a candidate. The ten minutes of silence seemed to be endless. Finally, at the last probable moment, Eugenio Cardinal Navaronne, Arch Bishop of Milan rose majestically to his full five foot two inch height, cleared his throat loudly to ensure proper attention, and then began speaking.

"My Lord Cardinals, in view of the singular virtue and probity of the Most Reverend Carlo Cardinal Constanza of Milan, I would judge him worthy to be elected Roman Pontiff, and I now choose him as il papa."

"Elezione," came the sparse reply, not surprisingly, exclusively from the Italian group.

"Inspired by God indeed... more like struck dumb with lightning," Fitzgerald whispered to a confederate who replied in kind; "We are not wont to eat fruit from a poisoned tree."

Ten more minutes of silence prevailed as the embarrassed Italians saw the final hold on the papacy crumble. Three Popes in succession, not of Italian birth, spelled the final end to the stranglehold enjoyed by the Romantia.

Cardinal Fitzgerald rang the silver bell at the end of the second ten-minute time period. He scanned the room for yet another "inspirational" nomination; a dead silence was his answer as he asked for the election process to continue. Fitzgerald was anticipating a request for a selection "by delegation" from the backers of Cardinal Wilhelm. He was more amused than surprised when none was forthcoming from either Botticelli or Avenel. Fitzgerald rang the silver bell once again as he addressed the assemblage.

"My Lord Cardinals and Most Reverend Brothers," he said, gaining everyone's attention. "Since no one person has received unanimous sentiment to be elected by inspiration, and since we have not heard a suggestion that we proceed by delegation, we now direct that the Sacred College begin the process of election of the next Pontiff by scrutiny." Upon that instruction, the Maestro di Cerimonia began to distribute a packet of cream-colored ballots to each Cardinal.

"It is time, Justin..." Cardinal Sun Yet of Korea said as he took the American's hand and held it. "Are you prepared to take your place where God has directed?"

"If it is the will of the conclave and the will of God, I shall serve as Jesus Christ directs my life," Justin replied. In his mind he felt as if he were rowing his raft towards the Titanic. Deliberations began immediately, each Cardinal speaking whatever was in his heart at the moment. None were forthcoming with a name to be put forth to the Cardinalship.

Cardinal Fitzgerald of Ireland moved the dialogue off dead center as he stood and began addressing the members: "In this age, we must consider fully that the man who will fill the shoes of the fisherman must be a man for all seasons... If debate and discussion takes hours, days or even weeks and nay, months, we must be prepared to take that time, for we would not be the true servants of Christ if we act in haste and regret in a sea of turmoil. But..." Fitzgerald's voice boomed over the gathering, "if we find that one among us is surrounded by the halo of God, we must act swiftly while the light is shining and giving us that beacon to lead us to greatness."

Many of the Cardinals looked around the room, some expecting a bright countenance around someone's head.

"We have already heard references by a few of our esteemed brothers that we must consider the race and nationality of the next Vicar," Fitzgerald continued. "To this I say; the only consideration must be that our Pope shall be bold, decisive and above all be able to move this Holy Church of Roman Catholics during the twenty-first century!" Fitzgerald bowed politely towards the smattering of hand clapping.

The majority of the Cardinalship knew in their own minds that they were collectively able to block an election but that they would have to eventually vote for someone. If their important vote was for a man of their own choosing who had absolutely no chance of succeeding, it behooved them to be ready to vote for the most papal of candidates from the front runners. Even though the Pope was considered above suspicion and void of rancor or spite, an assignment list prepared by the Pope elect would find his supporters receiving the most prestigious of positions within the walls of Vatican City.

Cardinal Avenel rose to his feet as the members hushed. It was no secret that he was the stalking horse for the German Cardinal. Wilhelm sat stoically as Avenel began his drum roll of dialogue.

"We do not need to see the light of which our beloved brother from Ireland has spoken. The sign we need is in deeds... deeds and accomplishments by an experienced leader of our Church. I agree wholeheartedly that the question of race or nationality must be brushed aside once and for all. Therefore, we now have a simple choice before us. We look upon one among us who has the credentials, the experience and the qualifications to assume the Chair of Peter. He is the most Reverend Cardinal Kurt Wilhelm from the Republic of West Germany." Avenel made a grand gesture towards the German Cardinal as all eyes followed.

In these few moments, the membership had the time to reflect upon the candidate... Did he ever do any injustice to them? Would he look with favor if I vote for him? As a German would he form his own clique of power brokers, form his own "Gestapo," as the Italians created their own in-house "Mafia" in past years? These and other questions drifted silently around the Conclave.

The vote began as each Cardinal wrote in his ballot. Each of them, tried to disguise their respective handwriting, an action totally unnecessary as the burning of the ballots would occur in any event.

The scrutiny of the ballots progressed rapidly, the ritual followed to the letter. The final tally showed that Cardinal Wilhelm had solid support for candidacy but fell twenty-six votes short of election. The voting did not attest that the Conclave was deeply divided; rather, the count graphically pointed out that Kurt Wilhelm was simply not papable at this juncture. Under the rules, his name could still be written on succeeding ballots.

Cardinal Sun Yet quietly proposed the name of Justin Kennedy along with the admonition that the world was awaiting a leader of his stature. Justin's participation in the finding of the Cross, was uppermost in the minds of all of the Red Caps. Cardinal Sun Yet's warning to seek, not debate, was met with nods of approval. Cardinal Wilhelm saw his candidacy disappearing as quickly as a wisp of smoke blown by a stiff wind. He shuffled uneasily in his chair at the thought.

"This man, Cardinal Justin Jerome Kennedy, has been sent to us by God," Sun Yet attested. "The words of Joel tell us, your young men shall see visions and your old men shall dream dreams. Let us tonight share in the visions of this man. We have had our quantum share of dreamers. Now, this hour, I call my brothers to act swiftly while the hand of God is upon us to break from tradition, break from the norm, break the chains that bind us." Sun Yet paused for a few moments. Justin sat uneasily in his chair as Sun Yet continued.

"When we elect a new Pope in the hours before us, we must realize that he will rule over a new Church, a Church that was once powerful, unified and monolithic. The division of the Church today is traced to our ineffectiveness. The Church of which the new Vicar shall rule will be vastly different from the one ruled by his predecessors. The very issues of fundamental belief will come under attack... he must be able to decide on issues never dreamed of by any Pope before." Sun Yet paused again, reached for a glass of water and sipped slowly giving time for his words to sink into the collective minds of the

Cardinalship. He was now assured of their rapt attention and began again.

"He must attack the acute problems facing the Catholic community, and assume a high profile among the leaders of the world. He must discard the political and financial weights hanging about his neck. We have received a message from Jesus that this is our final hour... if we fail... all is lost. Therefore, we dare not hand the shepherd's staff to someone who has not the foresight to rule with a strong hand and keen mind. We have this opportunity to change, change in the form of a revolution... a revolution, I might add, is already underway. The question of terrorism or Democracy will matter little, for our main thrust must be the levels of life and social values for all peoples of the world. If we fail, our immortal souls shall perish in the flames of Hell. We have such a man before us... He is our man for all seasons, a man with thirty years yet to serve. My Lord Cardinals' listen to your hearts. Allow not the pressures of outside forces to dictate our choice for Pontiff. Give this man your vote. Let us shout to the world that this very night they have a Pope. Let the chant 'Habemus Papum' ring throughout the square. Let us begin."

A silence descended over the place as each Cardinal bent over his desk and wrote his vote on a sheet of paper, their respective choice for the next Vicar of Christ. The laborious count began. The silver chalice on the altar, placed to receive the ballots from the Cardinal electors, gleamed in the bright light of the Conclave. Justin stared at the vessel with the knowledge that the object was destined to change his life forever. His faith gave him strength to endure the pressures building around him.

A trio of Scrutineers took their place on the altar as the Cardinals sat back on their individual canopied thrones. The will of the Conclave now was determined on the cream colored ballots, each of them held in their hand. In honor of him finding the Cross, Cardinal Justin Kennedy was asked to be the first to approach the altar. He genuflected quickly, rose to his feet, his throat dry and gave the oath, "I swear by this Holy Altar that I have chosen as best as God has given me to see." Many assembled wondering if he cast his vote for himself. He placed his ballot into the Chalice and returned to his position. He made eye contact with Cardinal Sun Yet, the Oriental Cardinal destroying his own mask of inscrutability as he winked. Justin could not believe the gesture. His heart leaped at the display of loyalty shown under the most auspicious of moments. The remaining electors, each in turn, began approaching the altar and performed according to ritual. Within half an hour, the balloting was complete. The tension continuing to build as the Scrutineers initiated the task of counting and recording the consensus of the Conclave.

The Senior Scrutineer, Cardinal Dominguez, reached into the chalice and produced the first of the ballots. His countenance did not betray the vote. Dominguez noted the ballot on a two-column sheet of white paper, and then passed the ballot to his confederate to his left, who also recorded the ballot on his own tally sheet. Once accomplished, the ballot was handed to the remaining Scrutineer who then announced the vote in a loud voice to all assembled.

"Placet, the vote is affirmative." The first, an omen for Justin Kennedy many felt. The ballot then dropped into a second chalice under the watchful eyes of the Cardinalship, each in turn keeping their own tally sheets. The next five ballots were announced as Non Placets, which caused consternation on the face of Cardinal Enrique Capelli, the chief architect of the plan to elect Justin as Pope under the direction of the late Alphonse. Cardinal Wilhelm stared down at his desk. He pretended not to hear the whispered remark directed to him from a confederate. "It is impossible to unscramble eggs. Kennedy is finished." Then, suddenly, as if the hand of Alphonse was directing the balloting from beyond the grave, a series of thirty-seven consecutive Placet votes were recorded. The magic figure of positive votes, two-thirds plus one necessary to elect a new Pope seemed within reach. The numbers continued to mount as the Scrutineers studiously marked the tally sheets. Then it was completed. Whispered murmurs of relief, rippled through the great hall as the three, each initialing the others sheets for authenticity compared the totals.

The tension was over. The Roman Catholic Church had a new Vicar. His Most Reverend Eminence Cardinal Justin Jerome Kennedy of the United States of America was thrust into the pages of history, his chapters yet to be written. The Cross of Jesus Christ and the mysterious link with Judas Iscariot were destined to become the quotation marks of his reign.

Justin felt his legs begin to tremble, his heart beating wildly. His mind attempted to fathom what had just happened. A state of shock reflected upon his expressionless face; some assembled mistook the look as the countenance of heavenly serenity and were thus assured their vote was proper.

"Dear God, what have you pressed upon this unworthy servant?" Justin asked silently.

Cardinal Fitzgerald was quickly appointed new Cardinal Dean as the Conclave erupted into applause for Justin Kennedy. The Irish prelate rose to his full six foot three inch height and strode toward the front of the gathering. "Habemus Papam!" he shouted. "We have a Pope! Whosoever questions the authority of the new Pontiff between election and coronation is automatically excommunicated. The election true and confirmed has been done in the name of Lord Jesus Christ as our judge," he said according to tradition.

The Conclave could no longer contain itself; a babble of voices spoke out in various languages of the countries represented. Excitement and relief reigned for fifteen minutes as they congratulated themselves on the rapid change of leadership. Even Wilhelm accepted and understood his chance would have to wait for another day and another time. Permission was quickly granted to the Secretary of the Conclave and other clerics to enter and witness the acceptance and adoration ceremonies. All notes were collected and placed with the ballots in preparation for burning. The only evidence to be saved for posterity was the tally sheets, which would be sealed and placed in the archives.

The huge doors of the Sala Regia swung open as the invitees took their places in front of the thrones of the Cardinals. Justin, approached by Cardinal Fitzgerald, was taken by the arm and walked to the high altar.

"Acceptasne electionem de te canonice factam in Summum Pontificem?" he was asked.

"Accetto," Justin replied. The Italian members of the Conclave could hardly contain themselves. Justin's use of the Italian verb quickly endeared him to them as they grasped for any indication that the new Pontiff would be attuned to their special needs.

"And by what name do you wish to be called?" Fitzgerald asked.

"We shall be called... Constantine!" Justin replied, and thus with the decision made, he would be referred to as Pope Constantine for the rest of his life.

The responses to his chosen name varied around the great hall. Some felt it befitting, others not quite certain of the connotation or reason for the choice. Cardinal Fitzgerald kneeled in front of Justin and kissed the hand of his new Pontiff. The canopies of the Cardinals' individual thrones came rustling down, some one at a time, others like cascading dominos. Each of the membership stood in line for the hand kissing ritual of fidelity, the first of the three adoration rites. Justin received each of them with humility, some receiving a spoken greeting, others a silent blessing and a benevolent smile.

The singing of Te Deum, the hymn of joy of the Catholic liturgies completed the second phase of the ceremony.

Cardinal Fitzgerald gave the signal to put the match to the notes and ballots mixed with a chemical in the small stove. The white smoke signaled to the awaiting world that a new Pope had been selected. The Plaza of St. Peter's would ring with the cheers of thousands assembled. At the sign of the white smoke, thousands began their pilgrimage to the Square as media sources flashed the news to the inhabitants of the Earth. At that moment, everyone became a Catholic, at least in brotherhood. The hundreds already in the Square were increasing in what seemed to be geometric numbers by the minute

Justin was quickly ushered into the 'Room of Tears' to be outfitted in Papal vestments. The same room used by previous Popes to remain alone to contemplate the momentous occurrence of being elected to lead the 1.1 billion Catholics worldwide and to become the Vicar of Christ. He could hear the noise from the Square as he proceeded through the palazzo in the direction of the loggia in the facade of San Pietro. He stood in the background as Cardinal Fitzgerald walked to the front of the balcony where the announcement would be made to the masses. Papal colors of maroon, white and gold had been draped over the front railing. Fitzgerald grasped the microphone, took a deep breath as the crowd became silent as if an invisible hand had stricken them mute.

"I announce a great joy. We have a Pope!" Thunderous applause and cheering erupted as Fitzgerald held his arms out flapping them slightly like a college quarterback pleading for the fans to be quiet so he could call an audible from the line indicating the next play. "He is our Most Eminent and Reverend Lord Cardinal Bishop Justin Kennedy, of the United States of America. He has chosen to serve under the name of Constantine The Second."

The words echoed across the cavernous square. A few faint cheers were duly recorded. Cardinal Wilhelm smiled knowingly at the muted reaction. Murmurs slowly turned into shouts and then into sounds resembling an oncoming tornado. Waves of cheers began to swell the decibel level of the crowd, each adding to the first until a crescendo crashed against the doors of St. Peter's. Cries of joy filled the air. Cardinal Fitzgerald turned to Justin. "Holy Father, the people are ready to receive you."

Justin knew he was not prepared for this moment. He silently prayed for direction as he stepped forth into the bright sunlight of the Square. He would speak from the heart. The crowd reacted while Justin Kennedy looked over the Square. Shouts of "Viva il papa" filling the air as he looked over the crowd, astonished at the size of the gathering. He began to speak, choosing English knowing his native tongue would best convey the very real thoughts of his mind; reassuring thoughts for the millions of Catholics awaiting his word.

"Today is an opportunity," he began in a firm, strong voice. "An opportunity to see and to hear and to understand. I will be straight to the point with you as you deserve nothing less," he continued. "Our former Popes had the opportunities to renounce temporal power and to return to the simplicity of the gospel and provide for the needy. This they failed to do. We must now return to this simplicity and give up the elements within our dogma which are a deadly cancer eating away at the very roots of our faith. We insist on masculine priests, yet we argue with celibacy! We fight for the rights of the unborn, yet we do little to stop starvation of babies across the earth! We no longer have the choice to make changes slowly. We must act boldly! We must do as our hearts dictate. We must face the issues confronting us with vigor.

Shall we pit one Catholic brother or sister against another because of the choice of a lifestyle? If a mass is said in Latin, what is in error? Does not God hear all tongues? We are carving the name of the Catholic Church onto our tombstone with each edict that fits well with the Church, but not with the people it wishes to rule. I am talking about a revolution... a revolution to begin today. At this hour, I shall ignite the torch and light the way." The crowd yelled and applause drowned out his voice momentarily, and then he began again.

"The Catholic Church shall become the beacon to guide upon forever. If we fail in this endeavor, we must resign ourselves to the fact that the institutional church is finished...dead! I refuse to officiate at the funeral, therefore, I pledge myself to be the lynch pin to connect this Church with all peoples. I have used up half of my allotted eight hundred or so months on this earth. This next portion, God grant, shall be dedicated to the proposition that all men and women are God's creatures. In the beginning, our Church was handed the task of creating equality for all. Our ancient Scriptures are the blueprints for this equality. The tools of our minds have been given to build, and yet, what have we created? We have helped spawn evil in the world where money is king. Greed and avarice the queen, and lost souls the inhabitants." At this, the crowd again exploded with applause. Shouts of joy chorused throughout the square. In the front row of the faithful, next to the barricades, Sister Mary Frances wiped away tears as her feelings for Justin Kennedy overwhelmed her.

"This spiritual death of which I speak is brought about when the people give up; when they no longer feel... and when they quit dreaming. We all are guilty of holding the smoking gun in our hands. We have been told by the past administrations of the Church that we can see the light at the end of the tunnel; it is time to exit that tunnel. We are, and will continue to be, the modern day Christ killers. For we have equated the stewardship which Jesus gave us with investments in oil and gold stocks. We were told to go forth into all the world. We have indeed gone into the world, where we have purchased all the real estate we could lay our hands on. Our wealth cannot be worth one single social injustice. As such, we must become involved in secular politics. The separation of the Church and State is nothing more than a lame excuse to remain quiet, while the world cries out for justice," the crowd listened in amazement to words they thought of but dared not speak.

"I pledge to you that we shall change this injustice and the Catholic Church shall become involved! From the parish priest in remote villages to the very throne of Peter, a new emphasis will begin with the words that shall become our standard: <u>Vox Populi</u>, the voice of the people." He paused while the crowd cheered, taking a sip from the glass of water on the table next to the podium.

"We shall have a relentless analysis of the Catholic Church. We shall rise high above Rome and take a look at the rest of the world. We shall change the rigid adherence to certain doctrinal points concerning contraception, the devil, women priests, and all other thorns that are pricking at the head of the Church. No longer will the Church cast a blind eye to clergy involved in pedophilia, by simply transferring the offending Priest from parish to parish thinking all is well as long as it is 'not in my neighborhood'. The highest members of the clergy who promote sexual abuse by failing to condemn and punish the offenders will no longer have the power to refuse to resign. That decision will be made for them and there will be no appeal. To those who are considered the traditionalists of our calling, I pledge that innovations in this modern age will not challenge the teaching authority of the Church. Nevertheless, the dogma of the Church will be tempered with reasoning and experience and we will throw away unrealistic rote used to force-feed Catholic theology to the masses." Justin paused to allow his words to sink in.

The reaction was one of stunned belief. Never in the history of the Church had any Pope the courage or the determination to speak of those things that were considered unmovable and unchangeable. Those who accept Catholicism must accept the intrinsic power coming from heaven itself. The infallibility of the Pope was now coming full circle. The single rule of the Church, never before challenged, was to be put to the test.

"We teach service to mankind." The American Pope continued, "and yet our poorest Catholic cousins are living in the most abject of poverty. They walk the dusty paths of villages in South America, their bellies swollen, eyes sunken, hearts heavy and bodies diseased as they enter the Church where our priest preaches to them about God's promises and love. If I were that priest, I would tear down the rich tapestries and use them to clothe my flock. I would take the golden crucifix and melt it into bullion. The silver chalice would be used to dispense rice to hungry mouths. And, I would know that Jesus Christ would have tears of joy in his eyes for I would indeed be about my Father's business."

Shock waves spread around the Square, like a ripple from a stone tossed into a lake, each wave building upon itself as satellite transmissions spread the words across Italy, the Mid-east, across the great oceans until it circumnavigated the earth. Peoples of different religious persuasions joined in the chorus and yet each heart knew this man of God was speaking the truth as no other man in Catholic history had dared.

"In conclusion, I pledge a new image of the faith. I shall, before this week is out appoint ten new Cardinals to assist the implementation of these new policies, all of whom shall be under the age of fifty. We have a laborious task ahead of us, and we shall be strong in our endeavors. Of the ten, I shall for the first time, appoint five women to the Cardinalship, those capable of bearing the responsibility to move us further into this new century. These appointees shall be the vanguard of a new emphasis fueled by input of Catholic women. We have for too long relegated many brilliant women to a life of servitude under the guise of service to God. We shall become the Church for all." Perspiration now trickled down Justin Kennedy's face as his mind shifted into higher gear. Reporters for L'Unita and il Manifesto raced to their respective city desks, for the biggest story since World War II was unfolding before them and the reporters were fully primed to massage the verbiage of the Pope.

Again, the crowd reacted as if in slow motion. The throng of over one hundred thousand began to chant, "il papa!" Many on their knees rose and shouted. Thousands more screamed their joy as the new Pontiff, raised his arms in blessing.

Justin's words were now soft and delicate, as if he had suddenly throttled back on his dynamic delivery. He felt the hand of God on his shoulder as he spread his arms to quiet the crowd.

"I ask for your prayers in the days ahead. I need your strength and love to open the heavy doors that have been closed for much too long. We need the new light to shine upon us, the stagnant air of indifference to be purged from the Catholic Church. God grant us the wisdom and the courage to do His will."

Pope Constantine ended his address with the Papal blessing in Latin: <u>Omnipotens Deus, Pater, et Filius, et Spiritus Sanctus</u>." He looked to the bright sky of Rome, feeling not unlike those Christians about to face the lions for their faith. Visions of the Roman Coliseum burned into Justin's brain as he retreated into his mind and visualized the thousands who had perished for their faith and the horror of being eaten alive by ferocious beasts. Now history would decide if the name Constantine would be ranked with Leo, Gregory, and Nicholas, the only Popes in Roman Catholic history who were termed great. Attention was now directed to the Coronation ceremony that was to take place on the coming Sunday.

CHAPTER THIRTY-ONE

*E*nrique Capelli headed up the programming for the pomp and grandeur of the impending coronation. The event was scheduled for 7:00 p.m. Rome time to enable audiences of Western Europe to witness the installation during prime time Sunday evening. North American viewers would spend their Sunday afternoon glued to their television sets taking in every aspect of the coronation.

Justin was adamant about the use of <u>Sedia Gestatoria</u>. He would not be carried into the Basilica or Piazza. "I will walk. . . . . give the throne bearers the day off." He directed. Capelli immediately crossed out the item on his schedule list with his pen.

"We must enter the Piazza from the Basilica to allow more of your people to see you and also stage better television coverage." Capelli said, not taking his eyes off the notebook, pen poised for a check mark.

"And if it rains?" Justin asked.

"Mother Superior has instructed our entire contingent of nuns across the world to pray for good weather," Capelli said, as if to finalize the question.

"I believe God and His angels would not be inclined to resist that kind of pressure," Justin chuckled then grew grim as a migraine started in his head.

"We must discuss security, Holiness," Capelli looked stern as if to convey his concern not only for his Pope but the various attending heads of state and the welfare of three hundred thousand people that would jam the square for their moment in history.

"We will have five thousand Carabinieri and special troops. The secret service contingents of the other world leaders will bring our totals to about eleven thousand... I believe this should preclude any major incidents," Capelli said with assurance.

"Eleven thousand!" Justin exclaimed his astonishment at the numbers. "I have decided that we will tell the world of the Cross on the day of my coronation. In fact, we will carry the Cross in procession from the Basilica and hold it upright during my speech to the people. At the conclusion of the ceremony, we will then return it to its place of permanent enshrinement. I would like for the carpenters who installed the Cross to release it from its guy wires and carry it from the Basilica. It will add meaning to the revelation when I make the announcement to the audience."

"It will be done as you wish, your Holiness," Capelli obediently replied.

They discussed the details of the program with Justin nodding or commenting as each item was noted. And then it was settled the fine points to be delegated to lesser notables.

The red phone in the Papal office, reserved for secure and direct access to the Pope, sounded its unusual ring. Capelli was immediately dismissed leaving Justin alone as he placed his ear to the phone and greeted the caller.

"Congratulations, your Eminence. This is Prime Minister Gold of Israel."

"I am honored by your call," Justin replied.

"I wanted to touch base with you regarding our security forces and latest intelligence reports from the Mossad," Gold said.

"I am aware of the offer of security assistance," Justin continued, "but I do not know the details and for what purpose Alphonse had in mind. He passed on before he confided that information to me."

"Then my call comes at the right time. Eighteen Mossad agents dressed as Jesuit priests have infiltrated the Vatican. Pope Alphonse advised of a security leak and they were sent to eliminate the problem. Unfortunately, we have not yet been successful in discovering the name of the traitor. We do have reliable information that Muslim terrorists are poised to attack the Vatican and destroy the San Petronio fresco sometime within the next two weeks. We are prepared to intercede on your behalf as we promised Pope Alphonse."

"Before I was selected Pope, I wondered why the Church was fighting for the life of this fresco. I came to the conclusion that few works of art were so important to mankind that blood of many should be spilled to save them. I asked myself 'why should this fresco that defiled another religion be saved?' The answer was straightforward it should not! I will announce at my coronation not only the discovery of the Cross, for which I will at last be able to publicly thank Israel for its assistance, but also, the pro-active role now being taken by the Catholic Church to quell racial hatred. I will do this by example. The Catholic's, not the Muslims, will destroy the fresco. This symbol of racial intolerance will be recognized and no longer tolerated. With all this in mind, I would like you to recall your security force. I do not want to take a chance of its discovery and possible accusations of hypocrisy."

"I would strenuously advise against that, at least until after the coronation," Gold insisted.

"I am not afraid," Justin argued. "God will not forsake us."

"It is not God I am worried about, it is man! These Muslim extremists do everything in the name of God to justify man's acts of violence. They do not care about Catholics or Jews or any free thinking society."

"I appreciate your counsel, Prime Minister, but that is what I have decided to do."

"Reluctantly, we will respect your wishes, although we advise against it. Our agents will return home. However, should you need our help, you can count on us," Gold promised. He knew Pope Constantine's inexperience could be very costly. His fears would become real much too soon.

CHAPTER THIRTY-TWO

$\mathcal{T}$he dreams of power Marcella de la Sant envisioned as mistress to the Pope were gone. However, information from her Vatican connection was even more important to Khatabi. If Khatabi could make hundreds of millions selling the Cross to OrloThompson, she would be sure some of those millions would fall her way. Wilhelm, a traitor without portfolio, continued his role as an unwitting dupe, revealing even the smallest details of the coronation to Marcella before and after feverish sessions of lovemaking at her villa. He no longer had a reason to subliminate his sexual desires and found comfort and compassion for his defeat in the arms of Marcella, a willing participant. She would now play out her hand matching wits with Khatabi, and it would cost him.

Marcella stood on the balcony until she saw the black limousine stop in front of her villa. Khatabi's driver walked to the rear passenger door and opened it and Khatabi stepped out. Marcella rushed to greet him as if he was a long lost lover. They walked into the house where a tray of traditional Middle-Eastern food was waiting on the coffee table specially prepared for his enjoyment.

"I have little time for niceties," Khatabi warned. "What do you have for me?"

"I have what you will need," she said coyly.

"Do not tease me. I do not have the patience to play your games."

"I will come straight to the point," she said. "There will be a procession at the coronation where eight priests, carpenters who installed the Cross, will carry it for the people to see for the first time. After Pope Constantine finishes his speech and the ceremony ends, the Cross will be carried back to the Basilica to be enshrined permanently for the expected onslaught of parishioners to view. The Basilica will be closed to all until the Cross is re-installed. You have a window of opportunity."

"What is the strength of the security guarding the Basilica?" Khatabi questioned.

"There are two guards stationed at each entry encircling the building. Other than the perimeter guards, only the eight unarmed priests will be permitted in the Basilica," she answered. "They will remain inside the building the entire night before the coronation. The doors of the Basilica will be locked. The keys will be held by Cardinal Lattimer, who will open it the morning of the coronation."

"Those doors must be built with reinforced steel...they are almost forty feet high. How do you suggest we enter the Basilica other than blasting our way through giving a wake up call to the entire Vatican City?" he said facetiously.

"You have a much stronger force than blasting powder," she toyed with him. "You have me!"

"Did I warn you about teasing me? You best get to the point." Marcella reached inside her blouse pulling out a small tin lodged between her cleavage. She opened the tin.

"Inside is molding clay of the type used in making impressions. As you can see there is an impression of a key...a master key that will unlock the doors to the Basilica," she grinned slyly with a look of pride. "It was at great risk that I obtained this impression. I did it for you, my love."

"You did it for yourself and nobody else. So, what is it you want?" His demeanor was now mellow. Without a thought, his attitude was now one of negotiation appreciating the value of her efforts and trying to pay as little as possible.

"I will make it easy for you. You pay me nothing...nothing, unless you sell the Cross. Then, you pay me ten percent of the price you sell it for."

"I can take it from you right now and you would be helpless," he threatened.

"You could," she acknowledged. "But, that's not your style. Not when I can be of further use to you in the future."

"Three percent," he countered.

"Without the key you have no possibility of success. Surely, it's worth eight percent. Eight percent of two hundred million is a pittance," she offered.

"Five percent of two hundred million is even less, and that is my number. You may take it and make money or you may say no and get nothing. In any event, I will have the key. The question is, will you have your life?"

"You are very persuasive, my love. A trait I have always admired. We will seal the bargain with your pleasure," she said as she started to unbutton her blouse.

"Another time. We have work to do. Now, if you will hand me the tin."

"Of course, another time," she said placing the tin in his hand.

* * * *

The days of feverish activity were coming to an end the day before the coronation. As evening approached, the crowds in St. Peter's Square went home for the supper meal. They would gather early the next morning to garner the best seats for the coronation. The

Vatican security guards were posted outside each entrance to the Basilica in units of two just as Marcella had predicted. The eight priests were already inside the building locked in for the night. Mustapha's team of ten assassins, as ordered by Khatabi, approached the Basilica having pre-selected the little used Sacristy door reserved only for notables, as the most vulnerable point of entry at the side of the building. One of the assassins walked boldly past the guards directly to the Sacristy door and inserted the key. The other assassin lagged slightly behind waiting for the guards to turn their backs to question his accomplice.

"What are you doing?" one of the guards questioned as both reacted exactly as expected. Two muffled sounds and slight puffs of smoke from pistols equipped with silencers and the guards dropped dead in their tracks, the accomplice firing to the back of their heads so as not to stain the clothing of his victims. Quickly, the remaining eight gathered at the doorway as the door was unlocked allowing the twelve to enter, ten assassins and two dead priests of the Vatican security force. Two of the clean-shaven assassins changed into the garb of the dead guards and took positions outside the Sacristy door as if it was business as usual. The rest stealthily walked the building until they came upon the carpenter priests bedded down for the night like ducks in a pond. Each intruder stood over the bed of a priest and with a squeeze of the trigger each bullet did its work. Only at this point, assured of success, did the assassins shave off their Saddam Hussein mustaches, a great sacrifice to their manhood, but required to better blend in for the morning coronation. They stripped the priests of their clothing and piled, the now ten bodies, into a closet and locked the door. The "newly ordained" carpenter priests then rested in the beds still warm from their victims.

CHAPTER THIRTY-THREE

*J*ustin was held in a small anteroom dressed in a plain white cassock and scarlet cape. On his head was the non-jeweled Bishop's Miter. He held the Shepherd's Crook in his white-gloved left hand as he blessed the various officials with his right hand. The small group joined Justin Kennedy in a short prayer as muted shouts of "Il Papa" entered the room. The moment arrived, hearts beating loudly, dry mouths and nervousness pervading the participants. Enrique Capelli managed a smile as he placed a pill in his mouth.

The procession began with a brilliant spectacle of rainbow colors. The initial appearance of the Swiss guards was breathtaking as they marched in renaissance uniforms of purple, yellow and maroon. There were followed by various representatives of religious orders. Next came the Dominicans in flowing white habits, and then the Franciscans in course brown wool who entered with purposeful strides. The master of the papal wardrobe carried a plain iron tiara on a black velvet cushion followed by clergy and Curia officers clad in clothes signifying their rank, capes of red, purple or gold over their shoulders. The assemblage looked in awe as the Sacred College of Cardinals strode majestically; gold chasubles over white surplices set off by ceremonial tall peaked white miters upon their heads. The Commander of the Grand Noble appeared to be almost seven feet tall in his gold and scarlet uniform. His steel helmet, of eighteenth century vintage, glinted in the bright lights. His mirror polished black boots, clicked as he walked forward.

The completion of the cortege was accomplished as Archbishops, Bishops, Generals and Patriarchs filed past.

The thousands grew impatient as the twenty-five minutes elapsed, all straining for a glimpse of the American Pope-elect as he walked from the Basilica followed by eight men dressed as carpenter priests in procession carrying The Cross.

Trumpeters stationed high in the loggia sounded the call as choirs sang on both sides of the altar. The master of ceremonies lifted a vessel of smoking hemp and swung it around the papal chair as he intoned the ancient warning:

"Pater, Sancte, Sic Transit Gloria Mundi," a reminder to all that men are mortal. The Cross was received by Bishops who held it high next to the Pope. The High Mass was completed in less than twenty minutes, a record according to Capelli who was nervously keeping track of the precise time schedule. "il papa" received the Cardinals one by one as they knelt and kissed his ring. Only Kurt Wilhelm squeezed Justin's hand as he kissed the ring, Justin wondering for a moment at any hidden meaning. Justin had chosen the youngest of the Cardinalship Paulo Cardinal Favarro from Milan, a singular honor for a forty-year old man, to crown him. The action flying in the face of tradition, as the oldest Cardinal usually performed the act.

Cardinal Paulo Favarro draped his Pope's shoulders with the caped symbol of becoming the Bishop of Rome, the woolen pallium, a reminder of humility. The magic moment neared as the Cardinal from Milan raised the triple tiered crown high into the air for the thousands in the Basilica to see. After a few minutes of thunderous applause, Paulo placed the crown on Justin's head and recited in a magnificent baritone voice the ancient formula in Latin, advising Pope Constantine, he was the Father of Princes and Leader of Kings.

Pope Constantine raised his hand and imparted the expected words; "Urbi et orbi." He walked to the microphones on the railing and raised his hand for silence, the crowd refusing as they shouted their joy of the occasion. "Love..." he allowed the word to echo throughout the Piazza. "Brotherly love..." He again paused. "Simple words for a complex world. Love is a powerful word able to perform miracles. A blessing when we give love and receive love in return. The immeasurable love of Christ, who died on our Cross. Yes..." he paused, "the very Cross being held high by your Bishops standing next to me. This is the Cross. It was found in Israel and, with the help of our Hebrew brothers, was returned to us as the most sacred relic in the Christian world." An unbelievable silence fell over the crowd as they viewed what they never imagined still existed. Pope Constantine continued, "The love of God who gave us His Son...Cannot this power be harnessed to cure the ills of the world? I say it can and shall be the flint to ignite the deep rooted emotion in every human heart, burning into a flaming passion for all God's creatures." Shouts and applause filled the square as nervous security personnel tensed as the crowd's emotional level doubled then tripled.

"We have tried words, treaties, alliances, threats, and even compromise in attempts to rid the world of man-created catastrophes and yet we again have brother pitted against brother in the Middle East. Starvation is still rampant in many areas of the world, crime ruling the streets, drug merchants so powerful they occupy high seats of government while ruining millions of lives. We call upon God to place the terrible swift sword in our hands. With this sword of love we shall smite the ungodly as we rally around our new symbol of love...the Cross of Jesus Christ,"

Constantine turned toward the Cross. "I instruct all who will heed my words to become individual laborers in the vineyard of our Lord to seek out all areas of injustice and remove them. Doctors and nurses to rededicate themselves to the unfortunate sick, lawyers and judges to fight with a renewed will to protect the innocent. My clergy will become involved with the laity and root out social ills by becoming involved in secular politics. We will no longer be relegated to taking care of only the religious needs of our flocks. We shall purchase newspapers and television outlets to expose those elements that feed upon the misery of the world. We shall work to topple governments who refuse to allow their citizens the basic human rights of freedom. We are today embarking on a holy war of love."

Embarrassed looks exchanged on the balcony. It seemed to the participants the world had stopped. Then it happened. To the west side of the square, a lone shout in Italian then a wave of excitement, energy exploding simultaneously as thousands roared their joy. Unrestrained cries of happiness as pure emotion gripped the mass of people. People began fainting as groups fell to their knees. A loud clap of thunder shook the Piazza, knowledgeable newsmen knew instinctively it was only a sonic boom from a high flying aircraft and yet the crowd heard it as the voice of God. This only adding to the hysteria which squeezed the assembly. "I will be the first to set the example of the future peace of all our brothers. Our forefathers are not without sin. For many years we have oppressed others believing that was what had to be done to survive. We were wrong. Today, I have ordered destruction of the fresco that defiles the Prophet Mohammad that our Church has protected too long. I reach out my hand to our Muslim brothers and seek forgiveness for past sins. I hope they will accept our sincerity and allow all faiths to practice religions as they choose. We all come from the same patriarch...Abraham. As such, we are all brothers in the heart and by birth."

The crowd stormed the barricades in a mad rush, reason absent from the faces of the now out of control mob that wanted to touch this man of God. Security forces quickly went into action forming an impressive human barricade until the crowd quieted. Constantine ended his coronation with a prayer and was quickly ushered away from the balcony. The Bishops returned the Cross to the eight dressed as priests who carried it back to the Basilica under armed escort of the Vatican police. Once inside the Basilica the doors were locked as the eight terrorists carried the Cross to the rear of the Basilica where the two who had assumed the guard of the Sacristy door were busy opening another door. The eight never broke stride from the time they entered the Basilica until the time they walked through the rear door and into a twenty-four foot refrigerated box van. They laid the Cross on the ice-cold floor of the van careful not to damage it. This was not done out of respect, but because of Khatabi's warning that any damage could depreciate its value. The rear door was closed to the Basilica and to the refrigerated truck. The driver then started the engine, engaged the gears, and slowly drove away with his cargo of assassins and the Cross of Jesus. People on the streets saw only a refrigerated commercial truck with artwork showing six flavors of gelato in cones colorfully painted as if they were dripping down the sides of the truck. Words printed in large letters in a half circle above the artwork announced, "Don Salvatore's Gelato...We Never Have Any Complaints." A slogan in a half circle below the artwork read, "Voted best by the Vatican...Rome's finest...First Choice of Princes and Laity".

Justin felt spent, totally exhausted as he entered his private apartment on the third floor, now alone, his mind numbed at the happenings of the day unaware that the Cross was being transported by truck to a small airfield outside of Rome where an aircraft was awaiting its arrival. Sleep came over him. This fateful evening dreams of the late Pope Alphonse and the place in Justin's heart for the revered man of God. Justin prayed Alphonse could come alive and release him from his fate. He drifted off into a twilight sleep once again.

At the village of Bethany, nestled in a hollow, 15 furlongs off the road to Jericho, was a nondescript place that was surrounded with olive, almond, pomegranate, tall oak, and carob trees. It was a frequent resting place of Jesus of Nazareth. Here the Chosen Son of God felt at peace with his friends. It was the home of Mary and Martha, and Simon the leper. This day a new visitor arrived. Judas Iscariot looked about the place, not knowing why he was there. Cries of anguish filled the air from the House of Lazarus. The wails of Mary, the sister of Lazarus, heart rending. Judas inquired as to the commotion and was told that the good man Lazarus had died four days previously.

Lamentations and sobbing filled the air as Martha attempted to comfort Mary. "If the master had been here, my brother would not have died." Heads were shaken in agreement as all assembled knew of the miracles accomplished by Jesus. And yet, I know even now, whatever is asked of God will be given."

Jesus appeared with his followers and walked to the entrance of the House of Lazarus. "Thy brother shall rise again," Jesus told them. Murmurs and looks of astonishment rippled through the group. To return one from death was a new dimension even for the mysterious man from Nazareth.

"I know that he shall rise again in the resurrection at the last day," Mary said softly.

"He shall rise this day, for I am the resurrection and the life. He that believeth in me, though he were dead, yet shall he live," Jesus said. Judas pondered the words of Jesus. He had many doubts of the things attributed to the man they now called Master.

"Come ye now to the grave," Jesus bid them. They walked to the cave and saw the stones laid upon it. There were protests when Jesus bid them to take away the stone.

"He has been dead for four days, his smell shall be of putri-fication," they cried.

"Have I not told you if thou believeth, thou shalt see the glory of God?" Jesus said, rebuking them.

The stones were rolled away as Jesus looked to the heavens, "Father I thank Thee that Thou hast heard me."

Judas wrung his hands as he and the others watched in wonderment.

"I knowest Thou hearest me always, but because of the people that stand here, I said it, so that they may believe that Thou hast sent me." Jesus raised his arms to the sky and intoned in a loud voice, LAZSARUS, COME FORTH!" The stone fell away; a figure suddenly loomed at the entrance of the grave, a linen cloth over his face, grave clothes binding him hand and foot.

"LOOSE HIM...LET HIM GO!" Jesus commanded. The grave wrappings fell away as Lazarus stepped toward the amazed crowd.

Word of this miracle quickly reached the Chief Priests and the Pharisees who began to plot for their fear was great. In the days that followed, there was a feast prepared, a supper of celebration six days before Passover. At this supper, Mary produced a pound of expensive spikenard, and anointed the feet of Jesus with the ointment. Judas Iscariot could not contain himself at this waste.

"Why was not this ointment sold for three hundred pence and given to the poor?" Judas questioned. Jesus knew Judas cared not for the poor and that he would become a thief, and he would sell something more precious for thirty pieces of silver. Jesus rebuked Judas and at that instant the seeds of betrayal were sown.

CHAPTER THIRTY-FOUR

*P*recisely at 5:30 a.m. the next morning Secretary General Lattimer arrived at the Basilica with a new contingent of eight priests who would aid the others in re-attaching the Cross to the pillars and would prepare the Basilica for the parishioners who wanted to be the first to see the sacred object up close. He unlocked the mammoth doors and they entered only to see an empty hall where the Cross had stood and not a soul in sight. They continued walking into the main room, completely dumbfounded, as they were drawn to a stench coming from a closet. Lattimer unlocked the door and jumped back as a human body stiffened by rigormortis, rolled off a pile of nine others, landing at his feet. He recognized the ten, clad only in undergarments, as his priests. The smell of death flowed from the closet as he turned his head as his body begged to vomit but could only produce dry heaves. He caught his breath as sweat poured from his forehead. After a few minutes he regained his sense of purpose and ordered the entire Basilica searched, relying on faith that the Cross was still there.

Pope Constantine was apprised of what happened and could make no sense of it. He placed an embarrassed call to the Prime Minister of Israel realizing that the Pope was not infallible after all. He now understood how naive he had been. It was jointly decided that the Israeli's would now tend to matters regarding the theft of the Cross. Pope Constantine would tend to the administration of the Catholic Church.

The day following the coronation was filled with a mixture of unrestrained praise and condemnation of the new Pope. The Catholic world community was torn asunder by Constantine's speech. They decided it was best to keep the theft of the Cross and the deaths of the priests quiet. The Basilica would be closed for a long overdue renovation in order to accommodate the relic. The public was again deceived, but for the good of the investigation into the murders.

Justin's use of power politics, propounded at his coronation under the authority of Jesus Christ, was a new dilemma faced by the ruling factions of the Church. They had no road map to guide them, no precedent to follow. If Justin Kennedy's vision of a new direction for the Church was correct, he would indeed be ranked among the greats. If incorrect, his name would be relegated to denunciation and infamy. Newspapers in Europe were comparing his address with the innovative early pronouncements of Mao of China during the 1900's, and predicted a gigantic leap forward that would, if enacted, destroy forever the Monarchic papacy.

Justin Kennedy, as new Vicar of Christ, lost little time making his presence felt. He called for a meeting with his advisors and began setting the tone of his papacy. "We must be forceful in our quest for immediate changes. On Monday, I shall have the resignations of the following Cardinals in my hands. It is time to clean house." Justin handed the list to the Monsignor.

"Holiness, you must not do this," Capelli cried out as he looked over the list.

"If bloodletting is demanded to purge some of the poison so it shall be," Justin's Papal response was met with grim faces.

"Visinni! San Filippo! Cassidy, and all of these others?" Capelli asked in disbelief.

"Visinni and San Filippo have earned the rest," Justin replied. "Old men cannot make reasonable judgments. As far as Cassidy is concerned, his personal bank account seems much too large for the size of his mind. We all know he is lining his pockets, using the Church as his personal umbrella of protection. He is as slippery as pond slime. Rather than an embarrassing inquiry, it is deemed best to dismiss him. Since Cassidy is an American, I would believe it would also dispel any accusations of favoritism."

"You also list Krameer and Danker, both from Germany. How are we to explain this to our German community?"

"They still have Wilhelm; that old fox is too clever for me to close up his den. Krameer and Danker are both up to their respective ears in the money markets of Western Europe. They must have at least ten relatives on the boards of prominent banks in France and Germany. I intend to stop this 'patrimony' of Peter," Justin promised.

"Do we not have enough problems besetting our Church? Capelli questioned. "Catholics are split down the middle. That picture of you with the Sister in that obscene newspaper is only adding to the hate building against the Church and its leadership.

God grant us the wisdom, Holy Father, we are about to embark on heavy seas. We may end by destroying the Church," Enrique Capelli offered.

"I share your concern, dear brother; but anyone can be a good captain on smooth waters," Constantine replied. "Problems have solutions, indecision has no solutions. Social and political as well as ideological boundaries are no longer relevant in this modern age. The gap of division between peoples of the world has continued to shrink with the advent of the electronic age. What is

said today is heard and understood today. Feedback is instanta-
neous." Justin paused, then continued. "With assassinations of
world leaders occurring with frightening regularity, we dare not
tarry in our tasks." Justin's words were intended to remind the
men of the near death of John Paul in 1981.

The cardinal red telephone, never more than seconds away
from the Pope and always carried by his top aide, shrilled out
three staccato-like rings. It was immediately handed to Justin
who listened intently to the voice at the other end then said, "I
will be expecting the phone call". He returned the phone to his
aide and requested adjournment of the meeting.

CHAPTER THIRTY-FIVE

$\mathcal{T}$he specially modified twenty-two passenger DeHaviland Twin Otter aircraft approached the abandoned airfield in the Sinai Desert near the ancient Muslim fortress of Ras el Gindi. The twin-engine turbo- prop was chosen because it was small enough to utilize dirt runways, if necessary for refueling, yet still maintain a respectable airspeed. The aircraft, with the Cross tucked safely in its belly, touched down on the pot hole ridden tarmac, and was greeted by warm desert winds, a scattering of sheep, and Mustapha the Assassin who arrived earlier by helicopter with a few of his select bodyguards.

Isolated, an almost impregnable place, <u>Ras el Gindi</u> had been built by Sultan Salah-el Din in the twelfth century; it was now the temporary home of the Cross pending negotiation of its sale. Mustapha the Assassin, had one thing on his mind, money. He had the Cross to sell, and Hosni Khatabi, had a buyer. Khatabi, always the smarter of the two cousins, now realized that there were two buyers. He could pit the two against each other and bid up the price. Orlo Thompson versus The Roman Catholic Church! His plan was to auction the Cross to the highest bidder, but pay the lower commission to Mustapha. He would cut off his cousin's legs as easy as slicing a pomegranate, if he could profit by doing so.

The phone call Pope Constantine was told to expect, came through as promised. A meeting was to be arranged between a wealthy Arab businessman and a high level official of the Roman Catholic Church. It would take place in Israel. The Arab, Hosni Khatabi, was labeled in international circles as "the Fixer". His involvement in arms trading and other illicit activities clouded his credibility, yet he was accepted in various capitals of the Middle East as a necessary cog in the wheel. Although ruthless and cunning, Khatabi had a reputation for accomplishing the impossible. After the self-inflicted death of Father Peter, Khatabi was now Orlo Thompson's only source of information regarding the relic. Now, both Pope Constantine and Thompson were informed that the Cross had been "reclaimed" from the Vatican, but was in the hands of Khatabi's agent and available for sale.

Within twenty-four hours the Pope met secretly with his advisors to formulate a plan to ransom the Cross. It was a situation not unlike the rumored efforts of the House of Rothchild, to purchase the discovered pieces from the Ark of the Covenant supposedly in the possession of King Hussein of Jordan during the last quarter of the 20th century.

Justin's waking nightmares began to reoccur as his thoughts of loosing the Cross became more frequent. The flashbacks episodes of a few seconds now grew to minutes. One incident lasted over an hour, and it left him physically and emotionally drained to the point he cared not even to bathe. He doubled the intake of drugs prescribed by Dr. Carlton, unconcerned that the substance would begin a new roller coaster of emotions that would dig deeper and rise higher with each hour throughout the night. The revelation came to him as he was sipping his third cup of morning coffee. The details of the meeting lay in front of him, challenging him. He would not trust the assignment to a clergyman filled with liturgical nonsense.

He decided he alone would make the trip to the Holy Land. He must be the one to negotiate for the return of his Cross. He had never met Khatabi and thought it best to keep it that way for purposes of negotiation. Khatabi would be led to believe that a special envoy from the Vatican would meet with him and could strike a deal provided he received approval from the Pope. Having a "buffer" was a common negotiation technique and understood and accepted by even less experienced businessmen.

Justin knew he could never leave for the holy land without first having a viable story for his disappearance from the Vatican. He requested a meeting at his apartment with Dr. Carlton. It was arranged for the morning.

"Thank you for coming, Doctor...It is good to see you." Pope Constantine greeted Dr. Carlton warmly.

"I am at your service, Holy Father." Carlton bowed and kissed the papal ring.

"Please...sit down. Would you like coffee, or perhaps something more stimulating?" He asked

"Thank you, no...I have just finished what the good sisters term breakfast," Carlton said as a smile erupted on both men's faces.

"I have asked you here, rather than consult with Dr. Sansone, to request a mild sedative. My migraines seem to be getting worse with each day. I live in a vacuum now that I am the Vicar and only you are privy to the secrets of my mind. Secrets which have me concerned and I need your counsel in the days ahead," Justin told him.

"I am honored for this confidence, Holiness. I shall be here at your request day and night." Carlton responded.

"I knew I could count on you...I have one other request which I am sure will not burden you." Justin's eyes narrowed slightly as he looked directly in the eyes of Dr. Carlton.

"You are my Pontiff...your directive shall be accomplished." Carlton said.

"I will need a supply of medication for a number of weeks duration, it seems the Vatican walls have not only ears but eyes as well," Justin's concern about the rumors surrounding his mental health were beginning to annoy him.

"As you wish, Holy Father,' Carlton agreed, a puzzled look showing on his face.

"Do you think it beneficial if I was to spend the next few weeks resting at Castel Gandolfo?" he asked, knowing the response would be positive.

"That is something I would definitely prescribe, but I was unsure of your acceptance of he idea. You need the rest." The doctor stamped Justin's suggestion with the approval needed to substantiate his whereabouts. He had served his purpose.

"Then I will make the necessary arrangements," Justin replied.

"The tragedy of the death of Pope Alphonse and the general excitement of the election and coronation certainly is cause for a respite understandable by everyone," Dr. Carlton stated with authority reinforcing "his" idea for the retreat to Castel Gandolfo.

"Thank you, again. I will not take more of your time as my time is becoming more precious as well. I'll walk you to the door," Justin said, as the doctor left the Pontiff's apartment.

The next few days he remained secluded in his apartment seeing no one. Meals were delivered and left for him by servants who were instructed that the Pope should not be disturbed for any reason, under doctor's orders. He packed a small suitcase with civilian clothes and opened his wall safe taking the still valid passport using the alias Justin Templeton. He went into the bathroom and dyed his hair so it was all gray. After several days of not shaving he sported a stubble of a beard which, when coupled with dark glasses was intended as a disguise. The world did not know the Cross was stolen but everyone now recognized Pope Constantine. This religious "double agent" was charged with retrieving the stolen Cross before knowledge of the theft was made known to the outside world. The persona of Justin Templeton had to escape recognition to afford him the opportunity to complete his task. He looked in the mirror and did not like what he saw. Someone, he thought, might still recognize him. He had to remove all doubts in the minds of everyone he would come in contact with. The solution was so simple he almost overlooked it. He needed a traveling companion. The person had to be a woman. He needed Mary Francis. If anyone suspected him as being the Pope, that thought would be sublimated quickly if he was traveling with a woman. His next phone call was to Mary Frances Templeton, who would again assume the role of his putative wife. Instructions were given to allow Sister Mary Frances access to the Pope in his apartment. She responded to the calling with the urgency Justin commanded. He was dressed in civilian clothes and answered the door personally.

"Please come and sit," this strange looking man who had taken on an exaggerated stooped over posture said. "His Eminence will be here shortly," he continued after ushering her in with the promise he would announce her arrival to the Pope. She did not recognize him though she wondered what this man was doing in the apartment of the Vicar of Christ. Convinced the deception had worked, at least for the moment, he stood erect and removed his dark glasses. She looked for his ring, saw it had been removed, and rushed to embrace him. Subconsciously she forgot he was Pope and remembered only what she had prayed for, that he was free to accept her as a woman.

He put his hands on her shoulders and gently pushed her away so he could look into her eyes.

"I guess an explanation is in order," he said. She looked up at him but was speechless. "Your passport has not expired, has it? The one in the name of Mary Frances Templeton."

"What have you done? Are you abdicating the Throne of Peter for me?" she said pensively.

"If I could, I would," his words were apologetic recognizing he had quashed her dream of running away with him. "I will be leaving Rome temporarily, but you are one of a handful that will know about it." He then proceeded to tell her about the theft of the Cross and the trip they would both take to retrieve it. He instructed her to go to her apartment, pack, and wait for his phone call. Capelli had purchased two tickets to Tel Aviv in the names of Justin and Mary Francis Templeton. They would travel by commercial airline in coach class, to blend in with the "great unwashed" who never tasted the luxury of first class accommodations. Mary Francis had been reassigned to Rome, having completed her latest archeological assignment orchestrated by Justin and commanded by Alphonse. However, the paperwork was not yet completed for the transfer and therefore, her arrival could easily be postponed and she would not be missed. The slight detail of money to be used in this high stakes game of poker was satisfied after requesting Lattimer to provide him with negotiable securities.

Justin and Mary Frances Templeton checked through Israeli customs with a perfunctory examination of his false credentials. Prime Minister Gold would see to it that Justin's covert operation in Israel would remain so. As they walked through the airport terminal, Mary Frances noticed a Franciscan priest looking quizzically at Justin as if he was familiar. He turned away as she reached for Justin's arm and planted a kiss on his cheek. "Say nothing," she whispered, that was for business reasons she smiled. I'll explain later. Their destination was a small hotel in Jerusalem not far from the King Solomon Hotel located at the intersection of the New and the Old City and within twenty minutes walking distance to all city attractions. Justin would leave Mary Frances at the hotel where she could explore the ancient city while he attended the meeting with Khatabi the next morning.

The meeting was to be held at the abandoned British Bank of the Middle East, its rusting shutters now imprisoning the musty

stale air of the once prodigious institution. He arrived at the East
Jerusalem bus station near the Damacus Gate and walked the short
block to the bank. Arab handbills were plastered on its walls. An
old woman stood by the side of the bank door, her basket of flowers overflowing with anemones and golden hyacinths. Only Justin
and the mysterious Hosni Khatabi knew the woman to be the contact person for the meeting. He approached her resolutely, handed
her a gold coin and said to her "Allah is Great" in English.

She replied in English, "God is Great ". She gave him the
instruction to return to the abandoned Bank when, "the chant of
the muezzin sounds from the minaret on the Mosque of Omar."
The old woman showed no emotion as she handed him a bouquet
of flowers in exchange for the coin, and disappeared down the
alley at an astonishing rate of speed for her age.

Justin felt the brooding quality of Jerusalem overpower him
as he walked aimlessly. The redolent smells of roasting lamb and
spice mixed with the unmistakable smell of hashish enveloped
his sense of smell; even overpowering the fly-covered feces of
donkeys. His travels took him toward the Via Dolorosa as the
noonday sun beat down upon his head. He was startled as he saw
the bare backed man struggling with a cross. The reenactment of
the "Walk of Jesus;" by a French evangelical group was complete
down to the actual whipping of the sobbing man by his associates
who took on the role of Roman soldiers. One stroke of the whip
by an over zealous participant brought an eruption of flame red
blood to the back of the portrayer of Jesus. This sight triggered
something in Justin's soul. His eyes glazed for a moment as the
flashback took hold, deeper and more real than at any time during his illness. Justin stumbled through the Arab marketplace,
blindly following the zigzag of the "Street of Sorrows." He stag-
gered and fell at the front of the Polish Chapel that marked one
of the fourteen stations of the Cross. Bewildered onlookers
shrugged their shoulders as the locals looked on indifferently.
They were used to the antics of the Christian pilgrims that

seemed to be everywhere twelve months of the year.

Justin struggled to his feet and stumbled, almost drunkenly, toward the Armenian Church and the spot where Christ had encountered his mother. He cried out in the stillness of the afternoon, "Mother...Mother, I have come home." The vision of the old hag at the village of Kerioth spread before him. Then the face of his real mother, Kate Kennedy, superimposed on his brain. Justin continued, as if some unseeing hand was pushing at his back. The Greek Chapel of St. Veronica suddenly appeared on the street. He felt faint as he remembered the wiping of the forehead of Jesus by Veronica. Symbolically and without hesitation, Justin wiped his own perspiration-streaked brow as the force again propelled him forward. He stumbled and fell at the entrance of the Coptic Church. A brown robed Franciscan monk came to his aid, unaware he was assisting Pope Constantine of the Roman Catholic Church.

Justin waved off the arm of his Good Samaritan, and continued toward the Church of the Holy Sepulcher. The rock of Golgotha was dimly visible near the entrance, a plate glass separating the viewing public from its spiritual attraction. Justin entered the Sepulcher. He was jostled along by a group of white robed Dominican monks chanting in Latin. The spot where the Christ was said to have been lain; was bedecked with trappings of a religious nature. Thin white candles burned in the dimness, giving an added dimension to one of the holiest places in the world. The sacred stone slab seemed almost alive as candlelight flickered across the smooth surface. Incredibly, beautiful Icons stared out from the ornate marble walls of the place. A hush fell over the gathering, even silent prayers and juggled rosaries were fused in silence. It was the week that the Greek Orthodox had control of the shrine. The gathering awaited the Greek patriarch's entrance and the ceremonial mass to follow.

The Church was darkened; all eyes were on the port-hold. Suddenly a lighted torch was thrust through the hold, its blazing holy fire changing the darkness to instant light, the light symbolizing the Resurrection of the Light of the world. The ceremony was not for the faint of heart. The emotional handhold of the attendees, when coupled with the shock of the torch thrust into the room, caused a heart skip to more than a few of the millions who had witnessed the rite over the years. Justin felt numb as he departed the place, his senses reeling as bright sunlight shocked him back to reality. It was mid-afternoon when he found his way to a café where he refreshed, ate sparingly, and reached in his pocket for one of the pills. He took a swallow of water and placed the pill on his tongue. Soon he began to feel much more in control of his faculties.

* * * *

At that moment in the small village of Yamit, another gathering had been whipped into frenzy by the words of Mustapha the Assassin. His words geared to incite the pent-up emotions of the Palestinian religious radicals. "Tomorrow we attack...death to the Israelis...death to the non believers...Almighty Allah shall wreak his vengeance and protect you from harm." A plentiful supply of hashish was distributed to the villagers along with weapons and ammunition. While Mustapha was busy drawing his blood bath of terror, his cousin Khatabi was thinking of the added money that would line his pockets if he could get his second buyer to increase Thompson's bid for the Cross, and cheat Mustapha out of a full commission as well.

Justin heard the mournful chant of the muezzin calling the faithful to pray and returned to the appointed place at the designated time. He approached the abandoned bank building and saw the side door was slightly ajar. He pushed it inward and stood in the entrance. A heavy accented voice bid him enter. A single overhead light bulb illuminated the dingy place. Its furnishings, a small wooden table set upon a dirty blue and gold rug, a rug too dilapidated to have been stolen. Justin immediately deciding this was not a fitting place for the barter of the most precious artifact in the history of Christendom.

"Shall we begin?" the heavyset Arab intoned. A huge ten carat diamond was sparkling on his little finger. The red fez upon his head was not totally unexpected, but did set Justin back for a few seconds.

"The price?" Justin asked, his voice husky.

"Five hundred million American," he was told as simply as if he had requested a glass of water.

"Five hundred..." Justin stammered.

"Million," his counterpart in the bargaining added.

"I must have time to decide...this is more than we anticipated." Justin stalled to give his mind an opportunity to drive a wedge into the process. His knowledge of the Middle Eastern mentality told him of their love for haggling. Except in this instance, the haggling would encompass a million dollars a point.

"Come now, my Catholic friend," he said, unaware of Justin's real identity, "time is short. The price is not exorbitant...in light of the billions you will garner into the vaults of your already filled coffers. Think of this as an investment. The shrine will triple your membership every month for ten years. Pilgrims will spend their life savings to come and revere the artifact. Also...we have expenses which must be handled." The man behind the desk lit a small black cigarette and exhaled the smoke out the left side of his mouth, a mouth beset by a wide grin.

"Fifty million. That is the amount authorized," Justin suggested.

"I would venture a guess you are toying with me...I have not the time or authority to negotiate for such a sum. Our meeting will be adjourned to another time...good day." Khatabi lifted slowly from his chair, grunted as a stiff left leg was shaken, then he looked to Justin.

Justin Kennedy was aware of the Muslim mystique and their oriental oblique approach to problems coupled with a preoccupation with saving face; a strong habit of saying one thing and meaning another. The reputation of being volatile and explosive by nature was reflected in the eyes, fierce and hostile as an eagle. And yet, he perceived the Arab's weakness...Justin incorrectly suspected his adversary was only the go-between, the Israeli Mossad intelligence unit having advised that it was Mustapha the Assassin who stole the Cross. He sensed that Khatabi was fearful that the negotiations might come to an abrupt end and there would be no commission.

"Four hundred," the Arab countered.

"Two fifty," Justin said firmly.

"Done," Khatabi said with finality.

Both principals felt they got the best of the other, as it should be in the scheme of things. Justin produced negotiable securities, laying the two hundred fifty million in bonds on the table, his fingers dealing out one twenty-five million certificate to which he had previously signed as Pope Constantine making the instrument negotiable. The rest he put in his pocket.

"The balance when the Cross is safely transferred to a Vatican aircraft," Justin said, now in control of the dialogue. The Arab's eyes bulged as he watched the remaining bonds disappear into Justin's jacket. The Arab wet his lips and wiped his brow with a dirty handkerchief as he quickly determined that he could have pressed for the entire five hundred million.

"Alas...we are both satisfied," his statement not quite hiding the thought of attacking the Catholic and taking all the securities. His innate fear of Mustapha the Assassin, pushed the foolish thought from his mind for the moment. While he fully intended to cheat Mustapha, if he could, he also realized compensation was expected and that would only come about by making a deal. The real bidding had just begun. Orlo Thompson would be a participant in the continuing auction process, but for much more money.

"You will begin at dawn," the Arab continued. "A driver in a military vehicle will pick you up at your hotel. He will deliver you to a place in the Sinai that will be the rendezvous with my people. The Cross will be loaded into the small cargo jet, which will rendezvous at an airport of your choice for the transfer. By this time tomorrow you shall have your Cross and be safely on your way to the Catholic fortress you call the Vatican." The Arab touched his forehead and his chest in a gesture of good-bye. He left quickly leaving Justin with his outstretched hand hanging in mid air.

Justin returned to the hotel. He related what he could to Mary Francis believing that the less she knew the safer she would be until they returned to Rome. Khatabi went straight to the bank depositing the twenty-five million dollars for transfer to a Swiss account. The account required one of two signatures. It contained the funds that were dispersed to Marcella for her day-to-day living. He forgot she was a signatory to the account.

CHAPTER THIRTY-SIX

$\mathcal{T}$he dawn was wonderfully uneventful. The birds were singing and flowering almond trees and pines welcomed another day in the ageless city.

"I will be back for you this evening," Justin told Mary Frances. "We'll have a quiet supper together after I am certain all arrangements are concluded and the Cross is again in our possession."

"I'll be waiting. Be careful and God go with you," she said.

Justin waited at the front of the hotel for about fifteen minutes before a dusty military vehicle sped up to the curb. The driver opened the door and with a hand gesture, motioned Justin to get in. The man said nothing as he put the vehicle in gear and sped down the deserted street. It was hours before they entered the desolate Sinai. The road was strangely quiet even for the early hour. Their attention focused on a billowing cloud of smoke in the distance.

"Trouble," the driver said.

Justin's heart pounded...he did not need any further strain on his mind.

"What is it?" Justin asked.

"Might be the Liberation front...we just wait and see." The driver bit on his lower lip as he decreased speed.

"Can we go around?" Justin quizzed.

"If it is just a demonstration...they will allow us to pass through the road block. They know better than to molest non-belligerents. If it were not for the U.N., they would all have died years ago along with their dream for a free Palestine.

"And if it's not just a demonstration...what then?" Justin asked, not really wanting to know the answer.

"I believe I know a detour...a little rough but it will take us away from what's up ahead," the driver said, fully aware of his passengers importance to the Arab Hosni Khatabi. Neither of them heard the impact or the resulting explosion as the front end of the vehicle lifted into the air, the blast hurling the driver against the unrelenting steel of the military vehicle. The driver's head smashed through the front window and Justin thrown against the passenger side roll bar before being jettisoned out the door, a deep gash on his head. The pair lay silent, the vehicle exploded into flames as the Palestinian radicals looked down on their quarry, each congratulating the other for their marksmanship with the Katusha rocket launcher. Within minutes, the pair was surrounded. A quick inspection revealed only the driver's head, pierced with shards of broken glass, was still recognizable. A rifle butt was used to prod Justin, who moaned as he began to fight for consciousness.

"Put him in the truck," Mustafa the Assassin instructed having no idea who he was, just that he was to be delivered to Khatabi, unharmed, and therefore probably had some value.

"He's bleeding pretty bad," the shortest of the group said through broken and stained teeth.

"Bandage him, then cover his eyes," Mustapha instructed.

Justin felt the cloth bandage tighten as it was wrapped again and again around his head and eyes. An explosion of sparks fired in his brain as the pain rendered him unconscious.

"We return to Yamit...the battle is joined!" Mustapha shouted as he fingered his <u>masbah</u> prayer beads, silently calling the
ninety-nine names of Allah.

CHAPTER THIRTY-SEVEN

$\mathcal{T}$he clock in the lobby of the hotel struck eight times. It was dark outside and past the dinner hour. Mary Francis paced the lobby waiting for Justin to return. There were no messages at the front desk. As midnight approached she realized he would not be coming back that night. Something was dreadfully wrong. It was unlike him not to keep her informed. All he told her was that he had a meeting with a man named Hosni Khatabi that morning. She went back to the hotel room thinking she needed help and tomorrow would not come fast enough.

Her inquiries in hotels and shops along Gordon Street were met with shrugs of indifference. Just the mention of Khatabi's name struck fear in the minds of the shopkeepers. She was unaware that she was being followed. It was after three days of fruitless search when she was approached in the lobby of her hotel on Dizengoff Street in Tel Aviv. "A thousand apologies please" the young boy dressed in Arab clothing said, handing a folded piece of paper to her. The youth disappeared into the hotel crowd as if a puff of steam. Mary Frances unfolded the note that simply stated "tonight 8:00 p.m. at Ahad's". She recognized Ahad's as an exclusive Tel Aviv restaurant. She knew she was in harms way. She had to get to Israeli intelligence. She remembered that Justin had written the name and phone number of an Israeli officer on a piece of paper and gave it to her to be used only if she was in danger. She placed a phone call to Gideon Lot, the Israeli captain encountered during the excavation for the Cross. She was instructed to go to the restaurant and accede to the demands of those who demanded her presence. An intelligence unit of the Israeli Mossad would take care of the rest.

She dressed slightly upscale, as she was aware of the semi-formal atmosphere of the restaurant. She directed the taxi driver to the restaurant at Ahad Ha'am St. The taxi took her past miles and miles of massive medium rise apartments. The arabesque art deco structures from the early twentieth century were accented by the streetlights.

The driver stopped in front of the upscale restaurant. Mary Frances was nervous as she surreptitiously noted the glances of men standing near the entrance wondering if they were friends or enemies or maybe neither. She walked assuredly to the front door. The place had the feel of the 1930's with Arabic floor tile and tables dressed with hand painted Armenian plates. She also noted the Biedermeire chairs presumably brought from Germany.

She was greeted with a gracious bow by the Maitre d' and directed to a table near the rear of the enclave. She noticed the tall Egyptian rising to his feet, a grand smile through perfect teeth that seemed whiter in contrast to his olive skin, a pencil thin mustache accentuating his full lips.

"Please be seated" he directed, as a tuxedo clad waiter performed the seating rite. A number of male diners looked to her beauty and luxurious red hair, disdainful looks from their escorts.

"May I please introduce myself...my name is Anwar Kaddiz and my employer has taken note of your inquiries regarding an American.

"My name is Mary Frances Templeton," and the man I seek is my husband.

"Our sources are many and we just might be able to help you."

"I am very worried," Mary Frances said.

"Forgive my manners, but my medical condition requires that I must eat first, please enjoy yourself and do not worry about your husband. I was sent to help you. The watermelon soup with feta cheese and mint is superb," he said knowledgeably.

"I am not very hungry," Mary Frances said politely.

"May I suggest the quail flambé' salad with pate? For the light appetite" he insisted.

Mary Frances nodded her head affirmatively, knowing she had to "play the game" with her host before he would get on with the matter of discussing her "husband". Dinner first, information secondary.

He ordered the saddle of lamb, rare, with stuffed eggplants so miniature to deceive the eye and herbed skin of the eggplant crisp and flavorful.

They ate exchanging pleasantries about Tel Aviv until he made an indiscreet inquiry as to her occupation, which elicited her response: "An archeologist" she told him.

"You have hardly touched your dinner," he said solicitously.

"It must be the climate change."

"Then you must have the fig crepes with grand marnier sauce" he insisted.

"I am sorry to be such a poor guest, but my mind is on more important matters" she apologized.

"I understand," he said as he reached across the table and patted her hand.

Mary Frances pulled her hand away slightly.

"I will arrange a meeting with my employer, Mr. Khatabi, of whom you have been making inquiries. He is at his villa awaiting my call. My task was to determine if you were on a quest for information or a possible foe of Mr. Khatabi. He is very influential and high profile and such must be very discreet about strangers."

"When may I meet him?" she asked directly.

"Our driver is awaiting us as we speak" Kadiz offered, snapping his fingers to the waiter to help her from her chair.

They entered a black limousine and drove along Allenby Street north toward the hills of old Jaffa. She could see the Tel Aviv shoreline disappearing in the distance.

Within twenty minutes they arrived at a villa. It had been a silent trip with only a few words spoken between them. The villa was nondescript. Clean with functional lines of international style, a front portico with a sculptured balcony and curvilinear corners.

She was led into a library, dark and foreboding with only a small lamp splitting the room in two.

"Good evening" a voice from the corner intoned in a Middle-Eastern accent.

She turned toward the voice as the man stepped into the light. She felt a fear as none other in her life as she looked upon the scar face countenance of Moustapha the Assassin.

"Mr. Khatabi"? Mary Frances asked.

"I'm afraid not" Moustapha leered at her. "I am his cousin. Welcome to my home."

Presently a woman servant took Mary Frances to a suite on the second floor of the villa.

The rooms were opulent, ostentatious, and odorous. The sweet smell of incense permeated every nook and cranny.

"You will be my guest until my cousin, Mr. Khatabi arrives," Moustapha invited.

The main room of her quarters contained a tall winged Isis, beloved goddess of Egypt, it's cultured marble with gold leaf and hand detailed paint of red and blue in it's 3 foot wing span, towered over it's marble base. Her sunflower bed was typical

Egyptian motif. Twelve delicate sunflowers with green stems decorated the ornate wrought iron, the black and gold headboard of aged patina. The only chair had inlaid ivory in the shape of lotus blossoms, leg paws of a lion supporting the cedar of Lebanon frame. Heavy damask curtains kept the iron barred windows from view. Arabic rugs were strewn about as if an after thought. A small set of pyramids etched in brass sat upon a chest that Mary Frances deduced was from the pre-dynasty period.

Her dilemma and fear grew by the passing hours. Her only visitor was a lady servant with one hand. Mary Frances attempted to speak to the woman and was granted a negative shake of her hand with a finger pointing to her mouth revealing the absence of a tongue.

The lady servant obliquely and silently pointed out the cameras in the room including the one in the bath. Her wristwatch had been removed and the absence of any clocks in the quarters gave her pause to the time of day or night. It was the second day of her captivity when Moustapha entered her room abruptly.

Mary Frances felt a chill in her spine as she looked upon the scarred face of her captor.

"I take it your accommodations are satisfactory – I took the liberty of bringing your personal effects from the hotel."

"Thank you" Mary Frances said almost inaudibly.

"I trust you are ready to answer my questions and discuss who you really are?"

"I'm looking for my husband and felt Mr. Khatabi could be of assistance."

"And what business does your husband have with my cousin? Moustapha said with a beginning volley of interrogation, the intent showing through his piercing eyes.

"I do not know, he is a simple archeologist," she answered.

"Your beauty is only surpassed by your treachery, the fraudulent passport attests to this fact." Moustapha asserted as he threw the passport to the floor.

"You are not the local authority and my passport is of no concern to you" Mary Frances said.

"I <u>am</u> the authority in my home and you will answer my questions" Moustapha said, exposing his well-known temper.

"You have no right to hold me here," she said.

"My informants have advised me you are a Sister of the Roman Catholic Church – is this not so?"

Mary Frances knew her cover was gone and felt it best to cooperate with her captor.

"That is true," she admitted.

"And why would a nun be trying to contact Khatabi?" he asked.

"I told you I am trying to locate my husband," she had programmed herself so well she forgot that once discovered as a nun, she would have no husband.

"Your husband? Do you think I am an idiot? Perhaps your lover, maybe? You must be of the Order that has dispensed with virginity," he laughed. "Fear not, your secret is safe with me. Now, let us get down to the business at hand. You will tell me why you are here and what you want with Khatabi?" he ordered.

"Or what—you will have me deported?" she said with sarcasm.

"Of course deportation is a possibility – perhaps the Sudan where huge sums of money are garnered for a beautiful woman – I know of one merchant who would pay tens of thousand of dinar for a virgin of your beauty" Moustapha leered.

Mary Frances shuddered at the very real prospect of being sold into the white slavery organization of the Middle East.

"I will give you until tomorrow to decide if you wish to cooperate" Moustapha said ominously.

"I might just keep you for myself," he added taking her face in his hands and crudely placing his hand on her breast he laughed aloud and left the room. After about fifteen minutes, the one-handed woman knocked on the door, opened it and handed Mary Frances a plate of Tabouleh, the Middle Eastern appetizer of parsley and cracked wheat salad. She left the room and returned with another plate of Djejad... chicken roasted with apricots and put it on the table.

"What time is it," Mary Frances asked her in Arabic. The half tongued woman went to the cupboard and took out a bag of sea salt and spilled it onto the table. She then used her finger and drew a number that resembled a 7. "But, it is light outside," Mary Francis said. "It can't be seven!" she insisted. The servant shook her head negatively indicating that is not what she meant. Then she wrote the word Dalet in the salt. Mary Frances instantly recognized Dalet as the fourth letter of the Hebrew alphabet. The Hebrew symbol for Dalet resembles the number 7, an upside down reversed "L". It was only four o'clock. The servant quickly cleaned up the spilled salt and wiped off the smudge marks left by her finger. Mary Frances was puzzled. Why would this Arab woman be writing in Hebrew? It would be sometime later when Mary Frances would find out that the half tongued Arab woman was recruited by Israeli intelligence to infiltrate the terrorist cell run by Moustapha.

CHAPTER THIRTY-EIGHT

*H*osni Khatabi was at one of his many offices. This particular one was located in Caesarea on the second floor of a two story building. It was directly above the business run by the owner of the building, an antiquities dealer. Khatabi used it as a place to hold clandestine meetings escaping from under the ever-watchful eyes of the Israeli government. The office was always cluttered. The smell of tobacco and strong coffee overcame the Arabs heavily scented perfume. A huge mahogany desk with cigarette burns, that had all but destroyed the antique vintage of the wood, stood guard under a window that overlooked the main entryway into the building allowing Khatabi advanced notice of those who might not be welcome.

Seymour, the landlord, paid little attention to the comings and goings of infrequent visitors, as Khatabi always paid the exorbitant rent.

Hosni Khatabi fingered the large diamond ring on his hand as he read the report regarding inquiries made by an American woman on the streets of Tel Aviv. Her abrupt disappearance orchestrated by his cousin Moustapha, added to his anger. Khatabi slowly sipped the coffee, his fifth cup of the day. "Send for Anwar now!" Khatabi growled to his manservant. The order, when relayed to Anwar, would be met by fear. Moustapha employed Anwar, but he was also a paid informer to Khatabi. Greed placed this servant of two masters in a dangerous, if not foolish position, but this was not uncommon when forming Middle Eastern alliances.

"He is already here...he arrived ten minutes ago," the aide announced.

Anwar knew he best come clean with Khatabi and the sooner the better. Bad news traveled fast in this part of the world and sources of information were not always loyal or reliable. An incorrect interpretation without the opportunity for explanation could mean his execution.

"Send him in, now!" Khatabi ordered.

Anwar entered the room bowing repeatedly in supplication to the Arabic power broker.

"You have information for me?"

"Yes Mr. Khatabi – it is of utmost importance."

"And why has it taken you three days to share this important information with me?" Khatabi frowned.

"I only found out it involved you this morning" he lied.

Khatabi's report indicated Anwar had dinner with Mary Frances at the Tel Aviv hotel and abruptly left in a limousine registered to Xtant Trading Company, a front for Moustapha the Assassin.

"She is well, but under guard at Moustapha's villa." He wants to know why she needs to see you."

"And why does the son of a dung beetle just not ask me?" I have very little patience with anyone who interferes with my business." Khatabi fumed.

"He is a very foolish man" adding "I felt you should have this information" Anwar again lied to protect his own life.

"I am pleased you are here as we need to effect her escape while keeping my affairs private." Khatabi's eyelids narrowed as he began formulating a plan to rescue her.

"Is Josepha still working for my cousin?" Khatabi inquired.

"Yes, the one handed woman is serving the American lady" Anwar replied.

"Good, she will assist us if we need her. I know she hates the filthy bastard. You will contact the American Embassy anonymously, and report a missing person, last seen with you. The Embassy will contact the police and Interpol and ask for assistance. The Tel Aviv police commandant knows you work for Moustapha. They will put 2 and 2 together and issue a search warrant for Moustapha's residence.

Meanwhile, I will give Moustapha a little task to perform away from the villa. You will be at the villa during Moustapha's absence and will protest loudly and strongly to the police in spite in front of the household servants so they may report your resistance to Moustapha. Mary Frances was told to be ready to move quickly by Anwar, as she was to be rescued by the authorities.

The plan fell into place the next day. Anwar's protestations heard by all in the household and recorded on the surveillance equipment as Mary Frances was ushered down the rear steps to an unmarked Mossad vehicle.

CHAPTER THIRTY-NINE

$\mathcal{M}$y offer is four hundred million..." Khatabi spoke into the speakerphone on his desk. On the other end was Orlo Thompson.

"Outrageous! The agreed upon sum was fifty!" Thompson said, and I already paid you two million. Thompson knew full well the agreed upon sum meant nothing to the Arab.

"The price has escalated somewhat. Do you wish to counter?" Khatabi said simply as if the difference of three hundred fifty million American dollars was a trifle. "The demand seems to have outstripped the supply."

"I shall hold you to our agreement or..." Khatabi stopped Thompson in the middle of his sentence.

"Or what...you dare threaten me?" Khatabi's tone of voice hinted of a stronger emotion forthcoming.

"I have powerful friends here and abroad...I'll not be the target of extortion," Thompson shouted into the telephone.

"And I would suppose these same friends have children...possibly little boys?" Khatabi smiled at the pregnant pause in the conversation.

"I'll get back to you..." Khatabi heard the phone click.

"Do not tarry," the Arab said to the broken connection, his eyes taking in the confidential report and photographic evidence of Orlo Thompson's pedophilic sickness.

Khatabi's smugness quickly turned to rage as he was advised of the death of his driver and the capture of the Roman Catholic emissary. He summoned his driver and they began the one and one half hour journey. His anger was increasing with every dusty kilometer as he raced to Yamit and a confrontation with his cousin.

Mustapha's broad smile did not mirror the expression on Khatabi's face. The expected Arab greeting was absent, a serious breech of manners by both parties. Mustapha and his followers were aware of the power of Khatabi, many of whom would only whisper his name.

"Where is he," Khatabi demanded.

"Who?" Mustapha said coyly.

"Do not play games with me...the man in the military vehicle. He was to meet with me on a matter of great importance". Khatabi said raising his voice and showing his disrespect. Mustapha kept silent as he pondered how he would treat this man who embarrassed him in front of his troops. His men were waiting to see their chief's reaction to the perceived insults. Murmurs and bowed heads met the gaze of Hosni Khatabi.

"The emissary...I demand to know what you have done with him!" Khatabi repeated.

"With the doctor," Mustapha hand signaling to the small-dilapidated house behind them built with mud, rocks, and straw on the outskirts of the village of Yamit.

Khatabi entered and went to a small room at the rear of the house. He approached Justin, taking in the swollen face and matted blood thinking that this mangled piece of humanity was worth at least $250 million dollars to him. He felt the anger filling his throat, stifling an exploding urge to scream at Mustapha.

"Forgive us, an unfortunate accident even though you were under my protection. These are difficult times and I beg your forgiveness." Hosni Khatabi apologized to Justin. Justin remained silent beneath the bandages and blindfold. The painkiller drugs were beginning to numb his senses.

"Remove the blindfold," Khatabi demanded. Justin heard the rasping of the doctor's surgical scissors cutting away the blindfold letting in a dim light. The Palestinian doctor moved the examination light back and forth across his patient's eyes looking for a dilation reaction.

"This man must be hospitalized immediately," the doctor shook his head and pursed his lips. Justin felt the urge to vomit as the realization of his condition set in.

"I cannot see...I cannot see...Am I blind?" The American Pope could not believe the awesome question came from his own mouth.

"It is only temporary. The fool who bound your head so tightly contributed to your condition."

"Your passport indicates your name is Templeton. Do you wish anyone to be notified," Khatabi asked.

"No...No," Justin shouted. It was at that moment, Hosni Khatabi felt he knew the man and the voice. Images of men he knew flashed computer-like in the Arab's mind as he searched for the identity.

"The Cross!" Justin blurted out. Then the last piece of the puzzle fell into place, as Khatabi recognized the Pope of the Roman Catholic Church.

"Great Allah...you have given us your prize." Khatabi said pleased with his discovery.

"The Cross...what does this man have to do with the Cross of the Vatican?" Mustapha's face took on the mask of a fox.

"It is my arrangement," Khatabi glowered.

"Correction...it is now our arrangement," Mustapha raised his rifle slightly as if to give emphasis to his meaning.

"Do not interfere in this matter friend of my family," Khatabi's bodyguard made the first move as gunfire erupted in the small room.

In seconds the bodyguards lay dead as Hosni Khatabi struggled with his breath. Bright red blood welled from his chest, a look of amazement crossed his expression as he shouted; "I take your face with me to Hell," he screamed.

"Then allow me to speed your journey," Mustapha said as he plunged his knife into Khatabi's belly gutting him like a fish.

"When you pull weeds, it is necessary to get all the roots," Mustapha laughed. "When ye encounter unbelievers, strike off their heads until ye have made a great slaughter among them, and bind them in bonds, and either give them free dismissal afterwards, or exact a ransom," he said quoting the Koran as he fingered his black masbah beads. He knew his men would follow him without reservation for the true believer of Islam eagerly would fight and die in a "Holy War" with a firm assurance of a heavenly reward. The Assassin then grabbed for the huge ten-karat diamond ring on Khatabi's finger. Unable to pull it off, he spit on it but it still would not loosen. He pulled the knife from Khatabi's belly and sliced off the entire finger placing it in his pocket, ring intact. He looked down at Khatabi's eyes they were dialated and fixed. Mustapha muttered to himself, "so much for the fixer".

"On to Ras el Gindi, the Cross is ours...my cousin seems to have abandoned his interest...the ransom shall buy a free Palestine, and I shall be its Chairman," he vowed after searching Justin's clothing and removing everything he thought valuable like a vulcher hovering over a dead body. His biggest find was the negotiable securities in the inside pocket of Justin's jacket. He counted three hundred fifty million, the amount Justin was prepared to offer, but overlooked the fact that none of the certificates were endorsed. He thought he would now be paid twice. He knew Orlo Thompson was his mark. He no longer cared about the second bidder who was on the verge of dying in front of him.

"And what of him?" one of his men asked.

"Tie him up and leave him!" The Angel of Death will soon take him from his blindness," their leader said. Suddenly, Justin was alone, the silence pounding in his ears, his fear mounting. It was hours before Justin heard the tiny voice.

"Allah is merciful to all creatures," the voice said.

"Who is there?" Justin spoke into his darkness.

"It is Shasha, from the family of Azhar...I am sixteen," the child spoke proudly in her broken English.

"Please help me," Justin asked softly so as not to frighten her off.

"I do not know what to do," she replied.

"Untie me, I must get help," Justin pleaded. The girl attempted to loosen the knots, her fingers not having the strength to accomplish the task.

"I will get a knife," she said with the authority.

"Please hurry, Justin implored. His head was still throbbing from the tight bindings even though they had been removed. Shasha returned in minutes with a large butchering knife and with deft cuts loosened Justin Kennedy's bonds.

"Are you the devil?" she asked as she stepped back and looked into the bland unblinking eyes of the Pope of the Roman Catholic Church.

"Of course not," a slight smile came across his face. "Why do you ask such a question?"

"We are taught the light eyes are the devils that have stolen our land," she said innocently.

"No, my dear" Justin replied, "I am a man of God and you are blessed for helping me."

"Are you a Mulla?" she asked. Justin knew the term for the Islamic priests and answered her; "I suppose I would be in my own country."

"Then you have my respect...even though you do not look like a Mulla or even an Imam." She said in a matter of fact voice.

"Please would you give me water, I am very thirsty." Justin was becoming more aware of the darkness. Sasha returned with a long handled ladle of water and a wash cloth. The ladle felt warm to his lips as he eagerly gulped the tepid water.

"God bless you my child," Justin said.

"Why did they hurt you?" She asked as she gently wiped the dried blood from the bridge of his nose. She patted him on the head. It was if some latent maternal instinct took hold of her.

"Thank you...I must talk to the Israeli's." Justin said quietly.

At this she stepped back, her gasp signaling fear. "Do not be frightened...you will not be harmed. I promise you." Twilight began permeating the small room,

"It will be all right. We will pray to God for his deliverance," Justin assured her.

"Should I try to find someone to help us?" she asked.

"No...do not leave me," a tinge of panic in Justin's voice. Shasha began sobbing as Justin held her hand as to give her comfort.

"You are my Angel of Mercy." Justin told her as even more pain began wracking his body.

"My mother is dead and my father is gone with the men...He is always angry," she said in a matter of fact voice. Justin began praying aloud. He felt God would soon take him from this life. He slept fitfully through the night with Sasha watching over him. Justin awakened as gunfire from the northeast broke the silence of the dawn.

"Be still." Justin said. The gunfire drew closer as they huddled closer together in the small room. A bullet ricocheted off the adobe walls just outside the single broken window. Shasha saw her father in the glassless window frame. The man had come back looking for his daughter. His eyes squinted as he looked into the room, a crazed look on his face. He at once recognized the western clothing on Justin Kennedy. "Infidel...Infidel" he shouted as he lowered his rifle and pointed it into the room. Justin made the sign of the cross. The girl screamed, "No!..No! Father," as she stood in front of Justin in an attempt to protect him with her body. The man seemed to freeze as a bullet thudded into his back, his rifle slamming down into the sill. A solitary shot rang out from his weapon, the projectile barely missing his daughter.

The Israeli troops poured into the room, search lighting the place with their weapons.

"Clear," one shouted as an officer entered.

"Commander," an urgent voice directed the Israeli officers' attention to the floor. A dead Arab with a finger severed was in one corner, a girl in another, and a wounded man propped against the north wall.

"God of Abraham," Gideon Lot shouted as he recognized the face of the wounded man. "Bring the gurney," he ordered. Justin was placed on a stretcher.

"Who are you?" Justin asked

"Gideon Lot...of the Israeli army."

"The tank commander, Gideon Lot?" Justin asked.

Justin saw the face of his rescuer in his mind's eye. "Thank God," he said. "Is the girl all right?" Justin cried out.

"She is fine, we must hold her for questioning. It is her father that was killed."

"Ras el Gindi", Justin uttered to Gideon and then lapsed into unconsciousness. Gideon Lot knew the real identity of Justin Templeton. He had been briefed by Israeli intelligence.

Within one hour an air ambulance arrived to take aboard the famous patient.

Mary Frances, under the protection of the Israeli military, sat at his side, courtesy of Captain Gideon Lot. The air ambulance headed for an Israeli hospital in Tel Aviv.

* * * *

Justin was in and out of consciousness the remainder of the night as he lay in the hospital bed. He saw the vial of pills on the nightstand and mentally reached for the entire contents and saw himself swallowing them to the last. He fenced with himself in slow motion, his mind pain-wracked and starved for sleep attempting to play tricks with him as he lay back on a pillow in total exhaustion. He did not feel the blanket of sleep conquer the emotions of wakefulness. It was almost as if another tumbler had fallen into place, an inaudible click transporting him to the land of the unconsciousness.

CHAPTER FORTY

$\mathcal{G}$ideon's men tracked Mustapha and his band to the airfield at Ras el Gindi and radioed for back up support. The airfield had long been abandoned probably due to the fact that it was in a valley surrounded by mountains. Strategically, it was a double-edged sword. Enemies would have to traverse the mountains to find the airfield, but once found, the mountains became a perfect vantage point. The commandos took their positions spreading out into a half circle, to eliminate the chance of being hit by cross fire from their own forces. Their view of the valley below was unobstructed; their movements' ninja like, bathed in silence. They were close enough to smell the whole lambs being roasted by Mustapha's men in a huge fire pit only twenty meters from where the DeHaviland aircraft and Mustapha's helicopter were grounded. Gideon watched as a half dozen of the terrorists removed the Cross from the Aircraft and attached it with ropes to the pods of the helicopter. Mustafa peered at the Cross and boasted, "Like a whore, we sell it but we still have it". He walked toward the helicopter and patted the hatch like a master would reward his dog.

Mustafa, encircled by the most demented of his cohorts, shot bullets from their automatic rifles in the air as sign of victory.

The call for supper was made by another of the armed terrorists who, following his master's example, pointed his automatic weapon to the sky and fired off seven staccato-like rounds bringing the contingent of eighty men to the fire pit anxious to consume their evening meal. Mustapha took his meal by the helicopter with one of his pilots and two armed guards. The window of opportunity was now. Gideon appropriately gave the incursion the code name, "the last supper" intending to serve these enemies their just desserts. The Israelis, in a coordinated attack, carefully crept down from the cover of the mountains. Snipers fired the first three shots taking out the perimeter guards. The plan was to pick off the terrorists one by one without endangering the Cross. Confused and surprised, the Palestinian extremists ran for their weapons and began indiscriminate bursts of fire at enemies they could not see under the cover of the darkness. The leader of the group yelled in Arabic to stop firing but not before an errant spray of bullets cut out a small portion of one of the rotor blades of the helicopter as well as hitting the rotor hub. The fuel tank was intact. If hit by one misdirected bullet the gasoline in the tank could transform the copter into a huge fireball consuming the Cross, themselves, and all hope of ransoming the Cross to the highest bidder. Mustapha would not take that chance. He threw open the door of the helicopter and ordered his pilot inside. Gideon had no choice, he had to attack to prevent Mustapha's escape with the Cross.

The pilot instantly revved the engines, the rotor hub turning the blades with increased speed. The commandos descended on the terrorists, whom still confused, were bunched together with their backs against each other trying to ward off their attackers. A bullet from a sharpshooters weapon rang out. It ripped through the glass cockpit hitting the pilot in the left eye killing him instantly. The dead pilot fell to the side of his seat, his body pressed against the controls. The assassin's men fired barrages of rounds at the Israeli commandos who now were on the airstrip finding cover wherever they could. A fierce firefight ensued with the Israelis getting the upper hand although death was not limited to the Palestinians. Mustafa retreated to the safety of the helicopter. A few of his men followed only to be met with Mustafa's boot kicking the first man in the face propelling him backward onto the others leaving the remaining Palestinian fighters to fend for themselves against the Israeli commandos. He threw the pilot's body to the tarmac. He closed the hatch quickly and increased power to the engine. Mustapha the Assassin was now at the controls. The Israeli commandos led by Gideon Lot ran toward the craft dodging hostile fire as they sought to stop it. Mustafa engaged the controls and the helicopter lifted speeding North, it's precious cargo strapped indecently to its landing pods.

Gideon looked up as he realized his failure. "Shit", was all he could say as he watched the copter fly out of sight. He looked around. The terrorists who were not dead on the ground had fled.

Mustafa felt the helicopter torque, sliding the craft dangerously to the left. One of the blades had been cut from bullets of his own men. He now felt the affect of the damage to the rotor hub that was being loosened with every turn. He fought to gain altitude as he flew for ten minutes toward the Horeb Mountains.

In the near distance, he saw the summit erupt from the limestone range to the Northwest. He looked for a landing spot but could see nothing but the peaks of the mountain range. Suddenly, one of the rotor blades disengaged hitting an oil pressure line that spewed its contents onto the plexi-glass canopy. He was unaware of his proximity to the Sinai Summit and strained to see through any part of the canopy not covered in oil in order to see an emergency landing site. The copter was five hundred yards away from the summit and on a direct collision course with the uppermost tip. The landing pods shirred off as if some someone had taken a surgical knife to them. The ropes securing the Cross split allowing the ancient relic to freefall to earth. The Cross thudded into the soft sand and burrowed under the soil somewhere near the inaccessible summit of an uncharted mountaintop. It was as if a giant hand had dug out the earth, laid the Cross to rest, and then covered it over, preparing to wait centuries to be discovered again.

Mustafa continued struggling with the craft for twenty-five seconds, then the engines caught fire and the helicopter exploded. Over the next few weeks, local villagers who witnessed the fireball made their way to the site of the crash. Remnants of incinerated parts of the helicopter were scattered for almost a kilometer across the mountainous summit. The torso of the charred remains of the pilot clad in a burned and ripped jacket and separated from its extremities including the head, was found smoldering next to a piece of the cab of the helicopter. A villager pulled the only means of identification from the pocket of the remains of the jacket; a huge ten-karat diamond ring still attached to a burned and severed finger.

CHAPTER FORTY-ONE

$\mathcal{J}$ustin was recuperating at the hospital in Tel Aviv when Gideon Lot arrived to see him. Two weeks had passed since he was admitted. Mary Francis rarely left his side.

"I'll come to the point, your Eminence," Gideon started, "Khatabi is dead, Mustapha is dead, sixty of the terrorists died in the fighting. The Cross was tied to the pods of the helicopter with the Assassin at the controls. The copter crashed in the mountains, its remnants found by some villagers. We sent search teams out immediately to locate the Cross, but there was no trace of it. Some of the mountains in the region are so rugged man has never set foot on them. We scoured the area by reconnaissance aircraft as if we were standing on a whale searching for minnows. I'm sorry." Justin looked directly at Gideon through his dim vision, his tear glands still so damaged he could not emote the feelings he had at the moment.

"Gideon, I owe you my life. It would be ungrateful if I said to you that I would gladly trade my life for the Cross."

"I understand, you need say no more," Gideon needed comforting himself, having failed at this most important assignment.

He reached out and held Justin's hand. "I promise you, we will not give up. If it can be found, we will find it!" he said, trying to mask his helplessness with a forceful sense of confidence.

"I must have time to think this out. Perhaps it would be best to return to Rome for a few days of retrospect." Pope Constantine said.

"We will make arrangements for you to return by private jet. From there, you can return to the Castel Gondolfo when you are ready, your identity has not been compromised. We will also make arrangements for Mary Francis to return to Rome. It is best you travel separately."

"I would like to leave as soon as possible," Justin requested.

"We will have everything in order for you departures," Gideon answered.

* * * *

The Alban hills surrounding Castel Gandolfo were verdant with growth. Justin was amused as he noticed ongoing repairs to the little-used tennis courts were in full swing. The exquisite trappings of the Papal retreat seemed befitting for a king, and yet a heavy loneliness seemed to pervade the place. It was here, the Vicars of Christ were supposed to regain inner and outer strength for the ponderous job of pontificating. Justin reluctantly fell into the diminished routine of Castel Gandolfo, fully aware as the other Popes before him that all papal edits and items requiring his attention would have to wait. Even the most urgent matters were shelved until he would return to the Vatican. The retreat was twelve miles distant from the Vatican and millions of miles distant from the burdens of state; the pollution of the motorized city of Rome left behind, the noise of thousands of Vespa motor scooters were now unheard.

Justin looked out over the sparkling blue lake of Gandolfo. The splash of colors from the hastily erected canopies in the garden gave the place even more serenity. To the southwest one could almost hear the grapes ripening on the vine, giving vintage to the new season wine, and wealth to the small villages of Frascati and Aprilia.

The presence of Pope Constantine was important for the residents of the village of Gandolfo, dependent on the heavy tourist traffic while the Pope was in residence. It was enough to know that he was there. Very few held out the hope of ever catching a glimpse of the Vicar.

Justin walked the balcony in silence, only his inner mind speaking. The events of the past two months were kaleidoscoping rapidly and forming a picture. It was as if he had just awakened from an unbelievable dream and suddenly found himself Pope. Justin had not heard from Mary Frances since he arrived at Castel Gondolfo. It had been three weeks. The search, discovery, and loss of the Cross, Father Peter, the others in the cast of players on the stage of his life, and of course Mary Frances, flashed through his brain. What fate or destiny had decided the events that held him captive? And, his headaches continued. Regression to another time and place became more and more real. He walked from the balcony to the parlor, his aides appearing out of nowhere to fulfill any wish he might desire.

"il periodical?" an aide asked, as he offered his Pope the latest edition of Vatican News, the four-language newspaper published by the Vatican.

"Mille grazie, Senor, eh café, per favor," Justin replied as he tucked the newspaper under his arm and entered the main hall of Gandolfo, proud of his Italian, one of six languages he had mastered in his lifetime. Justin sank into a large overstuffed chair in the private study of the papal villa. The tinted lenses prescribed by his doctors that now enabled him to read the newspaper remedied his sensitivity to light. He saw a picture of his Coronation as Pontiff and a feature article. He became somewhat piqued at one reference in his biographical sketch that he had once been a member of the honor society at

Notre Dame. An obvious fabrication; he had not been a member of the honor society. He perused the pages of the newspaper, skipping the articles that were nothing more than an update of the goings on within the walls of the Vatican. Capelli had briefed him daily on the happenings in Rome. The wheels of the dynasty seemed to be running smoothly without Justin during the past month. He flipped the page and his heart beat wildly as he looked at the name under the heading of Vatican transfers. He looked once more to be sure before he reached for the telephone that was directly linked to the Papal Secretary at the Vatican.

"Connect me with Mother Superior of the Magdalene Order, quickly," he ordered. Directly, the Mother Superior was on the line, her face flushed with excitement at the request of the Pope to speak to her. She thought of the slight hope that he might be making inquiry as to her thoughts regarding becoming one of the first female Cardinals of the Catholic Church. Her hopes dashed quickly as she listened to the request from her Pontiff.

"I shall see what I can do, Holiness. She may have already departed," the reply came back to Justin, his hands sweating.

"It is of vital importance that I speak to her before she leaves for South America," he asked, fearful that his voice betrayed the urgency of the request.

He looked at the newspaper article once again. The words piercing his mind:

"Sister Mary Frances of the Magdalen Order has been granted transfer from her duties in Rome to a new post in the South America. She will begin a new missionary station in a small village in the Amazon rain forest, bringing the Gospel of Jesus Christ to the people indigenous to the area. We ask God-speed and love for our Sister in Christ."

Justin felt very much alone. His single link with a woman, his best friend and confidant, the one person with whom he shared his innermost thoughts, was leaving his life forever. Whatever the reasons were, he knew that she had no right to depart without a word, without some sign of final recognition. Was it anger or was it the helplessness of the situation that made him feel dismayed? He walked back and forth from one end of the study to the other, his eyes focusing on the telephone; ears tuned to a ring praying his pace would soon be interrupted.

"I have contacted the airport, Holiness, the Rome police have been instructed to bring the Sister to Castel Gandolfo for your audience; may I be of further service?" Mother Superior asked.

"Thank you dear Reverend Mother, I shall remember this favor—go with God and my blessing." Justin retired to the Papal study, feeling his emotions had been rubbed raw, as if the grind-stones of the wind had worn away the last vestige of will to fight. His attempted reverie was immediately disrupted.

"Excuse me, Holiness, I do not wish to disturb you, but Cardinal Wilhelm is here. He insists it is most urgent that you grant him an audience. I tried to tell him you were not receiving visitors. He is very insistent." The Papal aide appeared flustered as he was caught between two heavyweights of the Catholic Church.

"I do not wish to be disturbed." Justin instructed. Thinking to himself, this was not the interruption he was praying for.

"Begging this intrusion, Holy Father!" Wilhelm said as he barged into the room. He was carrying a briefcase.

The two Catholics exchanged looks for a few moments, squaring off like two tomcats, their expectant pious demeanor nonexistent.

"Very well. Now that you have come to Castel Gandolfo, I would surmise your visit is of weighty substance. Please be seat-ed." Justin motioned to a leather chair.

"I must make this point clear...I have no quarrel with your election, Holy Father. Our peers have made the choice and you are the Bishop of Rome," Cardinal Wilhelm began quickly, his Germanic voice calm and deliberate.

"I would expect nothing less from you. Your services to the Church are of the highest reputation," Justin replied, knowing he would have to constantly be alert for hidden meanings anytime this man spoke.

"That is why I am here...it is my love for the Church which has prompted me to seek this audience." Kurt Wilhelm's eyes narrowed.

"I am always open for dialogue with the leadership of the Curia and I welcome this opportunity to strengthen the relationship of your Pope and the College of Cardinals,' Justin said, his political instincts honing in on the leather strop of reality.

"I have not spent my lifetime in prayer and fasting as some of our brothers have done...I have spent it in learning about those things which make the Catholic Church a power in the world. Finances, diplomacy, politics and all the other necessary elements which make for astute and practical judgments for the millions of Catholics who look to Rome for leadership, secular and otherwise," Wilhelm said.

"Is it a matter of patronage...some appointment you wish me to make for a worthy churchman?" Justin asked.

"Patronage is child's play...if I wished to place a friend in a position within the hierarchy of the church, it would be accomplished in a matter of hours." Wilhelm laughed at the suggestion. Justin knew Wilhelm's words were correct. He had the backing and the power base to do what he had to do almost up to the point of assuming the Papal Chair.

"If it is not patronage you seek...just what does bring you to Gandolfo?" Justin's voice became testy in the sparring.

"I ask forgiveness for my words, Holy Father...but, I must, for the love of my church speak my mind," Wilhelm said.

"Speak then..." Justin asked of his visitor.

"Very well...you are aware that an American Pope is suspect even before he issues a single edict. Even though the world is rejoicing now that we have filled the void caused by Alphonse's death. This feeling is likened to the father of a household returning from a vacation. The children rejoice until the father exercises his power to discipline, and then the mood begins to change. Rejoicing turns to routine; routine turns to suspicion. This suspicion needs only a small nudge from a hint of scandal involving the Holy Father and the Church immediately becomes embroiled in controversy while the affairs of state are put on hold." Cardinal Wilhelm had succeeded in gaining Justin's attention. Justin was already forming a defense for his relationship with Mary Frances.

"My dear Brother in Christ, I am not without human failings...even if the magic transformation from mere mortal to Pope is accomplished. The infallibility of the Pope is nothing more than a coverlet to hide the mistakes the Vicar is sure to make during his tenure," Justin replied.

"Human feelings are rooted from deep within. Secrets of the mind are best left alone. Public scrutiny of one's mental foibles give rise to nasty connotations of madness," Wilhelm said.

"Would you please get to the point?" Justin said.

Wilhelm nodded. He opened his briefcase, which rested on his lap, then turned it so Justin could view its contents.

"You see before you these disks, duplicate disks which came into my possession quite by accident. I have listened to them and felt compelled to bring them here at once." Justin Kennedy stared at the tapes, his mind attempting to equate why the German Cardinal had them and more importantly, what was contained in them. "Do you know what is before you?" Wilhelm said threateningly.

"I have no idea," Justin replied.

"Then let me enlighten you and then ask for your explanation," Wilhelm continued. "These are medical recordings of private consultations with the Vatican psychiatrist, Dr. Otto Carlton."

Justin, stunned by the revelation, instantly assumed a defensive position.

"Let me see them please," he said and Wilhelm handed over the disks. "It seems the labels clearly indicate these are private and confidential. You have made a grievous error in listening to them," Justin said, his anger barely contained.

"It would be more grievous a sin not to have listened to them. It is my duty as a protector of the faith to bring them here for your decision," the Cardinal said.

"And what is your motive in delivering these recordings?" Justin asked.

"I have no motive except to protect the Church. If the contents of these tapes ever become public, the Church would crumble, never again to rise from the ashes as a Phoenix. Total destruction of the Roman Catholic empire is contained in them." Wilhelm continued the cat and mouse game.

"You dare speak to me of these things, I am your Pope," Justin felt the anger rise in him.

"You shall no longer be the Pope if God in His wisdom speaks to you. You have no choice in the matter. I demand you resign, or I shall..." Wilhelm did not finish his threat. He saw the veins pump in the Pope's neck.

"You dare threaten me?" Justin stood and began to step forward in an offensive posture.

"I do not believe violence is in your heart, my American priest, therefore, it behooves us to remain calm," Cardinal Wilhelm said carefully choosing his words by planting the seeds of a demeaning demotion from Pope to priest.

"It is not violence which I seek, it is to look deep into your eyes to find the truth of your being," Justin replied.

"You sit here in your <u>Katholisch Schloss</u> while Rome burns. Perhaps you <u>are</u> Judas Iscariot, the living incarnate of the evil man himself," Wilhelm suddenly said.

"It is you who are mad. What nonsense is this you prattle about?" Justin replied not knowing the contents of the disks because he was under a form of hypnosis while being treated by

Carlton during the periods of time regression. Wilhelm was unaware that Justin had no idea what information the disks contained. Justin only knew that Wilhelm was attempting to blackmail him.

Justin looked directly at his nemesis.

"For your insolence, I place upon you the threat of immediate excommunication, for violating a sacred trust and breaching your vow of obedience," Pope Constantine announced with firmness.

The German Cardinal's face reddened. Even he, who was steeped in the traditions of the Roman Catholic Church, was shaken by the threat.

"Then I plead to your sensibilities. These recordings will destroy both you and the Church. You must resign," Wilhelm again insisted.

"You may leave these private recordings and retire. Your audience is at an end," Constantine announced, his voice demanding a hasty exit.

"The tapes will condemn you, the Church will not, and cannot accept the modern precepts of reincarnation. And, by the way, the originals are being kept in a safe place."

Justin eyed the mysterious disks, the words of the German Cardinal pounding in his brain.

Cardinal Wilhelm instructed the Vatican driver to return to Rome. He sat stoically in the back seat and contemplated the happenings of the past hour. A gnawing doubt worked his mind into a knot. It was not every day, one took on the power of the Papacy with a direct confrontation.

Justin began listening intently to the recordings of his sessions with Dr. Carlton. The voice was unmistakably his, and yet the strange pronouncements sent shivers through his body. Could this be the riddle to his strange dreams and awesome headaches? Was it possible he was linked to the betrayer of Jesus? His mind could not fathom the dialogue, his sanity ebbing under the assault of the damning words of the tapes. He surmised correctly why Dr. Carlton ignored his request for the recordings ten days earlier. He had no choice. The matter was too sensitive for consultation with others in the Church. Justin knew what he had to do.

It took him two hours to draft his letter of resignation. Once accomplished, he breathed a sigh of relief as he placed the document on the desk. He walked to the window and suddenly felt homesick for America. He felt a calmness cover him as his eyes took in a storm brewing in the hills. He walked across the main hedgerow road and entered the Gandolfo grounds. The air had the hint of rain to it as he stopped to visit with a small butterfly that had landed on a yellow flower. A small field mouse scurried in fright as he continued his walk. The weight had suddenly been lifted from his weary shoulders. His lungs took in the fresh air. A flash of lightning caught his eyes and he began to count the time that elapsed between the lightning and the clap of thunder that echoed across the valley. When he reached the number seven, he surmised the distance was less than a mile away, using the yardstick he had learned as a boy. Justin knew in his heart he had done that which God had directed him to do and yet many unanswered questions continued to bother him. Droplets of soft rain began to pelt his face as he looked to the sky, now growing dark and menacing. A distant rainbow arched its colors over the hills towards Rome.

He heard her while his back was still facing Gandolfo. He turned and saw her waving both arms attracting his attention. She could not see the look of relief on his face. Justin retraced his path quickly. He joined her in a matter of minutes.

"Thank God. You came," He blurted out.

"It seemed I had little choice in the matter," she replied, a glance over to the Rome Police vehicle added to her seeming dismay.

"But I had to see you before..." He started.

"I would have not missed seeing you if it were possible." She smiled, again sending him off balance.

"Then why did you not tell me?" he asked.

"Is it the Pope's position that every nun who seeks a transfer must advise him?"

"Of course not. But, you are not "every" nun. In your case, it should have been recognized. Our kinship must transcend politics."

"And I am now here, by your bidding." Her emerald eyes seemed almost a reflection of nearby Lake Gandolfo.

"My dear impulsive creature, swift to weep and swift to smile. The knowledge that you are close by me, even if we cannot see each other, is enough to sustain my soul. I do not know what will be in store for me if you leave taking with you that spark that assures me that the dawn will always follow the dark." The drizzle of the soft rain was now beginning outside the walls of Gandolfo and rapidly developing into a heavy downpour as it followed them. "Come, let's get out of the rain." Mary Frances followed Justin to the Papal Study.

"What is to become of me?" she asked. "Am I to sit on the sidelines pining for you as you carry on the affairs of state? It is better that I leave rather than live with a soul that cannot be satisfied. I can no longer bear to watch as you drift farther and farther away. The demands of the Church exact a price. That price is a slow torturing of my heart."

The pair sat quietly for a few moments, each of them grappling for the correct words. Justin was the first to speak. "Pleasure does not always follow pain. There is always hope. My pain runs deep as well. I need you now. The Church cannot give me the warmth and comfort I seek at this moment. You are the only one I can turn to," he said.

"There are no simple answers. Are we not both facing the same dilemma? The decision to seek a post away from the Vatican was the only decision to be made. I weighed my feelings for the Mother Church and for the feelings which you engender in me." She paused and lowered her eyes, then raised them again to his. "I would grieve in my heart if I remained and clouded your true resolve to unite the Church. The future holds only dreams for people like us. Hope is the reality of the today's we must face apart. This hope will dim as time passes. It is my fondest prayer that memories will forever unite us in kinship of mind and spirit," she tried to explain. "I have made my decision for the good of both of us. Someday, perhaps not too distant, you will know that I have chosen the correct path to follow," she said as she placed her hand on his. He felt the warmth, both physically and spiritually.

"I also have made decisions which will change my life forever." Justin glanced over to the letter of resignation on the oak desk.

Mary Frances walked over to the desk and saw the letter. She picked it up and read it not quite understanding what prompted the writing. Her dreams of his abdication and her life with him seemed frightening now that it seemed he was willing to do so.

"The people of the world need you more than I. Can you not see that which is happening around you? I do not fancy myself as a sacrifice on the altar of public opinion, but neither will I stand between the people of the Catholic faith and I feel the greatest man ever to sit in the Chair of Peter."

"And this coming from you further clouds my mind. If, in this hour, and by your presence here, you say that my life is to be dedicated to justice and fairness to my fellow man, then why do I still seek that missing ingredient? The vital something to make me complete?" Justin said simply.

She now found herself trying to discourage him, she didn't want to in her heart, but felt guilty if she failed to try. "I shall always be with you in friendship. Miles are nonexistent when true feelings transcend distance. You and I have somehow become entwined during these past months, and now the vines must seek a different direction, if only to grow stronger and search for the sun." She appeared to have come to grips with the reality of the situation.

"Without the nourishment of tender love, good earth and water from the heavens, the vine shall wither and die," Justin said.

"You have the love of your people. Your reign will have the deep tap roots which will find the earth and water it requires to grow." She said.

"Why is it that you force me to think more clearly, feel more intently? That remarkable facility to strip away the clouds of uncertainty," Justin asked her.

"Can you not see? I am not a Pandora's box filled with secrets. It is the love I have for you and for my Church," she replied.

"It is my feelings for the Church which have become suspect. I question my ability to rule, even to administer. These doubts have directed me toward resignation from the Chair of Peter," Justin said. He spoke of his plans, talking as he walked over to his desk. He paused, and then took his resignation letter from her hands. Suddenly anger overtook her. She glared at him for the first time, her jaw set.

"Well, what is it you wish me to say? Do you wish me to give it a stamp of approval? Is it well thought out? Does it have merit and substance? It has none of these! If you wish me to tell you what is wrong with it...I'll tell you. It is all wrong! She became increasingly angry. "Tear it up, mix it with chemicals and burn it in your fireplace...Signal the world once again that they have a new Pope, a Vicar able to unite the world. A Pope to change the course of history and yes...a Pope so filled with love and compassion for his Church and its peoples that he is even willing to give up the Papacy." Her voice filled with emotion, her face flushing as she looked directly into Justin Kennedy's astonished face.

"Do I consider myself properly chastened? Shall I change my mind every day? It is not so simple. God would have it no other way for me. All of my life I have been faced with decisions and these decisions were made based on my best judgments," he said adamantly.

"This decision is not yours to make!" Mary Frances argued back.

"Shall I consult a crystal ball? Is it necessary to study the entrails of a chicken to show me the way? Or perhaps you, my wandering queen, have the key to the future," Justin said, his voice mocking.

"Men...all they can think about is the problem. God bless the mothers of the world who teach their sons about solutions!" Mary Frances again turned from him and walked to the window. Her mind attempted to react to the dilemma.

"Before you cast me to the lions, hear what the letter does not say." Justin told her of the visit by Wilhelm, and the attempt at blackmail as he related the contents of the recordings. He also told her of the twenty-five million dollars in negotiable bonds that were no longer in the asset column of the Vatican balance sheet. The deception of the Father Peter "miracle" was next on the list of his confessional. It was as if a dying man was telling all to repent for his sins so he could walk through the gates of heaven.

She listened intently as she knew in her heart Justin's decision, though not verbally expressed, was also based partly on his desire to continue the relationship they both felt was beginning to consume them. Was her love for the Catholic Church stronger than the love she was constantly suppressing in her heart for Justin Kennedy? She knew she held the future of the Catholic Church in her hands. She could tip the scales to either side. Justin was second-guessing himself making him vulnerable. It would be easy for her to applaud his resignation, and then he would be hers. She did not want him by default. She would not let him succumb to blackmail. If the decision was to resign, it had to be made for reasons other than Wilhelm's threats. Justin left the room and walked to the balcony as he looked at the rain still pouring in the distance. She went to him, her arms encircling his waist, her head resting on his back as he stared at the hills.

"Forgive me, my heart...I have not the right to speak this way. You are my Pope, not my lover," she whispered.

"If only it could be different. If only our lives could belong to ourselves. But it is not to be. My decision must be made to save us both from damnation and God's fury." Justin took her in his arms and held her gently. They stood quietly on the balcony, eyes closed in repose and thoughts. A light drizzle continued to fall. The world no longer existed for the star-crossed lovers. Only this moment was important, for in their hearts they felt they would never again be as close. It was Mary Frances who broke the spell as she took Justin's face in her hand.

"Know this...I love you," she said.

"And I you...I shall always be near to you... you'll remain in my thoughts and my prayers for as long as I live." Justin looked into her face, his hands stroking her hair.

"I'll take these sweet memories with me, locked in a secret chamber of my heart. And when I feel lonely or sad, I shall take the key of this moment and unlock the sorrow, remember our love and be lifted to the skies," Mary Frances said as her soft eyes showed a strength of hope and resigned satisfaction. "I ask only one thing of you, for now. Wait a few days before you do anything. Do not submit the resignation yet. I must have time to think alone about a solution. Promise me that," she said.

"I promise. But my decision will not change. If I do not follow this course, the recordings will come to light and force the issue."

"We shall see," she responded. "I wish one other favor."

"And what would that be?" Justin asked.

"Call Cardinal Capelli. Tell him I will be contacting him about a delicate matter and that he should give me full cooperation. Don't worry, it has nothing to do with the recordings."

CHAPTER FORTY-TWO

$\mathcal{M}$ary Frances traveled the twelve miles to Rome for her meeting with Capelli arranged by Justin per her request.

"You are a most trusted confidant of his Eminence," she began. "He is concerned that there may be some in the Curia that might view the negotiable bonds entrusted to him as a squandering of Church assets."

"Let me reassure you, dear sister, issuing those bonds was a business decision. It has already been buried in the accounting records and will not be discussed again. Those approving it are as much to blame...if there is fault, and they will say nothing," Capelli answered.

"It is still another battle his holiness is fighting and he needs no more battles in light of the recent events. I would like you to find out the name of the person who negotiated payment. Can you do that?"

"Of course, but what do you intend, asking for return of the funds because there was no quid pro quo? That cannot happen. It has been decided that the public is to have no knowledge that the

Cross is no longer in our possession. We cannot risk making the truth known," he admonished her.

"No, that is not my purpose. Will you grant my request having given your promise of cooperation to his Holiness."

"I will do so, pursuant to his request and my promise," he said begrudgingly.

"And," she said politely, "I will need the information by tomorrow noon."

Mary Frances visualized Justin standing in the middle of a room watching as each of the four walls began to collapse upon him. She spent the evening strategizing what she could do to tackle each problem one at a time to relieve his pressure. The thought of everything coming down on any mortal all at once was overwhelming. Capelli would deliver her answer personally just before noon the next day. He telephoned her to meet him at the front of the Basilica.

"Good day, Sister," he said cordially. She responded by thanking him for his attention to the matter requested.

"The negotiable bonds had the guaranteed signature of Pope Constantine. Once endorsed by him they could be cashed through a transfer agent. In this case, I located the transfer agent, called him and gave him the specific certificate numbers of the bonds." He pulled out a folded sheet of paper, opened it and began reading.

"The securities were deposited in the Middle Eastern International Bank in Macao. The account is registered in the name of Ramadan Trading Company. There are two signatories authorized to draw on the account."

"Did you happen to get their names?" she asked.

"Yes, the transfer agent was good enough to ask the bank for the information. The signatories are Hosni Khatabi and Marcella de la Sant. Also, the money was withdrawn by Marcella de la Sant only days after it was deposited."

"Marcella de la Sant...she lives here in Rome doesn't she?"

"There is a Marcella de la Sant here...I don't know if it is the same woman. On the other hand, the name is not very common," Capelli added.

It took Mary Francis little time to locate the villa just outside of Rome where Marcella de la Sant resided. She decided to dispense with normal protocol and simply showed up at the villa without calling first. Marcella's servant was caught off guard when she answered the door and saw a nun.

"Forgive me," Mary Francis said. "I am here to see Countess Marcella de la Sant. I have no appointment but it is urgent Vatican business." She felt the white lie regarding her authorization from the Vatican might be the only way she could get an audience with the Countess.

"I will see if my mistress will see you, Sister." The mention of Vatican business worked. It was enough to engage Marcella's curiosity. Perhaps it involved Wilhelm she thought. She advised her servant to bring the Sister to her in the garden parlor. Mary Francis entered the villa thinking how it would take millions to keep one in the lavish lifestyle of such a Countess.

"Sister...this is indeed a surprise," Marcella said greeting her.

"I'm sorry for the intrusion without proper prior arrangements, but I am here on Vatican business and must speak to you alone. My name is Sister Mary Francis."

Instantly, Marcella recognized her as the same nun Wilhelm suspected as having a more than platonic involvement with Justin Kennedy, now Pope Constantine.

"May I offer you something, a refreshment perhaps?" Marcella asked cordially.

"Thank you no," Mary Francis demurred.

"Then how may I be of help?" Marcella asked.

"I have come for the money that belongs to the Church."

"What are you talking about?" Marcella replied coyly trying to find out just how much the nun knew.

"The Vatican has sent me to see if we could work this out without further incident," she lied, but continued. "Twenty-five million in negotiable bonds deposited to a bank account in Macao and withdrawn by you only a few weeks ago." Mary Francis was unsure where she was going or how far she was going to get. In the back of her mind was the possibility she could recoup some of the money and still keep the matter quiet. It was worth a shot.

Marcella reacted stoically realizing that the money was traceable to her and determining to keep as much of it as possible.

"You'll have to enlighten me...I made no agreement with the Vatican and certainly not for a sum of twenty-five million dollars."

"It makes no difference that you were not the principal, you have ill-gotten gains and we both know it. I'm here to avoid the unpleasantness that will certainly occur when you are charged with criminal fraud." Mary Francis' bluff would have placed her as a top contender in the World Series of Poker.

"I see," Marcella continued, "I am not inclined to part with the money no matter who was its former owner," she said buying time to think of something. "And, how does it feel to be the lover of the most powerful man in Rome? Don't deny it, I know of you and your liaison with Pope Constantine." Marcella always attacked when backed into a corner. "Never mind, you need not answer," she said indignantly.

"I understand that Mr. Khatabi met an unfortunate death. Does that not mean that decisions are now solely in your discretion?" Mary Francis countered. Mary Francis had carefully ignored Marcella's last comment replacing it with a seed of suggestion that Khatabi no longer called the shots. She had nothing to lose and everything to gain and continued with the game. "Do you have a proposition?"

Marcella thought for a moment and then responded, "you may be quite right my dear. Possibly I can offer you something more valuable than money," Marcella teased. "Then, maybe we can both solve this dilemma." She went to her wall safe, opened it and took out a manila envelope. "In this envelope is the key to the Throne of Peter, at least in your case," she said. She reached inside the envelope and pulled out the disks. "The information on these disks are sufficient to destroy your beloved Pope. They are private session tapes your Justin Kennedy had with the Vatican psychiatrist. These are the originals. They are no longer in the doctor's files. And... the only copy was given to your priest," she said degradingly. "The man is most assuredly insane!" she said abruptly.

Mary Francis finally saw the complete picture. The connection between Marcella and Wilhelm was now evident. The recordings Justin told her about were the very same Marcella now appeared to be offering in exchange for the twenty-five million dollars. But how did the money come to her through this man Hosni Khatabi? She didn't understand, but it didn't matter. A bargaining chip was offered by Marcella that was never expected.

"The Church has plenty of money. Accounting errors occur all the time. Let's discuss the matter as two women who each have a love beyond that of the Church...not as between a Countess and a Nun. Do I make myself clear, Mary Francis?" Marcella continued without waiting for a reply. "I happen to have a love of a material nature not quite as personal as yours. Nonetheless, who is to say your love is any deeper than mine?"

"Go on, I'm listening," Mary Francis replied.

"You will agree to drop all inquiries and report to the Church that I have no involvement in whatever dealings it may have had involving twenty-five million dollars or any amount. In exchange, you shall have the original of the recordings to do with as you like. Perhaps they will be of some value to you in the future, who knows?" she said projecting her own evil thoughts of blackmail. Marcella had taken the precautions of hiding the funds in multiple offshore accounts anyway. The only risk if Mary Francis reneged on such a deal would be the exposure of her relationship with Wilhelm. She could live with that if she had to. She could not live without the security of the twenty-five million dollars. Mary Francis did not have to contemplate the deal.

"We have struck a bargain, Marcella de la Sant. On my woman's word of honor I will be bound by our agreement." Just as those words flowed from the mouth of Mary Francis, Marcella de la Sant handed her the disks and said, "bonding is such a noble adventure...excuse the pun." Mary Francis smiled and Marcella showed her to the door. She would wait one day before returning to Castel Gandolfo, but called Justin to let him know that she would be there and to assure herself that he would make no decision before talking with her.

Justin put the telephone receiver back in its cradle. He felt a trembling take over his body. He was frightened, more afraid than at any time in his life, not knowing if he were going insane or having a nervous breakdown. He resolved to consult with Dr. Carlton. A phone call to the doctor was met with an immediate appointment. He would be seen by Carlton as soon as he arrived in Rome. He summoned his driver. Justin was ushered into the private entrance of the psychiatrist's office.

"Am I going insane?" Justin asked of his doctor.

Dr. Carlton thought carefully before he responded. He wanted to take care that the correct words were spoken so as not to alarm the Pope.

"It is absolutely necessary that you find a handhold, something to grasp. The changes in your life over the past months have hammered away at your physical and mental health. You must not succumb to the Silver Bullet Syndrome. You are as mortal as any man, and just as subject to pressures thrust at you from many directions," Carlton said quietly.

"But this latest episode...I was wide awake and suddenly, I was completely lost to some inner urging which transported me to another time, another place." Justin held his hands up in disbelief. "Doctor, I have listened to the tapes."

"You what?"

"I have listened to the session recordings. I know about Judas!"

"That would be impossible," the doctor answered in shock. "You will wait right here, I will be back in a moment." Carlton went to the adjoining room and to the vault. He opened the file marked "JK Extremely Confidential", opened it and brought it back to his office.

"I do not understand it, the disks are missing." The doctor had a perplexed look of embarrassment evident in his expression. "How did they come into your possession?"

"It doesn't matter," Justin answered, not wanting to bring Wilhelm into the matter. "Suffice it to say I have copies." Justin reached in his pocket and showed the disks to his doctor.

"You must answer my question, am I insane?"

"One's imaginations are as strong as the intellect which produces them. Your personal involvement with the Cross, coupled with a possible psychic connection with Judas, has created turmoil within your mind. We must sort things out and take them one at a time," the doctor said.

"The Cross is my treasure...I found it!" Justin surprised himself at the tone of voice he used, and of his use of the personal pronoun.

"That is the point I am making, Holiness...the Cross is still only the Cross. It cannot become the focal point of your every waking moment. Your fears regarding the safety of the Cross are unfounded. While few know it is no longer in the Basilica, those of us who do know must believe it is again in the custody of God, who moves in mysterious ways."

"And its powers... its curative powers?" Justin said, insisting on a professional opinion.

"I have consulted with my colleagues in this matter and it is the consensus that all of the supposed miracles and cures were brought about by the same hysteria which created the patients' ills in the first instance," Carlton advised dryly and without emotion.

"And what answer do you learned men of the medical profession have regarding Father Peter's miraculous cure?" Justin insisted on something other than a patented answer.

"I grant you, man could never conceive of a miracle if none ever occurred in the first instance. Some things will never be explained to the satisfaction of everyone," Carlton said.

Justin was still not satisfied as he retorted, "I believe you people do not know what you are dealing with. The Scriptures are filled with miracles manifested by our Savior. What about Lazarus, rising from the dead...the healing of the lepers, the blind, and the deaf? Jesus even reattached the ear of Malchus at Gethsemane? These and many more are miracles that we as Christians accept without doubt. Are we now so sophisticated in this modern day, that we cannot accept that which in the past was accepted without reservation?"

"I am sorry, Holiness...I do not have the answers you seek. Perhaps if I call in some colleagues to consult with me we may be able to ease this journey through the unknown."

"No! That is not necessary..." Justin responded fearful that others might be apprised of his illness." I am asking a simple question...am I losing my grip on reality, slowly losing my mind...or is this some passing emotional stress-related illness?"

"The question is simple enough to understand, it is the answers which are difficult to deal with. I could prescribe rest and medication or even more drastic measures such as making sure you are heavily sedated. I elect to do none of these things. Reality must be faced head-on, even with the risks involved.

"And what are these risks? Justin asked.

"You have had episodes of regression while you were awake. While this is extremely rare for the conscious mind to do, we sometimes all float between the conscious and subconscious at one time or another...it is called daydreaming, and could be caused by fatigue or something as non-esoteric as eating too many sweets," Carlton explained.

"And what happens if these episodes, as you have termed them, continue, pick up in intensity, become more vivid and real?"

"In that case, you would have to be committed for your own protection," the doctor said averting his eyes from Justin.

"Is it possible to slip into this phenomenon and not return?" Justin asked.

"Unfortunately...yes. Many mental institutions have at least one patient who believes he is Jesus Christ. In fact, the Jesus Syndrome is quite common."

"Your prognosis?" Justin asked abruptly.

Dr. Carlton cleared his throat for a moment, "I believe your problem is more than stress related. The tapes indicate a deep-rooted psychosis that can be controlled with therapy and mood altering drugs. One shock can produce a trauma and push you over to the other side. It is necessary that you keep in daily contact with me until we get through this period." Dr. Otto Carlton signaled an end to the conversation by handing over a vial of pills to his patient with instructions on their use.

Justin returned to the papal residence, his mind on his dilemma. What part was the Cross to play in the strange connection with Judas? He slept that night with the aid of the pills prescribed by Dr. Carlton. His last memory before he dozed off was the anticipation of seeing Mary Francis the next day.

CHAPTER FORTY-THREE

$\mathcal{M}$ary Francis arrived at the Pope's retreat promptly at 10:00 a.m. She saw Justin on the balcony, his hands behind his back pacing the marble veranda as if he was the loneliest man on earth. She called to him but he did not hear her. She entered the villa not waiting to be greeted, and walked the stairs to the study and out to the balcony. "Justin," she said softly, wanting his attention but not wanting to disturb his apparent meditation. Again, he did not hear her. She walked to him and placed her hand on his shoulder waking him from his trance-like state of mind. He turned and saw her. His eyes welled but he held back his emotions. Mary Francis was not so disciplined.

"I have lost you and I have found you. I draw from your strength, my dear Sister," Justin whispered, trying to maintain an inner strength that he knew was waning. He held her gently for a few moments more, no further words necessary. She took his hand.

"I have wonderful news," she said, smiling through her tear-streaked face. She took his arm and walked him over to the railing of the balcony. They stood in silence for a moment looking into the distance. Pockets of low mist surrounded the hills clinging to the valley slopes, almost as if the heavens had decided to visit the earth. A magnificent rainbow appeared asserting its colors in a manner that artists have attempted to recreate for centuries.

"I have spoken with Cardinal Capelli. You need not be concerned with the twenty-five million dollars in bonds. The Church has expensed the amount as part of its budget for archeological development. It is no longer an issue. The accounting treatment is perfectly valid. It will never be questioned. But, I have even better news." She reached in her pocket for the disks. "You will never be blackmailed by Wilhelm or anyone else. These are the original disks of your sessions with Dr. Carlton." She handed them to Justin and smiled with satisfaction.

"But...how? How did you do this?"

"It doesn't matter. I did it for you and God was with me. I was simply the instrument of His work," she answered. She saw a sense of relief in his face but the unabashed exhilaration she expected to see was missing.

"Are you all right?" she asked. Justin said nothing. He seemed remote and distant trying to make sense of what transpired.

"Come," he said as they walked into the study, a paneled room that smelled of ancient wood and new money that created an odor of sanctity. The fireplace was spilling its warmth over the hearth and down across the deep pile carpeting. Justin held the disks in his hands contemplatively. He went to his desk and picked up the letter of resignation and came back to Mary Francis where they both stood in front of the fireplace. Justin stared at the flames. The words of the tapes and the words of his resignation tumbled in his mind as he fingered them both. He was wrestling with a Solomonic decision.

"Burn them both," Mary Frances urged. "Throw them into the fire."

"It is an easy thing to do," Justin said with a renewed clarity of mind. "I could simply drop the disks into the fire and destroy the evidence needed by Wilhelm to dethrone me and embarrass the Church. Or, I could return them to Dr. Carlton, where they belong knowing they will be needed by the psychiatrist if he is to help me. I could be risking the danger that they might again return to the wrong hands. But, I can now make certain the disks would be afforded maximum security." He articulated the struggle within verbally, hoping the sound of hearing his voice might help him analyze the options.

"As to the letter of resignation. You and I are the only ones who have seen it. No one else knows it even exists. Certainly, that simplifies the problem of its destruction."

"Give it to me," Mary Francis insisted as she reached for letter of resignation. Justin pulled it away.

"You must understand. The disks, even if destroyed, do not erase the knowledge of their words imbedded in my mind. Am I fit to sit as the Vicar of Rome? Do I need help? What if my headaches and nightmares continue to the point that I am incapacitated? It is not the blackmail of Wilhelm that concerns me, it is the deception my mind encourages should I believe that I am infallible, and above the possibility of mental illness. It is not I who will be hurt; it is the millions of our Catholic brothers and sisters. A wrong decision places me in the same category of those priests who have covered up the sins of other priests. The Church was not better off by their acts, and the Church will not be better off if I cover up this monster inside my mind and find that I cannot perform what is expected of a Pope." The incredible realization that his age regression pointed to juxtaposition with Judas Iscariot weighed upon his already burdened mind. The mystical quality of the Cross further disturbed him. The happening with Father Peter, enhancing the distinct possibility of a curative Cross. What far-reaching effects would be manifested if the Cross, did have these powers? Could he or anyone deal with this new aspect of human history, he pondered? Justin's natural intellect directed that an inanimate object could not encircle mystical power. He reasoned quite properly, that people who fell under the spell were absolute fools or were in such an emotional state that they and all around them were easily victims of their own flammable imaginations, and yet this was no ordinary object. This <u>was</u> the Cross on which his Christ abolished the fear of death!

"I must deal with many unresolved questions and deal with them alone. There is no choice. Justin felt something strange come over him. A calmness he had not experienced for months descended upon him. His tensions seemed to melt as an ice cube on a hot pavement. He now knew, through direct revelation with his God, what he must do, once again bringing credibility to the old adage, "<u>Whom the Gods wish to embrace they first drive mad.</u>"

"I will resign," he said adamantly, feeling a great relief once he uttered those words.

"I do not deserve the love you have given me," he said. "I am grateful for everything you have done." Mary Francis looked up at him and said, "It is far from over, my love. I will be with you every step of the way."

"Go now, go with the grace of God, and the blessings of your Church," Justin said as he released his hand from hers.

"<u>Veni</u>, <u>Vidi</u>, <u>Vici</u>," she said as she left him.

The American Pope called for his personal valet and announced, "We return to the Vatican, arrange for Cardinal Wilhelm to meet me tomorrow morning at 10:00." With this, the commencement of a new age of Catholicism would begin.

Justin Kennedy sat quietly in the sanctity of the Papal study in Rome, it was one hour before he was to meet Wilhelm. To his left, like a group of dark suited pallbearers waiting for the body, sat the lawyers, all of whom assured him that the discussions about to take place were subject to an attorney-client privilege and would never be revealed. Their Pope sat quietly in a high-backed chair, looking very un-pontifical behind tinted glasses. The discussion was brief, with the Pope listening intently to the options and ramifications of an abdication scenario. He thanked them for their counsel and excused himself. He rang for his aide and requested a shot of schnapps. He looked at the magnificently carved wall mounted clock noting the time as 9:45 a.m. He had fifteen minutes to gather his thoughts. Wilhelm would not be late.

"Your schnapps, my Holiness," his aide handed Justin the drink and left immediately feeling the tension in the room given off by a strange form of energy. Justin sipped the drink as if to wet his lips then tipped the glass finishing it in one gulp. He had formulated his plan and awaited his adversary. The time was 10:00 a.m.

"Cardinal Wilhelm has arrived for the scheduled meeting, your Eminence," the aide announced.

"Please, show him in," the Pope requested. Wilhelm entered the study and promptly reached for the Pope's hand and kissed the ring in respect for the office, if not the man, then stepped back.

"I have had time to consider your threats of blackmail and my resignation," the Pope began. "Is it your wish that the College of Cardinals be convened?"

"I knew you would come to the right decision, your Eminence, for the good of the Church. Yes, it is appropriate to call upon the College of Cardinals for selection of your successor," Wilhelm answered.

"Then, I will give you the duty of contacting them and arranging for all to meet with me tomorrow at 1:00 p.m. in the Sistine Chapel. That is all we have to discuss," Justin said curtly dismissing Wilhelm, who left with a sense of victory. Wilhelm spent the rest of the day notifying the other Cardinals of the Conclave to be held the next day, and not too subtly suggesting that if the Pope should resign, he would be the logical successor. The following morning he met with several groups of Cardinals forming alliances that he was sure would bring him the Throne of Peter.

Sounds of hushed voices echoed from the walls of the Sistine Chapel as the Cardinals walked to their assigned seats. The call to order muted the sounds of their voices. Pope Constantine II entered the Chapel and took his place at the podium. The room was silent. The Pope nodded to Capelli signaling him to bring in the only outsider. All eyes turned to Capelli as they watched him open a side door and escort Dr. Otto Carlton into the Chapel and to a place beside the Pope. Wilhelm looked perplexed.

"My brothers," Justin began. "Many of you have had the pleasure of meeting my esteemed guest, Dr. Carlton, on a prior occasion. Some of you can attest to the quality of care he has given you when you sought his medical advice." The Cardinals looked cautiously at each other not knowing where Justin was going with this information that they all assumed was confidential. Dr. Carlton stood straight and tall exchanging smiles as he looked around the Chapel recognizing his patients but not dwelling on any one of them.

"I now ask Cardinal Wilhelm to please stand."

Wilhelm proudly rose smiling at his fellow Cardinals anticipating the endorsement from the Pope as his successor. He nodded affirmatively in recognition of the various Cardinals who had pledged their allegiance to him. He stood erect with his chest out and stomach in as if he were commanding a Marine Corp battalion allowing all to acknowledge his position of respect and unquestioned control.

"It is Cardinal Wilhelm who requested that we convene here today. He approached me earlier in the week to advise me that certain tape recordings of private and confidential sessions with Dr. Carlton came into his possession." Expressions of deep concern and amazement came over the Cardinals being treated by Dr. Carlton, or whom he had treated in the past. They all wondered silently if the tapes were theirs, precisely as Justin expected.Justin effectively isolated Wilhelm by forcing him to stand out among the crowd of Cardinals. Beads of sweat began to form on Wilhelm's forehead as his comfort level was diminishing quickly.

"A serious breach of the confidential relationship between a doctor and his patient has occurred. I will not mention which of us have been compromised. The theft of something so personal as confidential medical records violates the sacred trust we have all sworn to uphold. We confide in our doctor so he can help us. We make ourselves vulnerable when we reveal our innermost thoughts to him. In a sense, we confess to him hoping for absolution for sins of the mind. There is one among us who has betrayed all of us. He has tried to blackmail the Church. He has brought dishonor to the Church, dishonor to his brethren, and most of all, dishonor to himself. He is standing among you." All eyes zeroed in on Cardinal Wilhelm. The Cardinals looked at him with disdain, a few shaking their heads at the shame he brought into the sacred place.

"I have asked Cardinal Wilhelm how these tapes came to be in his possession. He refused to answer. I now give you one more chance to answer the question Cardinal Wilhelm. Name the person who stole the tapes!" The Chapel was deathly quiet waiting for the answer. Wilhelm was dumbfounded. If he said nothing he would be labeled as the thief, or at minimum, an accomplice. If he revealed the name of Marcella de la Sant, he would expose the relationship. He was placed in a box from which he could not escape. He stood silently trying to think of what he would say. Sixty seconds passed without a word. His hopes of being the next Pope instantly transformed to that of a Cardinal on the verge of excommunication. Justin had successfully held him up to ridicule ensuring that Cardinal Wilhelm would never be successor to the Throne of Peter. He had destroyed Wilhelm without disclosing that the tapes were his own, and without allowing him to utter a word in defense. Dr. Carlton's presence served its purpose causing fear of disclosure of intimate secrets to infiltrate the minds of the holy brothers. Justin now assumed complete control, his demeanor becoming more and more angry and vindictive.

"Cardinal Wilhelm," he continued. "I should invoke the punishment of excommunication. But, I have elected not do so. You will be saved by your one redeeming act of goodness, your efforts on behalf of the Ethiopian people and other starving nations. Your penitence shall not be a multiple of Hail Mary's or Our Fathers. It will be the looks of your fellow Cardinals each time they cast their eyes upon you, in the hallways, in the plaza, when you're dining, and when you are praying. You will not be stripped of your title as Cardinal, but you will be stripped of your rank. From this day forward you shall be a Cardinal Priest. You may now be seated Cardinal Priest Wilhelm. You have acted without thought and you will now live with the consequences. Raised voices filled the Sistine Chapel. It was clear that this Pope was in charge. After three minutes, Justin raised his hands to quiet his audience much like Moses did when the Red Sea was parted. He purposely waited the time to allow his words to sink in. The Cardinals looked at each other in silence each wondering what words would be spoken next by their Pope. Wilhelm was quickly "old news" having been dismissed as the one rotten apple in the holy barrel.

Justin began again. "I too have had the wise counsel of Dr. Carlton. I have suffered migraine headaches of a debilitating nature. While presently, they have only slightly interfered with my work as your Pope, the headaches are getting worse. However, with the help of our esteemed colleague to my right..." he turned toward Dr. Carlton breaking the tense atmosphere pervading the great hall and continued, "my care is in good hands and I know your prayers for my well being will speed the process". I thank you for your patience and support. God bless you." Justin and his doctor left through a side door as the Cardinals filed out the main hall of the Sistine Chapel distancing themselves from the disgraced German Cardinal. Wilhelm rushed for refuge away from the sight of his brethren escaping to an empty room of the Vatican Chapel. He reached for his pipe hoping to calm himself. His hand shook nervously as he tried to fill the bowl of his pipe with a tobacco blend that seemed to have a mind of its own scattering to the marble floor as if it also preferred to distance itself from the German. His frustration boiled as he screamed at the top of his lungs in anguish as the sounds bounced off the hallowed walls of Catholicism echoing over and over again as he covered his ears hoping to rid himself of his own voice.

CHAPTER FORTY-FOUR

$\mathcal{T}$he Papal Study was chosen as the meeting place. Justin and Mary Francis were alone. Justin came straight to the point.

"I asked you here to tell you that I have decided not to resign and...I will not allow you to leave my life." He looked at her anxiously for a response. There was none. Mary Francis silently awaited his next words.

"That is what you wanted, is it not?" he continued.

"How am I to compete with the Church?" she asked. "I will not put you in a position where you must choose...and...you do not wish to make me a jealous mistress. You need time to rest, and I need time away from you, and the Church. My feelings are too deep and beyond repair. No act of contrition can grant me the serenity I seek. If I cannot have you spiritually, physically, and as my husband, I must make a new life for myself. You have shown me the pleasures of a loving relationship between man and woman. How can you expect me to return to the life of a Sister? And do you really think I will allow you to compromise your emotions? We will not sneak to see each other hoping others will not suspect something. You are the Pope and as such your every move will always be watched as if you were under a microscope. Are we so clever to be able to withstand such scrutiny? I assure you, our emotions will betray us and place the Church in harms way."

"My requests are few," Justin began. He opened a file and took out a sheet of paper. "I will implement the policies I promised when I ascended to the Throne of Peter. Here is the list of the five women whom I will now select as Cardinals of the Roman Catholic Church." Mother Superior was first on the list followed by Sister Mary Francis and three others who had distinguished themselves in service to the Church. "I can have both you and the Church. As a Cardinal, you will be near me all the time. I'll arrange for a special assignment where you will report to me alone. No one will dare question what you do, where you go, and how your time is spent." Justin's desperation outweighed his judgment.

"Listen to yourself. Do you wish a scandal? Do you want me as your Marcella de la Sant? Do you really want to taste the deception of a Kurt Wilhelm?" She threw her arms around him as tears ran down her cheeks. "I will not allow it," she said sobbing. "I must abandon my vows of the Sisterhood. I will leave!" With that pronouncement, she left the papal study.

Justin was now alone with his aching heart and the fresh smell of the only woman he ever loved still in the air. He silently vowed not to give up so easily.

Three weeks passed without contact with Mary Francis. The medications prescribed by Dr. Carlton numbed his senses to the point where his dreams of a prior life were secondary to his longing for her. But the dreams still occurred. Justin summoned two of his most trusted advisors. It was time to plan for administration of the Church in the event he became incapable of carrying out the duties required of his office. A secret committee of three would rule the Church. They would include Capelli, Sun Yet, and soon to be appointed Cardinal, Sister Mary Francis.

CHAPTER FORTY-FIVE

$\mathcal{T}$he announcement of a major Papal address raced over the airwaves throughout the world as Justin laboriously drafted his speech. As Pope, he was aware that his words could calm the nations or further incite the tempers of revolution.

Dampness seemed to permeate St. Peter's Basilica as crowds began to assemble. Security was heightened as television networks created more chaos as they vied for vantage points. Millions of euro dollars were passed between television executives and the few greedy Basilica Sanpatrini to better position their cameras.

Pope Constantine dismissed his personal valet. He decided to wear a simple white peasant garment. Not withstanding, it would be met with horror by the Cardinals. The absence of the expected Papal appointments, the missing mitered pontifical cap, the shepherd's staff; these were all to be left behind. A procession down the wide aisles of St. Peter's was also abandoned; Chancel Choirs were dismissed, all at the direction of Pope Constantine. An air of expectancy filled the House of Peter as the hour drew near. Initially hushed conversations began to rise to a crescendo, the voices of a hundred different nationalities echoing off the frescoes of Michelangelo. Triple lines of people stretched all the way through the piazza, past the Via di Conciliazione and even to the banks of the Tiber River.

Correspondents and newscasters interviewed everyone who appeared to be in a position of knowledge. Pope Constantine entered the Basilica by a side door, almost unnoticed. He had walked thirty steps before Enrique Capelli recognized him.

"Father...God be with you," Capelli said aloud.

"Thank you, my dear friend...I shall remember your loyalty. As a new Cardinal, you must begin to bear the weight of responsibility for the Mother Church," Pope Constantine told him quietly. Justin disappeared down the cleared aisle and stepped onto the altar floor.

The crowd's cheering was so intense it took five minutes to quiet them as their Pope stood at the podium.

"Brothers and sisters of Christ..." He began simply. "I stand before you having dispensed with the usual papal vestments you deserve to witness. I do this to emphasize that I am no more than a humble servant of God, mortal in every respect, and not bound by ancient traditions that cry out to be changed. When the reason for the rule no longer exists, we must change the rule and adapt or we will perish. There was an instant elevation of noise from the crowd. They quieted quickly waiting for the next words from their Pope.

"I have met with the Ecumenical Council. Together, we have drafted a reformation of Church policy. I promised you at my coronation that I would be at the forefront of change for the betterment of the Church. I now am honored to apprise you of the two most important changes that are to be implemented immediately.

First, I have named five new Cardinals who have demonstrated their collegiality backed by deeds rather than mere words. Heading the list is Mother Superior of the Magdalene order. The others, all of equal importance, are Mother Teresa from the arch diocese of London, Mother Francesca from Rome, Mother Dima from India, and Sister Mary Frances from the arch diocese of Boston. Yes, we have broken the glass ceiling. For the first time, we welcome our Sisters as new Cardinals of the Roman Catholic Church and hope that others will follow in their footsteps." The crowd cheered as the media scrambled to communicate by satellite telephone to their respective newsrooms straining to hear confirmation of the transmissions above the noise of the crowd.

Pope Constantine continued. "Second, we must recognize that our priests and other clergy are mortal. They are subject to the weaknesses of humans. Our needs, in some instances, cannot be repressed. We are bound by the demons of man dating to the time of creation. Eve's first bite of the apple... Cain's slaying of his own brother... Jacob's conspiracy with his mother to deceptively take the birthright from his brother Esau...the sin of adultery using the disparity of title as did King David when consorting with Bathsheba...all of these and more are not new to us. Some of us have been bound to repeat them all through the ages. Confession and a thousand of "Our Fathers and hail Mary's" will not cleanse our souls if we know our penitence is temporary. To repeat our transgressions knowing words made without intent will absolve us is as much a sin as the act itself." The Pope's words hit home in the mind of every parishioner, as Justin knew they would. No one was immune from once seeking absolution knowing his or her acts would be repeated with the passage of time because that is the way with mortals. "If there is fault, perhaps the first stone should be hurled at the Church itself. In our zeal to bring stray lambs into our fold, we have overlooked human frailty in our own clergy. Some...are not fit to serve. They join for reasons of convenience to serve a different master...their own lust. This brings us to the issue of celibacy; the commitment to remain unmarried which today is more often associated with chastity. It is undisputed that although the Council of Trent reaffirmed the tradition of celibacy in 1563, it decreed that it was not a law that came from God but a Church tradition that could be changed. It is apparent that the Church's position on celibacy inadvertently brings the weaknesses of men to the forefront. The shadow of the sickness of immoral or unlawful sexual activity is cast upon the Church. Effective immediately, the Church will not tolerate being placed in a position that acts as an incubator for sexual impropriety of its clergy. From this day forward, celibacy in the clergy shall be optional. The vow of chastity taken by our Sisters shall be optional as well. God made man and woman to procreate. Who are we to limit that which the Holy One has decreed?" The Roman Catholic leader walked six feet forward, turned about, raised his eyes to the Crucifix behind him and made the sign of the Cross then prostrated himself on the floor before his God, his body face down on the cold marble of the altar, his arms spread out as he prayed silently.

Pope Constantine was lifted to his feet, blessed the crowd, and was quickly ushered to a side door, chants of 'Viva IL papa!' filling his ears. It was hours before normalcy returned to the Vatican.

CHAPTER FORTY-SIX

$\mathcal{M}$ary Frances looked at the white band around her finger where the missing silver ring had been removed for the first time since she had spoken her vows as a Roman Catholic nun. The un-tanned circle of white was a visual reminder of her vows and symbol of her marriage to Jesus Christ. It now played the role as a reminder of her fictitious union with Justin Kennedy while they were in Israel. It had been four months since she renounced these vows and resigned as a nun. Her Sisters in Christ could not fathom turning down the highest honor a woman in the Church could now attain. But, just as history was made in the appointment of five women and the acceptance of four of them to the formerly all male council, renouncing of the honor would also be recorded in the ledgers of the Catholic Church.

The transition was not as traumatic as Mary Frances imagined. Once the yoke was removed, she felt a freedom of both mind and soul. She could see more clearly, feel more intently and now looked to the future with hope and ambition. Human attributes, long stifled under the cloth of her habit, were now removed. A new aspect of her life was about to begin.

Her communications with Justin had been limited, not by Justin, but by protocol established by Vatican doctors put into place during his recuperation at Castel Gondolfo. Two more months passed. Justin's eyesight was now almost back to normal. His migraines had subsided, his ominous dreams now virtually non-existent. Dr. Carlton met with Justin twice a week, the treatment proving beneficial. Session tapes were always kept in Justin's possession, for safekeeping.

The last letter Mary Frances received from Justin stated he would be going to a villa in the south of France within a few days, to continue his recovery. She answered his letter asking if there was anything she could do to help him and telling him that she had accepted the position of Chair of Archaeology at the prestigious International University of the Antiquities near the Smithsonian Institution in Washington D.C. She received only a picture postcard showing boats in the harbor at Cap Ferrat, a small town between Cannes and Monte Carlo overlooking the Mediterranean, and Justin's handwritten note thanking her for being so thoughtful.

Her interest in antiquities brought a renewed meaning to her life. She found herself in great demand after the publicity afforded her in the quest for the Cross. A quest still deemed successful based upon public belief it was still enshrined in the Basilica, although currently unavailable for viewing due to "unspecified matters concerning its preservation".

CHAPTER FORTY-SEVEN

$\mathcal{T}$here are three parts to every chess match, the opening, the middle game, and the end game. The chess pieces ranging in power with the lowly pawn to the most powerful of all pieces, the queen. Marcella de la Sant was a master of each part employing the same deception, strategy, and cunning in the game of life. She would always be the white queen, the first to make a move. A safety deposit box in an offshore bank guarded the sexual tapes of the trysts recorded at her villa with the German Cardinal, a knight reduced to nothing more than a pawn in the scheme of things. He was destined to continue his position as a Cardinal, as long as he was in favor with Marcella. She had set up a bank account in his name as trustee and a Vatican charity as benefici-ary. The funds would be used for the noble purpose of feeding the poor of the world in exchange for discarding the threat of excom-munication Wilhelm would have otherwise faced. Of course, the real beneficiary was the white queen. Her direct channel for Vatican information would remain open. Wilhelm would be kept on a short leash and, as long as he was obedient, the sexual encounters with Marcella would remain undisclosed. The rumors of the German's manliness were not only true, but became some-what addicting. Marcella had one more diagonal move with her bishop. Just as a chess master, her thinking was six moves ahead of her opponent. This time the move would be to entrap the Bishop of Rome, Pope Constantine, without him knowing it. She was unaware the Bishop had already outmaneuvered her and would win the game.

* * * *

CHAPTER FORTY-EIGHT

$\mathcal{W}$orld attention was focused on the one hundred eight acres surrounded by the leonine walls of the Vatican as media scoured for details of the growing schism. Controversy reigned supreme as internal pressures mounted for the impeachment of Pope Constantine.

"We have no road map... This is new ground. He is indeed incapacitated but we dare not rush into this. Perhaps the situation will settle down," Enrique Capelli's nervousness manifesting as his cheek twitched.

"This is not the dark ages and yet I have...God forbid...heard a whispered rumor some would have him poisoned and blame his demise on his injuries." The room hushed at this startling statement from Cardinal Fitzgerald.

"He must be removed! If our Lord Jesus was here he would throw him out for the shame and dishonor he had brought upon the Church," Jacob Lattimer shouted, pointing a finger at his associates.

"We are planning our own liquidation and demise, holy brothers. Not by a firing squad, but by acts of stupidity...if we remove a Pope do we not set the precedent for all future Popes who can be removed for the least of reasons? We have set our own hair on fire and are trying to put it out with a hammer," Capelli shouted.

"Are we a group of ethical pygmies? Are we not empowered to take the necessary steps to right our listing ship of state," Kurt Wilhelm now feeling his influence in the matter was growing among the ranks of the Cardinalship.

Shall we have him put into the stock and have him pilloried also," Fitzgerald shook his head sadly.

"This is insanity," Capelli screamed.

"The insanity issue belongs to the one wearing the pontifical cap...not with this group," Wilhelm retorted as he waved away the pipe smoke encircling his head. The German Cardinal perceiving his associates now marching in verbal lockstep as if a group of pious penguins.

"Roman Catholic power rests in its undeniable permanency... If we pierce this we will surely bleed and die. The traditionalists will never, ever allow an impeachment. I have strange emotions in my heart and yet something must be done. His injuries both physical and emotional must heal, but will they? In the meantime, we cannot afford to wait as our Church begins to disintegrate. Constantine must abdicate..Yes, we could create a new position; Pope Emeritus... full honors, a villa to recuperate, funds for his every need," Fitzgerald suggested.

"A novel yet possible, workable idea," Wilhelm wedging his foot into the first crack in the resistance to remove the American Pope.

"I suggest we appoint our esteemed brother, Cardinal Capelli to discuss this matter with His Holiness," Fitzgerald offered not wanting to face his Pope with this seemingly preposterous alternative to impeachment.

"I will do what I can...Perhaps it is time for a frank discussion with His Holiness, Capelli said.

* * * *

The <u>Justice</u> newspaper was having record-breaking sales of their evening editions. The publisher churning the turmoil surrounding the Papal throne into a boiling frenzy. A recommendation by other Rome newspapers to name Kurt Wilhelm as Pope upon impeachment of Constantine was published in the <u>Justice</u> in an unusual sign of agreement with the diametrically opposed newspaper.

Marcella de la Sant, would have the final say in the matter of Cardinal Wilhelm. Through her attorneys, the countess offered twenty-million dollars in cash for the second largest newspaper in Rome; a secret bank account in Switzerland the receptacle for the twenty-five million dollars in negotiable securities, put there hastily and temporarily by Hosni Khatabi prior to his death... The same secret account, that also funded his annual payment to his former wife, the Countess. With his death, she remained the only living signator to the numbered account. The Papal chair of the fisherman would not go to Cardinal Kurt Wilhelm. He was destined to resign as a Cardinal, under the guise of ill health, which might have been the case after he became aware of the sexual tapes in the safe of the newly purchased newspaper; to remain there only as long as the Countess and the former Cardinal remained paramours.

Cardinal Capelli sat quietly in the sanctity of the Papal study, to his left, like a group of dark suited pallbearers waiting for the body, sat the lawyers. Their Pope sat quietly in a high-backed chair, Justin looking very un-pontifical behind dark glasses.

The discussion was brief, with the Pope listening intently to the options and ramifications of an abdication scenario. And then Justin spoke: "I have already decided my course of action...My only thought is for the preservation of the beloved Church, to this end I shall..." Justin paused as his throat tightened, "I shall abdicate with some specific proviso's." Murmurs were heard among the lawyers. Their pens jotting down notes on the ever present yellow pads.

"First and foremost I shall have the absolute right as reigning Pope to name any successor; second, I shall have a major voice in formulating Church policy and that is all I wish. Please summon Father Michael, I will dictate my letter of abdication."

Father Michael entered discreetly and walked to a large desk and produced a sheet of stationery, the papal crest with the name Constantine emblazoned upon its heading. Justin fingered the pectoral cross on his chest and silently prayed for guidance as he cleared his throat and began to speak the words destined to be the most startling document ever conceived by the Roman Catholic Church's titular head. Father Michael poised over the white papal stationery, his thin hands trembling, fearing his expertise at shorthand would fail him.

"I, Justin Jerome Kennedy, heir to the Throne of Peter, chosen by my peers to become the Vicar of Jesus Christ and called by my own request, Constantine II, do with sound mind call upon my Lord Jesus to guide myi hands in the preparation of this document." He paused and sipped water. "Your Pope has been ill-chosen. We of this modern age must rely upon a strong mind and will to guide the Church over perilous grounds. In me you have failed. Your leaders have failed and I have failed. The hour of destiny is shadowing over the Church, the Cross of Jesus was our final hope for unification of the peoples of the world. I feel blessed that I have had the opportunity to serve God during my lifetime. Your reward to me for this, while well intentioned, is not justified. I have been caught up in the drama of life and find I have not the total capacity to lead as one expects of their Pope. My love for the Church knows no bounds. I would gladly give my life for it, and its people, and yet my cup runneth over. To do less than abdicate would be the most grievous sin ever perpetrated on the Catholic Church." Justin wet his lips, then continued. "A Pope, while no less or more a Christian than his followers, sustains a special filial relation to God, and must discharge the duties and possess the feelings belonging to that relationship. The

Pope has no special interest from his followers. I am fearful for the honor of the Mother Church and the aspersions cast upon the real character of the Catholic Church. In your Pope, you have granted implicit trust, unbounded wisdom, obedience of his words, reverence of this mortal showered him with affection and love. So feels and so acts a Catholic towards his Pope. This awesome preeminent excellence of Christian love leaves me with a sense of humility for no man or entity save Jesus Christ should have this fidelity," Justin paused as memories of the past month passed through his mind. "Man's destiny or even the destiny of the beloved Church will not be decided by man, nor is it at the mercy of chance. We know that each of us is responsible to our Creator. He has shown us right from wrong. All of us seek a new dynamic in our lives and we resolve to do better next time." Justin continued. "The battle is the fundamental survival of the belief in God. This struggle must take precedence over our individual faiths. It is a battle between us and those who want to destroy all faiths be it Christian, Jew or Muslim. I therefore abdicate the Throne of Peter on this twenty-second day of September, in the year of our Lord two thousand and nine. May God have mercy upon me, Amen." The room was hushed as he finished.

"Please have the draft prepared immediately," Capelli whispered. Within the hour, Father Michael produced the document of abdication, prepared in the beautiful handwritten scroll by the Vatican scriptologists. Father Michael lifted Justin's hand and directed his pen for the signature. Once performed, the others signed as witnesses. Emotion as heavy as wet snow permeated the sacred place. The red wax on the bottom of the stationery began to cool as the pontifical seals were used to authenticate the instrument destined for a hallowed place in the archives of the Roman Catholic Church. The participants filed out of the room quietly as Enrique Capelli embraced his Pope...He shook with emotion as he bid him goodbye.

CHAPTER FORTY NINE

$\mathcal{M}$ary Frances was mindful of the missing silver ring on her finger that had not been taken off since she had spoken her vows as a Roman Catholic nun. The untanned circle of white around her finger a visual reminder of her vows and symbol of her marriage to Jesus Christ and also of her fictitious union with Justin Kennedy. It had been two months since she renounced these vows and resigned as a Roman Catholic nun. Now a new aspect of her life was about to begin.

The release from the Order was accomplished with the approval of the Mother Superior and Pope Sun Yet, Justin's named successor to the papacy. Her sisters in Christ could not comprehend her actions, only the wise Mother Superior, feeling empathy for her. The transition was not as traumatic as Mary Frances imagined. One the yoke was removed, she felt a freedom of both mind and soul. She could see more clearly, feel more intently and now looked to the future with hope and ambition. Human attributes long stifled under the cloth of her habit.

Her communications with Justin had been limited, not by
Justin, but by protocol established by Vatican doctors put into
place during his recuperation at Castel Gondolfo. The last letter
from him stated he would be going to a villa in the south of
France within a few days, to continue his recovery. She answered
his letter asking if there was anything she could do to help him.
She received only a picture postcard showing boats in the harbor
at Cap Ferrat, a small town between Cannes and Monte Carlo
overlooking the Mediterranean, and thanking her for being so
thoughtful. Mary Frances wondered silently if this was the
Church's effort to distance the former Pope from the Vatican.

Six months passed. Justin's eyesight was almost eighty percent improved. He could now make out ships at anchor in the harbor. His migraines had ceased, his ominous dreams now gone.
Justin took in the views and stared in wonderment at the hundreds
of bougainvillea surrounding the cliffs of the villa. The residence,
a gift from a grateful Roman Catholic Church and a fitting abode
for a Pope emeritus. Pope Sun Yet signed the edict to supply
Justin with every need including an unlimited bank account and
unrestricted use of the Vatican archives. The villa staffed with
servants employed by the Catholic Church, was an added bonus.

Meanwhile, Mary Frances, now back in the United States,
had accepted the department head and Chair of Archaeology at a
prestigious International University. Her interest in antiquities
brought a renewed meaning to her life. She found herself in great
demand after her success in the quest for the Cross. In fact, a
managing director of a blind Trust, had recently approached her
with assurances that unlimited funding would be made available
to her for research and exploration of ancient biblical relics. She
felt this to be the springboard to again pursue the symbols of religious artifacts, having turned down a six-figure advance to write
her story of her involvement in locating the Cross. It was not disclosed to her that the major benefactor of the blind trust was an
American television evangelist. In addition, the Board of Regents

of the University, in exchange for a large donation, already approved a two-year sabbatical for Mary Frances to work exclusively for the Trust, in exchange for a large donation.

There were no strings attached. She was also promised continued funding to be used for other quests of ancient relics as determined from time to time by the managing director of the Trust, with her input of course. She was to have full control of hiring her research team, the only restriction was that at least one member of the team was required to be proficient in linguistics and translation of ancient languages. Justin's mastery of ancient linguistics and keen perception of research, as well as a brilliant mind would be a perfect match with Mary Frances. She felt like a pair of shears about to cut out the pattern of their lives and allow them to enjoy the closeness long denied. She accepted the challenge. Her first telephone call was to Justin Kennedy.

The next morning, Mary Frances boarded an Air France flight at New York's Kennedy Airport en route to Paris, France. She was assigned window seat 2A. She relaxed in the Corinthian leather chair thinking of the possibilities in store for them. There were many treasures to be found. The lost cross was only one of them.

The flight land what seemed a short time later and Justin Kennedy was there to meet her. He saw her through the large glass picture window as she was being processed through French customs. She was a vision of loveliness in a soft flowered afternoon dress, a wide brimmed matching hat, and a flowered purse that completed the ensemble. She saw him and her smile was as bright as the clothes she wore. Justin stood paralyzed, mind racing, heart seemingly about to jump from his chest. She cleared customs and ran to his outstretched arms. "Justin, my love" she cried as she felt his strength envelope her in his strong arms. Justin placed his hands on her cheeks and looked deeply into her sparkling eyes. "This is the time and the place" he whispered, their lips coming together for the first time. They embraced for minutes in silence; both with thoughts only imagined a few short months ago as tears of joy gently flowed down her cheeks.

"I have something for you," she said wiping her eyes. Mary Frances opened her purse and produced a velvet bag; she opened it slowly to savor the moment.

Justin looked upon the two golden crucifixes, made of the wood splinters, which she had gathered from their odyssey, protected behind crystalline shields.

"I love you," she said as she draped the gold-chained pendant around his neck. She then placed the matching twin around her own neck. She held his hands and looked at him lovingly, "Is it a coincidence that fate has brought us together?"

He smiled at her and said, "Coincidence is God's way of remaining anonymous."

The Beginning

GLOSSARY

Accetto	Acceptance
Acanthus	Thorny bush
Bramante	Vatican Architect
Buon Appetito	Italian for Good appetite
Chaldee targums	Religious writings
Camerlengo	Title given to the treasurer of the Sacred College of Cardinals
Cnidian Aphrodite	Statue of Aphrodite
Constitution of Constantini	Edict by Constantine giving power to the Catholic Church
Carabinieri	Italian Police with civil and military duties reporting to the Minister of Interior or Minister of defense
Castel Gandolfo	Pope summer residence
Chair of Peter	Papal throne
Codex Vaticanus	Index of all Vatican manuscripts
Curia	Hierarchy of Catholic leaders
Elezione	Election
Extra Omnes	Everybody out except those authorized

Gian battista	John the Baptist
Gebel Musa	Mount of Moses
Gomorrah	Biblical city destroyed by God
Holy See	Rule or power of the Pope
Hall of Broken Bones	Place formerly used to store Vatican broken statuary
Habemus Papam	We have a Pope
il Manifesto	Rome newspaper
il Papa	The Pope
il Papal palazzo	Plaza of the Pope
In Pectore	Pope's power to name a Cardinal in secret. (Literal meaning, "close to the chest")
il Periodical	Newspaper
Imam	Reader of Koran-teacher
Index Libroum Prohibitorum	List of publications to be avoided by Catholics
Junto	Hebrew prosecutors
Katholisch Schloss	Catholic Castle
L'observatore Romano	Rome newspaper
L'unita	Newspaper of Rome
Latin Vulgate	Religious writings
Loggia	Balcony
Mossad	Israeli intelligence
Masbah	Prayer beads
Mille grazie	Many thanks

Mons Vaticanus	Hill upon which the Vatican is built
Mottu Proprio	A mourning period
Muezzin	Prayer tower/caller
Mulla	Muslim clergy
Nello	Inlaid polished stone
Pieta	Statue of Mary holding body of slain Christ
Placet	Yes
Papable	Capable of being selected a Pope
Pier Luigi da Palestrina	Musician (the arcade where musicians played)
Pontiff	The Pope
Romantia	Power of Rome
Raz el Gindi	Ancient Muslim fortress
Robespierre	French Revolutionary Leader (1758-94)
Rubicon	River in eastern Italy
Sanpatrini	Gardeners/custodians of Vatican
Santissimo Padre	Sainted Pope
Stigmata	Nail imprints in the palms
Sanhedrin	Jewish authorities
Sedia gesatoria	Papal throne carried by bearers
Septuagint	Ancient translation of the Old Testament from Hebrew to Greek
Sultin Salah el Din	12th century Arab leader

Summum pontificum	Supreme Catholic leader
Talleyrand	French Statesman (1754-1838)
Throne of Peter	Head of the Catholic Church
Uomini de fiducia	Man of trust
Urbi et orbi	Unto all the world
Voltaire	French Writer and Philosopher (1694-1778)
Veni-vidi-vici	I came-I saw-I conquered
Via di Conciliazione	Street in Rome
Vicar of Christ	The Pope